*BE WARNED THER
*AND WORDS OF E)
*TASTE,EXPLICIT SE, & GRATUITOUS
*VIOLENCE CONTAINED WITHIN
*THESE PAGES.

Small print.
      The author and publisher wish to distance themselves from this work and vigourously reject any liablity for any unexpected medical, moral, physical, or psychological breakdowns, outrages, or traumas associated with this material. (pre, or post). Read on at you personal peril. Of course this entire flight of fancy is fiction and not based on any individual, event, or actuality. . . OR IS IT?
Indeed the author, who wishes to remain Anon. E.Mouse for a very good reason is a reknown retrobate, an unscrupulous liar, thief and utterly beyond the pale, a complete culchie.Who is rumoured to have traded his Granny, Flora for some rancid butter, which he then sold to widows and orphans.
All is not lost, however, his redeeming features are a fondness for fallen women, cuddly toys, small furry animals, greyhounds and racehorses, as his bookie will gratefully attest.
Further, this indulgence is liberally laced with complete lies, incredible innuendo best ignored, half truths,red herrings and terrible trixsters. So best not read too much into it,as little of it is to be belielived, or trusted.
LONG LIVE ROCK!

Anon E. Mouse

© 2010.Anon.E.Mouse (A mischevious Mouse-Muse Fantasy)

IN THE BEGINNING IT WAS DARK.

Spyder got lucky and scored with Jill Bowman after several setbacks. She'd been a face in the crowd for a good few weeks now and he'd tipped her the wink more than once.But she was an untouchable poker faced super mod and colder than an Inuits todger.

As Frankie Clay's secretary at Shotgun, she was double trouble. He called the slots on the circuit, no band with any future intent got a gig unless it was booked through his agency and he was only crossed by madmen and those

with little regard for an untroubled and long life.

The Marquee was a real downer with the lights on in the afternoon when setting up, but come the gig with a packed house sweating buckets, finger popping and strutting their funky stuff when the band were really cooking, it was a whole scene going.

Although only seven months since 'Bangon' formed, they'd already forged a rock solid reputation for aggressive

and dynamic stageshows with an uncompromising attitude. It was no secret that the band hated each other and were as likely to kick seven shades of shit out of each other on stage as to play and entire set.

Rumour had it that Frankie wanted to exploit Bangon and the whisper was that Spyder was making things difficult. Recklessly letting it be known that he'd never sign and Frankie could only get the band when he was a stiffie.

But if Frankie really wanted something, Frankie got it and always on his terms. He was short in stature and surly, a belligerent blackguard who garned grudging respect rather than reverance.

True enough, Bangon had hammered each other and slaughtered the punters leaving them yelling for more, but the fact that Jill gave him the big come on, blew him away. Of course he'd heard that the birds got turned on by a hot band and were gagging for it in droves and would claw and scratch at each other to get their hands on the face with the pace, but to actualy be the object of her desire.

Sure he was a cocky nineteen year old and no stranger to back street girls with loose knickers and elastic morals, but they were mostly old dogs making the most of their fleeting charms in the hopes of blagging a trophy husband before the rot set.

Jill was something else. A willowy blonde with long legs that went all the way, bristols that hinted of things to come and a face that fanned the flames of fantasy; all things to all men with vivid imaginations and truly a girl for all seasons.

A more mature man might have stopped to question his unexpected and very sudden streak of seduction, perhaps praised his aftershave, but shit, hesitate and the moment is lost and forever a wonder what if?

She didn't even take any real chatting up, she was all over him like measles, snogging him and rubbing herself against him like a bitch on heat.

Well what could a poor boy do?

The back alley was a mess of dumped rubbish, discarded cartons, rats and overlooked by dirty windows and printing works, but late at night most buildings were empty, bar odd cleaners and there were enough secluded nooks and crannies.

After a few furtive kisses and a quick fumble with her bra, Jill lost no time in dropping down to blow both his member and his mind he was Jack the Lad and hard as nails.

Spyder closed his eyes, settled back on a pile of cardboard and praised his good fortune. If this was what being a pop star was all about, bring it on big time!

Spyder wasn't the only wanna be to have designs on Jill and the big time and this motherfucker had no compunctions about needs justifying ends. He'd had the audacity to beard the devil in his den and was now in the pay of the great trixsters dark force. He had nicked a motor to order, had no licence, and more to the point no moral qualms and was there to enjoy the mayhem, mop up the mishmash and redistribute the miscellany beyond retribution. He had the foresight to cover his arse in every way; was anonymous with a rock solid alibi, knew where the bodies were gonna be buried and had managed to record his masters voice as a class of an insurance policy. He might be a working class oik, but had street credibility, knew to be callous, ruthless and was more than partial to casual violence, rather enjoying a perverse kick that fucking somebody over gave him.

 Spyder never saw the shadows closing in, or the car at the end of the alley and knew nothing until Jill bit down in shock and swallowed more than she'd expected.

She puked, pissed and passed out.

Spyder didn't get a chance to cry out in pain as a hammer rained down on his head and split his skull, spilling his grey matter onto the now damp and sticky cobbles. There was no subtulty to the crime; this was sheer brutality and just for good measure he raped Jill, just because he was up for it.

A few days, later a bloated body was snagged in the Thames at Deadman's hole and although identified as Jill, her reputation as a pill popper with desperately depressing cold Turkeys counted against her. It was concluded that she'd lost it and committed suicide, although friends and relations questioned it. But Frankie 'co operated with the old Bill' and even had the good heart to make a 'donation' to the police widows and orphans fund.

The Gravesend messenger had a few paragraphs on the fifth page reporting a stolen car burnt out just off the bypass containing the charred remains of a tearaway. The local police had more pressing matters to fill their precious hours beside further investigation into hooligans nicking motors and wrecking them and duely shunted the file into a bureaucratic cul de sac.

DOWNTOWN BLUES.

Mutton Jeff and Sweaty Betty sat swatting flies in the drab waiting room, watching the wall clock away precious minutes of their ever decreasing life. Idly flicking through yesteryears Country Life, Betty drooled and dreamed over palatial Shire properties and estates,then glanced out of the window at the killing fields of Kensal Rise and sighed deeply. The yardies favored abatoir and the gateway to the once fashionable Victorian cemetery and Kingdom come,for the blessed and perhaps the damnation of fire and brimstone for the licentious and sanctimonious.

Even a poor girl can dream of how it might have been, if only?

Perhaps how it could be, if only that ever elusive lottery jackpot came their way, or ? She smiled as she remembered the secret and colourful days of her youth.

Lost opportunities, personal cul de sacs, fates false footings and the all too human misjudgments that we all make on the snakes and ladders of a life.

Betty had been around the block more times than a zealous traffic warden and if truth be told didn't really regret a single moment. Sure it was a rocky road in every sense and she had been on the floor and her knees (not to mention the bed) more times than eight miles high, but life is bitter sweet and you'd need one to balance t'other and give depth to experience.

She turned to Mutton Jeff, ' you did put the lottery on, didn't you!'

'You what?' Mutton fumbled with his hearing aid, turning it on clumsily.The infernal machine started to feedback and crackle as he unsuccessfully wrestled with it.

Betty leaned over, grabbed it and turned it off. In a louder voice ventured, 'I told you it was stupid to buy a second hand hearing aid at the car boot,' She snorted indignantly,' The lottery. Did you play our numbers? . . . It's a £32 million rollover!'

Mutton nodded and returned his gaze to the tropical fish tank and the kaleidoscopic colours of guppies and neons flashing around the wreck of Davey Jones locker, which opened periodically to allow a stream of bubbles to briefly break for the surface before bursting. In a rare moment of deftness he flicked a bluebottle that had been idling on the rim of the fishtank into the water and watched it struggle for life before and inquisitive fish snatched it gratefully. He fidgeted and shifted from buttock to buttock to ease his discomfort and occasionally stamped a foot on the ground to try and restore some feeling to the troublesome limb.

'Mutton.' Betty admonished, aware of the withering gaze of the owl like receptionist, who had obviously long

5

resigned herself to the curse of facial hair. Betty sighed and for a fleeting moment wondered if life was really worth the living, if it meant enduring the aches and pains of an aging body and the torment of youthful memories with the clashing emotions of agony and ecstasy.

Resting the open magazine in her lap ,she checked her watch and wondered how much of her life had been wasted in waiting for something to happen, Betty glanced around the room trying to second guess what ailed the other patients. She was annoyingly adept at it, now she was visiting the surgery all too regularly. The middle aged shifty looking guy in the greasy mac flicking through a copy of the daily sport was easy, Viagra, or the clap. As was the teenage girl with acres of provocative flesh and a tattoo on her right breast saying 'happy days' and on the left' cuddly nights'; fifteen Betty guessed, but going on twenty in her head. Betty knew the angst of wanting every fit young geezer to fancy you and the lengths a fun loving girl would go to, desperate to stand out and be noticed. The wonder bra, thong, false eyelashes, 6" stilettos and a pint of eau de toilette. Those anxious hours in front of the mirror, trying and rejecting outfit after outfit, almost suicidal because your nose was too long, you had freckles, or hideous blackheads and what if nobody fancied you? Yes she either wanted the pill, a pregnancy test, or more likely a brain scan and glasses, if the scruffy cretin with acne and the black cloud of flatulence wafting around him was her boyfriend.. But then the temptations of turpitude when one is a young, impressionable girl & eager to please are very appealing and all but impossible to resist.

It suddenly occurred to Betty that she was in no position to cast moral aspersions on others, when she herself was servicing three members of the youth club band at barely fifteen. Smiling as she thought ' those were the days,' and remembered the heady times and sticky moments of lost innocence, she glanced over at Mutton still transfixed by the passing cavalcade of colour in the aquarium and sighed. She was fond of him in many ways, but he wasn't the rock star she'd always believed she would marry and their mansion on a hill was a decrepit one bedroom council flat in a high rise block in the badlands of Ladbroke Grove. Her nearest neighbors were a family of rumbustious rats living in the rubbish chute and glared menacingly at anybody who challenged their authority.

'Ewe and Crocker ! The doctor will see you now.' The bird of pry posing as a receptionist peered over her severe glasses and raised her eyebrows to the ceiling in despair, 'Where do they come from!' Before returning to the shabby, sordid and shallow scandals of third rate celebrities in her hot gossip ragmag, a tepid cup of sweet tea, a Garibaldi and self righteous indignation.

PUMP IT UP.

The preposterous pink Roller; gold plated handles and personalized number plate, all cynically designed to draw the eye and proclaim status swept to a halt outside the Holland Park office. A bottle blonde bombshell sporting chauffers hat, lime hotpants, matching boob tube and bow tie leapt from the drivers seat to open the rear passenger door as if her life depended on it and not just her job.

A street beggar sitting on cardboard boxes with a handicapped mongrel for company and a sign begging for change watched in amazement as the pop god Rock Sturdy stepped gingerly from the limo anxious to avoid the turd in the gutter.

The great 'narcissist ' complete with shades,fake tan, dyed black hair that arrived moments before himself and the ego of self obsession and delusion was always a sight to behold and best avoided.

A flunkey opened the door of the plush building, kicking out at the beggar to clear the way,' piss off loser you're polluting the environment!' Instantly regretting it as the three legged dog snapped at his ankle.

With total disdain Rock ignored everything, intent only on his progress and appearance which was regularly checked in every reflective surface in passing. He was still chuckling to himself, having ordered his driver to slosh through puddles left from the hailstorm, so he could watch the faces of the footsloggers as they were soaked.

By the time Rock assended the penthouse, his manager Buck Silver was ready to receive him, the desk cleared of compromising documents, which were locked in the wall safe behind the gold disc for a million sales of 'NUN-SUCH'S' third album in Patagonia. By hook and by crook most often the latter, Buck had been the boys manager since the fledgling days of pubs and bar mitzvahs.

In the early days Buck had managed the boys affairs from a decaying slum next to the Italian chippie down the Golborne road. The damp walls were decorated with pages from the Melody Maker and literally dripped rock'n'roll history. Frequent visitors could watch a picture of Mick Jagger and one of Tina Turner morph into a damp blob and drip to form a paper machie penis on a well-thumbed copy of Razzle.

Acker Bilk and Sandie Shaw became a touch more intimate than strangers on a beach.

But the good old days when men were men and the boys were ripe for a nice ripoff were now the stuff of legend, it was much harder work now earning a dishonest dollar. At one time the boys had listened to him and his word was law, he guided them through the excesses of fame and fortune, much like a loving father, encouragement, support and where necessary tough love. But then it was Buck's masterstroke that transformed an energetic, if run of the mill group into something with attitude and bollockss when he insisted that the insufferably insolent singer from the recently imploded group Bangon front Nun-Such. Rock had a cruel streak and an infamous reputation, created more crap than he took, quickly muscling his way to supremacy, with glaring contempt.

True, he'd once held the bass player from a window by his well worn boot heals, but only in his best interests and of course that of the band.

You simply can't allow dissent in the ranks to jeopardize the groups future and Rock's prosperity.

Buck himself was teak tough, conniving, outmaneuvering a declining Frankie Clay and living to whisper the story behind locked doors to a select minority; once Frankie was burnt toast.

Time and tide mellowed the 'boys', now days they were content to socialize with the county set, jetting off on exotic holidays when bored.

Rock was different, there was still a world to conquer, he'd come this far, rags to riches and still craved the ultimate kudos. He wanted titles and the endorsement of the establishment. As life unfolded each plateau gained was briefly entertaining, but he was soon jaded, no matter how licentious, or outrageous. Every excess conquered must be superseded, the status quo can't be it, there must be more. Just follow the yellow brick road over the green hill and there will be jam tomorrow, always the goading of a restless intellect. If one could ever accuse Rock of having such an preposterous attribute. He was a driven man with a troubled history, but his view of the world was limited, superficial. If ever there was a man who'd visited the crossroads to sell his soul to the devil then Rock was a grand candidate. However,that being the case he'd been short changed, sure he had success, but never enough compared to others who he worshipped and loathed in equal measure.

More importantly he was all too keenly aware that his talent was limited and genuine articles like Geal, the inspirational main man in SMOKE & MIRRORS were self effacing, but manifested an all pervasive presence. Rock always seemed to be playing catch up with Geal who was several steps ahead with cutting edge ideas and themes. Even the media were flummoxed by Geal unable to find any dirt to dish, constantly having to acknowledge his achievement, fame and glory and by golly it was vexing.

A further thorn in his side was the multi instrumentalist and talented Nick, an erstwhile member of Nun-Such, who did his own thing with massive success, which dwarfed anything Rock could hope to achieve.

'Rock, my man'. Buck all slimy smiles and nervous twitches very much a Gollum, as Rock christened him of late, 'an unexpected pleasure,' he hated surprises,' always great to see you! . . . ' a pregnant pause as Buck momentarily struggled, wringing his hands and nodding like Fagin, in anticipation of another pocket to pick. . . We rarely meet these days, always the blower.'

'Cut the crap,' Rock snapped,' keep it for Johnny cum lately,' Rock deliberately seated himself in Buck's padded leather chair and snapped his fingers at a bemused acolyte,' GEMME A DRINK!'

Buck nodded obsequiously,'Champagne, well jump to it, don't linger like a stale fart in a bean can!'

' So Rock . . . What can I do for you?' Buck reluctantly settled into the uncomfortable guest chair. A deliberate ploy, make it uncomfortable for the visitor and they are unlikely to exact a good deal, or take up time asking awkward questions.'

'I want a knighthood !' Rock idly flicked a kinetic toy, watching a tightrope walker roll precariously around a loop before crashing to the desk, he grinned.

'A WHAT ?' Even buck was astounded, almost swallowing his gold tooth, ' . . . How the fuck do I do that?'

'How the fuck do I know? . . . You're the fixer, buy somebody. . . fuck a flunky, or something!'

 Rock narrowed his eyes and fixed Buck's gaze menacingly.

Buck was more than aware of how petulant and vindictive Rock could be if his passing whims and fancies weren't entertained. ' You are serious?' Buck dared to question, ' this isn't another baby elephants at Madison Square Gardens is it?'

Thirty seven years previously, when Rock was perfecting his arrogance and aggression, he'd been in the New York office as Shadow was putting together the rider for the Big Apple gig, when the tour manager asked if Rock wanted any special requests added to it. Without much thought and eager to flex his ego, Rock flippantly said the first thing that came into his head, ' baby elephants. . . Yea, three baby elephants,' and swept out of the door with Pinky, the groupie of the hour on his arm.

Besides the appearance fee, merchandising sponsorships and sales, the promoters were legally bound to provide every item listed on a rider; an integral part of the contract.

Even the vintage of the wine had to be exact, as had other novelties to excite, entertain and soothe jangled nerves and stage fright. Failure to do so allowed the artiste to cancel the gig at a moments notice, demand the full fee and with a sharp legal eagle a claim for damages, trauma and compensation for injury to reputation.

John Doe was a slick NewYork Promoter, bringing the brat pack to the Big Apple, the sixties beat invasion and every pulsatting ' sensation' since. He knew the ropes, had contacts from here to eternity, with a reputation for sharp shooting, feared no one, loathing freeloaders and fools.

But three baby elephants in Manhattan is a tall order and there were dry palms to grease and many sweaty moments. The crew took hours to set up, ready for a late afternoon sound check and by 5.30 the band had sauntered in, drifted off and been recaptured.

A cacophony of crashing cymbals, deep bass licks, screaming riffs,'ridiculous mic checks', adolescent tantrums, histrionics and a half hearted hit of bygone days.

Rock kicked his heals at the side of the stage, bottle of Remy in one hand, a joint in the other, between his legs a groupie was immortalising his erection for posterity.

John Doe blundered into the scene, no narrow minded prude, but he did attend his local synagogue and have a reputation as a family man to preserve.

'OH. . . Er Rock. . .' J.D. desperately wanted to be somewhere else, but he persevered and words didn't come easily, even for an articulate New York hustler, ' er Rock, I've got your elephants.'

Rock was unphased, even appreciating an audience, 'the price of fame, even I sometimes wonder at the demands and sacrifices of stardom,' ERE! watch it, you've got sharp teeth. . . you'll have it off!'

'ER Rock . . . I've got your elephants.'

'Elephants! . . . What bleeding elephants?' Rock was incredulous and nearing orgasm.

'The ones on the rider,' J.D. had a queasy feeling, ' what do you want me to do with them?'

'What do you want me to say . . . Can't you see I'm hard at it?' at that moment Rock came, as did a zealous Buck Silver, who rarely missed an aside, less it be conspiracy.

'Elephants you say. . .' Buck led J.D. away, arm firmly clasped across his shoulder, ' tell me, when was the last time elephants brought Times Square to a stop?'

BAD NEWS TRAVELS FAST.

'Hello Betty . . .hello, can you hear me?' Mutton heard the phone ring, but put it to his deaf ear, looking decidedly perplexed as he gingerly reseated himself, trying to ignore the urge to scratch his itching arse.

Betty, returning from the kitchen with fresh banana bread, smiled gently and thrust the warm plate into his lap and grabbed the receiver, ' Hello it's Betty, who's that?'

'Betty? . . . Betty, at last, it's Molly.'

'MOLLY! . . .Molly darling, good to hear from you, how's it going?'

'Yea good, not so bad,' Molly hesitated,' listen Betty, I've got bad news.'

Betty was silent as dozens of unpleasant scenarios bounced around her brain and she steeled herself for whatever came next.

'Betty, you still there?'

'Yes darling, yes, what news?'

'You remember Cornish John?'

A pause while names and faces rearranged themselves in her head,' Yea, John Treager?'

She slumped into a chair,' Why? . . .What's happened?' Although she had already guessed.

'I'm afraid he's gone, died yesterday. ' Molly waited for a reaction, knowing they'd been close in the eighties.

'How?'

'Cirrhosis,' Molly continued, the words came easily, it was her third phone call that evening,' been living in a hostel in Kilburn. When he came of the road with leg trouble he lost it, crack and cider,' Molly was pragmatic and not a little cynical, ' same old, same old, thirty years on the road, never his own place, living out of a suitcase, always the raver.' In truth Molly had never really liked him, thinking him flaky and selfish, but knew Betty would want to know and after all, Betty was her best friend.

'How long in the hostel?'

'Not long. . . kept getting nicked for stupid things. . . cracking meters, popping car windows,. . .you know, hustling for a high . . .' Molly felt awkward feeling both sorry for Betty and believing John got what he deserved.

'When's the funeral?' Betty felt sick to the stomach, needing time to get her head around it,' he was younger than me,' she said quietly, almost to herself.

'Yea, but he never took care of himself and had nothing sorted for when he couldn't hack the road anymore.' Molly didn't really have anything much better, living in a grotty studio flat in Croydon, working a supermarket checkout and reminiscing on facebook with yesterdays people.

'I know what you mean,' Betty said casting a resigned eye her around flat and then Mutton, who was playing with his XBOX,' do you know, I can't think of any of the old crowd who aren't struggling . . . When did you say the funeral was?'

'Wednesday week, 2.30 at Kensal Green crematorium,' Molly blew her nose,' Shadow organised it, he got Lucy and Bunty to pick up the tab.'

Betty remembered that both Lucy Lastic and Cuddly Bubbly, as Bunty was known had small legacies, ' lucky bitches', she found herself thinking and was embarrassed by her thought and hoped she hadn't said it aloud.

' o.k. . . . I'll guess I'll see you there, luv you honey.'

'Good crowd then'. Tic Tac Thomas said flippantly. In fact only 23 people had turned out, four at the wrong wake and another couple freeloaders in search of a free lunch.

'Leave it out Tic Tac, you make it sound like a duff gig,' Molly chanced her luck with a dubious sausage roll, having decided the vol au vents looked an odd colour. Mind you, buffalo wings, bloater paste sandwiches and a shameless pink dip weren't any better, only a fool would tempt fate and actually eat them. Drink had been taken this past two hours since retreating from the leaden skies and sharp showers. The drab nicotine stained tope colour of the bar only adding further dark clouds to the general mood of depression.

Never able to stand Tic Tacs company. His crude tongue, lecherous eye and generally offensive manner made enemies of friends.

Molly exited quickly joining the girls and a tempting bottle of Blue Nun.

While Tic Tac checked messages on his phone, ' Hey, Smokey Joe sends his apologies, says he wanted to come, but has to bring his own oxygen, cos he's got Emphysema and only got a two hour supply. . . It would have taken a hour to get here on the tube. . . So it's a big no no . . . that's a drag. . . he always had good dope.' smirking he returned to a porn site

The comfort ladies as they euphemistically called themselves, were both morose and euphoric, the conversation swinging from painful memories to hilarious anecdotes, fuelled by a steady stream of alcohol.

'. . . for my fifth birthday I got a Snow White outfit. . .' Betty reminisced thoughtfully,' . . . I was never out of that costume until it became Cinderella's rags. . . I can still see the bright blues, reds and yellows. . . I lived the fairy tale in my head. . . the cats and dogs around my street were my dwarves.' Her eyes sparkled as the light caught the tears as she mourned lost innocence and simple bliss.

'The original virgin queen, hey?' Molly chinked her wine glass against Betty's G'n'T, ' Yeah, so where did it all go wrong!' She giggled, her face flushing with the warm glow of alcohol.

' I discovered the agonies and ecstasies of orgasam!' Betty chuckled,' It was well alright at the time!. . . I couldn't believe a girl could feel that good. . . .and it got better every time, in every way!'

T.J. and Agatha sat in a corner nursing their porter and rolling grass joints, joined occasionally by Mutton who was having a problem with the old Father Giles frequently needing to soothe his grapes of wrath and shake a leg in the cannery row.

'I'm telling you it's win win, it can't go wrong,' Agatha insisted, sure didn't I think the thing through entirely. T.J. arched his eyebrow skeptically, ' You say you thought it through! . . you the man who wrote off two hired trucks in the one week.'

'Argh. . . fair do's, . . but I hadn't slept for a few days and those Mandrax were terrible powerful altogether.' Agatha grinned inanely, his yellowed and gappy teeth testament to the shambles of a man he was.

'Point taken, but when you got to Hertz to tell them why you were hard intent on scrapping their fleet of trucks, you drove the Avis truck into the wall of the yard.' T.J. pointed the fickle finger of fate.

'Right! . . . own up, you're a complete moron and you tell me you thought it through.'

'Sure I wouldn't have crashed the Avis truck, if Hertz hadn't banned me from driving their trucks, now would I?' The logic was simple in Agathas eyes, as was just about everything else about the lummox of a man.

'If it's so easy how come there aren't queues waiting to get one over?' T.J. was more than a little skeptical, especially as it was Agatha's idea' Think about it, who's gonna think a bunch of old geezers are gonna knock over a bank?' Agatha shrugged, His clothes were testament to the unending struggle to wrest breakfast, or indeed any meal from plate to mouth without spillage and were forever evidence, if indeed such was required that yer man was a walking disaster in continuum.

'Who are you calling and old geezer grandad?' T.J. snorted,' I still got all me teeth and most of me hair, which

14

is more than can be said about you.'

'I still say it's a good un, . . . We don't get a pension, cos we never paid the dues. . . so if we knock over a bank we get a good stash to see us through. . . and if we get slammed up we get bed and board in a warm nick for the duration.' Agatha grinned inanely and winked,' get it?'

T.J. smiled to himself wondering how long it would be before Agatha discovered the brown label with his name and address that T.J. had gaffered to the back of coat, just in case he forgot himself again.

'Hey T.J. man how's it going.'

T.J. looked up from his porter and saw the Bandit, a notorious blast from the past and a not entirely welcome one at that, as the Bandit true to his name was inclined to believe the maxim ' all property is theft' and act accordingly. He liberated anything that wasn't nailed down for the people and as the self-appointed representative of the people, also assumed that he should be judge and jury in deciding which of the community deserved the detached item. Unlike Robin Hood's legend, the Bandit invariably decided that he should be custodian of the item for the community, who rarely, if ever got a look in. Unfortunately he was rather lax in selecting his victims from the wealthy and privileged; therefore anybody careless enough to provide an opportunity for the Bandit was considered fair game.

'Yea canna complain. . . ' T.J. said.

' Tried it once, but nobody listened.' Agatha finished for him.

They both cracked up at yet another stale old tour joke, that refused to die quietly.

'So . . . how long you been out this time?' Agatha ventured winking at T.J.

'Agh, come on lads, that's all behind me. . . you're looking at a reformed man.' The Bandit grinned, ' The last time in chokey was enough. . .. three years for nicking some lead off a church roof. . . I ask you, is that fair?' He shrugged his shoulders,' I mean. I didn't even have it away. . . the bleeding motor had a flat tyre. . . . teach me to nick wheels from a van hire company. The filth were on me like flies round a turd. . . Three years!'

'Is that a fact!' T.J. replied patting his inside pocket to check his wallet was still there.

'So who's gonna buy your old mucker a drink then?' The bandit glanced around looking for a warm smile, 'Bit strapped for cash at the minute, but I've got some dosh due imminently.' The Bandit scratched his palm and everybody froze and rechecked that their few bob were secure, not a soul offered a drink.

' So much for a friend in need,' The Bandit was offended,' after all that water under the bridge. Whenever did I

15

turn my back on a mate?'

'That's the problem. . . whenever we turned our back for a second we was robbed blind, because he didn't.' T.J whispered to Agatha.

'Good one!' Agatha grinned inanely.

T.J. eyed the Bandit suspiciously and leaned over to whisper in Agatha's ear,' They say it was that bastard who legged it with Hendrix's guitar at the Roundhouse gig.'

'Oh yea, I remember it.' Agatha couldn't help but feel a little respect for the Bandits audacity,' Hendrix just finished his set and was back in the dressing room for a joint while the crowd cheered for an encore.'

Agatha sniggered,' Then the bandit leaps on stage grabs the axe and legs it down to Camden with a mob on his heels.'

'He got away with it, didn't he?. . bastard!' T.J. didn't share Agatha's juvenile admiration.

The bandit hung around getting up everybodies nose like a frowzy fart in the crapper, until like Scott of the Antartic he felt the icy wind of despair and was frozen out, leaving in search of richer pickings and innocent young fools. He passed the bewildered old folks, whose regular boozer had been polluted by this sinister crowd of infidels and ragamuffins, roughly and rudely blitzing through them with no respect for age and infirmity.

Lucy Lastic arrived clutching several lucky white heathers in foil twists and floated about presenting them to the gathering,' a gypsy woman said they were very lucky. . . they'd brought her great wealth. . . so I bought them all. . . Only a £1. each.

'I bet she did and no doubt told your fortune at the same time. . . you know cross my palm with silver and I'll tell you I saw you coming and how much your purse used to contain?' Molly mocked.

Lucy looked a trifle startled, which was not unusual, but chose to ignore the remark and said, ' They say there comes a time in your life when you go to more funerals than weddings, that's when you know you're over the hill.'

Lucy was the exception to her rule, she actually looked much as she always had. Still natural full length honey hair, no make up save turquoise eye shadow and her trade mark white fairy dress.

' Sweetie, I never went to that many weddings, nobody I ever knew got married. Much too passe.' Molly laid claim to the seat that Mutton had just vacated in a hurry, stopping only to grab his tube of anisole and she immediately rose to check it, as it felt a little too warm and perhaps a touch damp.

Betty was morose and worse for the G'n'T's, she too had inspected the sad excuse of a buffet and rejected it, so was drinking on an empty stomach. The sight of old friends, now truly old and increasingly decrepit had forced her to realize just how sad their lives had become. Most had no savings, little of value, lived on state handouts and had no coherent plan for the future. These days a wild night was a bottle of cheap wine and a swig of night nurse to ease the desperation of a cul de sac existence and yet another night fiddling and fumbling with 'he's at home' to get some satisfaction through the frustration of insomnia.

The few,like Lucy and Bunty living on a legacy, lacked close partners to share their magic sunset moments. True Lucy liked to think of herself as a free spirit, not to be pinned like a butterfly in a display case, but there were times when she felt desperately lonely and places she longed to share with someone special.

'Do you remember Miss Clawdy?' Betty lashed into her third G'n'T and was beginning to plunge into the depths of melancholia, as her mind filled with the recently departed and wondered who was next.

'Of yea. . . didn't she hang out at Klooks Kleek?' Molly was also getting markedly squiffy as she methodically emptied another bottle and scanned the bar for more.

'They both did, huge knockers she had. . . if she turned quickly she'd have your eye out!' T.J. remembered fondly,' agh the good old days. . . when she gave up servicing musos she became a porn star. . . I've got a couple of her videos if you wanna cop a look. . . man that chick had the deepest throat. . . . pity she only went for main men. . .she lapped 'em up.'

'Thank you and good night. . . I wasn't talking to you.' Betty snapped.

'oohh   meow. . .sorry was I breathing.' T.J. slouched back to the dark corner of strange thoughts,even odder actions and misdeeds.

'Anyway, as I was saying before I was so rudely interrupted,' Betty said imperiously,' She's dead. . . died of Aids. . . ' She added,' 'course she got religion when they told her she had it,' became all Lordy. . went to church three times a day and took up yoga and tried alternative therapies. . . no good of course, she'd burned all her bridges in the porn business. . . they said she didn't mind what she did as long as she got a packet for it.'

'These days I try not to think anybody's brown bread. . . better to believe they just doesn't do facebook anymore.' Molly smiled, almost apologetically.

A Billy Whiz of an idea popped into Agatha's feeble mind and he slipped off to the juke box grinning like an eejit, moments later 'My Generation' was blasting across the boozer. Agatha started wind milling his air guitar and leaping in the air as he returned to the table,' hey man remember that American tour in 69?'

'No. . . .I was doing six months ,' T.J. was pained at the memory,' I got busted coming back through customs after the Belgium tour, remember?'

'Oh. . . er, yea!' Agatha had a selective memory at best.

Oh yea is it you bastard! . . it was your dope!' T.J. rose from his chair, a long forgotten score to settle,'You fookin slipped it in my pocket when you thought they'd sussed you!'

Mutton was struggling to catch what was said, but leapt to restrain T.J. regretting it almost immediately, personal hygiene wasn't T.J.'s strong point. Pallid, creased and craggy features and clothes, a mess from morning to night, like his best mucker Agatha.

He normally looked like he had been repeatedly dragged through several hedges backwards and smelt like it, ripe, pungent and best viewed from a far field with a favourable wind.

Ever in debt and on the cadge, T.J. was best avoided, but always great entertainment, mad, bad and dangerous to know, but fun in a perverse way all the same. Something along the lines of banging your head against a wall; painfull in the action, but a blessed relief when you stop and then you wonder why you ever began.

'. . . and what about the time the holy terrors in Glasgow wanted to plant an axe in that thick skull of yours?' Agatha countered . T.J. flayed out in all directions,' What about it?' . . . you fucked off and locked yourself in the van!'

Agatha did his best to think quickly, no mean feat for the man,' . . and what about when I rescued you from the alligator's wrestler's wife in New Orleans before you blew it big time! . . .he was one mean motherfucker.' T.J. laughed, ' well it was my birthday and she had a southern drawl.'

'Sure and wasn't it myself that got you the job with Nun-Such in the first place, you habermagallion.' Agatha grinned disarmingly and chanced his arm for the secret handshake, the tension melted as quickly as was inflamed. Blessed, as ignorance is bliss, limited by a short concentration span and the constant need for both attention and action to ward of the acute pain of having to think for himself, Agatha twisted his head in search of the next prank. He spotted a little old lady sitting with a couple of friends sipping milk stout and gumming a ham sandwich, Agatha lurched over, ' that looks nice granny. Mind if I . . .' and with that he snatched a bite of her sarnie, grinned manically and skipped away. Mouth agape in shock, her dentures slipped forward, her horror

18

apparent as she stared wide eyed at her assailant. Never in her life had her snack been seized and she'd lived through austerity, the great depression and the war. Her consort Percy was as quick off the mark as his old war wound and rheumatics would allow,'YOU SCALLYWAG, if I wasn't 86. I'd have you. . . I was in the last lot you know, wounded at D.Day I was. . . up to my neck in muck and bullets and for what? . . . so you and your mob can act the maggot. . . Get off with you and get a haircut.'

Percy shook his fist,' alright Vera? . . . I showed him, young gangster.' Percy continued mumbling into his pint. Only he knew his heroic wound was accidently self inflicted, when he sat on his bayonet in the landing craft and sustained a nasty laceration to his right buttock. Just the thought of it still made his eyes water.

'I hope I die before I get old,' Betty muttered to herself and looked at the motley turnout, again wondering who'd be next and how soon.

Just then a sad sight shuffled in, self consciously peered around until she spotted a familier face and then smiled weakly.

'Roxanne!' T.J. hollered,' overe here babe.' He stood up and waved her over.

She looked a bit embarrassed and limped over.

'She looks a real state,' Molly said too loudly. Studying her unkempt greasy hair, creased and stained clothing, 'Christ Almighty,just look at her! Talk about the wreck of the Hesperus, reckon she just dragged herself outta the sea. . . She should have gone down with the ship and done us all a favour!'

Betty eyed her companion with unease and was embarrassed by Molly's lack of humanity and tact.

T.J. offered a seat,' What'ya done to your leg?'

'Nothing, it's just a bit sore.' Roxanne slummped down wearily and glanced around nodding as she spotted old friends.

'God she looks rough. . .' Molly whispered to Betty, enjoying her chance to kick a dog when it was down' she was always a slapper, but look at her now'.Molly gave a spiteful and insincere wave and a thumbs up.

T.J. nipped up to the bar to get her a drink and a plate of the meager victuals, while Agatha got stuck in to chatting her up, ever hopeful and always desperate for a leg over.

She wolfed the food down peeking about nervously, as Agatha and T.J. exchanged curious glances.

Between mouthfuls of food they managed to coax a pitiful story and the downward spiral of a girl in trouble; a shocking and a cautionary reality check. Moments later T.J. stepped outside, returning with a supermarket trolly stuffed with bags; her life in tatters; a pathetic testimony to abuse and excess.

Roxanne hung her head in shame and started to sob as her secret was exposed. Once she'd had it all, married to Freddy Clay, with all the trappings of success. The fast cars, mansion on the hill and jet set lifestyle, but she was arrogant and aggressive, burnt bridges, with few real friends and more enemies.

'Those that the gods wish to destroy they first make mad', for Roxanne it was too true, she took to sex, drugs and the gangster lowlife, with the relish of a beetle to dung. Giving no thought to the future, adding alcohol to the heady mix for safe measure. The downfall was inevitable and everybody, but herself could see it coming like a train on the track closing at speed. Freddy fuelled by drink and drugs, exploded like a volcano in a police investigation and sordid scandal that completely eclipsed any previous accusation. Such was the nature of his criminal behavior, they were both ostracized by friends and arrest was hours away. He committed suicide in a very public and extravagant manner, fuelled by cocaine and whisky he filled his Lamborghini with cans of petrol and crashed it into the offices of a Sunday sordid newspaper.

Roxanne fell to earth like Icarus with melted wings and descended into addiction, alcoholism and anything that would help her temporarily evade her demons, for permanent escape is impossible. When she had lost all self respect and sold, or had stolen all her possesions, she flogged her body and soul to fuel her cravings. Now homeless and hopeless, she was a spectre from yesterday at anothers wake, frail and frightened with no future and few friends.

'Look at us, not a pot to piss in and that bastard Rock scooped the loot and doesn't give a fuckin' hoot. . . You'd weep, you really would,' Betty said downing her fifth G'n'T and wishing the room would stop spinning,' Betty slumped in her chair feeling nauseous; she tried to focus on fixed objects to ground herself, reading and rereading the notice offering o.a.p.'s special rates for midweek lunches.

Passing out, she slipped under the table to miss the parting of the clan, as they reluctantly retreated to the small existences left open to them to endure their autumn years as yesterdays forgotten ravers.

Agatha glanced down at Betty and tutted ' I dunno some people just can't take their booze.'then weaved and wobbled to the gents. Whistling tunelessly he fumbled his flies,the pressing need was on him before he managed to unleash himself and a wet patch developed on his crumpled strides,' ' Argh shit, not again'. He looked up at the posters on the wall and carefully read one particular ANTI AIDS advert which proclaimed rather grandly,' THE FUTURE OF THE WORLD IS IN YOUR HANDS.' He looked down and saw he was dribbling from his drooped digit onto his boots and shrugged, sniggered and the fag dropped from his lips,'bugger, that's me last baccy !' He considered retrieving it, then saw it soak into soggy.

As he passed the girls on the way back, he saw Molly trying to revive Betty before she herself succumbed.

Vera and Percy watched the hooligans leave.

' ere Percy now that peace has been declared I'll buy you a pint of Old Battleaxe. . . ' Vera reached deep into her handbag and delved,' . . . OH MY GOOD GOD ME PURSE HAS GONE! . . . PERCY IT'S GONE. . . HEAVEN HELP ME. . . IT'S MY PENSION I ONLY JUST GOT IT FROM THE POST OFFICE!'

THE GHOST OF A CHANCE.

The road through Rock's Dorset estate was smooth, unlike his rocky road to riches. He was as brutal and viscious as an alligator with its tail trapped under foot. When confronted you'd never know what to do for best, remove your foot and free the 'gator to vent its anger. Keep it trapped and buy time, hoping it might cool out; perhaps better to accept the inevitable and resign yourself to a mauling. In spite of his negative traits, Rock was canny and calculating, although no philosopher, nothing was as it seemed in the complex web of deceit that was his raison d'etre.

Morals and truth had long been jettisoned, all was fair, no matter how cheap, or outrageous, as long as he got away with it, untarnished by the fallout; better to let some patsy take the consequences.

He had once been told that Hitler said,' the broad mass of the nation . . .will more easily fall victim to the big lie than to a small one.' Rock saw the sense in that and took it as a maxim, encouraging his PR lakeys to leave no stone unturned, no cock and bull story untold to promote his perfect rock'n'roll profile.

The public image of Rock was an outspoken, anti-establishment hell raiser who was the vox pop of the discontented and disenfranchised. In short he was the beat of the street, a city poet that had captured the zeitgeist of his age and become a true working class hero.

Of course the gutter press, set their hot gossip hyenas to crawl through the slime and rattle the bones to expose 'the facts and nothing but the facts' for the puerile entertainment of the great unwashed. There were many lazy Sundays in which the outrageous and sordid were exposed, as a good redblooded tits and bums scandal is an intrinsic ingredient of a 'healthy' rock'n'roll lifestyle. Who would take him seriously if he was a temperate church goer, faithful in all, a pillar of society devoted to works of charityand taking tea with the vicar?

However, Rock wasn't commercialy blinkered and increasingly aware of the power of the pink pound had cheekily titled a track on an album ' Buy Today Gay Tomorrow' & quietly encouraged a rumour that it might might just have foundation, while publicly denying it with a wry smile.

One time, the vocalist of a rival band died in true rock'n'roll fashion,choking on his own vomit, after another excessive lost weekend, Buck mentioned it was a good career move.Taking this on board, Rock spent time contemplating the early and spectacular demise of somebody in Nun-Such. He eventually gave up on the idea, unable to decide who exactly was expendable and how to do it

.Much like Churchill, who he greatly admired, Rock believed that ends justify means, nothing was ruled out and if required would consort with old clootie himself.

A born misogynist, his father deserted the unborn Errol and his mother Dolores, a fan of Errol Flynn, when told the fruit of their loins was growing. Despite her best efforts and several transitory' uncles' , Dolores failed to capture a live contender and slowly descended into the comforting haze of gin and a vacuous alternative reality of soap operas. Rock pretty much brought himself up, quickly learning street credibiity, as confidence and arrogance grew, aspiring to leader of the demonic doggery. A cock on the walk, he aggressively strutted his stuff around the 'manor' and gained a reputation as The Bad Boy. He was loathed and detested by the parents, feared by wimps and adored by rapscallions. Of course girls are fickle and quick to form a crush on the strong and powerful, no doubt some genetic conditioning. They are happy to overlook character flaws, perhaps encourage them, as a gangsters moll has a certain allure, and there is always the chance a girl can change the man.

Adolescence is a minefield for relationships, driven by emotion, craving acceptance and a desire to discover self. Infatuation can ignite immediately, burn ferociously and be extinguished as quickly, but the heartache may linger in smoldering resentment. Girls came and went easily for Rock, as he broke hearts and hymens,with no regard for the pain and turmoil created. He detested girls for their flutterby mentality and easy virtue.

Increasingly brutal and cruel, he used and abused them, exploring deeper and darker recesses of sexual fantasy. He watched his peers marry and settle down in their teens, often from dire necessity, often to girls fribbled, sucked dry and rejected by himself, he was incredulous. Why hitch to one bitch who will become a witch, with untold out there willing to give their all and spend their life happily wallowing in bitter sweet memories?

Shadow was a cut above the others in terms of security, having semi-retired from the road. He'd landed a desk with Buck's company PREDATOR, enjoying pay, perks and cash incentives for 'exceptional endeavors', accompanying Rock when he needed a discreet minion to manage his machinations. Shadow had organized a meeting with Rock and now drove a company 4 x 4, with Mutton and Betty to the crucial encounter with the future.

All threehad conspired over the previous months, since Cornish Johns wake, honing an idea Betty had woken to, along with the mother of all hangovers the morning after the hard nights wake.

Everything came together for Betty, when dawn roused her with an urgent need to pee, a mouth like an ancient Indian flipflop and some naff drummer kicking a snare in her skull. As she sat upon the cracked stained throne, strained neurons within her brain connected the magnificent Country Life houses, her degenerate band of losers,subsidized lunches for o.a.p.'s and then threw up.

Shadow reluctant at first,finally realized that there, but for the grace of God went he and accepted the idea. Once the worm of discontent enters the brain it gnaws away like a weevil spreading fear and anxiety and for all his swagger, he feared a lonely future. Being Rocks 'Percie' had left little time to live his own life and some of Rocks attitude rubbed off, as he feasted on the crumbs of the rich mans table. Shadow was happy to further exploit and violate the girls, stripping them of whatever dignity they still clung to before callously rejecting them.

With time came perception and he began to see himself as he really was without pretension, naked and alone among dispassionate strangers. What he saw scared him, now bald with deep creases, obese and suffering from the aches and pains of a fast life, he'd developed diabetes, a heart murmur and acrid flatulence.

He was also pragmatic, aware of Rock's insecurities and bitter hatred of Geal's insight and achievement. Shadow had learnt the crouched cunning of conspiracy and the resulting rewards from Buck, who was lower than a snake and sharp as a shark in shallow surf searching for a snack.

Betty complained every time shadow polluted the atmosphere,' you need to change your diet and kecks! keeping her window open, despite the icy wind, Betty was glad to arrive safely as Shadow drove like a boy racer on adrenalin.

Mutton had drifted off minutes after the journey began, snoring without respite, despite Betty's sharp digs in the ribs. Shadow had turned the radio up to silence Betty's nagging, Muttons snoring and the rumble of thunder between his legs, but to no avail, his discontent was pervading and pungent.

For Betty the journey proved an inconvenience on many levels, not least her bladder problem, which wasn't helped by the motion of the vehicle and the pot holed roads.

Shadow stopped once at a village fish and chip shop for food and an urgent comfort stop and was intrigued by the couple that served them. Although he only saw Kirsty,who kept shouting to Aaron in the back room, he insisted on loudly playing his 50's r'n'r . She looked like a runner from the Rocky Horror show and he wondered if the guy in the backroom had a quiff, drape jacket, brothel creepers,an articulated pelvis and funky attitude.

Piscepore Abbey, just out of Pokespuddle was a moated convent looted by Henry V111 in the reformation, after stripping it of ostentasious riches he handed it to a court favorite Darcy De Valerian. The De Valerians enjoyed mixed fortunes through the ages,often taking the wrong side in the murky political and religious struggles to rule the roost and believed might was right.

They were prodigious breeders and married for money and power. The family motto translated from Latin 'Something Will Turn Up', held true until the 13th Earl, down on his luck and running with the new rock aristocrats discovered acid and pot. Having inherited the family estate and the crippling debts imposed by death duties,he chanced his arm on a cast iron opportunity to change his fortunes in a flim flam. Borrowing heavily from a seemingly magnanimous Buck to invest in a Golden goose that only lay lead eggs His dead cert went wild, turning out to be so much pie in the sky and Champagne Charlie found himself even deeper in the crap. A bum trip on purple haze only added to the anxiety and the blood hound of depression dogged him. After a last blast at Blaizes night club grooving to The Crawdaddies he crashed his Lotus into the pretty coloured traffic lights in Fulham, wiping himself and Lucinda Lytchett out.

The music pumping out of the car 8 track, the only undamaged accessory, was 'The Last Time' by the Stones. Charlie looked surprised by death and Lucinda was a strawberry stain on the road having flown through the windscreen.

Never allowing sentiment to cloud his judgement, Buck snapped up the estate from befuddled and distant relatives, who were only to pleased to offload the burden of running the crumbling edifice, pay off the death duties and make a small fortune.

Buck then sold it to Rock who in the fudge of initial fame and fortune and completely amazed that the mass of youth would lap up his bilge, jumped at the chance to own a mansion. He invested in restoration, turning the outbuildings into a recording studio, swimming pool and gym, although he preferred to watch his 'staff' working out than exert himself beyond the bounds of pure pleasure.

25

'Oh my God!' Betty was astonished as they passed over the drawbridge and into the courtyard.

'Oh shit!' Mutton was bounced awake by the rumble of the bridge and immediately his nostrils were filled with a putrescent stench.

The jolt had found Shadow out and he followed through unpleasantly, his face reddened with embarrassment and his knickers were a touch browned off.

Putting pedal to metal he covered the last hundred yards in great haste and slewed to a halt, ' er.the boys and girls will sort you!' Shadow jumped from the car speeding uncomfortably to a side door.

Betty reluctantly followed and a pretty girl in a maids uniform opened the door with a smile 'Hello M/S Crocker, please walk this way.'

Betty thought she had over emphasized the M/S and watched her slender frame strain provocatively against her tight uniform as she walked and thought,' if I could still walk like that, I might be mistress of the house, rather than a charity case' sighing sadly.

Mutton followed on eyes firmly fixed on her rump fascinated by the sway, until Betty noticed and sharply elbowed him,' Behave , you'll do yourself a mischief!'

Both Betty and Mutton were astounded at the opulence, Mutton more by the girls he kept glimpsing and also bemused by the ladyboys that winked at him.

Neither should really have been surprised at the former backstreet boy who had stumbled across fame and fortune, lost the plot and become a parody of a popstar.

It was just that neither had seen Rock in domesticity, although domestic was very much a misnomer. They'd been closer to Rock when the press coverage was overstatement and hype designed to enhance and entertain without the complication of truth.

But nothing of Rock was genuine, from his stack heel boots, to his bottle black barnet, he was attachments, cosmetic enhancement and connived complications with arrogant attitude.

Anthea led them into a reception room, explained that Rock was returning from a weekend in the Jersey, asking them to wait, smiled sweetly, noticed that Mutton was fixated on her cleavage, giggled and fluttered her eyelashes coquettishly.

'He's been over to pat the cash.' Mutton said in a rare moment of wit. Then feeling a long forgotten stirring in his loins, he shifted, momentarily forgetting the unpleasant sensations there abouts,' I think I'm gonna like it here.'

'Mutton behave!' Betty admonished,' Your hard put to get it up, let alone keep it up.'

Both mooched around the room, examining various   rock'n'roll memorabilia, smiling in recognition at

some and wincing at others. Betty was drawn to the plaster cock on the mantelpiece,handled it and quickly

found the little pimple she remembered, stroking it a little too affectionately, wondering if he could still do the

business.She doubted it, at least without Viagra, when they had, oh so briefly been an item he was a disappointing

droop. For him it was no longer a sexual thing, it was power he pulled because he could, that was his

buzz,thereafter it was mechanical and boring unless the perverse occurred.

The Barbie doll in uniform returned with coffee and biscuits, while a secretary of indeterminate

gender in a neat pin stripped suit popped in to assure them Rock was in the air.

The walls were adorned with photos of Rock through the ages, here the rebel without a clue in a leather jacket,

Levis and a brylcreamed quiff and over nearer a desk the sophisticated and cool lounge lizard. In those rare

moments when self esteem was low and the spirit fragile, Rock needed these tokens and trinkets to bolster his

confidence and give him the strength to perform the charade another day in the same old way.

Fifteen minutes became fifty and Shadow returned in a fresh set of clothes,' Rock shouldn't be

much longer, you know how it is!' He settled in a padded leather armchair by the log fire and quickly dozed off,

although not so quietly as his little problem was still manifest. The novelty of the room was exhausted and Mutton

watched the dust swirl in a sunbeam tapping out the tick tock of the grandfather clock with a teaspoon on the

coffee table. Betty had found a gold embossed leather bound volume of Rock's personal press cuttings and was

engrossed in his back pages, laughing fit to cry at the gross exaggerations and blatant lies.

After about two hours the prissy 'missy' in the sharp suit returned, 'Mr Sturdy is hovering and will be with you

directly, the deep drone and heavy vibrations from without penetrated within and evidenced her claim.

'Hello children, long time no see!' Rock was at the door, 'how's life in the fast lane?'

Buck followed him in huffing and puffing, burdened by briefcase and box file, looking more than a tad concerned

and distracted,' I'll make those calls now, they'll just be getting into the L.A office.'

'Yea do that!' There was an edge in Rock's voice and his look withering,'And get it right, this time!'

Shadow guessed all was not right at the ranch, but then things rarely were, Rock thrived on other peoples

27

stress and tension and revelled in their discomfort and distress.

To his way of thinking people were to be prodded and provoked, until he tired of their presence, then swiftly discarded to be replaced by fresh faces filled with naive optimism. During their brief tenure among his entourage it was routine to embarrass and humiliate them.

While busy servicing his whims and fancies, however absurd, they had little time, or energy to conspire against him, or steal his loot and thunder. It was also a grand distraction, he hoped that none would dwell long, or deeply on his own foibles. Just to be sure, all and sundry that came within arms length had to sign, almost in blood a confidentiality agreement that would all but crucify them if they transgressed the letter of his law. Along with his glory came increasing alienation, insecurity and paranoia, he trusted no one, often with good reason as he made enemies of potential friends as easily as he goaded and vexed existing enemies. Perversely he sincerely believed that all he met were in awe of him, his power and manifest wealth and therefore more than willing to suffer the slings and arrows for the privilege of knowing him. This attitude was not exclusive to his underlings, he regarded the members of Nun-Such merely as appendages to support and exercise his incredible talents. Rock had the measure of Buck and Buck knew it, although old habits die hard and Buck was ever trying to get one under the wire. Although unknown to Rock, his manager was no also ran as regards sneaky secrets from the past waiting to pounce on the present,going to great lengths to know the yackety-yak and await his moment.

Nun-Such were a global brand, multinational companies were prepared to pay good money to be associated with the groups iconic ? Logo. Which Buck had acquired for £25. and a pass to a years English gigs, after Buck organized a competion at an art school.

As it happened, they only did three English gigs that year and two were in exam time and far up in Northern wastelands.

Everything imaginable from plastic fantastic novelties to ostentatious flights of fancy, taking in a range of sex toys were fair game ,as long as Nun-Such picked up a healthy wedge and some royalties along the way. There had been many a lonesome young lass who had pleasured away her dull evening vibrating away to Nun-Such's albums and more excitingly, Rock's rather over exaggerated electric, orgasmic juice extractor.

'So Shadow tells me you've cooked up something to my advantage,' Rock was brusque, ' it better be good, I'm a busy man and don't like time wasters,' his eyes rested on Betty and he inspected her,

28

'you've lost your looks and put on weight,' he sneered,' not such a good lay ,hey?'

Betty looked aghast, blushed and glanced at Mutton, who had missed the whole thing as he'd dropped his hearing aid and was fumbling on the floor.

Shadow grinned part in embarrassment, but more in memory as he once seen Betty naked and humiliated and couldn't help but silently break wind as the memory rumbled from head to hindquarters.

'Miss prim ' darted in to mutter to Rock's and Betty took advantage of the distraction to whisper in Shadows ear, 'maybe now isn't such a good time.'

'Great news children, www. Excessallareas.com is the most visited rock'n'roll website ever.' he punched the air triumphantly,' suck that and see Geal.' The cock crowed and reached for the phone to put some hustle in the bustle of his P.R. department, he wanted the moon and sixpence to know the news.

'No, you're alright, there's never a good time,' Shadow glanced over to Rock who was settling into a leather armchair having issued instructions,' now's as good a time as any.'

'You'd better do the talking, I'm too nervous,' Betty was having second thoughts and suddenly wanted to be anywhere else but here,' I'd only screw up our main chance.'

Shadow, although not exactly brimming with confidence, felt that the spin he'd put on the proposal would swing it and having spent the best, although it could easily be argued the worst, part of his life pandering to the beasts barking bite, believed he knew how Rock's mind worked.

Shadow had learnt the hard way and Rock was a master, well versed in the brutal and blatant art of look, listen and learn, only a fool failed to find the way things were and where one stood in the pecking order. Shadow had only been with Nun-Such a few weeks and like a kid in a candy store,hardly dared to believe that he was touring the U.S of A with a top group. The first gig in Boston was just a haze, America a culture shock , he seen it in films, but upfront and personal it was strangely different and being jet lagged only added surrealism. The mean streets of New York, armed cops on horses in mirrored shades and unbelievably huge cars with acres of sparkling chrome, white wall tyres and fins. The yanks had attitude, confidence and swaggered down the streets, everybody in a rush and seemingly intent on some vital mission, even if it was to grab coffee, pastrami on rye, a slice of cheesecake and oggle the pussyfooting girls.

As he and Rock stood outside the Algonquin hotel, home of many literary and theatrical icons stretching back to the turn of the 18th century. He was agog as the crowds surged by, yellow cabs stretching bumper to bumper and the sound of the streets as the vehicles drove over metal plates covering the potholes. Steam hissed from gratings in the streets as he had seen in many films, he felt he was on the set of some musical, or a gangster movie. Searching faces in the crowd hoping to spot Bob Hope, Cagney or some other familiar film face. A cat brushed against his legs, meowed and walked into the hotel as if it owned it , the doorman reached down to stroke it. 'Morning Matilda.'

Shadow was impressed and called,' So even Yankee cats stay in hotels in, hey?'

' This one does Sir. She owns the place, it's Matilda, the latest in a dynasty that goes back to the thirties, . . . You're with that pop group ain't ya bud?'

Shadow felt important, although it was reflected glory as he stood next to Rock, who was obviously a star in dress and poise, all leathers and arrogance, Shadow nodded vigoursly.

'Excuse me sir. . . '

Rock turned and saw a couple of teenagers wearing Nun-Such tee shirts, baseball caps and sporting all manner of band merchandise, some of which he wasn't aware existed. He suspected that Buck was pulling a stroke, quietly knocking out shmutter and raking in buckshee shekels. 'where did ya get gear?' He demanded.

' Gee Whiz. . . You're Rock Sturdy, aren't you Sir?' The boy asked,' I'm Randy and this is Kandy,' he pointed to the girl,'we're massive fans of Nun- Such. . . and of course you. . . you are Rock aren't you?'

Rock nodded ungraciously, ' That gear, where did you get it?'

'Far out. . . you're really you,' Randy was checking Rock out from head to toe,' you're much more. . . sorta real in the flesh. . . awesome. . . Kandy and I just got married.'

Rock turned to look at Kandy, thinking they weren't old enough to marry, Kandy was well fit, pert tits and a body ripe for harvesting, she wasn't beautiful, but had an interesting face, amazing blue eyes and brassy blonde hair. ' Married you say, h'mmm.'

' Yea we saw you were touring and thought it would be really neat to get hitched and come to New York for our honeymoon and see the band. . . We took the overnight greyhound from Idaho, awesome and now we've met you. . . we've been outside the hotel for hours.'

'Idaho? . . where's that?' For Rock, the States were L.A. and New York, everywhere else was nowheresville.

30

'Can you sign this for us, it'd make or honeymoon kinda neat. . . we've got all you discs and Kandy has a scrapbook. . . she's really hot for you.' Randy thrust an album sleeve forward.

Rock had eaten brunch earlier with Buck, who was anxious as the single was wallowing outside the Billboard top twenty and seats for the tour dates were disappointing,' we need something to kick shit.' he said, dashing off to meet the east coast promo man.

Rock eyed Kandy, who looked like jail bait and suddenly had an idea,' hey kids, how would you like to be my personal guests tonight . . . you say it's your honeymoon and I wanna do something special for you. . . something you'll never forget.'

'Oh wow. . .awesome. . . did you hear that Kandy, far out. . . do you ,mean it?' Randy was on cloud nine and Kandy, who had yet to utter a word was dumbfounded, but with a body like that anything she said would be a disappointment.

Rock turned to Shadow,' sort it.' And then checked his look in a plate glass window,winking at himself, 'That old black magic's got me in a whirl. . . ' He sung jubilantly.

The sound check dragged through the afternoon, Rock kicked his heels, as the drummer got a sound and then fell off his stool in a daze of dope and jet lag. The bass player was next up, moody but on the case, followed by guitarists who tuned, retuned and ran a few riffs. Rock was bored out of his box, but had time on his hands to plan the evening campaign. He called Shadow over and being uncharacteristically discreet whispered his orders,' get your arse down the village, there's a kinky knicker shop, get a basque and thigh high patent leather boots. . . . and make fuckin' sure no motherfucker knows. Got it?

Rock prodded Shadow in the chest with a stiff finger,' understand, if anybody knows before the number.You're dead meat, I'll cut your bollocks off and fry em for breakfast. . . right shift your arse!'

It wasn't until Shadow finally got into the shop having spent an hour searching the mean streets of Greenwich Village and getting embarrassed asking for the exotic knicker boutique, then he realized he had no idea of sizes, so guestimated.

Rock dispatched Shadow to meet Randy and Kandy and smuggle them to his personal dressing room, where he plied both with wine until Randy was out on his feet and Kandy was dizzied up for anything.

'Kandy girl, I want you to do something very special. . . I want you to come on stage, you're gonna do something that you'll never forget and help me make the States.' Like the spider to the fly, Rock slowly enticed her into his web of intrigue,' you'll be magic. . . just think of it, outa all the chicks out there, it'll be you up there on the stage.'

Rock showed her the knick knacks he had for her and stroked her hair,' you're gonna look great in these.. . . Ever heard of Annie Oakely coming around the mountain in the Deadwood stage?'

Kandy glanced at them, hesitated and said,' you want me to wear this stuff?'

'Yea, you'll look awesome. . . it's a kinda stage outfit, we all wear special things on stage. . . you can't go on looking like some local loser. . . nobody would bother coming if they thought you were just like them. . . you gotta make an effort.' Rock leaned over a kissed her,' what'd'ya say Kandy. . .it'll be fab?'

Kandy fingered the bodice and was quite taken by the boots, this was the stuff film stars wore, like Marilyn Monroe and Jane Fonda. You couldn't get clothes like this within a 100 miles of Riggins.

Then she thought, ' this'll show Sarah Lee Harper and Donna Marie.' Her high school days had been tormented by their bullying and cruel jibes that she was white trailer park trash.' Yea I'll do it!'

As Kandy struggled into her clothes, which were at least one size too small she hoped Randy would come round and see her dressed up like a million dollars, she knew he would be knocked out and it be a sight he'd never forget.

There was just one thing and despite searching high and low she was at a loss and Shadow was evasive and embarrassed, but like the Gestapo he was in the pay of a tyrant and only following orders, however odious. Kandy was nervous and nauseous, she had been plied with more red wine in the one night then she had ever previously drunk in her life,was perspiring copiously and butterflies fluttered in her belly. Shadow reassured her unconvincingly, in truth he had little idea what was to befall her. His orders were to lead her onstage in the darkened interlude between ' Rock and a hard place' and ' Painful Love'.

Buck stood in the wings of the stage anxiously, his worries and woes compounded by Rock's terse words as he bounded on stage at the onset of the show,' You might wanna have a legal eagle on hand!' He smirked and winked,' We're gonna be the talk of the town.'

They say if you can make it in the Big Apple you can make it anywhere, which may, or may not be true, it's certainly a fact that New Yorkers have seen it all, heard it all and mostly done it all. Perversely, America has a strong religious and moral undercurrent, especially in the bible belt and among the quirky pseudo snake oil salesman that quote the word of the Saviour while quietly emptying your wallet and telling you the Lord loves you and will provide.

In the darkness betwixt and between, the applause for the last number faded and an expectant hush followed, broken only by calls and chants, guitars retuned and tokes from joints.

Shadow did his masters bidding leading Kandy to her allotted place, as he did so Nick noticed the unexpected addition to the line up and turned questioningly. As did the others, as they saw and were equally perplexed, the road crew were bewildered, but not surprised, they were often the last to know as they were beasts of burden with attitude and treated thus. Buck was pacing the boards in the wing, wringing his hands in despair as he glimpsed the future and didn't like what he saw.

He tried desperately to catch Rocks eye and end it before it began, but to no avail. Rock was intent and would brook no interference or censure, he was top dog and his bark and bite were equally barbaric, as were his morals.

With the opening chords of 'Painful Love' the lights flashed on, at first few noticed the blindfolded girl handcuffed to a lighting Genie, but Rock screamed,' WIPCRACK AWAY' snapped a bullwhip in his hand and leered 'My love is too painful for you to. . .'

A sharp eyed follow spot operator picked out Kandy and pinpointed her in limelight,all eyes turned to her, gasps of amazement and shrieks of indignation drowned out the band who had began to falter anyway. It became increasingly apparent to those with a clear view that Kandy was not only bound to please, but bereft of knickers and hysterical, kicking and straining to free herself.

Buck hustled the roadies onto the stage, but they were only seconds ahead of a clutch of New York's finest who swamped the stage dragging off members of the band and vainly attempting to free Kandy as the fire curtain crashed to the ground, narrowly missing one or two in the confusion. A deal of consternation later Kandy was wrapped in Rock's sweat soaked towel by a female cop called Janet Kallametie and led away still sobbing.

A night in the cooler did nothing to dampen Rock's aggressive and arrogant attitude, for all his bluster and bombast, he knew that ultimately the golden rule would prevail (those with the gold will always rule) and it would all be so much hot air once a wedge of cash had changed hands. The only chaos and complexity was in establishing, whose palm to grease. But that's what expensive and eloquent legal eagles did.

There was a need for a sacrificial lamb to appease the vengeful public and much hyped media outcry and

Shadow was the fall guy. No shrinking violet, Rock had no qualms about delivering up the scapegoat.

Three days in the slammer and the imminent prospect of a trip down the river for an indeterminate stay in the

horrors of Rikers Island, was an unwelcome burden and he justifiably felt betrayed and all sold out.

Hearby was the first hard lesson direct from the streets of hard knocks, he was a vassal, only one rung up from a

slave and was expendable without a moments consideration.

But for Nick,shadow would have faded from the story and been a fleeting figure in the history of rock'n'roll; a

forgotten pawn lost in the great game, left to be raped and rot in the terrible nightmare of the pitiless American

penal system.

Rock insisted it was Shadow who conceived and contrived to execute the jape, a practical joke in bad taste

that had spiralled out of control and it was Shadow that had bought the risqué costume. Further, it was Shadow

that got her pissed and unexpectedly took her on stage and handcuffed her. Rock conveniently forgot to mention

the fact that he had a whip in hand, having never previously used one and fortunately nobody questioned the

fact.

Shadow was fortunate to get a $1000. fine for lewd and lascivious behavior and was bound over to keep the

peace and Nun-Such's single grabbed the number one spot in the billboard top ten holding it for five weeks and

the tour sold out, with three weeks of additional stadium gigs.

A lesser lad might have seen the way it was always to be and jacked it in, to forward their own life without the

torture to mind, body and soul that being Rocks lacky would entail, but life on the road with a band is a

mighty adventure, more a lifestyle than a job.

A STEP IN THE RIGHT DIRECTION.

Betty could hardly believe it, pinching herself black and blue checking it wasn't a stoned dream, months had passed like minutes and she now stood before 'the mansion on the hill.'

When Rock said do it, it got done bloody quickly, he aimed the gun, targeted the victims and was the main man, any others were merely crude mechanicals, at his behest.

Shadow presented the outline idea, which Rock initially ridiculed, but Shadow followed up with compelling reasons to which Rock gave serious consideration.

As a matter of course Shadow kept his ear to the ground and was party to every whisper in wind in Buck's office, it paid dividends to listen to the scuttlebutt.He was aware of Rock's desperate desire to be honoured, recognized by the establishment and get connected with the movers and shakers that mattered. He also knew that Rocks paranoia of a past attrocity beyond the pale of that already accepted as his norm would sink all hope. Rock had carefully invested time and money in rebranding himself as a lovable rogue with a heart of gold, who deep down was proud of good old British tradition, the Royal Family and the heritage of the nation. He was keen to keep 'the crew' in a tarnished cage, ring fenced from the preying eyes and carrion crows of the media. But the pivotal point was a folder of facts and figures, showing creative accounting and charitable trusts yielded considerable tax breaks. He was snared hook, line and sinker.

Rock was also buoyed by the success of his album, a contrived project called 'Up the Girls'. Realising that songs with a girls name in the title appealed to girls with the same name, he had some research done on the most popular girls names of twenty five years previous, as this age group were his target audience. Commissioned aspring songwriters to compose songs based around these names, with the proviso that he was credited with co writing them. With the release date a few months away, he was looking for a good P.R. boost and saw the establishment of the retirement home would be a stunning vehicle for it.

Rock was very much a man for all seasons, having no qualms about back tracking from a problematic cul de sac, his previous single, a male chauvinist anthem called 'Ditch the Bitch' had spectaculary bombed amid ferocious feminist protest.

A little over a fortnight later, having had the pros and cons investigated, Rock announced his idea a goer and he was going to generously fund a retirement home for wrinkly roadies and comfort ladies. On certain terms and conditions, to be negotiated and confirmed, which he along with Machiavellian legal eagles and accountants had concocted. The devil is in the detail and apart from Shadow the others weren't about to wade through the pettifogging jargon of the small print.

Opportunity knocked, which in this case was the security of home, a bite to eat for those rock'n'roll frequently forgets and the chance to rave to the grave.

REFLECTION.

Lashed by the icy rain of another Atlantic gale, struggling against a wilful wind, Geal howled with laughter at the absurdity of life and the living of it.

Here on the Western point of Eire, where land and sea began and ended, an uneasy balance held sway, wild and raw now, but profoundly tranquil and benign when the tempest faded and a gentle muse ruled. Whatever mood the weather favoured, served only to enhance another fabulous facet of the emerald land and sapphire sea. The light of steel grey skies gave luminosity to the landscape, broken only where the sun punctured the cloud to cast golden shafts bestowing a transitory magic of being to some distant cottage, copse, or field.

The accumulated fame and wealth of his life seemed meaningless here, this place and time were priceless and beyond the jaded pomposity of poets, saints and scholars. The rugged unforgiving cliffs and awesome Atlantic waves relentlessly driven to dash violently against solid stone, having travelled over 3000 miles, were fleeting and ferociously free.

No life form could own another; only the body was prisoner, the soul was free to roam at will on a whisper of wonder.

Geal had long felt a prisoner, albeit in a gilded cage, and was all too painfully aware that his youthful ambition and astounding success had created it. His greatest strength his biggest weakness.

Here he was free, no appeals or demands on body, or soul, his time or money, no gleeful recognition, or pen and paper thrust at him. Here he could be still, think and swim in imagination and inspiration.

Geal let the gale blast the detritus of his frantic lifestyle from his mind. From this vantage point nothing was important, all merely illusions, who would know or care about him a hundred years hence?

Perhaps a line or two in some long forgotten dusty tome discovered in an attic during a house clearance, or an epitaph in the electronic ether of the internet.

Thirty two of his fifty two years had been spent riding the serpent of success, with all its sweet and sour twists and turns. He had tasted the heady brew of adoration and affluence, and wallowed in glut and glory.

Geal had grabbed all that was available and stretched for the forbidden fruits that were always tantalizingly just out of reach. But all had a price and more often than not, the actual cost is vastly different from that first perceived and almost always beyond measure.

The first fifteen years, or so had been nomadic, roaming the world with no fixed abode, a night here, maybe a week there and sometimes a month, or two somewhere else. Recording and tour commitments held the call, his life managed and manipulated by the sharp suits in agency, management and record companies. He knew not who to trust and his lack of self-confidence made him both defensive and unpredictable; a pig in a poke most of the time to himself,as much as to others.

Stepping back from the cliff he huddled in a hollow among the rock of ages to remember and perhaps regret more than a few immature bloopers and blunders, as he blindly fumbled for his true character and identity.He felt very much a fool among bufoons and knew that he was both deceiving himself and others as he fought the fears and fantasies that threatened to thrust him into a bizarre and surrealistic void.

THE BUSINESS.

There were more in need of Rock's largess than accommodation and Betty was overwhelmed at the choice. Forced to be pragmatic she and Shadow had to reject the terminally ill, seriously infirm and outright lunatics, as there could be no provision for their care and support.

Betty found it heartbreaking and spent nights crying into her pillow, coping out in as much as she got Predator to issue the rejection notices, avoiding the phone, lest it be a desperate appeal for clemency. She wasn't wholeheartedly in agreement with the final list, but Rock and Predators dictates were paramount and although she was allowed a say. There were 32 occupants for 23 bedrooms, so some sharing was required, but old friends were happy to have a pillow to lay their head and accepted compromise in good spirits, often 40% proof.

Nothing enjendered by Rock was without complications and the negotiations of purchase were brutal for the sellers. Rock's team could offer cash as an incentive and demanded a knockdown price and grudgingly received it. Rock also required a neon sign at the entrance stating this was the ROCK STURDY FOUNDATION, this was rejected as a hazard and distraction to roadusers. The local council were slow to embrace the unwelcome invasion of wrinkly wasterals and concerned about a drain on overstretched resources. Eventually Rock settled for a brass plaque naming the place DUNGIGGIN, although the locals dubbed it KINKY WRINKLY.

As Cathel O'Dowd said at the planning meeting,' Rock is it ,sure we've no shortage of such here about and the importation of foreign stone is a scandal ,entirely befitting the worst excesses of the E.E.C. and more than a man might stand.'

Even the suggestion that a donation to the G.A.A. & the sponsorship of the beach racing day was eventually rejected as improper by a majority vote of two. A Ms Plunket, who'd long since taken every pledge, was strictly teetotal, celibate and believed drink, fornication and gambling to be the labours of the very devil himself. Whom she frequently glimpsed parading triumphantly in the wee small hours, from the relative sanctuary of her net curtains, as she fingered her rosary and sought the protection of the blessed virgin.

Most often waving his willie provocatively and singing outrageous Republican anthems as he staggered back from the pub to his homefire in the bowels of the earth.

Miccal O'Coilcanin, a staunch Fenian whose family had fought and died through the ages for freedom from oppression, was adamant that no further Cromwellian plantations were required, or indeed welcome and he for one would continue the battle for independence. Of more relevance was yet another application for capital grants for Gaeltacht regions afforded by central government and the imperitive procurement of such.

The debate was heated, intense and continued long into the night ending whith a vote to retire to the bar for ham sandwiches, liquid refreshment and a session in which Eimeid Dalton played a major part, he was a hero of the hurling field, a powerful seanchai,and a cracking accordion player.

Ms Plunket abstained and retreated to her sanctum and study her bible and pray for the salvation of the sinners.

The inclusion of Dapper John Cox was controversial, a famed guitarist for Hypnotic, another of Bucks stable stars, he was yesterdays man, bankrupted and arthritic and not qualified to take up residence as neither an attitude adjustment therapist (groupie), nor roadie. But Buck insisted and apart from chattering into their coffee, the decision was absolute.

Dapper was over sexed, obsessed, reckless, feckless and a rampant dog with a silver tongue that sweet talked ladies into bed. A dandy in bespoke suits, pink shirts, striking ties and hand crafted boots, he frequently excersised a fertile phallus, which proved to be the root cause of his insolvency. He begat too many children by too many women and his scatterlings and castoffs crushed him under the weight of successful paternity suits.

It is as well to bear in mind that according to Anthropologists the entire human race can be traced back to around six hundred fecund people in Africa in the distant past & thus far science has yet to explain the origins of this fruitful family. Doubtless, Dapper had a strongblood line and DNA link to these fructuos folk and was endowed with the energy and passion to entertain the opportunity to extend the family tree.

Once asked how he would like to be remembered by Patsy Prurient, pop gossip reporter from some daily fluster and bluster tabloid, Rock said,' as a philanthropic visionary, a humanitarian giant and a sympathetic spokesman for the common people.' He'd stumbled across the words in the obituary columns of the Telegraph and thought it sounded like the sort of thing that would impress the elevated society he aspired to join. Although no regular reader of any paper, he had suffered acute constipation and been confined in a convenience with no other distraction and with no toilet paper, wiped his arse on the article.

Charity begins at home and for Rock his charity retirement home was a means to an end for him alone and the actual residents were meaningless detail.

Among the basket cases was 'Agatha' Christie O'Loone, a sad and disappointing result of an evoloutionery experiment that had foundered on a reef of despair. Darwin would have considered returning to the Galapagos to see what else had crawled from the sea with a notion of reviewing his theory, had he the misfortune to discover Aghatha.

Perhaps the Neanderthals had not entirely died out and a rogue strain had defied all the odds to endure and create madness and mayhem among modern man, but then, this may well be an unwarranted calumny on a grand generation. Another thought is that the notion of the Neanderthal having any direct responsibility for the likes of Agatha may well be a foul slur on an early branch of mankind, who any modern man would be happy to have a pint with down at the dog and duck.

His mucker was T.J. who was creased and stained from birth and perpetually looked like he'd been dragged through several hedges sideways and then across recently manured fields and was best viewed downwind from a distant landscape. His one saving grace was as a reasonable drum roadie, who could often play better than those he served, being able to hold a beat without slowing, or speeding as the tune progressed.

Another to mention was Tic-Tac Evans, a dimunitive Welsh pain in the fundamentals; cold as a witches tit, brutal, fiscally tight, uptight by nature and able to create and argument in an empty room. Emanating from a Borth caravan park, Emanuel was the result of a loveless union, a knee trembler in a shop doorway and born to be a hustler.

ROOTS.

Geal finally felt he had come home, it had been a long and confusing quest, perhaps a journey better sidestepped, had he known the cost of his ticket to Ryde at the outset.

His dad had been a tunnel tiger, one of thousands who left their native Ireland to seek work in England, many travelled to the new found lands. A native of Donegal, Padraig had followed the other young men from his village to London and the further constructions of the London underground.

He became one of the elite among the other navvies, a tunnel tiger, which in itself was an oddity, as a man would be lucky to find a depth of six inches of dirt before hitting bedrock in County Donegal. He had cousins who'd emigrated from remote Achill island in Mayo to New York who became, along with Mohawk Indians the men who built skyscrapers. Working away thousands of feet above the bustling streets, seemingly fearlessly, a crowd of them had been immortalized in an iconic photo picturing them lunching on a swinging girder with a dizzying view of the street below. All brothers and cousins and not a one of them having ever lived above ground level in the humble two roomed cottages back home. Evidence of Irish versatility, or perversity desperate to earn their daily bread, but deprived of opportunity on home turf.

At first his life was work, drink, eat, church and sleep, but youthful urges to sow wild oats led to the Irish pubs, clubs and dancehalls of Counties Kilburn and Cricklewood. The craic was indeed mighty at the Crown on Cricklewood Broadway and the Galtimore, a ballroom of romance with a sticky carpet soaked deep in spilt Guinness and Baby Sham, a little further on was almost a home from home. Here after many futile attempts Padraig finally plucked up the courage, with drink taken, to invite the vivacious redhead with flashing green eyes to dance. It wasn't the most romantic of offers, in fact it was rather terse,' You'll dance then.'

Looking up from the massed ranks of wall flowers, she saw the wild haired Irish rover she had dreamt about around the turf fire in the Kerry cottage, she smiled gently, 'That I will.'

But then Padraig was down to earth and not given to flights of fancy and the fripperies of society.

His proposal of marriage months later was equally prosaic,' You'll marry me then.'

Mary replied, with a beguiling smile,' That I will.' And tossed her mantle of flaming hair provocatively. She had her man for better, or worse, in sickness and in health, with a hope of a little wealth,until death would part.

42

The marriage had lasted forty eight years and as good Roman Catholics, produced nine children, seven of whom survived into adulthood and varying degrees of maturity.

Scouring the newsagents cards for accommodation was depressing and often fruitless as most of the cards had a postscript; no dogs, no blacks, no Irish, no kids. They eventually found a squalid damp basement in Westbourne park owned by a nice man called Rachman, rearing their family as best they could.

Mary a devout Roman Catholic Kerry girl, Padraig fond of drink, tobacco and pub conviviality were often in conflict and troubles were inevitable, but their bond survived until Padraigs kidneys, liver and lungs could tolerate no more abuse.

For Geal and his siblings life in the fifties and early sixties was drab, almost black and white with bleak Sundays, closed shops, after ten when the newsagents shut having sold out the Sunday sordids. Without fail weekends saw around half a dozen pitiful people emotionally and physically torn apart for the titillation of the masses. Some deservedly, others just hapless victims of circumstance, but all with human failings, foibles and flaws that all endured.

Padraig was a man of routine, Mary and the kids knew exactly where he was at any given time of day. Sunday he would rise around nine, having slept off Saturdays session in the pub, wash, put on his best suit and then the entire family went to mass at St Mary of the Angels. Catholic Herald in his back pocket,they chatted and joked with friends and neighbours, safe in the protective hands of the Lord, having paid homage to the sacred heart. Duty done, she returned to cook the lunch and he was back over the pub by twelve for a pint, or four and the mighty craic with the boyos before the Sunday roast at home. With the pubs closed at two, the kids were sent out to play and Padraig and Mary had a crude mechanical and for her dutiful fumble and fuck, once spent, he rolled over and snored and farted through the afternoon fug until the pubs reopened.

Monday, he was off to the tunnels by 6.30 am and Mary took his best suit down to the pawnbrokers for the cash to get through the work. On Friday the pledge was redeemed from his wages, ready for the Saturday frolics, the money was always spent by the Sunday night and the relentless routine resumed.

Like all the other slum kids none knew they were slum kids and just lived the life, making their own amusements. With WW2 bomb sites still grim reminders of all too recent conflict and human tragedy, few cars on the road and the freedom to explore, the only constraint was lack of imagination. Inspired by Saturday morning pictures, Geal could be the Lone Ranger, Geronimo, or Flash Gordan, as it suited. Cricket and bootball were played in the road, interrupted only occasionally as the odd car pootled down the otherwise empty roads, or some film company staged a car chase. What radio heard was 'Take it from here', ' Family Favourites', 'the Brains Trust', and 'Workers Playtime'. All wallpaper for the rude mechanicals with crude dreams, conditioned responses and few viable aspirations, beyond surviving another day.

'She'll be coming round the mountain and the Deadwood Stage', 'I love to go a Wandering, the Ugly Bugs Ball and How Much is that Puppy in the window,' were the hits of the time and hummed on buses and sang badly in baths, if available. Clubs and pubs often had ad hoc and enthusiastic entertainment, although the nature and quality offered often stretched credulity and enjoyment.

Then Geal heard Lonnie Donegan, Elvis and Gene Vincent and was blown away,he began to see colour and reason to be.

The older brothers followed the father and a dynasty was founded underground, pics and shovels were relegated to the apprentices while the seasoned stalwarts took to the mechanical diggers and earthmovers. Geal was fourth in line and determined not to spend his days in artificial light deep in the bowels of the earth. At every opportunity he and three school friends wangled their way into ever concert they could. Just to hear that wild rock'n'roll music was to be liberated, freed from the mundane, in his mind he could travel route 66, ride the rock island line, or gyrate in the jailhouse with the king.

Chuck Berry, Bo Diddley, Buddy Holly and Ray Charles knocked his socks off and focused his resolve, he knew what he wanted, but not how to get it. However, once it is possible to visualize an objective the subconscious kicks in and a road opens up, although it isn't always entirely straightforward.

Now a regular face in the right places, Geal was mixing with like-minded guys and quickly learning about soul, r'n'b, blues and the historical hotchpotch that was the beating heart of humanity.

Around this time, Geal won a victory at home, in light of good exams results he was accepted at the Slade Art school and his proud parents happily gave their consent.He was the first O'Neill to gain any grand titles and that meant much to Padraig and Mary, the family were going somewhere.

The piercing skreel of a gull wheeling and diving into the angry sea paused his thought and allowed the chilling wind to penetrate his bones . Away over the fields, near stunted and sparse skeletons of thorn trees, ten standing stones stood silent witness to the passage of time, and the transitory temerity and paradoxical tenacity of mankind.

Geal knew the myths and legends of his birthright, his blood ran rich with Celtic pride, the enduring blood sacrifice to nationhood and the resilience to endure the oppression of occupation in the pursuit of freedom and identity.

Through his formative years Mary told of kings, battles and the origins of things magical and fabled. Although her education had been rudimentary her father came from a long line of seanachi's and his storytelling and knowledge of all things historical was the talk of Dingle.

Fir Bolg, De Danan, Wolfe Tone, The Flight of the Wild Geese, Cromwell, the Easter Uprising, Michael Collins, the names, events and romance of tragedy tumbled around his brain, bereft of sequence, or consequence. These had been the source of his lyrics, the stories passed from generation to generation by the likes of Peig Sayers and Sean O'Crohan from the Blasketts, all he did was take the familiar themes of life in the raw and reinterpret them so a new generation could understand and find empathy.

His thoughts drifted through some of the faces of his days, the other guys in the band, the rag tag of roadies and the suited sharks of power. In the main the gods had smiled on him, bestowing gifts of creativity and imagination, which he hoped he had used wisely.

No, luckily maybe.

Geal remembered that Napoleon wanted lucky generals and then Shakespeare;

'. . . there is a tide in the affairs of men, which taken at the flood, leads to fortune, omitted, all the voyage of their life is bound in shallows and in miseries . . .'

He remembered Mr Wilkes drumming it into the unruly middle third year at Holland Park comprehensive one depressing January afternoon, with Christmas well over and nothing to look forward to until Easter. Mr Wilkes, a forty something wreck of a man in a crumpled jacket, his youth and spirit spent in the horrors of a Jap prisoner of war camp in the Far East. His shaky hand and tendency to falter and wander in mid speech a schoolboy howler.

A wave of shame touched Geal's conscience, now he understood and had sympathy, but it was all too late now, his cheap laughs had very much been at Mr Wilkes expense.

Later that bleak damp January afternoon, the hell of enduring his devastated life proved too much and he jumped under a tube at Notting Hill Gate, to the annoyance of untold rush hour commuters, who were consequently late home for Coronation Street.

Mr Wilkes was one of thousands damaged by the atrocities of war and unable to make the transition to civvie street, but offered a drab demob suit, the possibility of mushroom farming, or teaching as a way ahead, with no further emotional, or social support.

Pity both teacher and pupil.

Geal recognized and was grateful for the accident of birth and a youth spent in the slums of West London, with its crucible of cultures all rolling and tumbling in the austere post war poverty of rationing and recovery. In retrospect,Geal felt privileged to have spent his formative years in Notting Hill it was exciting and all he experienced developed his creative muse and an empathy with real people, who had aspirations, not pretensions.

In time the family qualified for a council house and moved up to Oxford Gardens, just off Ladbroke Grove, neatly betwixt Portobello Road, where upon reaching the age of reasoning, the O'Neil lads got Saturday jobs on the market and became street savvy.

Geal's sister Meave eventually married Ronnie, a barrow boy who lived just off Wormwood Scrubs, but spent as much time inside the prison as he did on the estate outside.Ronnie was just another likely lad looking for the easy option, ' a rough diamond', as his mother was fond of saying. The local coppers and magistrates had a more prosaic description,' an unremitting and unscrupulous villain.'

Still, Meave loved him and that was enough for the O'Neils, they stuck by him through the ins and outs of Ronnie's years. It was in fact through Ronnie's enterprise that Geal's first band 'Flahoola' obtained their instruments and some while later the old Commer van that transported them. Ronnie yearned to be their roadie, but old habits die hard and he was hardly ever able to make the gigs.

PHOTO OPPORTUNITY.

Pugnacious Patsy Prurient was reluctant to venture far from the sleazy and putrid troughs of self indulgence she frequented in search of fresh manure to reveal about the racy rock stars her shallow readers lapped up to fill vacuous lives. She had done very nicely out of wallowing in the triviality and hyped hogwash that she portrayed as normality in their dissipated world. She would have refused the assignment out of hand had it not presented an opportunity to delve deep into further depravities of her nemesis.

Striding purposefully through the accumulated muck that had been washed off the hills by the several days of torrential rain, Patsy viewed her mud splattered designer wellies and sighed sadly,' why on bloody earth did you have to park the O.B. so far from the pub?' She berated the foppish director, who trailed in her wake like a bedraggled puppy, with cameraman and soundman in toe.

'Patsy love, Patsy. . .' Julian implored, ' Rock's man was most insistent that our trucks should be out of camera shot.'

'The bastard . . . He's done it deliberately,' Patsy had a cruel glint in her eye and her lip was curled in contempt, ' he'll pay for this. . . ' She slipped and slithered, eying a questionable deposit on the drive suspiciously, ' I suppose you didn't think to ask why it was only our facilities that were barred from the carpark ?'

'Patsy sweetie, Patsy,' Julian blustered, blundering through what Patsy had avoided, 'oh shit!'

Eric the camera and Steve the sound sniggered, neither of them particularly fond of either Patsy, or Julian and much enjoying their obvious discomfort.

The service yard was a confused carnival of vehicles. Eircom engineers, electricians and removal men vied for access, all at sixes and sevens and the intervention of Agatha did more to complicate things, his basic grasp of Gaelic was lost in translation and raised hackles. His command of English was little better, as was his sense of logic and organization. Muddle and mumble was his forte, which presented a marvel of misadventure and misunderstanding.

On the front steps preparations for the main event were not quite as envisioned, or indeed hoped for. Betty held onto Beaver (the house cat) who had taken exception to travelling in a basket and was intent on retribution, also juggling her much prized diary. This one item was instrumental in securing Dungiggin in the first place as Betty had always kept a diary and besides her souvenir plectrum necklace every tryst and turn was recorded there. Those

47

Betty hadn't personally laid had graced the loins of her many lady friends and girls gossip. It is said,' keep a diary and one day the diary will keep you', many with an untoward history they'd rather forget had long feared the notorious black book.

Strutting his stuff with attitude Rock steamrollered into this important P.R. exercise and photo opportunity, preening and peering at his reflected image.

Nothing was left to chance, his hair was freshly dyed and coiffured, his nails sharpened and polished along with his regular botox injection. His people had been on the case for weeks coercing and cajolling all and sundry on both sides of the Irish sea to do the masters bidding.In the best rock'n'roll traditions the entire affair was late kicking off, because of Rock's tantrum, for no good reason, simply because a practiced showman knew it added dynamics.

Finally and with a flourish honed on the worlds stages, Rock stepped up to the microphone after Shadows hyperbole.

'Ladies and gentlemen it gives me great pleasure. . .'

'That it does. . . .' a Kerry man called from the crowd, ' t'is obvious'.

Rock glared at the crowd who were laughing, but he was not about to let heckler put him off his stroke,' So much for the cabaret. . . O.K. who let the dogs out?' The dogs were supposed to come later, a mutt's strayed.'

'Rock. . .' Patsy piped up,' can you confirm that you applied for a lottery grant and were rejected.'

'Yea, so what?' Rock glowered through his shades, if looks could kill.

'Can you also confirm that you applied and were elbowed by Age Concern, Alzheimer's and Arthritis Research, community hygiene and 27 other charities?' Patsy; mutton dressed as lamb, a formidable female hack who had seen it all and tried a bit herself, although she'd never inhaled, or swallowed anything of a compromising nature. Through the years she and Rock battled verbally and in print battles and their feud endured as both protaginists looked for every opportunity to wound the other.

Patsy's mission was to ultimately destroy Rock and he had previously employed private detectives and court injunctions to gag her and used interviews to harangue her reputation. Their enmity was legendary and everybody enjoyed and were entertained by each bout, which was symbiotic. Rock knew the only form of defense with Patsy was attack and he mixed sweet'n'sour charm with some success.

' Patsy, sweetie, as you know I'm a visionary in a world of limited imagination. I know only too well the pain of rejection and it is for this very reason that I came up with the idea of 'The Foundation'. These boys and girls gave their all for Rock'n'roll and I just couldn't't sit back knowing they needed comfort and succor. I simply asked those organizations for advice and support in my quest to comfort and cheer those that society has shunned. . . Sadly none felt able to extend the charitable hand to soothe and relieve the dilemma of my people.'Rock smiled sweetly,' next question.'

A dozen hands shot up and Rock eyed the scene contemptuously seeking familiar faces and safe questions, but patsy was again quick off the mark.

'Rock, we've all seen the bumph, just another transparent press release and photo opportunity for your greater glory.' Patsy's eyes glinted as camera and lights focussed on her,' What's the real deal?. . . Why are you doing this?'

Rock sighed audibly and deeply as if visibly wounded by Patsy's attack on his sincerity,'Patsy, Patsy darlin' you know me, we've both been around the scene, more than a few times since God invented the electric axe. . .' He eyed her scornfully,' and it certainly shows on some!' Rock smirked,' Hey cats, I'm straight from the heart, give me a break!' and then as an acid afterthought,he again fixed Patsy ' still with the weekly fuss and feathers, luvie?'

Patsy was stung, buzzed for a moment and then waspishly went for the jugular,' about your Bangcock gig. . . would you like to comment on the persistant rumour of the Lady boys at your hotel?' Her eyes blazed and she smirked.

Rock was flustered and visibly squirmed like a ragworm on the hook, then as in all good cowboy films the cavalry charged in the form of the brouhaha and hullabaloo twins.

Patsy was blown away in the whirlwind like one of her Sunday sordids the other side of midnight as Monday mornings mournings rolled hot of the presses to tittilate a depress the commuters in equal measure.

A siren and incessant car horn interrupted and all eyes turned to the drive where a gardai car, hearse and white stretch limo vied for position. Chaos, confusion and congestion reigned supreme and Rock angrily looked for somebody to blame for the past and seemingly future humiliation.

Shadow shrugged and watched, all attention focused on the melee and cameras tracked the travesty that had stolen Rock's thunder, then it came to him and he whispered in Rock's ear.

'Hey, think about it. No publicity is bad publicity and this will guarantee you get a slot on the evening news.'
Rock thought for a second,' yea your right, but it'll look like something outta the Keystone Kops. Not a good look and Patsy almost stuck it to me big time.'

Over on a nearby hill and old silverback fox ate the remains of fish and chips discarded by a removal guerilla, he'd once had the run of the peacefully deserted pad and was now having to adjust to a radically new regime. With a swish of his brush, he sniffed about, positioned himself and contemptuously crapped, took a final glance at the rumpus and set off to chase rabbits.

The rabble arrived at the steps where a bemused Rock and entourage watched two Gardai officers, O'Casey and O'Connor release Agatha and T.J. from their car, the hearse driver in sombre black emerge from his Daimler and Dapper John tumble from the limo.

Once more eyes and cameras panned to Rock, who smashed a bottle of fizzy water against a column raised a glass of champagne to his lips and announced, ' Cats and kittens give it large for Dungiggin and remember there's dog in the old life yet! ... Oh yea and don't forget my best ever album,''Rock on the line.''
is just out, buy it now and do yourself a favour and make sure you don't forget your uncle Brian's birthday, he'd love a copy!'

BACK PAGES,

Out at sea a small fishing boat pitched and rolled, homeward bound and happy to be so, as it braved the Blaskett Sound in temper and turbulence. A pod of dolphins pranced and pirouetted in the bow wave and wash, spinning and splashing to port and starboard, alive and playing in the moment.

'For those in peril on the sea. . .' Geal sang the phrase to himself and remembered his school assemblies singing the hymn, it meant nowt to London kids, whose only experience of water was watching Thames ebb and flow, or the cut. Fascinating and foul ,drowned kittens in sacks, dead dogs eyes staring from bloated and bleached bodies, dumped guns and the gunk and garbage of wanton waste in the mephitic effluent of the canal. Now and again some shipping disaster made the news and if dramatic enough might hold the public attention for the duration, or if the stuff of legend for millennia. But life is crammed with catastrophe and there's always another one lurking in tomorrows shadows and reflections, to shatter comfort and complacency.

Geal now knew some of the superstitions of fisher folk, respecting their lore, but was adrift of the merciless reality and content to accept their word.

Those unfortunates who fell overboard expected no help from others, to steal the prey of the sea was to invite retribution. Many a scatterling and orphan was created by such cruel luck and beware the redhead seen by sailors before a voyage, she was the harbinger of disaster. No rare vision in a land of flame haired Celts gathered in close communities for comfort and convenience.

Here and now he could appreciate the capricious power and nature of the element, for aeons the dashing waves had lapped and smashed against the coast. The courageous lunacy of mankind to boldly launch forth in relatively fragile creations, to ride the back of the awesome oceans, in search of the unknown and perhaps sail into an eternity just over the horizon, or drop off the end of the world.

The playwright Synge had spent a few summers on the Aran islands, thirty miles out from the mouth of Galway Bay, during which time he collected the oral folk memories and stories of the islands.

He was told,' The man who be not afraid of the sea will soon be drowned, for he will be going out to sea on a day he shouldn't. But we do be afraid of the sea, and we do be only drowned now and again.'

Whenever he had stage fright he remembered those words and found the comfort and courage to confront his demons. On the odd occasion his misgivings had proved correct and the gig an embarrassing fiasco,he then reasoned that you needed the downs of duff gigs to measure the glorious lift of triumph and a hard lessons learnt.

Like most of humanity he was searching for order, routine and reoccurring patterns in the chaos of the planet and never sure if it actually existed, but he had a fragile faith however futile at times and trusted that everything had a time and purpose.

Padraig was such, convinced that if he studied form he could win the pools, or pick winners at Cheltenham. Like fishermen, mug punters abound and talk of landing the big one that slips away through bad luck, or the conspiracy of knaves. On the other side of the coin, the fish and the bookie see only good luck. For all concerned the game continues and all will again tilt at windmills, no matter how the wind blows, in search of serendipity and the elusive fickle finger of fate that twists and twirls, always to return to a natural source.

The fishing smack was making slow progress against the heavy weather, once or twice Geal thought he saw Lowry like matchstick figures on deck and waved to communicate empathy and fellowship. Maybe they didn't see him.Perhaps he only imagined the fisherman. Most likely they couldn't be arsed to wave at the eejit perched precariously on the cliff.

Soon the gourmets in Dingle would be cracking crab claws, picking mussels from shells and selecting live lobsters from the tank in the restaurant. The dinners, restaurateurs and fisherman in pubs would toast a tasty treat and the spot of profit.

As for the crustaceans, if they could reason? Perhaps they can and find little comfort in conclusion.

With weather and wondering, Geal felt as if in a washing machine, his physical being soaked, windswept and chilled, his spiritual equally storm tossed on a spin cycle of emotion and memory. Some neurons sparked and he conjured up a vision of people packed into the mobile metal tubes of London underground like sardines in putrid oil. The smell of stale sweat and halitosis, probing eyes and sordid imaginations, the invasion of space, groping hands, stray jabs and prods with bag, briefcase, or brolly.

But paramount the dilemma of where to focus eyes, more than a passing glance invites embarrassment, usually a glare is returned, rarely a smile. However, what can a poor boy do and how to resist when a plump and pert pair of boobs, or legs that go all the way are forced into vision.The city can be a mean and menacing place, threatening, but always intrigue and interest. How could a boy born in the Donegal wilds of unrelenting rock and hard times endure and excel as a tunnel tiger boring through the claustrophobic clay deep under London, to create a transport hub that brought so much freedom to travel and so much misery of repetition? Geal felt pride for his father and pity for the commuter.

Copeland did well to compose his homage and salute, 'Fanfare For The Common Man', as did the Stones with 'Salt of the Earth and Factory Girl', even if the latter viewed with cruel contempt. Arguably judged uncouth, vulgar, shallow and cheap by those with an assumption of superiority, the backbone of any country are those that grease the wheels, check clogged cogs, tap the trunnions and wheedle the widgets. It was the' nobody knows' of this world, the anonymous heroes and heroines of drudge and humdrum, living in quiet desperation with no visible light at the end of the long dark tunnels that perversely most deserved honours and recognition.

Once very much the former, Geal had now reluctantly to admit, with wealth and fame he was apt to judge the book by its cover. It was almost instinctive and he invariably cursed himself for his snap sagacity moments later, but he jotted down these odd moments of insight and observation with a view to a tune. True he still maintained a house in Notting Hill, but it was atop the hill at the posher end of Ladbroke Grove, rather than the families former council house at the bottom, nearer to North Kensington proper. Then he also had a studio houseboat on the Amsterdam canals, a log cabin in the Canadian wilderness and now this old automated lighthouse complex on Cathedral Rock. His own island, now there's a thought, all 2 miles by 3 miles of rock constantly harried and tormented by the Atlantic intent on reclaiming it. Vegetation was sparse,but extremely tenacious and took advantage of any nook, or cranny to gain a roothold. Fuchsias, Escallonia, Montbrettia and Gunnera, a few twisted and tortured thorn trees seeming to grow towards the mainland in hopes of rescue and the old walled home garden in the lee and protection of the lighthouse cottages. He'd heard a tale of an old lighthouse keeper who one stormy night had seen his precious cabbages lift one by one to be blown by the ferocious wind way out into the wild Atlantic. Geal could fly at whim by private charter to any of his properties and spend as much time there as he desired. Nowadays he wasn't shackled to composing, gigs and recording at the dictate of management, agent, or record company, but his own capricious creativity drove him on. Geal viewed money in the same way he viewed hammers, mearly a tool with no inherent intention to create good, or evil. A hammer could help build a hospital, or in malevolent hands provide a patient there in.

Such is the penny in the piggy, the pound in the pocket, or the millions in the Swiss numbered account and offshore trust. Like most Geal like to think he was wielding a benevolent hand and had inflicted little harm with his wealth and power, but who could be sure, certainly not governments and multinationals.

For more years than he cared to acknowledge he had been like all youth, brash and insensitive and with fame came the 'great I ams'.

An ego in overdrive, fixated with a delusions of self importance and completely convinced by the publicity generated by incredible success. No different to untold others who gained the fickle gifts of fame and fortune early in life, initially the thought was it could never end and then anxiety and insecurity edged in and conviction began to become concern.

Geal had lived a false face for nearly ten years, during which time he began to appreciate the rocky road he was travelling was not all it seemed, the once smooth and golden pavement was cracked, treacherous and tarnished.

Sex had become mechanical, routine, his lovers faceless and nameless, just another body to abuse for the ever decreasing rush of orgasm and the high of personal possession.

At first cantankerous and increasingly curmudgeonly, Geal alienated those closest to him, questioning their relevance to his existence.

Who true friends and which were merely fair weather acquaintances along for the ride and rich pickings?

Who a loyal and trusted retainer and who a parasite taking all with nothing returned?

He remembered a report he'd read in a magazine from some psychiatrist observing that the age success was achieved was the age of maturity there after.

A mild cramp broke his train of thought and he struggled to his feet stamping his left leg on the ground to return feeling, the twin pleasure and pain of pins and needles, he limped along the cliff top.

In the distance on the sandy strand he glimpsed a figure walking with three dogs frisking and romping with the Atlantic breakers, he paused to watch and wonder.

BRAVE NEW WORLD.

Mutton stepped blearily into the bright new way and day treading deep in doo doo. Scrapping it from cowboy boot to nettle patch he was joined by a jaunty Lucy Lastic returning from a walk and carrying a wild flowers, nestled within a dove in distress, 'Look, I found this bird.' She offered it,' I think it's broken a wing,' her words were tender.' It's so lovely here, the birds and wild animals, how can this happen?'' she smiled sweetly, smelt her flowers,' don't worry little bird I'll love you.' Lucy piroutted, 'I've seen rabbits and foxes, don't you just feel so alive?. . . Have you seen anything?'

Mutton looked at his boot, 'yeah, you could say that.'

'It was so much fun yesterday, really. I didn't want it to end,' Lucy had her usual white fairy frock on, a headband of daisys and white high heeled shoes, much mud splattered,' I'm so going to like it here, that policeman Mr O'Connor told me they have dolphin called Fergie in the harbour.'

'You mean Fungi. . . yeah me and Betty saw him when we were first over,' Mutton though briefly, ' he was alright for the fuzz, letting T.J. and Agatha off, mind you, it was a misunderstanding, nobody got hurt and the bus company got there money back.'

'Oh that's so good,' Lucy pointed quickly,' look a butterfly. You know they say, butterfly morning, wildflower afternoon!

'Yea, I fancy a bacon butty and some black pudding,' Mutton was bored and turned to the door,' see you.' he glanced at his boot, knowing Betty would go ballistic if he trailed fox crap through the house,' Fookain fox!'

Betty sat at the Kitchen table with Molly drinking coffee and casually wading through heaps of junk mail ; stair lifts, copper bracelets, bulk deals on incontinence pads, vitamins and Viagra and a brochure hand delivered in the previous days fiasco by Jerimiah Stixe, the creepy undertaker.

'. . .yea I'll have another cup and banana bread?' Molly snorted suddenly.

'what's up Molly, you alright?' Betty looked concerned.

'No, no.. . it's the . . .' she sniggered and then burst out laughing,' . . . that little zombie funeral man is offering two for one on burials as an introductory offer.' Molly paused and laughed more loudly,' . . . and it say's here. . .' she looked again at the card through tearfull eyes,' anybody catered for' she was all but on the floor and doubled up,'Don't, oh don't,'too late. . . oh dear I wet em!

Both herself and Betty were convulsed as Mutton entered, 'any chance of a bacon but…',

He was bemused at the sight of Betty doubled up and Molly slapping her hand on the table,' what did I say?'

'Nothing luv, nothing important,' She added softly and with affection,as one has for an old damp mongral with a tendency towards flatulance' as usual.'

Dapper John Henry Cox awoke in a fug with an erection and urgent need to pee, instinctively he glanced to his side to see who else was in the bed and reassured saw a mass of black hair, he couldn't't see a face and had no idea who it was. But it was definitely female and he was heartened to know he could still do the business, even if he couldn't actually remember who with. Every women was magic, the sway of hips, that certain look in the eyes, the fall of hair, a deep cleavage, the bounce of boobs maybe just the fact that they were female. Being female was most important as once or twice, when pissed he'd made mistakes and discovered on waking that the night's love of his life was a transvestite.

He loved them all, the problem was, there were just so many of them and with the best of intentions, he was easily swayed by the next fancy. He never stopped loving the last, but loved the next as much and doubtless love the latest equally. He also knew that sometimes it took a lot of time and effort to find the true magic in some women and in truth he just didn't have those precious hours to waste, when he could be loving instant beauty.

Only once at Dapper John stayed long enough, his only marriage, to realize that when a woman starts wanting to wash your clothes, change your habits, hair, clothes and tidy up your home it's getting time to scuttle off into the next amorous adventure, before emotional barbs ensnare you. Dapper John had two talents, he had been a better than average guitar player, before increasingly arthritic fingers had cramped his style, but above this and beyond his reason, women were besotted by him. Another gift, perhaps a mixed blessing was his high sperm count. Of course he could have had a vasectomy, but it scared the pants off him and he'd heard that it could lead to impotence.

Having eased the urgent call of nature, he returned to his bed and breakfast, as he called his morning quickie, to discover that last nights mystery seemed destined to remain so, she'd done a runner. Dapper was not downhearted, he hated goodbyes and it saved him the diplomacy required in discovering her name. The the unmistakable noise of a blown exhaust jogged his memorie. The limo that transported him across Eire had been forced off the drive in the skirmish with the Gardai and undertaker and taken the exhaust out on a rock. The driver, Caitlin, who had a wonderfully sexy accent, a pert bosom and a very inviting arse, had explained that she couldn't make the return journey with a dodgy rear end and arranged for it to be repaired the following morning at a local garage.

Dapper hastily agreed and ever the gentleman offered her a bed for the night and a something for her trouble, which she had eagerly agreed to, as Hypnotic were a legend in her parental home .Her dad, had all their albums and proudly proclaimed he had seen their Dublin castle gig and had a drumstick and plectrum as proof. Caitlin couldn't wait to tell him that she had given Dapper a ride, she knew he'd be very proud of his 'darlin' little girl'. A pride that was tainted nine months later when she delivered a more enduring souvenier of her one night stand and was called a slut. Although the very beefy and bouncy boy child was called John and her dad was chuffed, on the quiet, as he now had a unique momento of Hypnotic and was now a distant relative.

Betty was a new age earth mother, delighting in good home cooked wholesome and organic food, although a confirmed meat eater. She soon established a vegetable garden, got a few dozen chickens and a few goats for milk. Such ventures didn't come easily to the undomesticated, but the girls were keen to learn. Mutton liked the idea of pigs and Agatha and T.J. were keen on home brewing and home grown weed.

But these ambitions were not achievable overnight, or indeed without some disasters in the making, fools rush in where the wise give thought before action and perhaps decline the challenge. The fookain fox appreciated free range birds, as did the rabbits and slugs tender vegetable shoots, Mutton discovered there's more to pigs and goats then meets the eye and the foot. The menagerie was further expanded, when it became apparent that the extensive lawns required regular mowing and nobody fancied the job . 'Mutton,' Betty demanded, having consulted the free community magazine ,' West Kerry Live' the font of all local knowledge,' we need sheep!'

'We do?' Mutton was taken aback, but warmed to the idea as he liked hanging out at the livestock mart and the idea of bidding with the boys in the auctions, although his deafness often meant the action was a little too quick for him. Their sheep soon became a souce of amusement and some affection, gaining the names one would expect from eejits like Agatha, who thought some had very attractive faces. Ba Ba and Black Sheep were

57

obvious, as was Lamb Chop and Basheba and although not quite a Doulton shepherdess, Betty was often seen far from the maddening crowd counting the flock before bedtime.

The nearest town, fifteen miles down the road was Dingle, a pure delight with its rumored fifty two pubs, the boys quickly settled on Dick Macs,it was easy to find. For Dick Macs was opposite the church and the church likewise was opposite Dick Macs. Many a birth, death and marriage and doubtless a few divorces were celebrated, or commiserated in both establishments.

Like many a pub in Eire the establishment could serve several purposes, sometimes grocers, or hardware stores, or funeral directors. Dick Macs had also been a cobblers and although no shoe had been made, or repaired for years, half of the establishment was still set up, with all stock. Not a large bar by any stretch, although several rooms led off from the bar, but cosy, if rudimentary. In one corner was a small booth, the snug, where gentile ladies could benefit from a glass of iron rich Guinness, without enduring the good natured hurly burly of hard drinking and important men's talk.

Free to chat, gossip and discuss the circumstance of domestic bliss, or otherwise, seek solace, advice, sympathy and bitch about those other women who didn't have decent standards, or were carrying on outrageously

Both ambiance and décor were surreal, much like a deserted film set awaiting cast and crew; most movies a pastiche of reality, no matter the character and quality. The cliental, perhaps to give them an over grandiose title were the eccentric and colorful, regular and transitory. From the salt of the sea, through the men of the sod to the bizarre from the stars and bars, virtually all earned the accolade of unique.

One could get merry with genuine cowboys looking up the family roots, crazed celebrities, outrageous authors and the common man who routinely faced the sublime and ridiculous of the mundane in pursuit of the daily bread. Tales of daring do, trepidation and woe, cheered and thrilled and storytellers required copious lubrication. Blind and crude bestiality of desperate lost souls swimming in hatred, frustration and obsession, drinking to forget, shared bar space with compassionate, human, noble and self-effacing seekers of a better way to lead a positive life. But within these walls, with a pint of the black stuff and the warm welcome of comfort and the craic, these barriers dissolved and a common thread established.

Dapper was the exception, favoring Foxy Johns bar and hardware store on main street which he deemed more appropriate and as it transpired closer to the doctors surgery, an increasingly important fixture in his diary and present raison d'etre. Of course with the reputed 52 bars in and around town no man really needed to rely the one place. But as creatures of habit and unless one gets banned from one establishment, the urge to circulate is not strong.

SKEETER.

Skeeter had also lived the hurry up and wait lifestyle that one fumbling for a footing in a fools paradise does and accumulated the complicated baggage of mistakes and recriminations that snare and endure. Born to a middle class Dublin family the O'Haras, Moirai her given name was all respectable parents could wish for, almost the model child, enrolled in ballet and drama classes to encourage poise and confidence, the brownies because that's what little girls did and just the right private day school.

She was around fourteen when she began to discover that the cosy secure bubble of her family's life was merely a façade. Her father was bedding his secretary and her mother in revenge the tennis coach, both knew of the other's affair, but chose to be mature about it. In some ways it spiced up their own sex life, as her mother's tennis coach was female. Moirai's sister Wendy was older and soon heard not so discreet rumours and remarks among the children of family friends, who overheard their parents commenting on the indiscretion, as it was an common knowledge in their social circles.

Wendy was appalled and embarrassed, retreating from society and finding solace in her eventing horse, Wild Goose. When Wendy blurted it out during a sisterly cat fight, Moirai was initially bemused, but quickly found
+
it hilarious, she had vision of her parents; HER PARENTS! screwing like actors in a theatrical romp, all sofas, standard lamps and farcical fumbles in furtive cupboards.

Having discovered the fraud the family lived, neither daughter could obey, or respect their parents and both slipped the leash and set out to make their own mistakes.

Wendy embraced the equestrian set and rode the circuit, both on the course and in the hay, taking the tumbles in her stride.

Moirai rejected her parents tarnished values and ran with 'The Bad Lads' from the estates on the wrong side of the tracks seeking cheap thrills and mayhem.

Within months joy riding and booze, drugs and aggressive vandalism were routine, her first brush with the law was quietly forgotten courtesy of the lodge.

But Moirai, now nicknamed Skeeter for her penchant for speed refused to toe the line, aware that she had stung the family in the most sensitive place; reputation and status, it seemed swinging was cool, but teenage rebellion taboo.

To her such blatant hypocrisy was a spur and she increased her wilful and damaging dance with destiny.

The writing had long been on the wall for all to see, wallowing in the rich kid blues. Skeeter, refusing

to acknowledge her given name, overrode her misgivings and crashed a stolen car into a chemist. They might

have got away with it, if fat George hadn't dropped the letter from the county court about unpaid fines in the

car, amusingly, it took the Gardai months to solve the case. The tear ways got a year each, Skeeter had sheaf's

of psychiatric reports detailing her mental condition and the consequences of imprisonment on an

impressionable, intelligent and fragile girl.

As one door closes another opens, the trick being to recognize the revolving doors and

began the next chapter. A professor of psychiatry pioneering a revolutionary American therapy based on

confrontational encounters with other disturbed adolescents, was on a fact finding trip from London. Skeeters

father and Professor Learie had been University roommates and in reminiscing about the good old days over a

meal in Lord Edwards they got around to marriages, affairs and kids.

' So Hugo you never did tie the knot then?' Enda was intrigued, as his Trinity College friend had been popular

with a free thinking and sexually liberated girls around the campus.

' This is a very fine Burgundy,' Hugo raised his glass to the candle and studied the colour, before sniffing the

bouquet.

Enda laughed, ' As ever elusive Hugo.'

'Some things are better left unsaid, but if you insist,' Hugo was briefly thoughtful and his brow creased,' no, no

I never married,' he hesitated,' do you remember Susan. . .Susan Laing?'

Enda searched his memory, ' yes, yes I think so, that pretty redhead from Fermoy. . . Yes, of course she

was studying, let me see. Was it Philosophy?'

' Near, Fermanagh and psychology' they both laughed, clinked glasses and sipped,' we met again in London a

couple of years later at a conference and after a whirlwind romance moved in together.' He stroked his chin,

pondering, the memory still hurt.

'And. . .?' Enda was impatient.

' She died of a brain tumour about a year later,' there was a tear in his eye,' the loss tore me apart, I loved her. . .

I truly did!' Hugo looked away, watching a waiter pop a cork from champagne for a loud American couple, then

turned back,' I could never face the involvement. . . the commitment again.,He quickly spun the conversation,'

61

and you and Sarah?'

Enda explained, deliberately missing several embarrassing and sensitive points, but soon Moirai and her problems were discussed. The upshot was Hugo offered to take her to London as a patient on the new course he was introducing at The Maudsley.

This seemed the perfect solution, it got Moirai of the legal hook, removed her from temptation and any further embarrassment for Enda and Sarah, and Moirai had long been fascinated by swinging London.

Here she met Charlie, the son of a County family with connections to the aristocracy and debauchery. Between sessions Charlie introduced Skeeter to Bohemian society.

The beatnik scene offered Skeeter the illicit lifestyle she craved, her days free and easy, with scant regard for the conventions of society. Hitching around the country, spending a few days here and there, crashing on friends floors, drinking scrumpy and smoking dope. She was of course kicked off Professor Learie's course, not that it mattered to her, she thought it too embarrassing and crazy anyway. In London she hung out at Finches in Goodge street, or Portobello road discussing Ginsburg, Keroac, Zen Buddism and C.N.D. dressing in blue polo neck jumpers, levis and a duffle coat, letting her hair hang long. She demonstrated against the madness of nuclear weapons, The Vietnam war and railed against the establishment.

Skeeter embraced free love and counter culture and blissfully loved the one she was with, only the moment mattered. She lost touch with Charlie, but heard he overdosed in a sordid squat, after getting a hotshot from dealer, who's chick he was screwing.

FLIM FLAM .

Tic Tac met a man in the bookies. A regular in Fureturs, a fairly basic affair, just the front room of Joe Fureturs home on Dykesgate lane. Joe stuck up the racing pages from the sun newspaper on the wall, tore plain paper into small squares as betting slips and got the results either from television, or a phone call from a friend in one of the grander bookmakers in Tralee. Under normal circumstances this quirky set up would leave him open to any amount of scams, but Joe had a system; no bets five minutes before the off and no payout until fifteen minutes after the result. It wasn't an exact science, he didn't have a gaming licence, but it was a father to son dynasty that had endured four generations.

Joe competed with two other licensed big bookies in town, but Fureturs had an ace up his sleeve. His relatives in the remoter areas of the Connor pass had developed a grand and specialized skill, the product of which was much sought after. His father,Joseph, the grandfather and way back into the boggy mists of yesteryear had produced potcheen. That magical spirit of moonshine and potatoes that cured all that ailed humanity, whether applied as liniment, or internally it did the trick. But five generations couldn't be in the way of it without the gardai knowing of the thing. However even servants of the law, are presumed human and sicken, with natural and illicit cravings.
Now and again some eager Dublin jackeen with an eye to the main chance for promotion, decided a new broom might sweep clean and order a crack down on the illicit spirit.

It was in no ones interest to kill the goose that lays the golden egg, but sacrifices must be made to pacify the soft city cops who are ignorant of culture and tradition. The local gardai would as courtesly inform the felons in good time of a convenient date to raid the still. A battered excuse of a contraption and the few bottles of low grade waste would be found in some remote spot. Never a distiller found, but with a creative report to Dublin city all would be pleased and the matter could rest.

The boys of Dungiggin hadn't been carousing around town that long, but had a nose for places where the craic was mighty and wild and the local boyos knew their own right enough. They might be English, they were beyond the pale, but they were good skins and brought fresh blood and fierce adventure. That strange crowd were the talk of the town, but a good scandal is welcome and a grand distraction from home grown irregularities, it helps if there is no complicated local history attached.

63

The arrival of Betty for the shop in Supa Value was eagerly awaited and reported widely, a few local ladies discreetly following them to see what sort of a thing they would buy. Often Betty noticed a knot of women around the post box at Holy Ground watching intently and guessed that they were the subject of speculation, delighting in greeting them warmly.

Equally the boys adventures and misdemeanors were discussed over pints and some even shared a roll up of rough shag with them and talk of the strange ways of pop folk was much appreciated and an intense curiosity.

Tic Tac and Joe got to discussing a castoff from O'Brien's stable with a good pedigree, but an unreliable leg that had only raced the three times, but never out of the frame and a bargain for a man with a few bob. He'd been bought out of the Ballydoyle stable for a song, but the buyer met a financial hurdle and needed to raise cash quickly to settle an outstanding gambling obligation. Joe also knew of a good brood mare in West Meath that also needed a new stable.

Joe crooked a finger and ushered Tic Tac into the back parlour, where a bottle of moonshine was produced, the cork popped and flicked casually into the corner, ' we won't be needing that again.'

Tic Tac liked that sort of talk and settled into a sofa and cast an eye around the room, which obviously hadn't been decorated since Pope Pius X11 was called home in 1958.

'You've a good bit of land back over,' Joe mentioned as he poured a steady measure into an old cracked cup. Tic Tac quickly knocked it back, gulped as the liquid fire scorched down his throat, visibly flushed and his eyes watered.

Joe chuckled, ' Slainte Agus Tainte.' He raised his favoured glass in salute and drank.

Tic Tac cleared his throat, took a deep breath and with as much nonchalance as he could muster, offered the cup again, ' what did you have in mind.' he had a feeling it might be a long afternoon and the following morning might be missed for good reason.

UP THE DUFF.

Early February, with England locked into a prolonged cold snap, Skeeter braved the chill and went to Eel Pie Island, a smudge of an island in the Thames close on Twickenham to see a couple of new bands with big futures. Crossing the bridge to the island, she was confronted by the two heavily muffled old biddies, collecting their toll, she fumbled in her purse for the few pence and was relieved when a boisterous crowd of moddy birds tottered along on their dolly rockers. Although by no means a mod in appearance, she managed to pass along with them, as the old ladies, bless 'em, got a tad confused. Like most girls, Skeeter was liked mini skirts, but given the big freeze, wondered at the wisdom of wearing next to nothing, with only white tights to warm their fundamentals.

Skeeter went alone, meeting friends at the gig, smoked a couple of joints and got hopelessly pissed on rough scrumpy. Needing fresh air she went outside to clear her head and promptly threw up, settled on a damp wooden bench and rolled into a foetal ball to let the world cease rotating.

Inside the gig the second group took the low stage for their set and the Thames flooded in ,forcing water up through the floorboards of the dance floor, developing an inch, or so of water at the audiences feet,to compete with the sea of broken glass.

Skeeter woke up in her own sleeping bag around Midday with no memory of the night before at the gig, she had the mother of all hangovers and spent the entire day in bed. It took a few days to shake off the affects of that night and she still felt odd a few weeks later, it wasn't until she started having morning sickness that the penny dropped. She was in the club, knocked up without the faintest idea who the father was, she suspected one of the friends she'd met on the island, but felt she couldn't confront him, as he was married. Skeeter became desperate, barely twenty one, pregnant by person, or persons unknown, alienated from her family and essentially homeless. True she could always find a space on a floor to unroll her sleeping bag, but wild as she was, she knew it was no way to go through a pregnancy. Her friends gave what little support they could, but their nomadic lifestyle couldn't offer the long term commitment she really needed.

You may not get what you greed, but sometimes the fates conspire to offer what you need, although it may well be a blessing disguise.

The isolated stone cottage on Bodmin moor was spartan, all but derelict , with no connected services. Water came from an outside pump and when it rained, through the roof and was discolored by the peat, oil lamps and candles the light and an open fire and primus, heat and cooking.

Morganna, three cats and two dogs actually lived there permanently, but there was a constant turnover of beats travelling through. Morganna, now fifty was something of an earth mother, once lithe and athletic, now rotund, but still enchanting. Her life and times were often so outrageous as to be barely believable. She'd travelled the world alone, when such behavior was frowned on by polite society, crossed deserts in camel trains with nomads, canoed along crocodile infested rivers with tropical forest Indians and climbed in the Himalayas. Morgana had been a sometime whore in Paris, brothel madam in South America, a cowgirl in Texas and a dope smuggler in Europe. Her travels were prematurely terminated by asthma and a severe heart condition and retreated to her beautifully bleak moors. In less enlightened times her knowledge of Wicca and the old ways would have her burnt at the stake. But nowadays open minded individuals visited to seek advice, herbal cures, or just some floor space for the night. Married twice and swinging numerous times as the gender embraced her.

Morganna had tea and sympathy, an empathic ear , a nourishing meal, a fire to warm, a bed for the night and often the comfort of tender loving.

Here in the company of Morganna and two itinerants one wintery November night, Skeeter went into a labour. As her waters broke so blew up a mighty storm that tested the tin roof, whistled through the gaps in doors and windows and rearranged the countryside according to whim .Morganna administered a potent broth which included magic mushrooms to ease the pain and release the mind.

Water boiled in a blackened kettle suspended on the iron cradle above the fire, cleanish sheets were placed on Morgannas bed and all meditated, while cats and dogs watched with curiosity.

As the contractions increased Morganna set amulets and herbs in special places, burned incense, all the while mumbling auspicious incantations. The two travellers had known Morganna for years and marginaly younger, both stoutly built with full beards, they looked like brothers, although one was Ebony Black with ginger hair and the other white and bald, both with sailors caps. They were jolly, uncomplicated with a tendancy to roll on the balls of their feet as they walked, more at home on the deck of a ship. Travelling and when necessary working at whatever presented itself, over the years they'd worked deep sea trawlers ,sailed the seven seas, driven road trains in Oz, logged in Canada and farmed. Birth and death came easy, having nursed animals through both and seen accident and incident. Within the hour of the wolf, with dark of night fading out and the light of dawn reaching for the day, the storm intensified as if the anger of all the gods boiled and fermented into an unruly battle for supremacy. Fire and tempest, wind and water, the deep rumble and roll of unrelenting thunder as the fingers of lightning cracked and clawed at the earth.

Seeking . . . Seeking?

With a final scream of agony Beeswisp was birthed, a mere slip of a baby, wrinkled red, with a fine quiff of black hair and looking like a small bundle of washing when wrapped in a pinkish towel.

Morganna said she was like a bees wisp (Irish slang for a small untidy bundle) and the name stuck.

Within seconds of arriving in her new world Beeswisp opened her green eyes and intensely surveyed her new surroundings with an all knowing look and Morgana swore she gave a wink and a smile.

'Good God, this child has been here before,' Morgana nodded wisely, before cutting the umbilical cord and passing her to an exhausted, but blissful Skeeter,' she's a very old soul returned here. . . . you should eat your placenta it'll prevent depression.'

Skeeter wasn't so sure, but Trusted Morgana and was in no doubt of her wisdom.

William searched in his rucksack and fished out a bottle of brandy, Benjamin found some old mugs and a generous tot was poured into each,' a toast to an old friend, treat her kindly, she's very special.'

'Health, wealth, happiness and wisdom,' William offered and Benjamin added, 'confidence, creativity and compassion.' and all four glasses were drained in one, at which point Beeeswisp cried out, as if in gratitude.

All laughed.

SETTLING IN.

Betty and Molly were pretty much the only residents actively involved in the house keeping, so it was quickly agreed that local hired help was required. In retrospect this had shortcomings in the shape of Nuala O'Keefe, a pretty 18 year old colleen, who along with a friend helped out as Mrs Mopps. They were cheap, enthusiastic and if they ever got the time to work unmolested did a grand job.

Nuala had already succumbed to Dapper John and given her strict Roman Catholic home and family, it had produced problems. She confided in Molly that her period was late, between deep emotional sobs and that she was scared and didn't understand why he had gone off her.

Dapper had henceforth found many other local ladies to greet and cheat and although as warm and charming as ever, had lost interest. Sean O'Keefe was not a man with a broad mind, or much experience of life beyond Tralee, very much a culchie, who entertained ambitions for Nuala to become a bride of Christ, like his sister, Mary Kate, now Sister Consumpta.

Rory Flynn, sometime jack of all trades, font of all local knowledge and general factotum, was rapidly losing the plot, easily distracted by the huggermugger of activity and loonacy that abounded. There was constant demand for his attentions and labour, Tic Tac wanted to renovate an outbuilding and fence a field, Betty erect a chicken coup and Mutton wanted to do up the barn as a rehearsal space for a band he was forming and Lucy quietly fancied the man.

'Would it be possible,' Lucy ventured as the remnants of a gathering sipped their third cup of tea and finished off the last of the banana bread,' I Think we've got Leprechauns at the bottom of the meadow by that little hill near the brook,' she smiled nervously, ' Agatha say's he saw them the other night after cycling back from Dick Mac's.

He says that's why he fell off his bike. . .'

'I'll bet he did,' Betty chided,' unfortunately it's only a few scratches and bruises.'

Molly laughed conspiratorially. ' More's the pity.'

'No really, it's so lovely down there,' Lucy continued oblivious to the cynical undercurrent,' I just wondered if we could make it a special place.' she smiled sweetly,' you know, tell the boys they can't fish down there and shoot rabbits.'

' I think your Leprechauns are more likely stalkers, I was down there last Wednesday skinny dipping and I'm telling you there was somebody lurking in the bushes,' Titbits always head to foot in black leather, adjusted her shades, to block a shaft of sunlight which seemed determined to dazzle her,'I think we should tell those two guardai, before one of us get's molested, or raped!.

Betty and Molly glanced at each other and raised eyebrows,' I'd think you could easily teach any local amateur rapist a thing, or two and wear out the poor creature!'

'Yea, they'd be more scared of you!' Molly followed,' and I think you'll find it's Tic Tac and his candid camera capers. . . Check out the next issue of Reader's wives, you'll be the centre spread.'

'BITCHES!' Titbits screamed as she jumped up and stormed out.

Tic Tac smirked sheepishly and shuffled in his seat.

'Sure he doesn't he doesn't have a camera anymore. . . I broke it!' Agatha blurted out.

Tic Tac leapt from his chair angrily,' SO, it was you. . . you cunt!'

'I was only looking at it. . . and I class of dropped it, honest.' Agatha was up and on the hoof.

'I'll drop you. . . you motherfucker!. Tic Tac called after Agatha in full retreat.

'Never Mind Tic Tac, you still got the camera in your phone and that cheque you got the other day from Nutz would buy you a nice new one .' Lucie said innocently.

Molly and Titbits had lived the good life on the London music scene and were known to many bands as 'Fun and Frolics'. Working a double act, they were infatuated with each other physically, each trying to outdo the other to look the more attractive and always wanting to be that bit more outrageous than the other. Neither were strictly lesbian, never thinking it anything more than pure pleasure, gratifying and satisfying for both themselves and the lads they serviced. Which made all the difference in the dressing room when it was make your mind up time and the place was a teeming meat market of girls with attitude, ardor and ambition. It was a good thing for a couple of years and they even achieved a measure of notoriety on the party society scene, getting invites to record company bashes and pop bacchanalias which featured in hot gossip magazines. One that never got published, although photographed and became a cult legend was an orgy at Rocks gothic house in Fitzjohns Avenue, Hampstead. Which became a lost weekend for many, some never made it back mentally, one only after two weeks in hospital and another tried to sue for deformation and damages;

unsuccessfully.

Fancy dress was very much an understatement, a bevy of big breasted ladies cruised the throng invited all and sundry to snort coke from their boobs and everything else was catered for, however unusual, unorthodox, or unique. In many ways this romp set the standard for a good few years, and although many tried to emulate the debauchery, most failed and it was only the advance of technology that bettered it.

But this was the event that caused Fun and Frolics to become feisty and feud, it was one fetish too far for Molly and she was convinced that Titbits enjoyed the humiliation and pain she inflicted just that little bit too much. More than egos were bruised and in some circles their reputation for outrageous and degenerate debauchery and erotic exhibitionism was enhanced. Their were many who were disappointed when the best show in town upped knickers and legged it. Lock, shock and bondage, to become something of a painful memory, but a great pleasure to remember for all voyeurs and bon vivants.

PAST PRESENT.

Geal was smitten with Dingle the moment he crested the Connor pass and first glimpsed it shimmering in a rare heat haze, with the sun sparkling off the Atlantic.

Mary had talked of her home town, but always, as if avoiding something in the telling,any mention of why her parents left and never returned, or why she herself never revisited.

Padraig had twice taken the family to Inishowen to meet the relatives, but then the drink diminished any idea of returning and when those over passed on any incentive evaporated.

Alone with his thoughts one barmy autumn day in October, Geal wandered the streets of Dingle in search of a muse. Something from the gradual grind to reflect yesterdays passing in todays reality, the daily basics of working, eating, drinking, crapping, fucking and sleeping had occupied all since the first. The names and faces have altered and rearranged, but only superficially the zeitgeist,ambitions and ideas are always in motion and always a work in progress, but basic humanity remains the same, whether good, bad, or indifferent.

Just before the rows of houses morph into the rocky fields to the east along goat street, a large rock with around half a dozen small smooth round, so called cup holes bored into it, nestles into the gutter. One legend would have it that the retreating ice age deposited the Holy Stone, as it's known and early man worked the holes. Another less romantic explanation, but perhaps more likely, was that in the ice age small rocks would get trapped between the sheet of ice, and the rock and the movement of the glacier would spin the small rock over thousands of years grinding out the holes before being released from the pressure, or pulverised. Whatever, there it sat over thousands of years unmoved and increasingly revered, although at some point some authority saw fit to place a pump, now painted fire engine red beside it. The town was built around it, people moved out of caves and eventually created concrete and glass cities. Thankfully far from Dingle, but the life and living of the day was also reflected out on the rocky edge of Europe, for Dingle the next parish west is the Eastern seaboard of America.

The stone had soaked in the trials, tribulations and triumphs of thousands and for Geal resonated with the story of humanity, just to sit on it, swimming fingers in the rain filled ancient holes was to draw upon the memories etched deep within the rock itself. Smoke'n'Mirrors seminal album, a seamless statement of poetry in motion within the soul of humanity was called 'Stories from the Stone' and

rested in the top five of the U.S. and U.K. album charts for an astonishing twenty three months.

Rock was mortified, bewildered and astonished as he tried to comprehend the simplicity and yet complexity of

the concept and its construction. He could never hope to even match it, yet alone supersede its subtle structure

and chose to return to basics and produce a retro album of classic standards.

The warm earthy smell of burning peat wafted around Geal as he wandered the town conjuring up an

ageless sense of the continuation of comfort,community and custom.

A way down from the stone on a road back into town was a junk shop, which kept irregular hours, many times

he passed the door and peered through the dusty windows at the eclectic mix of bric-a-brac, hotchpotch of old

clothes, religious statuary, books and pictures. He was bewitched and fascinated and his imagination raced as he

half glimpsed trash and treasure, saw white elephants jostling for trunk room with the blessed virgin and rows of

dead mens shoes waiting for new souls and heals to cradle and protect.

This day the door was wide open, airing shop and stock before the cold withering winds of winter returned to

chill the cockles of a warm heart. In disbelief Geal tentatively entered, finally banishing from his mind the

suspicion that the shop was a front for bandits or British intelligence. At first glance he was disappointed there

was much ado, but mostly about nothing of consequence, further searching unearthed several interesting dusty

books.

The most intriguing was a private press printing, a numbered run of thirty two copies, each apparently signed by

the author, according to the legend on the frontispiece.'The Saturday Book of Absurd and Outrageous Truth and

Lies', by The Fools Magician,' was the only clue to contents and author?

Geal was captivated by the cover, an intricate and compelling series of whirls and spirals hand tooled into

midnight blue leather in silver and fascinated by the legend and enchanted by a perusal of the contents.

Kitty O'Flaherty sat knitting a tea cosy, or scarf behind a fifties style kitchen table serving as the trade

counter, a radio in the background chattered in Gaelic and a stray spaniel popped in and pissed against a fine

suit hanging by the front door.

Maybe Kitty hadn't noticed, perhaps Kitty didn't care and Geal thought better than to bring it to her attention,

anyway it would soon dry in the pale, but warm autumn sun.

72

'The Book,' Geal asked, laying it on the exotic vegetable printed oilcloth that adorned the table.

'That's a grand book, sir,' Kitty knitted with dogged determination, the devil very much in the detail.

'How much,' Geal thought again, maybe it was a cardigan and he was sure red and green clashed.

'The brother in law had a book once. . .' The uncle found it in the road on the way back from O'Shay's bar the day the gale blew down O'Briens barn over Ventry ways.' Kitty tugged the wool ball which promptly rolled off her lap and into piles of stock to be sorted.

'This book?' Geal ventured, wondering if Kitty's sight was all it could be.

'Not the very same, sir, no,' Kitty continued to knit,' but a book all the same, pictures and stories.'

'How much for the book.?' Geal pointed, increasingly amused and feeling the beginings of a tune.

'T'is a fine book altogether,' Kitty laid her knitting aside and picked the book up, handling it carefully, placed it back on the table and stroked her chin momentarily, then considered her customer cautiously. Now that he looked, Geal thought he could see the beginning of a fine beard, maybe it was just the shade cast by the low watt bulb.

'Nine?' Kitty decided.

Geal quickly handed over ten, 'keep the change, luck money.'

'You're a gentleman sir,' Kitty smiled, winked and returned to her knitting.

Geal fancied the wink a touch too conspiratorial for his comfort and an image of the French women knitting happily as they watched Madame Le Guillotine working through the nobility during the glorious revolution sprang to mind. Then he remembered that Marie Antoinette was offered the chance to cheat the guillotine and escape to the sanctuary of Dingle,an offer she nobly declined as she would have had to abandon her husband and children and perhaps the ozone rich sea air wouldn't have agreed with her.

73

PARTY PLANS.

'What the fek!' Rory had been unloading his much abused Nissan van for yet another Billywiz of an idea that Mutton had to build a stage in the barn for a evening of sound and lights, to which an open invitation had been extended to any and all who wished to attend in the locality. Himself and Betty had been mulling over ways and means to meet and greet the many in the area that had heard false rumours, inaccuracies, downright lies, or a gloss and glitter beyond the truth of those living at Dungiggin.

T.J. pootled up the drive revving a battered old Lambretta, which sounded much like a fart trapped in a rusty baked bean can.

'Were you at Beehive autos by any stretch?' Rory laughed.

'How did ya know?' T.J. was rather proud of his bargain, he'd haggled for over an hour and beaten Seamus down by nearly seventy five Euros and despite its indifferent performance, was inclined to hope it was due to a misunderstanding about the fuel mix.

Rory was in two minds about the true origins of the scooter, having seen Seamus salvaging the thing from a bog, where it had been long abandoned by some scallys who'd had it away from a German tourist way back yonder. But decided it better to leave T.J. in fools paradise, after all, who was he to destroy a man's love affair.

T.J. was basic, flaky, creased features and clothes, always looking as if he had been dragged through a good few hedges backwards several times before breakfast. He looked and smelt stale,was terminally broke and on the cadge, and many goldfish were attributed with a broader intellectual capacity than he could boast.

But nobody born is totally limited and somewhere lies a redeeming feature, for T.J. it was drumming. He was no Keith Moon, or Art Blakey, but he could hold a beat, didn't speed up as the tune progressed and knew a paradiddle from a roll. Mostly they are mad as hatters in a glue factory, life is one long absurd practical joke and their only reliable feature is their unreliability. As his ship steered through life's tricky passage, captain consequence was rarely at the helm when disaster loomed large and any port in a storm was a regular if desperate occurrence.

Betty and Mutton decided a barn dance to celebrate harvest festival was appropriate, they had all reaped what they had sown over time and whatever window it was viewed from Dungiggin was a result. They had settled in to a greater, or lesser degree, made friends with many in the area and enemies with

74

fewer and felt it was time to firmly establish their presence and scotch false rumours. Flyers were printed and placed in appropriate places, Dick Macs, Supa Value, Fureturs, the church and many bars and places of gathering. Personal invitations were passed to those with local influence and valued opinion. A full programme was planned with a local ceildh band and any session players invited,traditional Irish storyteller, Cormac O'Siochain, a seanachai of great repute, Irish dancers from Dunquin, a home cooked buffet and Up All Night of course.

Betty and Molly fretted and fussed about the catering,' do you think they'll be enough eggs?'
'The slugs have decimated the lettuce,' and ' we'd better be sure the celler is well locked, or Agatha,T.J. and Cuddly Bubbly will have us drunk dry.' were a sample of their concerns.

Mutton and his boys rehearsed, discussed and dissected the songs and running order from dusk to dawn, smoked ounces of home grown grass, crates of beer and a near hog of bacon butties, but still felt the severe pangs of uncertainty.

The huge wooden barn was ideal for rehearsal, had surprisingly good acoustics, an ad hoc stage three foot above the ground, courtesy of Rory and his devout acolyte Tomas, who would work doggedly on whilst seriously doubting that a follower of the Roman doctrine would be safe among these heathens and Visigoths. He kept his rosary around his neck, a bible in Rorys glove compartment and made a point of averting his eyes when Lucy Lastic wafted about in her diaphanous frock. She especially found Tomas, fresh faced naivety a delight and desperately wanted to show him her hollow by the river, which she seriously believed was a portal to a wonder world where the fairie people now resided.

'Please come with me and see for yourself. . . You'll love it, you really will.'' Lucy had clasped Tomas' hand and was gently tugging him.

' You don't mind do you Rory?' she pleaded, all doe eyed and alluring.

Tomas looked desperately at Rory hoping that there was some pressing reason he couldn't be spared from the toil,' Ye said I needed to finish the steps.'

Rory enjoyed the moment. Worshipping nothing himself , but a pint, or two, a cigar and the prospect of a couple of winners on a Saturday. He had an eye for the women, but was too canny to get seriously involved, liking the chase and subtle seduction, almost more than the actual sex ,anyway all the loose women hereabouts were old enough to be his mother, or younger than yesterday.

'No you're alright Tomas. I can spare you for half an hour,' he laughed,' let Lucy here show you her delights. . . I guess it's time you felt her enchantments.' He added for good measure.

As Lucy dragged a reluctant Tomas out of the barn they passed Betty arriving intent on a mission,'Rory, I'm glad I caught you, I've had an idea,' She smiled and winked.

Rory wasn't as pleased she'd caught him, having heard more of her bright ideas, then any man should have to endure from a wife, let alone any other woman,' Is that right now?'

'You've got a long ladder haven't you?' Betty confirmed rather than questioned as she gazed at the cross beams.

SHADOWS AND REFLECTIONS.

Sitting by the turf fire in her humble stone cottage nestled into the cliffs south of Clogher, Skeeter listened to the radio, mostly she listened to North West radio, but as it often was in the gaelic which she neither spoke, or understood, she'd tune to B.B.C. radio 2 now and again. The traffic reports and mundane banter, often London orientated brought mixed memories, familiar street names and golden oldies were all evocative, like many, the hits and misses of pop and rock mirrored her own erratic life.

Outside a gale was blowing off the Atlantic, rattling gates, loose tiles and nervous souls suffering from an all too familiar Atlantic depression and melancholia. A news report talked of a third traffic warden in London being found dead on duty in bizarre circumstances leaving the police baffled and in search of a motive. The newscaster talked of inquiries into urban degeneration, a rise in teenage pregnancies, further economic decline, a food scare and finished off with a feel good story about a hero fireman who risked all to rescue a cat from a hot tin roof, despite the protestations of elfin sayfty officers.

It was nearly eleven years since Skeeter had last visited London for Beaswisp's wedding to Julian, the product of a Cotswold county family with impeccable breeding and status. Julian was something in the city, a keen point to pointer and a thoroughly decent chap with a cut glass accent and a sense self importance. Skeeter was blown off her feet when Beeswisp first told her about Julian, visions of her yesteryears and the social nightmare of her parents scandal and dysfunctional upbringing haunted her days and nights. She feared any media interest might free the hideous ghosts she had been running from, inviting awkward questions and further recrimination.

Although they had kept in touch by phone and letter, Skeeter didn't have a computer and the web and email were an alien concept and contrary to her nature, they had rarely met and then only for the very odd and uncomfortable long weekend. Skeeter had twice been to London, but felt intimidated and uneasy, appalled by the chaos and confusion, thereafter Beaswisp dutifully flew to Shannon and hired a car. It was a difficult relationship, Skeeter an aging hippie in Beaswisps view and her daughter a narrow minded and bigoted social climber in her mothers eyes.

Skeeter blamed the ever so nice born again Christians who had fostered Beaswisp after she had been taken into care as an at risk baby, only a few months after her birth. They changed her name to Wendy by deed poll,

77

transforming her life and prospects, further enhanced by the nature and nurture of her formative years, which shaped her character.

Just days after her birth, a concerned farmers wife had informed the social services of the birth, a midwife turned up, was appalled by Morganna, the dilapidated cottage, Skeeter's obvious frailty and just about everything else. Next to visit were social workers to confirm the nurse's horrendous report, followed by a return visit with a court order and embarrassed constable. Skeeter lost her baby, self confidence and a nervous and physical breakdown quickly followed.

They were her lost years with many more snakes than ladders, each time she climbed out of one pit of despair she was quickly thrown into an even deeper one, hopeless men in desperate relationships. Dope and booze ravaged her mind and body, she seemed locked in an ever increasing downward spiral and tried several times to end it all.

Even now Skeeter still didn't know how, or why she survived and if she hadn't a belief in spirituality and something more powerful than basic humanity before, she certainly had now.

She'd found herself standing in the middle of London bridge around three a.m one bleak January morning, having been taken for a ride in every way by the latest real charmer in her life, no money, no dope, no hope. Below her the Grand old River, black, swirling, cold, gurgling and sucking at the bridge, seemed to reach for her, there was no sense of comfort or promise of something better,just the prospect of an end to her bitter suffering. Looking back from the depths below at the city foggy in the sulphur yellow glow of the streetlights still Dickensian in many ways, yet the silhouette of St Paul's rising above the concrete and glass of modern office blocks. A city, vibrant with life for more than a millennia, countless millions of people living and dying, rich and poor. A history comparable with any other in the world; Rome, Paris, Istanbul, but cities are more than buildings and land, cities are built for people to live and work in and the character of the place is but a reflection of those that dwell within.

That misty morning she saw ghosts of every age passing through the street, there was no sense of time, nor purpose. Their costume showed the period, their faces betrayed no trace of good, nor evil, but all had a story of intensity of spirit to tell, the highs and lows, challenges, opportunities, rewards and failures, mistakes and missed opportunities.

Skeeter fell to the pavement as defeat, deep depression and despair overwhelmed her, but then she felt lifted as courage, tenacity and vigor to endure and rise above all that could subdue her returned, she was now defiant and inspired. In the end, what doesn't kill you makes you stronger,perhaps that is how it should be, tough love and hard lessons. Nothing of worth comes easy and all that does is cheap, shallow and soon forgotten, but that achieved with blood, sweat and tears endures and the success is all the sweeter.

Skeeter and Beeswisp tried more times than they cared to remember to bury the hatred, misunderstandings and guilt, but all quickly faltered after the goodbyes and futile promises at the airport. The wedding itself, best forgotten as far as Skeeter was concerned, a pathetic day of bitching, backstabbing and social engineering, which only confirmed her antipathy to breeding and privilege of so called birthright. Skeeter agonized and philosophized, turning to the East and the laws of karma trying to come to terms with the cruelty of history repeating itself so quickly in this seemingly repetitive and recessive circle of deception and distress.

A mighty gust of wind howled menacingly outside, like the big bad wolf at the door, summoning up darker memories and misgivings. She remembered her teenage bedroom, a wonder wall filled with posters of the pop face of the moment, a sea of clothes, stained knickers, grubby bras and cuddly toys.

The wind used to whistle and wail through the old dying elm in the garden, Owsly, as she childishly named the local barn owl who'd hoot on his hunting trips, terrified and comforted in equal measure.

She would lie on the bed with the pink candlewick bedspread and listen to Luxembourg initially and then the pirate stations Caroline and London. She dreamt of the warm embrace of the Fab Four, Walker brothers and P.J.Proby, bought Bunty and Fab magazine and thought her parents incredibly square and very weird. Even in her early days she was perceptive, but naive, innocent maybe and her idea of what sex and love were rather in the romantic tradition of Romeo and Juliet, Prince Charming and Cinderella, with everybody living happily ever after.

Skeeter curled up into the old and lovingly worn chintz sofa and glanced at Faith, Hope and Charity, her three border collies and felt genuine untarnished affection. It all seemed so much simpler with animals, trust was perhaps more about basic instincts and feelings, less complicated. But maybe this was because she was supposed to be the superior intellect in the relationship, after all, wasn't mankind the crown of creation? When she was about six she was struggling to understand what the Autumn harvest festival was all about and was out in the garden with her dad feeding the fish in the pond. Delighted when the goldfish rose en masse to feed,

79

she suddenly had a profound thought, ' Daddy . . . you know God gives us all that harvest festival stuff!'

Enda viewed fatherhood rather like a banker thought of his customers and maintained a formal and aloof presence, leaving affection to Sarah, such that she could spare. Taking his distracted nod as a signal to continue,' does that mean the goldfish think you are God because you feed them!'

Enda laughed uncharacteristically, ' No my dear child, not quite. . .your mother will explain.' not that mother had ever taken either the time, or trouble to explain anything that really mattered.

Reaching for her rolling tobacco, Skeeter smiled as she watched Faith drumming her paws on a cushion, twitching and quietly whimpering through a chasing dream.

Skeeter mentally chanted a favorite ditty;

'Row, row row your boat gently down the stream,

merrily, merrily, merrily, life is but a dream.'

As a nine year old she had wondered if her waking day was the dream, and her night dream the actual conscious life, but gave herself a headache when she sat by the pond and tried to reason it out. Sleep had always been her way out when the burden of living her life became unbearable.

Through her teens and twenties she had copped out, dropped out and doped out at every opportunity, always on the run, vainly seeking escape from the inescapable. She now knew you can't outrun yourself, or the thoughts, words and deeds of a life lived. It had taken over forty years and even now she wasn't sure she knew where she was at, her life, like all was a work in progress. She could go for days, months sometimes, content and at peace with the now stilled small voice in her head that constantly analyzed and challenged every thought and deed.

Then with no warning she was back with her demons, wallowing in angst and self doubt, alone in the dark, listening to Leonard Cohen and Simon and Garfunkle. She was the bird on the wire, longing to be a rock devoid of emotion and feeling, homeward bound, still waiting for the miracle and wondering why the act of birth is the start of an indeterminate death sentence with no reprieve,or respite.

At forty nine, her red hair noticeably streaked grey, Skeeter was still an attractive woman who turned heads, both male and female for very different reasons. For the most part she wore bright colourful dress's which emphasized her slim figure, full breasts and caught the eye of men. She had once been told by a well oiled second division thespian that she had just missed being beautiful, but had a charismatic and ethereal face which would send men mad, she still spurned his advances.

Women regarded her as a threat and Skeeter's bohemian lifestyle further alienated her, she was the subject of much gossip and speculation and her penchant for red petticoats earned her the title of 'the scarlet woman'. Not that one scrap of evidence, even circumstantial linked her to any man in the area, but malign tittle tattle feeds on itself and like a hurricane grows organically The more open minded who paused to chat with her found something completely different. Skeeter was happy to be sociable and pass the time of day, but evaded direct questions about her personal life and let it be known she had no interest in the affairs of others real, or imagined.

BARN DANCE.

Mutton sat on the side of the stage reading fabulous furry freak brothers comix with his guitar resting on his lap while T.J. replaced a drum skin on having hammered the previous into history. The band, true to their name had been up most of the night rehearsing and although dog tired were enthused enough to give it a couple more hours before dawn. Most of their equipment was cast off remnants and other odds and ends, cadged, borrowed, or simply nicked over the years from various groups. Not all the band were resident, Fingers Fahan was a local import, discovered by Mutton at O'Flaherty's bar, when three sheets to the wind . His day job was as a plumber, so came in handy when on site to deal with blocked sinks and overflowing bogs. Once Titbits dropped her phone down the pan when caught texting mid pee by a playful Agatha, who'd noticed she'd forgotten to lock the door and fancied a perky peek at her pretty. Fingers reluctantly chanced his arm to retrieve it and was rewarded royally.

When Fingers stumbled across the old Hammond C3 organ complete with Leslie speakers in the barn he was in seventh heaven and it was as much his idea as Mutton's to jam with the fledgling band, just for the chance to play the C.3.

Under Betty's direction the barn was festooned with foliage, bales of hay,buckets and baskets overflowing with fruit and vegetables, light ropes and strings of coloured Buddhist prayer flags. Trestle tables set along one side ready for the cracking spread planned and prepared over the previous few days lay heaving and sagging. Against her better judgement, but under pressure, Betty allowed Agatha to mix the punch and like a demented alchemist he busied himself with potent elixers and intoxicants. Which he bravely sampled at every stage, to be sure.

Betty and Molly were busy laying out the bowls and plates of food, leaving the minions to bring it from kitchen to table when Lucy hurried in,' I've just been throwing the runes and consulting the charts. . .'

Betty looked at Molly who shrugged,' And?'

'We have to expect the unexpected,' Lucy was quite concerned,' there will be people here who we should be wary of. . . they will not have our best interests in mind. . .A Gemini and Virgo will arrive together and cause trouble!'

Both were bemused, but not surprised,and nodded gratefully, ' Your right there Agatha and T.J. are already here. But we'll keep it in mind, thanks for the warning, you couldn't do us a favour and get a few things in from the kitchen.'

As the afternoon drew on, Betty began to fret increasingly, getting snappy and short tempered finding fault in the smallest thing, for her everything must be perfect and she was mindful that this was the main opportunity to win over the neighbors' and establish sound relationships.

A MUSE.

At Dick Macs, alone in the snug with a book and pint, afternoon became evening, as Geal absorbed the book which seemed to be about everything and nothing. On the one level it was an uncollated mishmash of folk wisdom, eclectic legend and ancient myth. A loose history of Irelands trials, tribulations, triumphs and tragedies.

On another a romp among the bizarre, outrageous, weird and shallow schemes, dreams and crude sexual and wealth creation adventures of base humanity.

But there was an element a thought, perhaps a plan charting and exploring the potential for progress, if that wasn't an understatement and contradiction in terms, given the propensity of humanity to screw up the world. Geal was so engrossed that he was oblivious to the comings and goings within the bar, many he knew in passing, greeted him, but for a nod, or grunt he didn't notice their presence and most could see the man was distracted.

There was heartache ,horror, perplexity, all manner of enigma and emotion within the covers, some answers, but for every one a raft of new observations and questions. For every truth, a lie and always the tantalizing promise of enlightenment. For no truth is absolute and all truth is subjective and often transient in nature.

Late into night, the empties accumulated and who knew where the time had gone, even Dick Macs diehard drinkers turned out into the chill of night, divorced and devoted equally ,to wander where ever minded by circumstance and sobriety, or excess, along with Geal still transfixed by the written word. His next moment of recollection was to find himself sitting alone on the metal statue of Fungie among the lobster pots, under harbour lights, book in hand. What looked like the same spaniel from the junk shop had just pissed on his leg and stood grinning and wagging his tail expectantly, looking for adventure.

Two or three trawlers were kitting up ready for the turn of the tide early the next morning, engines throbbed and figures,huddled in yellow oilskin jackets against the chill night air stowed nets and boxes.

The constant discordant clatter of rigging battering masts in the gathering wind, bringing an eerie quality to an already surreal scene. Geal sat quiet and still, returning from light presence into a misty orange tinted darkness and the underworld of strange reality.

The spaniel sat and raised a paw doggedly a few times, barked insistently and stared deep into his eyes as if trying to communicate some pressing message. Geal reached down stroked the dog a few times, then noticed a collar with a thinning metal name tag, Buck, or Puck was the Spaniel.

A few seconds thought and a brief perusal of the hound confirmed it, Puck it was and Puck was up and ready for the off. The creature was mad, bad and dangerous to know, mischievous in the extreme and totally self sufficient.

He begged, stole, or scavenged his food, raiding the dustbins of some of the most prestigious of Dingle's restaurants. He slept where he was when tired, or bored and kept his own company unless it was to his advantage to do otherwise. Puck was known to everyone within the area and treated as one of Dingle's fixtures and fittings, liked by many and tolerated by butchers and fishmongers as long as he kept his paws out of their premises. Seen by people more frequently than Dingle's more famous resident, Fungi the friendly dolphin, they were both enigmas and both as baffling in their attitude and behavior.

The first remembered sighting was of a half grown spalpeen of a mutt legging up John street with a salmon in its mouth, freshly liberated from the rear of the Gailic fish stall. A quick witted tourist took a photo which appeared on the front page of the next days local paper, such quirks of life are the stuff of legend and Puck was now, a notorious thief, a good craick and a quirky novelty for tourists.

A sometime yachtsman and oxford professor of middle English and ancient Norse, sailing around the coast of Eire sheltered his small craft in the harbour for the night and fetched up at Dick Macs after a fine meal in Lord Bakers. A very palatable bottle of claret and a couple of glasses of grand single malt already consumed. Prof Robin Goodfellow was a merry old soul and listened enchanted as several equally well lubricated local characters joked about the dog and the fish. As ever fantastic tales of other rogue dogs and legendary beasts from the dark folk memory began to circulate, each more bewitching and chilling than the last. Drink was taken and a conspiratorial atmosphere descended, as that best remaining unspoken was recklessly ushered into the light. Sly nods and winks circulated the inner circle hunched over the bar, pints became shorts and then doubles, smoke wafted upwards to form a grey fug over their heads as fact and fantasy morphed.

At first just a curious voyeur subject to the suspicious glances of the usual suspects huddled around the bar,

Robin was soon drawn into the intrigue. It was apparent he was well educated, speaking with some authority on history and legends of Britain and Eire. Better still he was ready enough to get a round in. With a fondness for stimulating conversation and a tale told in the great traditions of the raconteur the congregation, for such was the reverence accorded to the eminent visitor, listened mouth agape as he rattled through myth and mayhem like a well oiled Bren gun. He was after all the don of the history and languages department and knew of angels, devils, demons and fickle Gods, as well as he had thought he knew his now estranged wife, Madeline. Before she ran off with a visiting French linguistics professor with a silver tongue on him.

It had proved a critical turning point in his life and led him to a new and intriguing mistress, his ketch, 'Cytherea'

Robin was now a happy and contented man, alone to sail in peace and enjoy books and bonhomie. At some point the dog and fish re entered the conversation and Robin likened the Mutt to other hounds from the murky world of spirits and sprites. Eventually some wit drinking on borrowed time and others money insisted the the little fucker with the fish should be called Puck because it rhymed. Some ten minutes later he slid from his stool and three fading fisherman dragged him, over, under and sideways down, home to 'Darlin Morena', a sharp tongue and a not so rosy dawn.

Roused from his concentration to rejoin what passed for accepted reality, Geal walked along the pier still half minded to muse and noticed five seaweed encrusted blue fingers reaching from the flotsam and jetsam, in the harbour waters like the lost souls of all who perished at sea reaching for just another snatch at life. Closer inspection proved it to be a rubber glove with trapped air in the finger tips, just another piece of once vital fishing paraphernalia now surplus to requirements. Like the rusting hulk of the once proud trawler DRAIOGHT NA MARA, now permanently tethered to the quay, quietly returning it's base elements to the sea it had once exploited.

FOOD,MUSIC, MAYHEM,

Molly was worried, it was two hours past the get go and only a handful of locals had turned up. 'This isn't looking good,' Betty confided in Molly as she surveyed the fifty, or so souls in the barn, mostly gathered around the impressive mounds of food on the overburdened trestle tables. With not a bloater sandwich, chicken nugget, or buffalo wing in sight the early birds had launched into the cracking spread with relish. Anxious to be a sensitive and welcoming hostess, Betty had consulted old Irish cookery books and the few locals that visited Dungiggin, about what few traditional dishes she could supply 'crubeens, bacon and cabbage and ham sandwiches' Rory was quick to reply, these being all but his staple diet. A liitle probing and Betty discovered , much to her disgust that Crubeens were pigs trotters, she ruled out bacon and cabbage as impractical and also considered the social implications of cabbage flatulence in a confined space, especially as a good few, such as Shadow already had complications.

One or two pensioners who habitually cruised the social circle of weddings, funerals and anything else they could gatecrash in pursuit of a free lunch, desperately searched for the customary beef, or salmon alternative, so beloved of Irish caterers.

'Don't worry, they'll turn up soon enough, they're in no hurry here about,' Old Mrs Docherty mumbled in passing, a ham sandwich and cup of tea in hand, on route to a knot of worthy widows and words of comfort. Molly smiled,'Thank you luv,' Then turned to Betty and raised an eyebrow' they'd better, the vultures have landed and there won't be a crust of bread spared soon.'

Betty laughed with relief, ' . . . and the way they're staggering from Agatha's punch they'll not be on their feet too long either.'

'They're managing to get back for a second and third glass so far,' Molly eyed a fusty looking local lady who was closely inspecting a nut rissole, pinching it up between thumb and forefinger, sniffing it suspiciously, before dropping it back on the table and moving on to crubeens, which Betty had reluctantly added. 'Those things are a mystery entirely,' Fanny Higgins pointed to the rissoles and Biddy Mulligan nodded in agreement,' I hope it's not solved in my time. . . ' She sniffed her fingers,'I just ate one!'

'I'm just hoping Agatha hasn't slipped a Mickey Finn into the mix and spiked them,' Betty was seriously worried as the thought brought back memories of a gig at the roundhouse in London back in the mid sixties. Agatha supplemented his meager income by dealing acid and was a roadie for Yellow

Looselife, an ad hoc ensemble of untalented and very stoned hippies, who got a few gigs by playing for nothing as a statement of counter culture. Money and possessions were theft, food and unrestricted sex should be free to all, the government should legalize marijuana and doctors should prescribe it for anyone struggling to understand society.

Already tripping out of his tree, Agatha was a mite paranoid and thought he saw sergeant Nobby Pilcher of the Chelsea drug squad, the most zealous of the heat, sneaking about dressed as an arab. Nobby was adept at plain clothes duty ,believing he easily morphed into the wallpaper at whatever event he and his chums decided would best produce a good bust.

Looking for somewhere to lose his stash of yellow sunshine, the best acid he'd gotten hold of in months and as it was a benefit for starving artists there was a free cup of punch for each punter through the gate. Suddenly it all became clear, God meant him to turn the world on, or at least those who had come to experience the cream of the music scene, move with the action and of course get mighty stoned as the beat rocked on. With the fuzz hot on the trail and the word of the lord in his head, Agatha turned his stash into the punch and unleashed mirth and mayhem in unequal measure, many who tripped out that night were never the same again and a few unfortunate space cadets are still out in intersteller overdrive. Even Nobby was seen gyrating like a whirling Dervish with a sickly grin on his face and later staring in wonder at the liquid lightshow.Although nobody beyond the immediate circle knew the real rascal and they would keep the truth within, however they we're ever loathe to trust Agatha again.

'I must have been out of my mind!' Betty was getting seriously worried.

'No just another senior moment!'

' John!' 'No Betty!' she replied, surveying the barn of a man who was obviously in drink ,' . . . and who might you be?'

The place was heaving, from famine to feast seemingly in seconds, Murphy's Marauders were full of it with jigs and reels and a mighty Hooley was afoot. There was hooting an a hollering, fancy stepping , toes tapping, feet shuffling and a fierce craic breaking out wholesale. The first wave of comestibles had been consumed with enthusiasm, fortunately reinforcements arrived with every guest. It seemed that word had got out and every women had taken it as a challenge to outdo her neighbor and show the flitterjigs the best of Irish country cooking South of the Shannon. Molly was surrounded by a gaggle of hearty agricultural ladies competing to have her try boxty, barm brack, farls, soda breads along with drisheen,, champ, colcannon, carrageen, coddles, Dublin lawyers and a dozen other specialties and acquired tastes.

The heavy burden of serious drinking was ongoing with much determination, in a discreet corner a bevy of experienced locals were engaged in a boisterous match with one or two from the house to discover who would be first to slip away under the table.

'Show me John!' Betty was still perplexed, ' you mean the john?' Betty's first thought was that he needed a pee, or perhaps a safe haven to enjoy a technicolour yawn.

' If that's the fella!' The man was battling with gravity, weaving and wobbling, speech did not come easy and the accent was thick, but his anger was plain to see, as was his frustration at not running his quarry to earth.

In spite of the lateness of the hour there was a good few children and teenagers present, a rumour had swept the area that it was a pop stars home, although none were sure if it was somebody from a boy band ,Bono, or Van The Man and his street choir.

Such was the rumour and speculation about the place that even the holy father and a posse of nuns from the Gyddie Little Sisters of Vurtigho led by the redoubtable sister Aloopeshia whose saw it as her mission to save the heathen Visigoths from the claws of the cruel clootie himself.

Dapper John ever the suave lothario, had taken a full four hours to prepare himself for the event, bathing, making sure that his ironing was precise, his make up (a habit he'd picked up from television and video filming) exact and presenting his best profile. Half the time had been required in trying on three different suits, half a dozen matching shirts and exactly the right shoes.

For the past few months Dapper John had been swanking around the area letting it be known that he was the main man and it was his benevolence that allowed his former minions to pass their autumn years in his charitable care.

This occasion would set the seal on his status and he was determined to play up to the role, despite his increasing aches and stiffness which the Atlantic dampness aggravated and eucalyptus embrocation eased.

' Will ye show me the John then?' Sean O'Keefe was getting increasingly unsteady and irritable since Betty had slipped away, and had accosted several people in bouncing between the bar and the bog.

89

Murphy, who actually wasn't Murphy at all, but Bainbridge Cluny which didn't quite swing and Bainbridge knowing of the marauders who captured St Patrick himself and with a liking for the history and and name, wanted, 'something marauders' and he preferred Murphy's to Guinness. So it was Murphy's Marauders, it all made sense to him and nobody else much cared anyway.

Although burdened with a challenging name, God, as if in compensation had gifted him with a larger than life personality, once met he was not easily forgotten. He could have played all night and given half a chance would do so, usually needing to be dragged off the stage still midway through some lilt,or shanty. This night he was full of it, spurred on by the ambiance, company, venue and a nearly depleted bottle of Tullamore dew whisky. Or as Murphy would have it, the vital waters of his life, he was now fully tanked up and in no mood to lay aside his bow. Such was his confidance and humour, with fire in his mountain he'd have taken on the very devil himself in a fiddle dual for possession of his own soul.

'D'ye know the John?' Sean had stumbled on stage and laid claim to the microphone, Murphy refusing to be upstaged and upset by the intrusion, extended his elbow and caught Sean squarely on the jaw. Spiralling amid the Marauders, Sean knocked Pat Burke and accordion into Joe Fitzpatrick who lost his grip on the Bodhran and all became a babble of confusion.

Excited by the unexpected, the audience faltered and began to encourage Sean, who although far gone knew an enthusiastic encore when encountered. Andy Warhol is credited with saying, 'in future everybody will be famous for fifteen minutes.' and this, although not familiar with the expression himself was his allotted slot and he seized it joyfully and drunk fully at the trough of celebrity. It is also said the God looks after little children and drunks and as often as not, drunks are little more than small children when in drink.

Murphy, ever the professional and not one to take readily to being upstaged retaliated with a stirring jig, frantically bowing his cherished violin,fit to start a blaze, while his marauders marshaled matters accordingly. Playing up to audience and rhythm, Sean started to dance after a unique and much exaggerated fashion to much merriment, this was true entertainment, spontaneous side splitting surrealism.

Even the seen it all, done it all rock'n'roll runaways resident at Dungiggin were impressed.

'Is it always like this?' Titbits asked Patsy O'Regan, share fisherman and part time plasterer.

'Early days, early days,' he replied laconically ,' the blood isn't up yet, I'd say .'

Titbits was quite taken with the local talent and many of them with her, having rarely glimpsed the like, even in her advancing years she cut a swath through the local ladies of the same age, who had surrendered to the increasing ravages of time and were resigned to sagging breasts, varicose veins. weak tea and shallow sympathy.

Dressed entirely in black from dyed hair, leather mini skirt and thigh high patent leather boots, Titbits was a complete fantasy for man and boy, no red blooded male could easily fail to let imagination run wild and give in to self inflated machismo.

Gathered in a darkened corner, a gruesome gaggle gossiped gleefully in hope of splendid and sordid scandal.

'Would you ever look at that!' offered a blatherskite

'A brazen hussy!' countered a flibbertigibbet

'A flahoola if ever my eyes saw one!' Spat out the third wayward sister of sordid intent, thin in lip and thinner still in the warmth of human compassion, with a triumphant cackle.

' Isn't that your fella, Morena?' Toxic in torment, simple minded without doubt and an acute ability to speak before thought, the third mother of impure invention intoned.

Such was the clishmaclaver and joy of those with little else to mark the passing of the day, beyond the cruel comment and malcontent of malevolent mischief. They were alone in their dark thoughts, shunned by respectable society and more so by those with no reason to risk repute, or be damned by the presumption of proximity.

But then Titbits thrived on the drama of demonization, knowing that with a casual flash of thigh, a hint of nipple,or a wicked wink she could bedazzle and bewitch most men, stealing them away into the night and misadventure.

Giggling and laughing like a scandalous schoolgirl at the corny, horny come ons and witty wisecracks she heard a million times before and hoped to for ever more. She casually glanced at the sneering discomfort of wives and girlfriends, themselves unable, or unwilling to offer anything as provocative and tempting. Sadly, her glory days were in terminal decline, only she knew the awful truth of her condition, she could captivate and lure, but like a black widow to lay with her would be the kiss of death. But sex, drugs and Rock'n'roll had been her life, it was all she knew, all she cared for, she'd run in fear and loathing from suburban mediocrity. Music and laughter was all she was after and she'd traded her body to play the game among the names, but now paid the devil his due. Titbits was addicted to the adrenalin and thrill of the pursuit, the seduction and now could only be a Teaser, if she had any regard for a potential lover, for anything else would be tantamount to murder.

SINISTER SOLITUDE.

Geal read warmed by the crackling and sparking fire in the light of oil and wax, gifting a mellow,almost' Wind in the Willows' cosiness to the former lighthouse. Apart from 'Nine Lives' the stray black cat that visited him when in residence, Geal was alone with his books and music and moreover content to be so. A westerly wind howled and shrieked like a vengeful banshee, blowing through cobwebs and redistributing the settled dust of calmer days and past times. He paused to ponder and reflect, only then aware of the progress of Holst's planets on the sound system and through the window high in the heavens.

Pausing briefly he looked out to see the moon before it clouded over and thought about the dark side of the moon, the fabled home of devils, demons and all manner of unwelcome heebie-jeebies.

Did man truly walk upon the rock that shadowed this earth? Long had he watched its progress and wondered. A shiver ran up his spine and he felt the hairs on the nape of his neck rise, then shuddered for no apparent reason and reached for the poker to provoke the fire into white heat, before returning to the book.

Dark is the night with no light of dawn in sight, for there in the shadows both sinister secret and sweet serendipity vie for supremacy of imagination and intrigue.

Geal had a telescope, night vision scope and various other equipment to better know the land, sea and sky from the glass dome of his lighthouse. He passed many a night lost in the sheer awe of revelation and vastness of visible universe and longed to share the wonder with somebody. Much of his life was that of the global gypsy and he had liked it thus, in the manner of anthropologist, he was a voyeur, an observer of other's lives.

Aware of the follies, foibles and failures that haunt each and every face that passed on the street, there but for the grace of God went he and the luck, as such was in the draw of the deck, the cards were dealt by an unseen and unknowable hand and the way of play was arbitrary and abstract, if not absolute.

Like most he instinctively prejudged everybody, mentally concocting a who, what and where of strangers as he moved among them. On the odd occasion that he discovered more about the face, he was embarrassed at how wide of the mark he so often was. But as a song writer, such artistic licence was his daily bread and often the muse for lyrics that saluted the small victories fuelling the lives of the worlds humble spear carriers. Stuff happened, shit hit the fan, some stuck, much was washed away, but too many suffered from the indignity, trauma and torment of perceieved and impercetible consequence and inner conflict. Often aghast at the brutal, brash and boldness of those limited by failures of education,intellect and social interaction, Geal felt humbled by their stoicism in disaster, celebration of small miracles and intensity of being despite inevitable adversity. The binmen, checkout girls and factory ladies clocking in on a drab Monday morning to stand on the production line at an Edmonton industrial wasteland , moulding yellow plastic ducks for nameless bathroom frolics, in a numbing mindless charade of life, precious in the passing.

He might once have been part of that sphere, but success had changed him numerous times, spinning him through a multitude of variations on the theme of life and now he was. . . ?

He knew not what, or who.

But better knew what he was not.

With effort he could remember times past, who and what he thought he was in those naive and headstrong days when mindless action took precedent over considered thought. These recollections served to emphasis the distance travelled both materially and spiritually, but he was fully aware there was still a great distance to go, for like all he was ever a cavalcade of characters in search of his true role. Who would he be a month hence, a year, god willing ten years further and then perhaps beyond this incarnation and onto eternity. On nights of such intensity, when the maelstrom held center stage and mere mortals danced in blind attendance to the wild symphonies of wind and rain, Geal felt charged, energized by the sheer power that nature could unleash, seemingly by whimsy. The frequency and magnitude of the weather was a definite plus when Geal had been toying with the idea of a wild and isolated retreat from the prying ears and eyes of the paparazzi.

He had a notion that given the choice, they preferred swanning around the celebrity holiday hotspots of the tropics and fashionable cities, rather than sloshing through the rain in rural west coast Eire.

'Nine Lives' glided from slumber to full alert effortlessly as he rose to paw, stretched lithely, had a quick spit and lick and moved to sit staring at the stout wooden door.

'Hey nine lives, not even mad dogs and Englishmen are out this night!' Geal smiled as the cat turned to face him, ' even the Banshee's sheltering in Dick Mac's for the duration. You really don't want to be going out that door.'

The black cat rose to all four paws again and pattered over to Geal, tail snaking elegantly and leapt to lap, landing atop the book. Gently meowing nine lives arched his back and dug his claws into book and thigh,' YOU MOTHER FUCKER!' Geal shouted as he snapped to his feet, sending book, cat and candlestick flying from a side table.

Simultaneously the door knocker hammered thrice and the hairs on the back of Geal's neck stood up as an uneasy feeling pervaded him, he was, or should have been alone on his island, living in splendid isolation cut off from the unwelcome intrusions of strangers.

The cat initially arched glaring fiercely at the door, then scooted as if scalded and disappeared hissing wildly somewhere among the junk and genius of his life awards and articled achievements.

Geals gift was his imagination and ingenuity, the ability to observe the dull and pedestrian so often overlooked by the mass and paint a lyrical melodic picture that intrigued, impressed and resonated with others. This talent, however can also be a burden, sometimes ignorance of fancy and fantasy can be bliss and most often the anticipation and fear of the future is far worse than the actuality. As is often the case, the Germans have a grand word that goes beyond the urbane in conjuring up a delightful picture in the mind of a mood in man. Vorfreude, a rough translation of which comes close to serendipity, a pleasurable, yet unmeasured anticipation.

The flickering tawny yellow light of the lamp cast menacing shadows and the raging gale crashing and banging all and sundry, further increased the potential malevolence adding an oppressive threat to life and soul. The passage of time seemed to slow and each and every second hung pregnant as if prepared to pounce with profound and pernicious intent. Images flashed through his head as he remembered the myths and legends associated with the island, which long ago was home to more than seventy simple souls who precariously extracted a living from the little land and vast ocean. Their demands were small, food to fill, a cup of tea, a drop of the hard stuff on occasion, the warmth of a turf fire and conviviality of companionship. This did not come easy and each and every day was precious and precarious, daily tasks such as plucking gulls eggs from towering cliffs, catching herring ,mackerel, shellfish and seaweeds easily turned from custom to catastrophe. Tragedy and drama were also not the exclusive reserve of the islanders, ships in a storm, planes with problems and other extraordinary events claimed life and limb over the fullness of time. Spanish galleons from the Armada had foundered here, both world wars had taken their toll of humanity as had the general rough and smooth of everyday risk. Places such as this soaked in emotion, the trauma of sudden loss and the recrimination of how such a silly,unexpected miscalculation, or mistake could change things so dramatically in an instant, were seed beds for supernatural events.

Geal had briefly considered this when mulling over the pros and cons of buying his island sanctuary,but the more mundane and perhaps relevant factors like basic services, getting to and from in all weathers and how to cope with emergencies were more pressing. Such thoughts occupied him for what seemed minutes, but only seconds had passed, he was still uncertain, reluctant to respond staring at the door every nerve alert for any sense that might better tell what was unfolding.

The wind still shrieked eerily, rain battered the windows, shadows and reflections continued their macabre cavorting in the half light,as he continued to dwell on the ominous overtones of intrigue and imagination.

Again the knocking, perhaps sharper and more urgent.

Geal began to lose it, apprehension and panic were increasingly calling the tune, he eyed the door and saw the key was in the open position, it was unlocked, he was vulnerable and increasingly scared.

He swallowed hard, aware of the cold clammy sweat on his face, the chill in his body and the pounding of his heart and wished he was away over on the mainland, or anywhere else but here. It was such a grand idea, a hideaway from the endless intrusion of the world,. A monster of his own, creation that had increasingly threatened to devour him.

Fame and fortune, who wouldn't reach for it given the opportunity?

His greatest strength and gift was his weakest link, he couldn't fart in the street without the chance that it would make the news, with endless speculation on the state of his digestive system. A stray smile at a pretty girl ,or a spur of the moment compliment and he was all but married, if the rabid dogs of the media were to be believed. The thrill of recognition and the first million in the bank, were an adrenalin rush, a high that quickly faded, never to be repeated with such relish and so quickly became almost unbearable burdens. Now, he'd paid a fortune by anybody's standards to escape from that treadmill, to seek the solitude he so desired, but even this achievement seemed to have turned on him.

With a horrible feeling of apprehension, an empty dread felt deep in the pit of his stomach and a very dry mouth he approached the door and slowly reached for the latch, snatched images from dozen Hammer horror films swam through his head, as did more terrifying urban legends.

Again the rapping on the door, urgent and demanding.

This time he summoned up the courage to open the door, albeit cautiously.

RAVE ON.

Dapper John was all but doubled up by the hoot on stage, as Sean and Murphy got to rollicking around the stage like Keystone cops as the Marauders joyfully produced a spontaneous sound track. Both Sean and Murphy were the worse for drink, although many thought exactly the reverse, with no sense of self consciousness and intent only, on the first to run and the other to give chase.

Dapper had noticed an intriguing lady in a red petticoat and he was not the only one, a good few men were giving her the eye, a few more chatting wildly using all their guile.

The ganders of gossip who had never knowingly said a decent word about anybody were in their element, wagging crooked fingers and conjuring up toxic talk.

Had Dapper John known who Sean was and the nature of his quest,he'd have not lingered anywhere close, but even if he had an inkling, given the stormy weather outside he might still have chanced his arm in the barn.

'Hello John, feeling better?' Dapper wheeled around on his heel.

'Dr Cahir. . . Shabin,' John smiled   'I'm glad you made it.'

'Not at all, not at all. How could I resist, after all you've told me about your home. . .' The Tibetan doctor looked around at the throng,' it seems that the weather hasn't deterred anybody from your house warming.'

Dapper saw Betty and Molly in a huddle glancing at him, knowing they were talking about him, he caught their eye and winked. They smiled back, seemingly a touch embarrassed that he'd caught them in the snoop.

'You haven't seen Nuala about have you?'

'How funny, I was thinking the very same thing myself, Molly!'

They both laughed, as it was obvious Dapper was chatting up the doctor,' you don't think he'd try it on with her do you?'

'Of course, but it'd be something else again if she was up for it,' Betty almost doubled up laughing,' Oops. I wet 'em,' but continued unabashed,' Imagine, she gives him the script for his viagra and then takes advantage of the extra stiffie, She'd have to be totally naive. . .!'

98

'. . . .Or desperate, she can only be about thirty odd. . .' Molly said morosely, only too aware that own age and beauty were quickly slip-slidding away, whilst for Shabin, the best was yet to come.

Molly had another reason to bitch about Shabin, or any new conquest that Dapper might make, as she had herself fallen for his charms, all be it a good few decades ago and like an untold and unsung list of his other seductions, had only been flavour of the week, without even the dubious accolade of mothering one of his offspring, which at least a dozen had. It was also quite vexing that Shabin was both Betty and her own doctor as well and knew the tedious and uncomfortable feminine problems that were increasingly affecting their lives. It was well over a year since Molly had been laid and indeed since anybody had shown any interest in doing so, even when drunk.

Shabin noticed and smiled,' It's so wonderful that you are so casual and friendly with your staff.' She had only been practicing in Dingle for a few months, her first overseas posting in an exchange programme with Dr Quain, who taken Shabin's place in Tibet.

Dr Quain was a legend on the peninsula, an old fashioned doctor who shunned most new fangled medicines, preferring to rely on traditional cures, common sense and was loathe in to send anyone to hospital, as most people died there. He stood no nonsense, swore by a daily pint or three of Guinness and an odd medicinal whisky, drove like a getaway driver. Was as happy to treat animals as well as people as they all eat, breathe and shit in pretty much the same way. His exchange trip to Tibet, was his last great adventure, as he was sixty and not getting any younger and had long been fascinated by Buddhism.

Shabin found the local practice a culture shock, but less so then the locals themselves, having never had anyone but an native Irish doctor before and a male one at that, and Dr Quain for the last thirty two years at that. He treated the grandparents when parents, eased them out when their day came, delivered the parents as babies and their babies and knew the story of every family on his patch, including the relatives that had emigrated and where in the world they were.

For her part Shabin, whose father was an Irish rover, having left Dingle on a sailing boat he fetched up in Shambala, via a shipwreck in the Indian ocean and an abundance of adventure, it was a homecoming. Joseph Patrick Cahir was known for the telling of tales and Shabin had listened intently throughout childhood to his story of the old country where leprechauns, St Patrick himself and giants lived among emerald fields and the rain was fine and soft, with a rainbow to top the mornings magic and a pot of gold in every far field.

Shabin was graceful and delicate of feature,with almond eyes, coffee skin,a long black pony tail,intelligent, polite and possessed a warmth of spirit that quickly won hearts and minds.She was genuinely interested and intrigued by each person individually, regarded each as special, so much so that even the skeptical and suspicious suspended their initial caution and were captivated and enchanted.

J.P.Cahir had embellished and gilded the rose, for Shabin's expectations were far removed from the reality, although in retrospect she wasn't really sure what she had really been expecting. Certainly not the Atlantic weather, or the sheer magnificence of the coast and sea. Coming from a landlocked country, with stunning mountains and valleys, it is one thing to hear about oceans and see film, but to actually see the real thing is vastly different.

'Have you eaten,' Dapper indicated the weight of food challenging guests and tables, the selection had changed and changed again several times with each new influx and further tendered ,' a drink?'
'A white wine would be welcome,' Shabin laughed lightly as Dapper offered his arm to escort her through the crowd, 'why thank you.'
' Well I'll be. . . Holy Mother, would you look at that!' Betty and Molly weren't the only ones to notice Dapper and Shabin sparking. Morena sharp as a sharks tooth, had seen the doctor and the decadent dandy and was satisfyingly outraged and more than pleased to be on her high horse of righteous indignation. Mutton and the rest of 'Up All Night' were kicking anxious to take the stage, having watched Murphy's Marauders set turn increasingly to farce. Sean, who although hardly able to maintain equilibrium was still intent on both amusing his audience and finding The John, although the reason for his quest was fast eluding him. In the past the boot had most times been on the other foot, with local promoter, police, or some other authority desperately trying to curtail some lewd, outrageous, or degenerative performance by whatever group he was working with. Mutton was skilled at fighting the sheriff, jobsworths and frenetic freebooters who sought to disadvantage his boys, but somewhat at a loss as to how to clear the Celtic kerfuffle.

Having finally enticed Sean, Murphy and the Marauders off the stage, which in itself was no mean feat and taken the combined efforts of Lucy Lastic at her most enchanting, Betty with a plate of ham sandwiches, a bottle of Powers whisky and the promise of exotic dancing courtesy of Titbits.

' Ladies and gentleman, there will now be a short intermission of around half and hour while we reset the stage for' Up All Night,' Bodger announced, having assumed the role of master of ceremonies, a role he was more than proficient at. Then glancing behind him, continued with a sheepish grin, ' and so that we can keep you all entertained for the duration and in the great style to which you just have been by Mr Murphy and the lads, we have an added delight.'

Mutton ambled over rather uncomfortably as his Farmers were playing up at a typically inappropriate moment, he whispered into Bodger''s ear. With a suppressed laugh Bodger addressed the gathering crowd, 'as I was saying, a welcome addition to tonight's, er grand event. Give it large for Titbits who is. . .'

Mutton again whispered urgently in Bodgers ear,' er. . . Titbits was going to do the dance of the seven veils, but due to the weather it'll now be the dance of the seven raincoats.' The crowd roared appreciation and a warm ripple of applause encouraged Titbits to sidle from the side of the stage in shades, raincoats and kinky boots to Strauss's music for Salome, which Bodger had conjured up from the internet and channeled through the sound system. She was in her element as the centre of attention, adding dramatic little twists and turns as she tantalizingly began to peel of the first mac letting Mutton and the lads get on with the rearranging the equipment. As each came off, Titbits became increasingly provocative, much encouraged by the men in the crowd. While the female morale minority were delighted to discover their initial disgust, when first they heard of the degenerate and depraved pop people who had moved into the big house, was correct.

'A flippity gibbet, if ever I laid eyes on one,' Mrs Mclish said with relish, almost drooling on her ham sandwich.

' . . . and would you look at the age of her!' Nora O'Driscol continued with satisfaction, although secretly saddened that she had only once in her entire life contrived to seduce one man, let alone charm the better part of the peninsula.

' and wasn't I saying when there was talk of this crowd arriving, that they were trouble, sure would ye look at that harlot ' Kitty was dutifully incensed,' and isn't that your fella cheering at the front , Morena?'

With one raincoat to go there was intense speculation as to what lay beneath, those that knew Titbits were well aware that she was no shrinking violet and had form with this class of a turn. Those that hadn't clapped eyes on her before the evening, were more than hopeful that there was little of a material nature between herself and her birthday suit. Titbits played the moment admirably, lingering over the final garment provocatively flicking her tail and the shaking her money maker. All but revealing, then tantalizing and teasing, flexing and flashing,baring a glimpse of breast and a touch of thigh. T.J down on his knees to nail bass drum to floor was suddenly tented by the raincoat and looking up discovered that Titbits had indeed gone commando and was aware of muffled cheers from without. T.J.was no stranger to the decadent and depraved, as some of the righteous would have it, in his view it was more a case of when the cow stands over the bucket he'd be a fool not to milk it. Morena's fella had never seen the like and like it he did indeed, whooping and cheering, stamping his feet and yelling encouragement, he was all for climbing on stage and elbowing T.J. from within.

This class of a show was not to be sniffed at and would linger long in his imagination and local legend.

Betty and Molly could never have been called prudes, indeed they'd done as much themselves and often pushed beyond. But they were young then, impressionable and without inhibition in their mission to pull and be pulled by the young radicals who dictated the way ahead for the voice of youthful revoloution and kicked against moribund moral attitudes. But now they had mellowed, accepted that they had been used for easy pleasure, with no real affection, or commitment and discarded when they became surplus to instant gratification. It would be disingenuous to say that hadn't been willing and enjoyed the experiences and wild times ,often using fantasy and imagination to entice and enchant. Neither was entirely sure if the frolicking was appropriate to introduce themselves to the local community, given the controversial nature of rumour and speculation already rife, however it was obvious it went down well. Apart from a Shakespearian brooding of old witches waiting in the shadows, in search of sin, smut and shame, to fuel their salacious sense of scandal and satisfy their sanctimonious sang-froid.

'Grand turnout altogether,' Jeremiah Styx smiled and bowed, getting a peek at her ample bosom.' Your cup runneth over,' he quickly indicated the food and crowd. The grim reaper gathered his harvest relentlessly, often without warning and for Jeremiah he prided himself and proclaimed on all his advertising that he provided a 24/7/52 service. To that end he had arrived in a hearse with an empty coffin in the back, just in case and as he moved through the throng, he kept a wary eye for any that might seem unwell. Mentally measuring and guestimating their weight, to be ever ready for the drop off, even rumoured to catch the deceased before they hit the deck.

Betty, viewed Jeremiah with wry amusement, but was troubled by his constant attention, he'd call up for a chat every few days, enquiring after the health of all, often popping in unexpectedly on the chance his services might just be required..

'Mr Styx. . . Jermiahah how good of you to turn out, especially in this weather.' Betty forced a smile.

'Not at all, not at all, think nothing of it,' he surveyed the crowd,' these are the days that carry many off and we like to be close at hand just in case we can step in and ease the passing of a loved one .'

Hooked and crooked in nose and back, thin and angular, Jeremiah had all the charm of a voracious vulture, his sharp beady eye forever roaming for the first sign of distress, ever ready to pounce.

'How considerate, I do hope you haven't spotted any potential victim.....sorry possible deceased!'

She did have concerns that Agatha's punch and the wild nature of the freak out might well induce some untoward health and safety issues in a number of the more vulnerable revelers.

Betty also felt uncomfortable, having noticed on previous visits that he eyed her, as if assessing her terms and condition for future reference,' Why don't you pop over to the bar and get a drink, you'll have to excuse me I must check if there's . . . ' She hesitated, aware that he was transfixed by her cleavage,'if there's enough food.'

' Oh I never drink on the job and I rarely have the time to relax. the only things one can guarantee in life are death and taxes, and one is best to avoid both as long as possible.' Just then Jeremiah spotted old Mrs Harpy, a regular fixture at most funerals, she made a point of listening to the death notices on the radio, noting down the details and turning up for the funeral, no matter if she knew the dear departed or not. This practice had not only given her a new lease of life in her declining years, but her interest had considerably widened her social circle and ensured that she had free food and drink at least three times a week allowing her to stretch her meagre pension and save on her energy costs.

'Oh yes, and of course the third certainty over there. Mrs. Harpy there has yet to miss a funeral on the peninsula this ten years past, sure the women has seen more off in those years than she ever knew in the years before. If there is an afterlife, they'll be a fierce strong crowd waiting to meet her at St Peter's gates and a good few would still be wondering who she was altogether.' Jeremiah rinsed his dry hands together as he continually did and smiled thinly and unconvincingly, as he continued to examine the assembly much like a hyena searching a herd of gazelle for the vulnerable and weak.

GODAGURU.

'You must see this,' Lucy Lastic interrupted Betty and Molly in the midst of their daily coffee and cake making, the kitchen table had fresh banana bread and brownies. Although a great cook and an outstanding cake maker of repute,Betty was akin to an environmental disaster in the kitchen as regards tidying up and the end result was often very much like an explosion in domestic science class at a secondary school. Pots and pans piled high, perilously threatening to fall and inflict lethal injury.

Lucy had laptop under arm and was even more excited than normal, ' I found this site last night after Bodger left my room. . . he's so handy and sorted out my problem in no time.'
Betty and Molly exchanged knowing glances and giggled. 'Isn't he just.'
'What is it, did I say something?' Lucy looked a little taken aback, ' oh I see, you're teasing me again. . . he only put me on line, I've been having massive problems.'
'Haven't we all?' Molly said flippantly, with a sarcastic undertone.
'Oh, sorry Lucy, it's Molly she can't take anything seriously.' Betty said without conviction.' so what have you found?'
'Well. . . ' Lucy laid her laptop on the kitchen table, .'ooh, are those brownies?'
'Yea, help yourself.'
'It's called Cosmicguru, it's wonderful. . . so reassuring, he just seems to be so in touch. . .all you do is type in a question and he knows exactly what you mean!'
Molly and Betty again exchanged glances, suppressing giggles this time, although Lucy wouldn't have noticed as she was intent on establishing contact with Sidarthur Dallylarm.
'What have you asked so far?' Molly ventured.
'Oh just the usual, the meaning of life and other spiritual things, he's so cool. . . he answered straight away,' Lucy looked a little bemused, ' he sort of gives you a mantra.'
' What did he say?' Betty asked curiously.
'The secret of life is to take deep breaths and let your heart beat regularly ,while meditating on the rhythm of the solar system.' Lucy felt a hot flush coming on as she so often did, but knew it only happened when she was tuned in to the great cycle of energy and purpose.

'Sounds about right,' Betty agreed.

'Yea, can see it makes sense, two great habits to live by.' Molly was a cynic by nature and experience, but loathe to abandon belief in the hereafter, just in case. She crossed her legs and tried hard not to snigger, knowing her bladder could let her down, a problem that was increasingly frequent and malodorous.

'Ask him why men are so promiscuous.' Betty asked after glancing out of the window and seeing Dapper striding across the grass all cock of the walk, with T.J. and Agatha.

'OOh, I don't know if I can ask that,' Lucy blushed.

'Go on, if your guru is so wise he'll know the answer,' Betty insisted.

'Yea, don't forget the temples in India are covered in erotic statues and pictures.' Molly chimed.

'Oh, really, are you sure?' Lucy was surprised and thought about it for a few moments,' isn't that sacrilegious?'

'Depends which God you prey to and how you practice your faith really.'

'You're right there Betty. . . strangely enough a good few religions recommend sex as the path to enlightenment and there were untold harlots hanging around temples to satisfy demand.' Molly smirked.

'Come to think of it, all religions were dreamed up by men!'

' All right then!' Lucy typed in the question.

While they waited they ate a few brownies and poured a second cup while watching with amusement the lads trying to bump start T.J.'s old banger, ' you'd think T.J. would know better by now, he swapped that old scooter he had for that heap of scrap with Rory, if it wasn't for the bailing twine and Gaffa tape the whole thing would be a trail of spare parts along the drive.' Despaired Betty.

'That's about right, Agatha and T.J. have always been spare parts in search of a scrap yard anyway!' Molly scoffed gleefully.

Just then the computer chimed response and they eagerly scanned the message;

'If you cannot catch a bird of paradise, better take a wet hen.' They read and reread it and then an additional message popped up, ' For a premium rate service please insert credit card details and go to our payment page.' followed by,' Discounts are available for students, organized groups and senior citizens.'

A further message popped up,' the older you get, the better you get, unless you're a banana.'

'Did you pay anything for this poppycock?' molly sneered.

'You have to pay £32. to join, but get 23 messages for that' Lucy replied.

105

Betty typed in 'wisdom' and a few moments later received,' Ask the opinion of an older person and one younger than thyself and then return to thy own opinion.'

They spent the next hour engrossed in the guru's wisdom, forking out a further £32. when their credit ran out and learnt.

Betty and Molly were skeptical to say the least, but Lucy was convinced and felt she was closer to the path of enlightenment and decided to go down to the brook to communicate with her inner spirit.

She always felt close to the nature divas with the tinkling and gurgling of the water over the rocks and the wind dancing through the cotton grass. Already a firm believer in astrology, numerology and tarot, which she regarded as sources of wisdom and advice never making any decision until she'd consulted all three.

Lucy lay back in the grass to think, closing her eyes and just letting thoughts and images drift across her mind. Before long she had drifted off with golden gurus and celestial certainties conjuring up utopian landscapes and cotton soft warmth, wholeness and wellbeing.

Increasingly Mutton considered what his life might have been like, if he'd got the breaks and been the guitarist rather than the roadie, to his mind he could play as well as many who had won fortune and fame. He'd felt fortunate that he'd managed to spend a lifetime in rock'n'roll, with all the associated fringe benefits and trimmings, he was first to recognize that without being part of the scene he'd have been well lucky to get laid, travel the world, or live life in the fast lane.

Beaver strolled in sniffed the air and sashayed over to rub her side against his leg coquettishly. Mutton stroked her and scratched the base of one of her ears, which instantly produced loud purring.

She was a floozie and a sucker for the soft touch, if you found her weak spot, which all females have; all need lovin', just like a woman.

Mutton started strumming Stray Cat Blues and was reminded of a wild child that used to hang around the London scene in the late sixties, jail bait for sure, but it took a strong man to resist her allure, Flirty Girty by name and nature.

'Bet your mama don't know you scream like that'

'I bet your mother don't know you can spit like that,'

Fourteen maybe, but a dressed up eighteen, mini skirt barely covering her arse, suspenders and stockings straight out of St Trinians, tottering on her dolly rockers with those big round innocent doe eyes.

Mutton wondered what happened to her, probably married a stock broker and settled in suburbia, he liked to hope it all worked out fine for her after her lost years as every bodies playmate. Lucky was the man that married her as she had developed talents that could satisfy even the most adventurous , but then she had trouble containing her promiscuous thoughts and actions for one man for very long and was hardly likely to remain faithful.

A man with a roving eye might bed hop with impunity and be applauded by the lads and often envied, but a bird bustling between beds and blokes was a bicycle that everybody rode and nobody wanted to own, or respect. Just pump up the tyres now and again, oil the chain and for a few the odd sniff of the saddle was all the servicing required.

Then he remembered another little beatnik chic that hung around Eel Pie Island in the early days, another wild child, flaming red hair. If memory served she had a quickie with Rock, or was it Geal? He caught them at it outside the gig, she was pissed as a fart, he'd gone in search of his missing frontman as they were due on stage, they left her throwing up on some old bench, he still felt bad about that .Was it Geal, or Rock ?

Mutton had worked for both of them in their early bands, did it matter now?

He shrugged, funny the things that spring to mind for no apparent reason.

ON THE TOWN.

The boys were back in town for the first time since the barn dance, the fact that they were mostly balding old men was of little concern. You are as old as you feel and if fortunate the age of the lady you manage to feel, or at least imagine you might get the chance to wangle into compromise and carnal comfort. Dapper had an appointment with Shabin for a repeat prescription, but was intent on seduction, lately Shabin featured large in his thoughts. Sex is as much in the mind as the body. Dapper had laid many hundred, if not thousands of ladies in his life and apart from size and feature, the female form was essentially the same. Boobs, bum, bewitching beauty and that magic triangle of pubic hair that pointed to the holy of holy's, the honey pot where a certain magic, real, or imagined beckons and beguiles. Science has it that love is a chemical addiction that builds, some might say it is in the genes and is what drives procreation, others don't give a Donald and just seek it out and enjoy.

Dapper was aware of function and consequence, it would be a very thoughtless individual who had taken three wives, numerous concubines and untold one night stands, producing at least a dozen known offspring, who would still be ignorant of consequence. But even at 64 the drive, imagination and perhaps blind lust was still active and he was still smitten by the next lady he laid eyes on and unable to rest easy until he had satisfied his curiosity and desire.

T.J. and Agatha made directly for Dick Macs and the craic, their cravings being easily satisfied by a few pints, the odd furtive joint and a good larf with the lads.

'Argh it's yourselves lads, fine gentlemen the pair of you. . . so, would you be interested in an investment?' Squirreled beneath an oversized and well worn overcoat and a stained flat cap a craggy face that had last seen water when last it rained. Short in stature and semantics and born and bred to bemuse was Wilde. He may well have been given a Christian name, but if that was the case nobody knew it and he had never consented to readily divulge such information. The guardai, with whom he often collided, were equally confused by his tendency to dream up a different Christian name each time he was questioned. Apart from numerous brushes with the law no trace of his existence was to be found on any other list or record, he paid no taxes, nor any other demand for his cash, which he only dealt in.

Agatha had long had time to ruefully ruminate and regret the first & only time he'd fallen for Willie's ruse and lashed out on a pint for the freeloader.

'I'm still after yer man John!'

'Sean!' Agatha recognized the voice and turned from the bar and the pint he nursed,' t'is yourself sure enough.'
'That it is and my girl is getting bigger by the day and I'll no rest until you find me the John.' Sean smacked a
blackthorn shilllelagh on the bar next to Agatha,' my Nuala was to be the bride of Christ, not the whore of
Babylon, you're man John ravished her, you'll know his whereabouts!'

Agatha gulped and glanced at the dent in the bar,' er, is it a Murphy's Sean . . . ?

'Just the one then,' Sean wasn't a man to turn down a free pint in any circumstance,' mark my words and
mark them well, that John has played fast and loose with Nuala and she's in the family way,' Sean was
waving his stick about menacingly,' now what steps is he going to take?'

'Bloody big ones.' Agatha thought, ' are you sure it was Dapper?'

'Dapper?' Sean was puzzled,' What's dapper?' Thinking it might be some unholy sexual perversion.

'Jasus what's going on up at the old bar?', Sean muttered to everybody and nobody in particular.

'That pint you mentioned,' Willie intervened, already tasting the bitter sweet beer.

Just then Tic Tac arrived fresh from Joe Fureturs,' Ruby rode a treble for Mullins, then broke a leg in
the fourth at Fairyhouse,' I was robbed he was second at the time, cruising with two fences to go.'

Agatha smiled wearily at the barman,' I only dropped in for a quite pint.'

Over on the other side of Town, Dapper was staring deep into Shabins eyes,' it's my heart
Shabin . . . and my blood pressure has gone through the roof.'

'Oh really John, severe pain, palpatations, panic attacks?' Shabin sounded very concerned.

'More of a flutter really. . . . especially when I see you!' Dapper laughed and winked.

Shabin blushed,' John really, be serious.' She was embarrassed, but perhaps a little flattered as she had
reached her early thirties without romance of any consequence touching her heart, or life in any way.
As a doctor there was no aspect of the human body, or relationships she was not familiar with, but she
was very much a stranger to close personal emotion and couldn't help but yearn and dream that it might
happen to her. She had long felt uncomfortable and inappropriate in advising her patients on sexual matters,
when her only qualification was that gleaned from dry and clinical textbooks. In truth she was lonely, a stranger
in a strange land and as a woman she had all the natural desires and wishes.

109

She wanted to discover what love was, be in love and she was almost desperate to be a mother and find her soul mate.

But even Shabin could see how odd it was, there was she Dapper's doctor fully aware of his health problems, prescribing drugs for his arthritis and impotency and aware that he was 64, twice her age, yet she was attracted to him. She also knew she had possibly transgressed the BMA's code of conduct, but then again did it apply to Eire? In truth she knew she was fudging the issue, but love is a many splendid thing.

'I'm serious Shabin,' Dapper was besotted.

Shabin felt she was losing control both personally and professionally, the woman and the doctor were no longer separate and she had never felt this way before and wasn't at all sure she liked or understood it.

Dapper leaned forward and clutched her hand,' Shabin you're a beautiful woman.' Such sentiments came easy to him, but always sounded sincere and spontaneous,' You must know that . . . you must know that I. '

Just then the phone rang and Shabin grabbed it, just a bit too quickly, partially relieved, but still very much unsure of her emotions, 'Hello... hello Dr Cahir. . . ' Her eyes were still locked on Dapper's and she smiled sweetly, ' Yes Morena, I do know there are other patients waiting, thank you Morena. Yes Morena I do know that Mr Cox has been in my office for over twenty minutes.' Shabin laughed and shook her head in disbelief making her pony tail swing behind her.

'I love it when you swing your hair!' Dapper grinned,' there goes my heart again.'

Shabin put her hand over the receiver and giggled like a schoolgirl and then removing her hand,' yes Morena I do know that the guidline is ten minutes per patient, thank you for reminding me. . . yes Morena,   Mr Cox IS just leaving.' Shabin replaced the phone,' John I do appreciate your visit, but I do have other patients, you really must go, and some of them are actually ill.'

'What about my heart?' Dapper pleaded,

" I think a little rest might be beneficial and a little less brandy.' Shabin gave Dapper an old fashioned look.

'More rest, less brandy? Dapper visibly wilted.' Shabin what are you saying? . . . .What are you doing to me?'

'Now John, I do have other patients waiting, please!'

'I'll only go if you promise to have dinner with me tonight.'

The waiting room was heaving with a good few sneezing, something untoward was going around, but not all were in to see the doctor. Morena was queen wasp in her hive and her drones swarmed in the waiting room, as the juciest gossip could be gleaned here. Morena had been Dr Quain's receptionist, although the good doctor ruled his roost with a firmer hand and didn't tolerate the gathering of the coven, or scandalous tittle tattle. But with the cat away, the mice could play and Morena had never been one to let the grass grow under her feet as far as rumour and speculation went.

Nora O'Driscol, Kitty and Morena were as thick as thieves and thieves in a very real sense as they stole the intimate details, dilemmas, mistakes and problems that beset the lives of all at times and are best left untold within the community. Such spicy scraps were there to be chewed over, dissected and inspected, to know the secretive and sensitive specifics of another's life was to have a power over them. The toxic trio were known for what they were and distrusted, with none happy to spend time in their company, many were reluctant to visit the doctors unless it was desperate, as their problems all too quickly became the talk of the town.

Shabin didn't notice at first as she had no idea how many patients were an average turnout and the new arrivals from Dungiggin boosted turnover and masked local decline. Morena and her coven had noticed Dapper escorting Shabin at the dance and now considered it their moral duty to monitor their relationship, discuss the ramifications and speculate on any salacious sin.

As Dapper left with a smug smile on his face he noticed the extra interest from the receptionist.

'Goodbye Mr Cox, did the doctor satisfy your demands?' Morena enquired, with just a hint of sarcasm.

Dapper just nodded, noting the strange way she had asked the question.

Immediately the door closed, the trio went into a horrendous huddle.

'He's old enough to be her father.'

'I said as much when she arrived, you'd expect that sort of a thing. . . . a lady doctor indeed, well really whatever next?'

Nora glanced out of the window as Dapper walked up to Dick Mac's,' isn't that your fella talking to the scarlet woman, Morena?'

The bus to Tralee stopped outside the back of Supavalue and the boys from Dungiggin parked up in the harbour carpark across the road.

111

T.J. had to wait until the 11.am bus pulled out before he could cross the road, he noticed a bag of groceries and a sack of spuds leaning against the low wall. Stopping to chat to Sheehan who often got into Dick Macs, T.J. kept his eye on the groceries pointing them out to Sheehan.

'Ah that'll be Brosnan he has a farm over the other side of the pass, he'll be having a pint in Geaney's, I'd say he's missed the bus again.'

HOME GROWN.

Agatha and T.J. sat on the wall blowing a joint, idly watching a rat eat a toad and letting the day pass through, as they acted the goat in their own inimitable style, as true rapscallions.

'D'ye think the rat will get warts?' Agatha tilted his head to better see the last of the toad pass from this world into the digestive juices of the rats stomach.

'Don 't be soft. . .everybody knows. . .'

'Boys there's somebody here who wants a word with you.' Betty interrupted sternly.

They turned to see a Gardai officer giving them the severe eye of authority and Agatha immediately fell backwards off the wall and stubbed the joint into the manure, before reemerging grinning like the village eejit.

'Good morning gents,' The officer scanned the rough garden beyond and smiled,' I'd say you're keen gardeners lads.'

Both Agatha and T.J. looked a bit sheepish knowing what he was getting at and not relishing the nature of his visit,

'Gardening you say, no not us you must have heard wrong, sure we wouldn't even know which way up they go.'

Agatha said unconvincingly brushing off something that looked and smelled remarkably like fox crap, he sniffed his hand and muttered,' fookain fox!' before wiping it on his trousers.

Betty stood back watching in sad resignation, but little surprise as they both had track records for blundering from embarrassing disaster to petty criminal catastrophe and on to aggravated accident.

'Is that so? The gardai tipped his cap back with a finger,' o.k. lads shall we take a stroll.'

Agatha and T.J. exchanged nervous glances, considered a quick getaway, thought better of it and with a shrug followed the gardai.

'Now lads we might be a bit off the beaten track here abouts, but we do know what that is.' He pointed to the few plants waving around provocatively in the breeze.

'There stinging nettles aren't they?' T.J. chanced his arm.

The Gardai tilted his head and nodded with a wry smile,' and I'll be the next pope, nice try.'

Betty had followed on and was keen sort things out,' Tell me officer, how did you come to know about these plants?' She smiled sweetly.

He pointed to the low wall that separated the garden from the main road and then pointed to the plants which were some 3' higher.' Officer O'Hagen spotted them as he was cycling by, he's a keen horticulturist, he had the largest marrow at last years village fete. He wasn't sure what they were so he took a photo, grand things these digital cameras. Don't ye think?' The guardai noticed that Betty was quite attractive with a winning smile and when she flicked her hair from her face it was quite beguiling,' He thought he might grow some, so he looked them up on the computer. . . Quite spectacular plants altogether. . . totally illegal of course.' He added quickly. 'You'll come in for a cup of tea and a bit of cake, I'm sure we can sort this out,' She smiled warmly and touched his arm,' actually I keep chickens and fowl you know and I get these packets of seed from that shop in town. . . ' She led the way pointing out features of the grounds, T.J. and Agatha followed on bashfully.

Seated in the warm kitchen with the comforting aromas of coffee and banna bread wafting from the range, Gardaí O'Connor settled in a wheelback chair by the open door of the range where the warming flames flicked and danced within.

'Would you like some cake with you coffee officer?' Betty took her coat off, quickly checked her look in the mirror and smiled sweetly yet again,' and please call me Betty.' She suddenly had a frightening thought and leaned over, quickly removing a plate of space cakes, making sure her ample and provocative cleavage proved a grand distraction.

Gurdai O'Toole couldn't fail to notice and was suitably impressed.

The two scallywags seated themselves at the far side of the table nearer the door just in case the opportunity to escape proved necessary.

'Geal, long time no see!' T.J. exclaimed,' you don't often get in, how's it going?'

'Yea, not bad and yourself?' Geal winked at Sheehan,' is it a pint lads?'

'Sure, that's good of you, I'll have a Murphy's if it's all the same!' Agatha called out from the snug and then his head pocked out through the cubby hole with a big grin, ' alright Geal, remember me?'

Geal thought for a moment and then said,' yea, you're that Irish Bastard that dumped my gear in the Thames!' Geal looked stern.

Agatha swallowed hard and thought back.

In the 60's any band playing Eel Pie Island had a problem getting the gear to the gig. The narrow bridge to the island wasn't wide enough for a van to get over and the van had to back up and transfer the gear to

114

a little open back mini van, taking several trips to get it all over.

Agatha was working for Flahoola, replacing Ronnie who was once again banged up in the Scrubs for a touch of petty larceny.

In backing the old battered Commer van down the slope to the bridge, blew it and all but drowned himself along with van and gear.

'ER, Hang on mate that was a long time ago and it was an accident,' Agatha blustered,' sure, wasn't I nearly drownded myself and I nearly got phenomenonena from it,' he thought hard,' it's a lucky thing I wasn't poisoned by the river itself and I didn't get uppity about it, did I?'

Geal admired his choice of word and had to agree, better a freak show then a lung infection,

Staring at him,with a smile breaking across his face which slowly became a laugh, Geal elbowed Agatha in the ribs,' you're still a bastard, that Gibson was my first real guitar, I saved up for the deposit and still had to pay the H.P. on it for months after . . . It wasn't the same again,the neck was warped and it never stayed in tune.' Geal winked,' and you fucked off without so much as an apology. . . is that right you ended up working for Nonsuch?'

'Sure and why wouldn't I?' Agatha invariably looked as if he was struggling to understand what was going down even if he was the instigator.

'Nothing, it's just I'm beginning to sympathize with Rock that bit more now.' Geal said wryly. The others in the bar watched and listened unsure as Geal tormented Agatha mercilessly,but enjoying it none the less.

'A thought popped into Geal's brain and he said it without thinking it through properly,' Wasn't it you that married that Asian whore Laylay and had those couple of kids? . . . Her face cropped up among the demonstrators in Tinnerman Square.'

Agatha was wide eyed in surprise and gave it some thought,' No, no. . . I don't think so. . . I'm sure I'd have remembered that. . . although there was that time I was at this Asian girls house and screwed her as she was at the window talking to her mum who was hanging out the washing in the yard. . . but I'm sure I didn't marry her, I'd know that for sure.'

Sheehan leant on the crowded bar, nursing his empty pint glass and kicking a foot idly against the Garryowen Plug metal advert screwed to the bar, as he regretted the smoking ban in the pub. He was a patient man, as any man that chanced his life and fortune on the sea must be, for each and every trip was a voyage into the unknown, so many that sailed with the tide returned with nothing of consequence, or just failed to return. As had Sheehan's brother some twenty years before, lost in a squall out on the Blaskett sound leaving a young widow, two toddlers and no body to bury.

T.J. wasn't as patient as Sheehan and had a mean thirst on him, so he coughed and cleared his throat meaningfully,' Shall order up?'

'Yea go ahead. . . ' so what's it like?'

'What's what like?' Agatha said anxiously.

'Dungiggin!' Geal nodded to the barman,' an Irish coffee please. . . I've heard the talk in the town, a good bit about Dapper John. . . That right that he's the main man and you're all attitude adjustment and crew?'

'JOHN, did you say?' the voice came from the old kitchen and Sean appeared disheveled at the door,' you know the John?'

Parking up in the harbour car park Nick crossed the road to walk up to Dick Macs,

'The Tralee bus,' a crooked man in a flat cap, creased and stained brown jacket, obviously worse for the drink enquired,' it's late?'

'No gone this ten minutes' Nick smiled, having passed it on the road as he neared town.

Momentarily perplexed,' it's gone!. . . . Jeez, I've time for a drink then.' he knocked into the spud sack scattering a few and reached down swaying slightly to retrieve them.

'I'd say you've had one already,' Nick Observed.

'Only to keep the chill out, the wind gets into a mans bones here abouts and having to catch the bus.' With that Brosnan swayed away to get a warming drink.

Nick grinned and then strolled up to Dick Macs glancing into the shop windows as he passed, one or two of the arty craft novelties grabbed his attention and he briefly considered buying a mirror in a driftwood frame for Christine,but she could be a bit tetchy about more clutter. Like most couples that stayed together over decades, they'd weathered the good, bad and indifference of each other and although many of their individual habits and idiosyncrasies still grated they tolerated them, perhaps out of lazy habit, or maybe that little thing called love.

They enjoyed their time together, but equally relished time apart and space between, a balance that had been hard won and was much different to their early days, when hours away from each other were painful and seemingly empty. He'd often thought long and hard about relationships, considering how few species mated for life and wondered if it was actually unnatural to do so and in attempting such, one was breaching some instinctive code. On a more pragmatic note he was more than aware that a divorce would be unimaginably traumatic, financial suicide and just too much hard work. Nick had watched Rock over the years, never a steady relationship, a libertine and lothario, with no regard for the emotions of the people he ravaged in an ever increasing pursuit of sadistic pleasure and sordid degradation. He'd often pondered if Rock had ever had misgivings, felt some form of guilt, mulled over any moral implications, or feared any form of karmic punishment, or retribution.

Not that he would ever claim the moral high ground, as he had well sown his wild oats and had not been reluctant to indulge his carnal appetite for sexual excess. or abuse the naive willingness of the girls. He laughed as he thought how something so simple as a fleeting impulse to buy a novelty mirror could trigger a tunnel of deep reflection.

Geal and Nick shared many moral and spiritual values, which was the main reason they worked together so well, but whereas Geal was much more the dreamer tuning in to the ever transient zeitgeist. Nick was more forensic, continually probing and analyzing the undercurrent that drove each and every person to construct, or destroy their lives and those they came into contact with. Geal could soar to dizzy heights of fantasy and Nick was more grounded and pragmatic, it was this dynamic where both could equally give, or take which set them apart from the main stream

'Hello lads can I join the party?' Nick butted in to an intense debate between Geal and T.J. about bands playing for free back in the halcyon days of love and peace. Rock had done it once in Hyde Park, but thereafter refused, despite the protestations of Buck and the rest of Nun-Such, insisting that he was a professional and should be paid for his artistic integrity.

Whereas Geal had embraced counter culture and was more than happy to play a benefit concert if he could emphasis with the cause, such as Release, CND and where he was outraged by the abuses of the establishment in gagging free speech and the demonstration against the war in Vietnam.

117

BEACH RACING.

Tic Tac had been busy in the paddocks with his old nags, once pampered bloodstock that cost a keep and train were quickly dumped if they failed to win.

Many were slaughtered for the continental horsemeat trade, some returning as pet food and others discretely in cheap ready meals for the great unwashed. A few luckier ones were foisted at bargain basement prices on farmers who enjoyed amateur point to point racing, or aspired to stumble across a good thing that might just spring a sporting surprise at a grand price in the right race. More often the bargain buy was little more than a candidate for a dubious donkey derby, or at best a hunting hack.

Beside being a complete bastard, the considered opinion of most of the others who were condemned to spend any time around him. Tic Tac was an optimist, a chancer who would ring the last teardrop out of a sobbing girls hankie if he was thirsty and just for the perverse pleasure of rubbing salt in her wounds. 'So this 'orse of yours,' Agatha had been leaning against an old gnarled oak watching the action.' is it any good?'

'Cheap trick,' Tic Tac dressed for the part, in jodhpurs, flat cap, binoculars, 'He's no Shergar, but he's tidy alright.' Tic Tac grinned and showed Agatha his stopwatch.

Agatha studied it, looked at Tic Tac and back at the watch,' two minutes and thirty two seconds. . . is that good?' 'Not bad and with a week to the races I think I can improve him,' Tic Tac talked the talk with impressive confidence, or so Agatha thought,' I'll canter him on the sand and swim him over the next few days.'

Agatha was not slow to spread the news telling T.J. and Mutton,' Tic Tac reckons he can do the business on the beach next week.'

Beach racing had once been common around the coast of Eire, although with a few exceptions very much a local amateur affair, but still taken seriously within the area with heavy betting and often bitter rivalry.

Sure enough Joe Furetur had made small fortunes over the years, ranking it along with the Grand National, Derby and Cheltenham Festival as lucrative. It was something of a tradition for two, or three different crowds of conspirators to collaborate in preparing a coup and rumour and speculation was rife.

Joe had pulled off a good few nice touch's over the years, as indeed had his father and grandfather before him and was known locally as nobody's fool.

Tic Tac also played his cards close to his chest, ' Of course Cheap Trick is in with a chance, but there's talk that Flash Forward the Doran's colt is no back number and there's a crowd from over Tralee way that have a good thing in What A picture.'

Given the deviousness of Tic Tac and his track record for stretching the envelope to confuse and confound, none could be sure of the way ahead, although it did increase anticipation and expectation for the race day.

The day dawned bright with only an outside chance of a slight Atlantic squall and the first race was scheduled for 1.30, but due to a misunderstanding between the organizers and natures tidetable, was then postponed for an hour to allow the tide to ebb. During which time the slender prospect of an squall arrived to wreak havoc among the assorted tents and booths. A couple of tractors cruised the draining sand to deposit cones, spikes and tape to mark the course.

Quads bikes sped around with officials measuring the distance from sea to dunes and place the furlong markers for the races. Horseboxes and cattle trucks unloaded the runners and riders who were tacked up, or donned silks depending on species.

Groups of shady characters in crumpled brown jackets loitered, casting suspicious glances at horses and riders chatting amongst themselves. This was it, all the months of hard work and shrewd preparation had honed the contenders for the day and little could be done,but hope and pray all would be well and that the favourite might not be cherry ripe on the day. Money and pride were the prime factors and men would pull major strokes to achieve the result, with the end justifying the means.

Jockeys, trainers and owners most often had a deep bond of affection for the horses and ponies and when all was huffed and puffed were just happy to get their mounts safely home and hosed.

A dozen bookies set up pitches with satchels and chalkboards on stepladders and met in a huddle to arrange starting prices and sip at flasks of whisky.

Tic Tac had Cheap Trick cherry ripe, but if talk was to be believed so was just about every nag that arrived at the beach and some would proclaim that theirs were above and beyond the common herd.

The real shrewdies after a long price from the bookies planted whispers bemoaning the condition of their horse, or the course and could be seen weeping crocodile tears when they viewed the opposition.

119

Tic Tac strutted his short stuff around the compound of horseboxes sneaking a peep here and there and keeping a long ear to the tittle-tattle looking to get a good punt on. Like most gamblers he was looking for the main chance and liked an interest in every race, but as a born bad loser he hated to see his wedge sliding into the bookies satchel.

'Isn't it so wonderful, I can feel that this is a magic place...' Lucy twirled on the sand laughing, 'Molly I just know that the little people are watching us and giggling.
'
Molly raised her eyebrows and turned to Betty who shrugged,' The only little person I can see certainly seems to be watching everybody,' she pointed out Tic Tac who was creeping around the back of some horsebox earwigging on a crowd around a horse.
'Oh how amazing! . . . I simply must go and see her.' Lucy was ecstatic as she gazed at Mother Shipton's colourful tent, decorated with pentangles, stars, moons and other heaven sent magical symbols. A star shaped sign declared Mother Shipton was the seventh daughter of a seventh daughter born to a seventh son and thus had the insight of a born psychic and a clear sighted seer with an accurate vision of the future.Further still she proclaimed grandly, she had been born with a caul, which she still retained and this amplified her powers infinitely.

Betty and Molly saw her from a hollow in the dunes where they'd settled with plastic cups of tea and a dash of vodka,' I bet Mother Shipton saw her coming.'
'You don't need to be psychic to see Lucy coming!' Molly laughed.
'As long as she tells Lucy who'll win the race in time to get a bet on I don't mind.' Betty fidgeted and then reached down to scratch her arse, ' bleeding sand gets in yer knickers, don't it?'
'If only it was just sand. . . mind you, that's about the size of it these days, if I'm honest'
They both fell about giggling.
'Oops I wet em!'
'What can a poor girl do,' Betty shrugged,' there's always something going through yer draws if it ain't sand. it's men . . .' If only, she rued.
' Then your pipes needs replumbing. . .,' Molly said, thought for a moment and added,' mind you if Rory was working away with my waterworks. . .'
'Steady girl,steady!'

120

They were now giggling and shrieking like pre pubescent schoolgirls on an illicit jolly.

The tent equipped with two tables served as a bar and was doing a roaring trade, although little bigger that an average suburban living room, around a hundred people were crowded together desperate to prevent the rain diluting their beer. A good few regular faces from Dick Macs featured in the throng and Mutton and others from Dungiggin were not shy to mingle.

The nieve, or just plain foolish, could easily have done their stash on any number of dead certs who struggled to turn up for the races with three sound legs, but glorious uncertainty is very much in the game.

Billy Boots looked forlorn and frozen in his silks, but was a lion at heart, for him this was the big time. He was born and bred to ride, the latest in a dynasty of horseman stretching back into the mists of mythic, when history was very much a leap of imagination and not constrained by the fact of the matter. Who would have the time, or indeed the materials to write the actuality, which in any case was both boring and inconvenient to the cause, motive, or progression of the ultimate goal. Sure the entire peninsula would know that the Fureteurs had been alongside Graine O'Malley, Wolfe Tone and Michael Collins at the pivotal moments of Irish history and all had been horsemen of great repute, although their prowess in other skills might have been less reliable, or worthy.

Great Uncle Marty had spent two days before the Easter uprising making sandwiches for the duration,only to miss the Dublin train, arrive late and be forced to sit out the event in Mc Daids, eating his ham sandwiches, nursing a pint and waiting for the glorious outcome. But the year after he lifted the Dunquin cup in a fabulous fashion, for a third famous victory, which wouldn't have been possible if he'd arrived on time for the siege, been arrested and spent the following years in a welsh prison eating humble pie. Way back beyond the days when oral history became muddled and then forgotten in a haze of tobacco and purified potcheen the Fureteurs had enjoyed a coat of arms and family motto 'Ever a slim chance.'

It might easily be said the the Fureteurs had endured rather than enjoyed the tumbling turbulence of the years of Irish history, most often ending up on the wrong side of a successful outcome.

Although given the morals and motives of many of the victors it could be argued that the Fureteurs were viewed as noble and beautiful losers. Whatever, they were not quitters, no matter the apparent odds and obstacles they'd give it a go as a stubborn, maybe plain stupid gene coursed deep in their blood.

'Well Billy what d'ye think?' Tic Tac patted his jocky's back,' I could piss it on a rusty bike,' he joked.

'. . .and on Cheap Trick?' Tic Tac looked concerned.

'No problem !' Billy Boots had a wry sense of humour,' As long as' Flash Forward' breaks down, Declan falls off, 'What A picture' and the other nine don't go on the sand, we've a fighting chance.' Boots grinned inanely while secretly quaking in his jock strap and boots.

'So all's not lost then?' Tic Tac, glanced down, fished a drowning wasp out of his warm beer, which promptly stung him,' fuck, you little bastard!'then toasted his jockey ' I'll lump a wedge on then?'

'That was so wonderful, she knew everything about me, it was like I was talking to my mum.'

Lucy had caught up with Betty and Molly in the dunes,' Did she tell you who'll win the big race?

'No !' Lucy looked mystified,' do you think she knows?. . . but she'd did tell me the secret of winning money on the horses.'

Betty and Molly were all ears and glanced at each other, both intrigued and extrememly skeptical,' Well!'

'Apprantly you always get more if you collect your winnings before the racing starts.' Lucy replied innocently. Again the girls looked at each other, before bursting into laughter,' really!' Betty spluttered,' She might be on to something there.'

'What!. . .What?. . . Did I say something funny?' Lucy's genuine innocence was disarming and very beguiling.

Smiling warmly, Betty reached out and gently stroked Lucy's arm,' No, you're lovely. . . it's fine. I'm sure you're gypsy lady was right.'

'But she did say musicians had a big part in my life and I'd known many famous people. . .' Lucy twirled on the sand blissfully, the stars in her eyes sparkling,' she even knew I came from London.'

'No shit Sherlock!' Molly chimed in sarcastically and then caught sight of Titbits strutting her stuff in a tight leather bondage style suit and knee length patent leather boots by the bar with an entourage of lustful lads, their eyes a poppin' and their tongues hanging out like panting hounds. One of whom was down on his knees, with a wide grin on his face repairing the heel of her boot which had snapped off in the sand, looking for all the world like the willing slave of a dominatrix.

' Who let the dogs out?' Molly pointed at the incongruous sight on the beach and wistfully thought,'If only I could still get a crowd of lads to gather around me, maybe I'd go naked with a purple plume up my pussy.'

'This really is horse and hounds.' Betty was having a grand time and the cabaret was top class in every respect, a day at the beach races in Eire was ever a sight for sore eyes.

'Look what I got from Mother Shipton,' Lucy produced a small plastic container, ' she's a herbalist and a white witch and has ancient wisdom and secret knowledge of herbs and special potions.

Betty took hold of the jar unscrewed the lid and looked at the brown paste within and then tentatively sniffed it, it smells of fish !' she looked quizzically at Lucy,' what's it for?'

Molly put her hand out,' let's have a look.'

'Mother Shipton say's it's good for arthritis, bruises, sprains, headaches and toothache and if you use it like conditioner it makes your hair look super.'

' Is there anything it's not good for?' Molly said sarcastically.

'Well. . . she said that I could always go on line in an emergency and she could arrange next day delivery, or if I give her a call she'll give me an appointment to visit her cottage, it's just over the other side of the pass.' Lucy was still dancing around excitedly.

'What did you get it for?' Molly took a little on her fingers and rubbed them together, sniffing at it warily.' 'Nothing really. . . it was on special offer at half price when you had your fortune told.' Lucy fished in her shoulder bag and produced a withered piece of something that wasn't immediately identifiable.'I got this as well.'

'Urgh, what the fuck is that!' Betty recoiled.

'Oh silly,don't you know a mojo when you see one. ' Lucy laughed lightly,' This one is special for me and my star sign and numerology number.' Lucy stroked it affectionately,' it'll protect me and bring me luck.'

'It'll need to,it looks like a dogs dick to me.' Molly smirked,' you handle it well, I'd say you've played with one of those before.'

There was no response for a moment, as if Lucy hadn't heard and then ,' what do you mean? What are you saying?' Lucy was visibly shocked.

Even Betty was taken aback, but not really surprised as Molly was prone to mouthing off and was catty by nature,' Molly !'

'What ? . . .What I say?' Molly was unrepentant, in fact she genuinely didn't appreciate how tactless and wounding she had been.

Shabin was the designated race doctor and Dapper was her self appointed escort, having thus far failed to lay her, a first disappointment in his living memory. Which was fast failing, having long past the stage of climbing the stairs on a mission only to forget once he got there why he had gone to the bother in the first place. Senior moments were the rule rather than the exception and he had taken to writing long lists of reminders, only to forget to carry them with him, often returning from an urgent mission to collect vital items from Dingle, empty handed and bewildered. But he knew for certain he had yet to bed Shabin and it bothered him, in fact he had become obsessed and fantasized about how, when and where he would actually achieve his ambition.

'Do you know about horses, John?' Shabin and Dapper were wandering around the horseboxes peering in as the horses were saddled and the jockeys changed into their silks.

'Not a clue, but Tic Tac swears on his mothers life that Cheap Trick is nailed on to make the frame.'

As it happened, Dapper guessed that Tic Tac was an orphan brought up in an institution, knew he was a born liar and every third word would curdle milk in a vicarage.

No social, or sporting event on the peninsula could claim to be worthy of a place on the third page of the local paper without the attendance of the toxic trio and this was a three star show with a grand opportunity to inspect and dissect a larger percentage of peninsula people. Gleefully Morena, Nora and Kitty noticed there was a mighty crowd with many familiar faces plenty of which had a track record of scandal. With so much opportunity to be outraged, the gossips spun and wobbled with self opiniated moral indignation, unsure where the greatest sordid exasperation was to be found.

'LADIES AND GENTLEMEN I'M PLEASED TO ANNOUNCE THAT THE LOGOS BIG BANG STAKES ARE DUE TO START IN TEN MINUTES.' The crackly tannoy announced from the rather tired and forlorn caravan that had been dragged onto the beach by the even more used and abused land rover.

'WILLTHE RUNNERS AND RIDERS MAKE THEIR WAY TO THE PARADE RING.' Which was in fact a rough circle of sand ringed of by many strands of twine knotted together and wrapped around spikes driven into the beach.

The boys studied the race card, printed by the local paper, which was filled with sponsored pages of adverts by local businesses.

TAURUS - Ridden by Ox Heffenhan.
LEO THE LION - Ridden by Isaiah McGuire.
SCORPIO EAGLE - Ridden by Jeremiah Styx.
REVELATION ANGEL - Ridden by Angie 'Aquarius' Farrell.

It was a novelty race with jockeys ages ranging from 16 (Angie) to 66 (Jeremiah) and the horses were in fact donkeys and in aid of the local hospice, but the betting was still fierce with serious money wagered.

'The word is the Eagle will swoop.' Tic Tac stated authoritivly in passing to the bookies.

The others were Sceptical having seen Jeremiah skulking around Dungiggin,scavenging for the newly departed, looking somewhat like a cadaver himself, but on second thoughts decided it would be appropriate given the nominated charity.

'Look it's Faceache O'brien over there with Mary Dwyer.' Kitty watched Faceache like a hawk trying to lip read their conversation. Faceache visited the surgery once a month to collect his prescription for arthritis of the jaw and tended to wear a scarf knotted around his face to ward of the ill wind that did him no good. As the result of Morenas's painstaking research in delving through the surgery patient files, she'd discovered he once had NSU and he on the church committee and to this day unmarried.

' Did you hear anything about herself?' Nora nodded towards Mary.

'Not a thing.'; Morena said and then caught sight of the Scarlet woman striding onto the beach from the gap in the dunes,' Would you look at that, herself in the red petticoat again, the flahoola!'

There was a sharp intake of breath and a certain amount of self righteous indignation and cruel satisfaction at so much potential infamy and shame there, but for the discovery.

The opportunity for enterprise with a good crowd gathered was not lost on a few shrewd local entrepreneurs and a handful of colourful and intriguing banners and flags were snapping in the fierce wind whipping of the Atlantic.

'IF IN DOUBT CALL TOMAS HE HAS ALL THE ANSWERS.' unfortunately Tomas had neglected to specify what he did, or indeed what questions he had the solution to and there were no contact details.

Jermiah Styx's banner proclaimed, ' LET US HANDLE YOUR DECEASED. HOME, OR AWAY DISTANCE NO OBJECT. WE'LL GET THEM TO THE CHURCH ON TIME.'

In the distance a black and white file of nuns, like so many penguins progressed towards the main event led by the redoubtable Sister Aloopecia, her arms folded into voluminous sleeves, accompanied by Father Gorgeous, as the local ladies had dubbed the young handsome priest with a certain reputation. The senior priest Father Cayetano had arrived early, as was his custom to bless the runners and riders,get the inside information and a bet on before the prices shortened and as a special favour he blessed the beer tent in return for the afternoons drinks on the house. Mother superior, being an agricultural class of a country woman, brought up on a farm that had racing in her blood.

She had a small arrangement with the good father to place a wager to boost the contingency fund for the poor and feeble of the parish and knew the likes of a winner when she saw one.It was also rumoured that she was a class act with a billiard cue and had won many a championship, primarily against her arch rivals in London's Tyburn.

Nora had a soft spot for the holy father and when her turn to dress the church flowers arrived, she always wore her best frock and most expensive perfume and put extra effort into the display by the lectern, to which the father himself always commented most particularly.

The was a crackling and a staccato voice rose and fell with much background commentary, from the public address system,' LADIES AN . . . bloody thing I said it was, GENTLEMAN, THE FIRST, there it goes again,' 'you got to hold that button in.' All eyes turned to the lacklustre caravan,' O'HALLORAN IS TODAYS STARTer, blast I've dropped the racecard. . . .' AH THERE IT IS . . . IS THAT WHAT I THINK IT IS ON THE FLOOR? . . . JEEZ IT IS, YOU BROUGHT IT IN ON YOUR SHOE, YOU EEJIT!' Down at the start the donkeys lined up, then Taurus turned and took the Ox off to the tideline despite the desperate urging of rider and O'Halloran who waved a stick, Then Leo the Lion broke rank and took off, the two remaining donkeys followed suit and Taurus bayed mournfully before twisting violently tossing the Ox to the white horses that lapped at the sand.

'Is that a race?' Agatha asked Tic Tac who looked on dismally as Jeremiah trailed in last of the donkeys that had consented to run,' OBJECTION, OBJECTION!' Tic Tac shouted, a cry which was gleefully taken up.

Over the next twenty minutes a carnival of confusion continued, with neither bookie, or punter certain as to the actual nature of the race and no guidance emerged from the caravan where debate and denial reigned.

The next race up was the Spare Rib fillies handicap, which was upon everybody before the previous race was eventually ruled void for betting purposes, although there were eleven runners it was deemed a three horse affair.

BLUE MADONNA ridden by Madge Monahan was a narrow favourite, with BOON'S ROMANCE and CARTLANDS MILL joint second favourites, with local amateur rider Barbara Love on the latter.

The favourite had won over the distance, but Madge had yet to go that far when it counted, having fallen on her only ride in public. But her mum owned and trained BLUE MADONNA, which she usually rode and insisted her daughter get a leg over this time, for what was viewed as an important social outing.

Morena and her coven were venomous by nature, easily taking offence and only ever seeing the negative side of any circumstance, or situation. Satisfaction in any form had eluded them all their life and they were possibly well past their sell by date as far as any salvation was probable. Much like tarantulas, they had ensnared their long suffering husbands in a web of deceit and distrust and as Roman Catholics relied on divorce being abhorrent and forbidden to retain their victims. With no escape Willy, Pat and Keivan had turned to the drink and betting and were often to be seen rollicking around Dingle several sheets to the wind. There were many around who were delighted at the turn of events and the boot was very much on the other foot when Morena, Nora, or Kitty were seen in Supavalue, as tongues would wag and contemptuous stares would follow their progress. But their skins were thick and they were very much in denial, believing the idle rumour was a conspiracy conjured up by thickos that were jealous of their superior standards.

Down at the start a crowd of men had gathered to view the fillies and lasses in their silks, considering themselves good judges of flesh equine and feminine and were glad of the chance to inspect that on offer. The three miscreants had slipped the noose and were as keen as any to peruse the pretties, as these last few years the nearest they got to actual sex was page 3 of the Sun..

But then any beauty that the toxic trio might have enjoyed was very transitory, and their libido was even more fleeting, more an obligatory service required, if rather repulsive to catch a man. Unsurprisingly their were no offspring, which might well have been a blessing for humanity as the perpetuation of such genes would be a disservice to femininity and natural justice.

'I like the look of Lysa Coffen on LOVIN' SPOONFUL,' Willy liked to think he could spot a good thing

127

when he saw it and he quite fancied the horse as well.

'Don't I know the girl, sure she's Jeremiah's niece right enough,' Pat confirmed,' but 9 CC comes late for a strong finish and goes the distance.'

There was a riotous assembly in the bar and Cuddly Bubbly had established herself in a comfortable corner, where a crowd of equally thirsty aficionados gathered to drown their sorrows in convivial company. Agatha was in and out like the sun on a cloudy day, between the booze and the betting with neither satisfying his wild cravings and both rapidly draining his limited resources.

Since the Dungiggin house warming the residents had made many good friends from locals who thought their rock notoriety was a grand craic, rarely tiring of the unorthodox lifestyles and fund of tall tales. They took all with a strong pinch of salt, never quite knowing the gloss and glitter from the genuine, but that was of no matter as a tale told well.

With barely two races run, Cuddly Bubble was already well oiled, having risen early to buck's fizz's and bacon sandwiches in preparation for a day at the races in a style she deemed appropriate.

' Oh yes, I once had a Beatle for breakfast, a Stone for lunch and Who for dinner,' She claimed loudly, 'Oh Seamus do be a darling and see if they've any Champers at the bar.'

All had a plastic beaker with larger, or Guinness and the only alternative was a drop of Paddy Powers. The hamper that Cuddly Bubbly had got T.J. to transport lovingly was now drunk dry as many a mouth can quickly drain a few bottles of champagne in the time it takes to pop the cork.

'EMILY MUFF just won at 11/1,' Agatha dismally announced, although only very few had ventured from the tight circle of hard drinkers to get involved in either the betting, or viewing of the race. The racing was merely an excuse for a days outing from the usual haunts, a chance to see nature in the raw, blow away the cobwebs and get a breadth of fresh air in the lungs.

'LADIES AND GENTS, THE VERY NEXT RACE IS THE EGG AND SPERM RACE, crackle did they hear that, is it working?' the door of the caravan swung open and Ted Maloney peered out at the cone speaker on a long pole.' ONE, TWO, ONE TWO,'crackle, whistling feedback, HELLO AGAIN, SORRY ABOUT THE MISPRINT ON THE RACECARD. CORRECTION THE EGG AND SPOON

128

RACE, that's better, THIS IS A COLTS AND FILLIES MAIDEN HANDICAP OVER A DISTANCE OF FIVE FURLONGS, A THRILLING SPECTACLE I THINK YOU'LL AGREE.'

Feedback and distortion, crackle and earth hum continued throughout.

'Bloody hell it's bleedin' Townsend,' Agatha hurtled out of the tent wind milling an air guitar, singing "My Generation at the top of his lungs, jumped in the air for a scissor kick and crashed into a guy rope.

'Did you ever hear the like?' Nora snorted indignantly.

'Sure the man should see the holy father and confess his blasphemous words, he's an outrage to common decency indeed.' Morena puffed herself up as only a God fearing modest and respectable woman could or indeed would.

'Isn't that the holy father giving that girl a leg over on that 'orse ?' Kitty exclaimed, ' sure and isn't that your fella with him holding the holy father's ale Morena?' Kitty was rightly vexed,' you wouldn't credit it would you? why whatever next, Nuns racing in wimples and habits?'

Nora was disappointed and felt the holy father and the church had let her down, her beacon of good faith and Catholic mentor was interfering with a young floozie in front of the entire congregation and not a trace of shame about him.

Enoch Charon was known locally as the joker, although as one of Jeremiahs employees he exhibited considerable empathy in the undertaking of his somber duty to carry the deceased to their final destination. But once out of his black mourning coat, grey stripped trousers, polished shoes and if the occasion warranted top hat, with drink taken and away from the hearse this acolyte of the angel of death had a wicked sense of humour and an endless river of jokes. He also had an infuriating habit of turning a coin, quite skillfully it had to be said, across the fingers of his hand.

Just in case his services might be urgently required, Jeremiah had parked a hearse complete with empty coffin discreetly behind the sands of time and had Enoch on standby as the grim reaper might swing his scythe without warning and in wanton disregard for the nature of the event.

But Enoch was often on standby and only occasionally required and was only paid 'peace work' as Jeremiah termed it, so the odd guarded warmer from his hip flask, which he carried to revive any relative that was

129

overcome with remorse was always welcome and he passed the time flipping his lucky indian silver dollar, sent over from a cousin over the water in the States.

'What initially walks on four legs, then two and finally three?' Enoch had accosted Mutton who was evading Betty, as she was constantly nagging him about his foolish notion that Tic Tac knew what he was talking about when it came to horses.

Mutton ummed and arghed for a few moments, only half thinking about the answer to the riddle, in truth he wasn't that interested, but having seen Enoch knocking around town was being courteous.

'Don't know!'

' A human being, a baby crawls, becomes upright and if ye live long enough will need a walking shtick,' Enoch cracked up and slapped Mutton on the shoulder,' get it? it's a good un init ?' Then he raised a finger, 'did you hear talk of the man in drink rescued by St Mungo's?'

'Mungo's?' Mutton questioned.

'Sure, the fella was a stranger to the Catholic church these many years and they told him of the miracle of Christ. . . it was the same as St Paul on the road to Damascus.'

'Damascus?' Mutton was baffled.

'True, true enough and yer man went on his way with the light of the Lord in his soul,' Enoch rolled the coin, then he chanced upon a Jew and smote him rightly and The Guardai did see him. . . They were on him and asked why he hit the man. . . because his kind killed Jesus was the reply.' Enoch paused to swig from his flask and passed it to Mutton.

'The guard replied in wonder, but that was 2000 years ago. . . Argh yes say's yer man, but I only just found out about it!' He elbowed Mutton playfully in the ribs.

'Yea great.' Mutton said weakly and then spotted T.J. sitting in a pocket in the dunes obviously rolling a spliff,' nicely, look I've just seen a mate, I'll see you later, good luck.'

Enoch flipped his Indian Dollar,' Before ye go, will it be the chief himself, or his arse end?'

Mutton looked bemused,' erm. . . ' and made great play of tapping his earpiece,' Sorry, it's on the blink again. . . I think I'm getting RTE.' With that he beat a retreat, still tweaking his hearing aid.

DO YOU BELIEVE IN FAIRIES.

'I saw Geal in town man,' T.J. and Agatha had been in town carousing, it was a week since the races and they needed to get out and let off steam, three days away from the cut and thrust of populace and they started to get cabin fever. ' He was coming out of that junk shop with some bit of a poster in his hand. . . Dunno what he see's in that old place, all that dead peoples gear gives me the creeps.'
'Unless you can drink it, screw it, or smoke it, nothing makes sense to you.' Mutton said dismissively.
'I'll tell you what don't make sense to me and it gives me the spooks,' Agatha retorted,' dem lights I keep seeing some nights down by the stream.'
'Yea Lucy keeps on about them, she won't go down there after dark,' Mutton added,' but she tells Betty there's quare folk down there in the daytime, she's seen them and talked to them.'
'That's about right, she's been away with the fairies all her life.' Agatha smirked, ' but dem woods still give me the heebie -jeebies.'
'You give me the willies,' T.J. poked Agatha in the ribs,' specially when you drive pissed outa yer skull.'
'Yea, what about you nearly killing that old biddy on the way into town and you hadn't a drink taken.'
Agatha and T.J. bickered like an old married couple from dawn to dusk.
'Yea well, if she will wander around in the road with that donkey like there's no tomorrow.'
' She'd be all her yesterdays if there wasn't a few feet in it between the car and herself.' Agatha snorted,spluttered and spat out a glob of phlegm which engulfed an astonished ant.

'Do ya remember Geordie Joe?' Mutton was away in yesterdays memories.'
'Yea now that you mention it, he's brown bread, died of a heart attack on a plane in the States didn't he?' T.J. interrupted,' weren't you his axe man?'
'If you could call it that. . . real sad, he was brilliant, but got totally strung out on uppers and downers.' Mutton's eyes glazed,'I was real close to Jo, you know? . . . When he got into rock'n'roll he was only sixteen. . . a real athlete. . . totally clean. No drink, no drugs.He could have made it in sport if rock'n'roll hadn't enraptured him.'
'I was good at hurling when I was a kid back in Cork.' Agatha pipped up, but as ever nobody listened, why would they?'
'I put it down to Terry Balls, that flash bastard from that Croydon band, ' Sharp Eye'.He was like a chemist,

131

had so many pills on him he rattled like maracas when he walked. He turned Jo onto them, he was a soft lad easily led, came from some little country village. Couldn't handle the bright lights,big city no street savvy.'

Mutton nonchalantly scratched his arse,' The last tour in the States was terrible. . . most times if he played at all it was all over the place. I had to turn the standby switch off and when he sussed that I'd nip around the back and pull the speaker leads out. . . poor bastard knew, but was so fucked up he couldn't do anything about it. . . I reckon it was a broken heart that really killed him.'

'I'm amazed that more of us didn't die. . .mind you once you got past the 27 club you'd have a good chance.'

T.J. said in one of his more rational moments,' Hendrix, Brian Jones, Jim Morrison.'

' Thirty two's a bad age for drummers, Bonham and Moonie!' Mutton chimed in.

'Nice one, I needed to know that. . . I'm a drummer!' T.J. protested.

'Yea, but you're well past 32!'

'Oh yea, I forgot.' T.J. said with relief.

'Stupid eejit,' Agatha shouted and got elbowed in the ribs for the effort.

'Remember that song they did with us in the barn,' Mutton said toT.J. ,' what did they call it? . . . Alchemists? . . .Geal said he got the idea from some old book he bought.'

'There was a funeral over at the church, they all got into Dick Mac's for a drink before heading out to the wake.' Agatha piped up cheerfully,' That Styx fella was doing it, gave me a wink and said he'd be out to see us soon enough.'

'He gets over here a mite too much for my liking, he's always offering Betty special deals, he reckons he's the local agent for stair lifts, wheelchairs, Zimmer frames and the like. . . .Gets 'em cheap from China.' Mutton muttered.

'If I never see him again it'll be too soon!' T.J. exclaimed.

'and if you kicked the bucket and he buried your body, you still wouldn't see him,' Agatha fathomed, ' cos you'd be dead . . . Lord have mercy on us.'

'More like the devil gleefully rubbing his hands as he claimed his own.' Mutton added in half jest. ' Shhh. . . if you're quiet you can almost hear him'' Hello T.J. we've been waiting for you'' and then you'd get a warm reception and meet a good few old mates.'

Betty and Molly were into the daily bake, the washing up was towering and the banter and coffee flowed liberally, now times this was seventh heaven, all those teenage kicks, twenties raving and thirties good times were just too tiring to contemplate. Getting stoned, laid in the fast lane and hanging out with the big boys of rock was full on and required imagination, dedication and stamina and wasn't for starry eyed kids. But that was then and this was now and a warm kitchen with the welcoming aroma of fresh baked banana bread and coffee was infinitely more comforting and desirable than that of spent spunk ,sweaty bodies, dope and stale booze.

It seemed the same was true for many of the other residents, as the kitchen was a Mecca for the thirsty and hungry and those that just fancied a gossip in the warmth of the Aga, and Betty was often hard put to cope with the demands on her baking.

'So how often do you see these lights then?' Titbits had been listening to Lucy babbling on about the lights and the little people in her woodland glade for months with some disbelief, as she inhabited a world that was much more hands on, sensual, laid back to service the lads or down on her knees to please and tease.

'Maybe once a month I can see lights down there from my window, but in the daytime when I'm down there I feel all tingly and weird, as if I'm being watched,' Lucy shuddered at the memory,' I've seen funny things as well, shadows and shapes.'

'You got it right there!' Molly chimed in sarcastically, ' I used to see them myself after too much gin or a good smoke. . . now everything looks a bit fuzzy and funny.'

'How do you mean?' Titbits asked.

'The weird and fuzzy bit.' Molly sneered winking at Betty.

'Are you having a go at me again?' Lucy was a little precious and easily hurt, but Mother Shipton, who Lucy now visited on a weekly basis had advised her to be more assertive.

'Why do you hate me, what did I ever do to you?' Lucy said tearfully, her eyes visibly reddining.

'Hey ladies leave it out . . .' Betty had always been a bit of an earth mother and the years had mellowed her ever more, ' we don't need this, any of us. Isn't life tough enough,? . . . we should support each other. . . . Not bicker like old wrinklies.'

Betty went to Shabins weekly yoga class and although she'd only been going for a month was already feeling

133

the benefit. Her rheumatics had eased and she was coming to terms with the anxieties that had increasingly dogged her days and nagged at her in the nights.

'You could both handle a bit of anger management and I think you should sign up to the yoga class I go to.' She appealed to both of them,' what d'ya say girls?'

Lucy had never carried much attitude, being very much the opposite and playing the hard bitch didn't come easily to her.where as Molly had always had an edge to her, which had hardened over the years in the harsh world of bad breaks and tough luck. She had also increasingly felt that her future had little worthwhile to offer as her body aged and the aches and pains of her daily routine became more of a burden. When she was with Betty she laughed off her bladder problems, but having to wear what amounted to a nappy on a daily basis was not just inconvenient, but embarrassing, even if it was only herself that knew it. She found herself sniffing the air around her in case the smell of stale pee was noticeable and had developed nappy rash. Like Cuddly Bubbly she'd taken to buying cheap cologne in industrial quantities, just in case someone had caught a whiff of wee.

Titbits problems were more challenging and still a secret which she struggled to come to terms with, she'd dealt with the initial feeling of denial, was part way through private anger and the sense that she was victimized and abandoned by God, although she'd never believed in him until she needed someone to blame. Why her?

Was she really so bad?

Had she really sinned more than anybody else she knew?

She had started quietly slipping into town, going to the church, even praying that the doctors had made some mistake and she didn't actually have what they said she did. After all, according to the internet her symptom were common enough and covered a wide number of other, less serious illness's and diseases.

Doctors are only human and can make mistakes.

Can't they?

As she listened to the battling babes and mother earth she wanted to scream at them and shout how stupid they were, but feared she would let her cat out of the bag and in no time everybody would know and start to avoid

134

her.

Maybe even try and kick her out of Dungiggin, which offered her some degree of companionship, even if nobody else knew her isolation and despair. Here she could still pretend to be the old Titbits with the touch of theatrical magic in dress and attitude which seemed to work like a magnet to attract the men, even if she could never follow through on the promise she seemed to proffer.

'TITBITS!'

Cuddly Bubbly swayed out of Dick Mac's and was crossing the road to Holy Mary's grotto when she caught sight of Titbits sitting on the bench next to it contemplating, or perhaps praying. 'What are you doing here?' 'Oh er. . .' Titbits was startled and obviously embarrassed,' . . . I was just passing and my legs started to hurt. . it's the hill, so I was just resting on the bench for a bit. . . and if you twist around a bit you get a good view of Dick Macs and can see who's got in for a bevy.''

Despite drink being taken even Cuddly knew hogwash when she heard, 'Oh yea. . . and I suppose you saw the tears dropping from the virgins eyes as well!'

'What are you saying?' Titbits replied defensively.

Cuddly seated herself on the bench and studied the Holy Mary,' I didn't know you believed in all this stuff. .you always said all this was mumbo jumbo and only those who were stupid would fall for it.'

'I told you, I was resting.' With that Titbits was on her feet and striding away down Green Street.

'Was it something I said?' Cuddly called after her as she watched Titbits disappear into the distance.

Once safely out of sight Cuddly closed her eyes and began to silently pray, she was only too aware that eventually lifestyle would track you down and demand retribution, however embarrassing and excruciating.

THE GLADE.

'Bacon, Francis?' Betty said with a huge grin on her face and a pan of sizzling rashers in her hand.

Bodger was back in Dungiigin for a few days and Betty and Molly had discovered his actual name after years of only knowing him by his nickname and were determined to wind him up in the extreme.

Betty and Molly were making breakfast butties and Bodger was one of the few to make it down to the kitchen before ten.

'No, cheers. . . Hey you called me Francis!,' Bodger answered with a start,' How d'ya know that? . . .Nobody knew that!'

Molly laughed wickedly,' Your dirty little secret's out, we know the truth.'

'How? . . . Who told you?' Bodger was genuinely upset, in many ways he hid behind his nickname, as to be known by his real name was too close to what he was trying to blot out from his life.

Betty was more forthcoming,' Orenda called from A.L.W.L. she's trying to sort out your visa for the trip to China.'

'China indeed, hark at you!. . . Molly sneered ,' talk about the jet set . . . If you're not over on Geals island, you're half way around the fucking world.' She was totally miffed and jealous, ' it's alright for some, bet you don't know you've been born.'

To the casual bystander, Bodger was a gentle soul, most often lost in his intellectual puzzles and pursuits, but he was no robotic character devoid of feeling and Betty's barbed comment was not unnoticed. 'I am fully aware that I have incarnated and at this moment am being tormentented by a wizened old witch with precious little wherewithal remaining from a dissipated and wrecked life.'

'Oooh.'Betty uttered and gave Molly and old fashioned look,' so the cat does have claws.'

Molly felt shattered, recognizing the truth of his words, but more over it had more impact coming from such an unexpected source as she had always thought of Bodger as a pushover and burst out crying.

Betty was unsure, Molly was her best friend, but she was only too aware of her bitchy nature and knew it all too often put peoples backs up. Betty had also been instrumental in the initial wind up, although she had no evil intent and only meant to be playful and felt remorseful,' I'm sorry Bodger. . . I was out of order.'

136

Bodger stood feet firmly aside fixing both women with a firm stare,' look at you both, two thirds of a scene from the play that cannot be mentioned and neither with the talent to carry it off, just washed up witches!' with that he turned on his heel and strode purposefully out.

Lucy was tending the seven rose bushes she had planted in her fayrie hollow and marveling at the shaft of sun that had broken through the canopy of trees and cast a rosy cross of light on the ground. This was indeed her enchanted haven, to which she escaped the often unpleasant mischief that could too easily manifest among the ever monkey minded masquerading as mature men and the one, or two wichitty women. T.J. and Agatha in particular were Dungiggin's Tweedledee and Tweedledum, they often finished each others sentences, conceived capricious capers and were always in pursuit of precarious pleasure with little, if any fore thought for the humiliation and pain that others might suffer. Lucy was an obvious target as her fragile and fey nature were always a temptation to take things too far.

Lucy was convinced that the birdsong was sweeter and more intense in the glade and that gentle creatures gathered in grace and gratitude to gambol in secure warmth under the protection of Pan. Pan had horns, the legs and hindquarters of a goat and was no stranger to the delights of sex and was suitably well endowed; not for nothing were goats reputed to be horny.
Sometimes as Lucy dozed and daydreamed through lazy afternoons on the soft turf with the aroma of herbs wafting in the breeze, she drifted into an erotic ecstasy, often waking to find herself embarrassingly damp and soiled with her clothing in disarray. Oft times, the sex in the head was above and beyond the sex in the flesh that she had experienced all her life, which in many ways was just casual carnal violation of her body for the transitory gratification of jaded hedonists, who often couldn't remember her name.

She often wondered what the trees in the woods had witnessed, some of which were hundreds of years old and had lived through the turbulent times of outrage and unrest that too often were the zeitgeist of Irish history.
With half closed eyes and the ability to see beyond the obvious, the trunks and branches appeared to have an imprinted visual record of face. Here perhaps was a lovers tryst, a deadly ambush, political and emotional intrigue, or maybe just saints, or scholars pausing to mediate and contemplate the simple beauty of nature before

continuing their path to enlightenment.

Since our early ancestors first walked this earth in fear and wonderment certain places have felt sacred, making the hairs on the nape of the neck rise and creating feelings of both anxiety and enchantment. Often these became sacred sites surrounded by strange and seemingly ethereal apparitions and manifestations and were marked out in wood and stone as places to worship uncertain powers that had a strength and wisdom beyond mere human understanding.

As tribes and civilizations rose and fell and the control of areas and dominance of gods and reverence to them ebbed and flowed, so sites once sacred to yesterdays religion were replaced and rebuilt to enshrine the newdays deity.

This emphasized that the new God was that bit more powerful than the predecessor and was a powerful tool to conquer and dominate the vanquished and subdue revolt.

Here abouts the ancient tribe of Fir Bolg ruled, to be defeated by the superior skilled Tuatha De Danann, only to be replaced by the Milesians, each left traces on earth and in spirit. The Tuatha De Danann moving underground to become the magic fairies known as Aes Sidhe, their presence seen only on the surface in the fairies mounds. Some might also know them as leprechauns, the little people, or if less bewitched, de little devils, but few would have the temerity to dismiss their existence out of hand for fear of the wrath of retribution.

Popular folklore had them chiefly engaged as cobblers, as for who this mighty industry of shoes was for is unclear, but all the gold coins earned were stored in crocks at the end of a rainbow. The like of which was much sought after by children and drunks who had unfettered rashness and enjoyed the protection of the lord. Solitary small bodies, or half brogues, the literal translation of leprechaun might be seen wearing red jackets and breeches buckled at the knee with grey or black stockings and always seven buttons to the coat. Although it would seem that the style of dress was regional, as could the local name for this fella . In Kerry he'd be known as The Luricawne a pursy little fella with a jolly round and red face.

Lucy lived in hope of meeting such a magnificent little creature but only in daylight and never ventured to the glade after dusk for fear she'd be enticed away into the underground kingdom never to return to the surface.

But from the window of her room she could just see the tree line and very often the dancing lights which betrayed the presence of something, or someone the like of which she couldn't be sure of and was feared to discover. Lucy had moved on as far as her quest to realize enlightenment was concerned, or at least her light fantastic trip through the inscrutable fakeers and incredible fakers that populated and in many cases polluted the true path of the seeker.

She was now regularly in touch with Professor Marduk, who lived high in the clouded Atlas mountains and claimed to have insight into the Akashic records and knew all that had been and all that would be. She would now only ate a strictly vegan diet, much preferring the exotic flavours of the east and frequented an obscure little restaurant called Pansophy, which had a plaque over the entrance saying Deo Volent'. It was just out of town run by two very friendly and polite fellows called Sammy Khya and Mahab Huta whose every delectable dish was liberaly spiced with a generous sprinkling of Eastern wisdom.

Betty and Molly who were less airy-fairy easily, dismissed the lunatic ravings of Lucy, as did most of the others, although Agatha, as a sound Irishman wasn't about to shrug off their existence in private, but his public stance was that of a skeptic, in name only as he hadn't a clue what it actualy meant. However both Betty and molly were desperately in need of a little magic in their lives, the seemingly arbitrary and cruel injustices of advancing age and infirmity were catching up with them and they were becoming increasingly crotchety. Their world had been lived fast and loose and had been great fun, if one didn't stop raving long enough to actually think how wild and pointless it really was and that it was merely a feckless adventure of youth and unfettered energy.

139

DOWN THE DOCS.

'How d'ya get on, Betty was sitting patiently in Dr Shabin's waiting room, very aware of Morena's piercing stares and probing mind, every now and again she'd look up from the much thumbed copy of Take A Break magazine and give Morena a theatrical wink. For one who's stock in trade was scandal and slander, Morena was easily affronted and considered Betty and her sort to be so much low life and beyond the pale.

'Yea, alright I suppose,' Molly sounded downbeat,' same old, same old.'

Betty nodded towards Morena, who was in very serious danger of disjointing herself, or toppling from her perch as she leaned forward straining to overhear every word. ' Was that your husband I saw falling out of Joyce's bar again yesterday lunchtime Morena . . . He's a terrible habit on him, wouldn't you say?'

Morena snorted and very pointedly buried her beak in the register mumbling under her breath.

They left giggling at Morena's obvious discomfort.

'So come on spill the beans, what did she say?' Betty hooked Molly's arm as they walked towards Supavalue, stopping briefly to window shop a craft shop,' well?'

'Nothing new, they haven't discovered a magic potion,' Molly sighed,' keep doing the pelvic exercises, ease off caffeine. fizzy drinks and alcohol,' she had a tear or two in her eye,' lose weight, don't smoke . . .get my eyes tested. . . and stop breathing.' she added as a bitter afterthought. 'Still I did get some mother's little helpers to go with the pep talk.'

Betty put a comforting arm around her friend,' So it went well then?' she quipped. hoping to cheer Molly up.

'You cow,' she laughed,' and yourself?'

'Stiff as Rock's cock in a brothel and spreading,' Betty put a brave, if slightly painful face on it,' Shabin said that the West Coast of Eire wasn't the best place to live with rheumatism, as if I didn't know.'

'So where is?' Molly spotted a cute artsy fartsy bit of frippery, 'look Betty, I like that.' She pointed.

Betty peered at it blinked and looked closer,' what is it meant to be then?'

Molly looked again then shrugged her shoulders,' how should I know, but it's sweet isn't it?' She giggled,' so go on, did she give you anything?'

'Just the usual repeat prescription for embrocation and painkillers and told me to get Mutton to give me an aggresive rub down with the exchange and mart.' Betty was at the age when every new ache and pain gave her

140

acute cause for concern, with so many friends and others of her generation falling likeTommies on the Somme her anxieties and imagination were hideously heightened and cancer was a constant concern.

'Betty, did you notice Shabin had an engagement ring on?' Molly was all conspiratorial,' you don't think that . . . you know.'

'You don't mean . . .' Betty put her hand in front of her open mouth in mock shock, 'They couldn't. . .she shouldn't. . . he wouldn't. . . isn't he still married?'

'To half the women in the world, as far as I know and if my memory wasn't so bad I'd swear he'd proposed to me sometime in the seventies.' Molly was in her element exploring and examining somebody else's life.

'D'ya think we'll get an invite to the wedding?' Betty thought for a moment, ' make a change from funerals. Although the foods always pretty much the same, as are the speeches. . . Come to think of it. . . marriage and death aren't that much different. . . a beginning on one level and the end of another.'

No matter how difficult life can be, it is a grand diversion to trawl through the possible indiscretions and scandals of other people and goes a long way to raising self esteem and confirming one's own righteous indignation.

Coming up to the rear entrance to Supavalue Betty almost fell over a bag of groceries and a sack of tatties leaning against the low wall by the Tralee bus stop,' Shit I think I've pulled something !'

'Mutton. . . you soft cow and a good few years back at that.'

'You alright?' Molly kicked out at the spuds,' Bloody stupid place to leave the groceries.'

At that moment an old stray spaniel bounded up, sniffed the bags, peed on them and lopped off, tongue hanging out of the side of its mouth and grinning broadly.

They looked on incredulously and turned to watch the hound sniff and occasionally pee its way up towards town, stopping now and again to meet and greet somebody in passing.

'It's got a lot of attitude hasn't it?' Molly said with a degree of admiration.

'Reminds me of Agatha with a wrap of coke out for the night on the piss.'

They both giggled hysterically, like silly empty headed schoolgirls.

'Ooops I've wet em!'

FULL CIRCLE.

Skeeter had noticed the influx of 'weirdies', as many in town had affectionately named the crowd from Dungiggin ,who had most definitely enlivened the environs and excited the jaded passions and pleasures of many people. She had gotten use to being the scarlet women, a source of scandal and supposition, but nowadays she was secondhand news and of little interest, as there had never been substance to the smears. Skeeter was on nodding terms with them and had passed the time of day with Betty and Molly in the queues at Supavalue, but talked of nothing of consequence beyond weather and why.

Walking the dogs on Inch strand, she'd seen Dapper and Shabin walking hand in hand, but they were engrossed in each other and unaware that they shared the same world, let alone the sand with anybody else.

Skeeter had felt pangs of jealousy, even though she knew neither of the lovers, in many ways she longed for the close intimacy that radiated from their raptures. Over the past few months, she had developed a talent for painting, finding the muse a great escape from the ghosts that often haunted her.

It was all too easy to see herself as a victim, born under a bad sign, or simply just another beautiful loser struggling to come to terms with the fickle finger of a cruel karma, punished for the misdemeanors of some long forgotten past life. But applying paint to canvas was all absorbing and the world quickly shrunk to the size of her canvas and her problems diminished in proportion, as the scale of nature dwarfed the frail human condition.

The fall of light on land and sea was inspiring and she would often set her easel by the harbour, cliff edge or strand and attempt to capture the shifting shafts of sunlight as they briefly escaped cloud cover.

The leaden grey skies were a perfect backdrop for whitewashed cottages, relections in rain soaked roadways and rocky mountains ways and for Skeeter, a bumbling amateur, the little feat was to capture the elusive impressions on canvas, before rain returned.

'Alright there Geal sir, what time will ye be wanting to get back? Sheehan was mooring his boat as Geal strolled along the pier, when he noticed Skeeter, 'Mind out there sir!'

He turned back to face Sheehan and crashed into Skeeters easel, reached out to steady himself, knocking her masterpiece onto the ground,' WHAT THE. . . !'

'Watch out !' Skeeter slipped off her stool and sprawled next to her easel and best effort to date, she was sure she was painting her masterpiece, the painful and punishing culmination of all that had gone before and now painting and artist were as one. An ad hoc catastrophe of untamed beauty and colour spontaneously created in the gutter amid the cast offs, dog ends and loose litter of life, evolving organically into a work in progress. 'Argh too late'. Sheehan shrugged and poked his cap back with the tip of a finger, 'sure t'is a fine how do altogether.' He climbed the metal runged ladder from boat to pier, trying hard to hide his humour.

'Now look what you've done!' Skeeter crawled to her damaged canvas and stared at in tearfull disbelief,' I've spent a month , a whole month. . . it was my best yet. . . .the sea, the light on the boats,' she sobbed, ' even the seal by the crabber.' She looked accusingly at Geal,' Now look at it!'
Geal reached his arm out to help her up,' here let me. . . '
Skeeter angrily pushed his arm away,' you've done enough damage already, leave me alone,' she looked back in disbelief at her painstakingly painted landscape, now sadly more symbolic of the destruction in art symposium than the school of Constable or Turner.
'I'm sorry, what can I say, it was an accident,' Geal didn't know what to do for best and glanced at the painting,' You're right, you did a grand picture and I screwed it up. . .'
"Oh God men!' Skeeter stamped her foot angrily on the ground,' now you're patronizing me. I'm not some pathetic little woman you know,' Her eyes blazed with fury,' if you had an ounce of artistic feeling in you, it's just possible you might understand. .. . you. . . you lummox you!' She burst into a tearful rage and then thumped a fist on his chest in frustration.
"Whoa steady on there you'll break my heart !'Geal laughed and then glimpsed a hint of something, a distant memory he couldn't quite place,' have I met you before? . . . you know you're very pretty when you're angry.'
'You bastard, you complete bastard,.' Skeeter glared at Geal,' Who do you think you are, you pompous
. . . you pompous. . You're all the same. . . bloody men!.' She was all but speechless and utterly exasperation..
'Geal, pleased to meet you and you are?'
Skeeter spluttered,' I know you. . .I've seen you somewhere before haven't I?'
'And I know you,' he winked,' You're the scarlet woman aren't you?'
Sheehan watched in amused amazement, he knew both, enjoyed their company and was intrigued by

143

confrontation.

'How dare you!' She was incensed, almost incandescent with indignation.

Geal couldn't help but laugh, here was the scarlet women lighting up like a bulb in the red light district.

Skeeter was fit to burst, lost for words, knowing not what to do, fight or run. Then she exploded into uncontrollable laughter, tears cascading from her eyes, trembling with raw emotion.

'Hey steady on girl.' Geal was quite concerned and seriously considered slapping her face and turned to see Sheehan grinning like a Chesire cat.

Sheehan raised is arms as if to say how should I know what to do.

Geal noticed that the scene wasn't un noticed and feared the onlookers were thinking he'd assaulted her and the guardai would turn up. Briefly he imagined the ballyhoo and lurid headlines that the idle speculators might conjure up, but quickly dismissed the thought.

"Hey look, maybe I could buy the painting, I kinda like it, He glanced at it again, half finished, smudged, ripped with a footprint on it and all but regretted his offer, 'maybe I could buy lunch and we could talk about it, what d'ya say. He put one hand in the air, palm outstretched in a peace gesture, 'Pax veinieit? . . . come on,I'll buy you something a bit special for lunch at Ashes.'

TO BOLDLY GO.

Agatha had taken drink, in fact he'd had a skinful and it was just short of a full blown miracle that he'd made it back from Dick Mac's without incident in T.J's much abused vehicle, all be it in second gear. It was a fact that Agatha was still struggling to master the finer points of knife and fork, let alone the fundamental requirements of the internal combustion engine and the basics of maneuvering along the highways and byways. He'd slyly liberated it for the people, him in particular in this instance and very much an anarchist statement of freedom and a rejection of societies imposition of limitations on personal equalities, as he'd lost his provisional driving licence for the third time a good few years ago.

He'd actually pranged it just short of the house into a ditch and sat dazed and confused wondering how best to tell T.J. that his pride and joy lay side on, like some upturned and helpless beatle.

Then out of the corner of his eye he saw the dancing lights in the glade, blinked and blinked again, they were still there, ' Jaysus, it's the little people!' he mumbled to himself and made the sign of the holy cross, even though he wasn't a practicing Catholic, in fact he wasn't practicing anything in a religious sense. But right now he was seriously considering there indeed might be a God and it might just be a wise move to start praying, he made the sign of the cross again and tried to remember the Lords Prayer. Curiosity is a dangerous beast, it killed the cat and all but made Alice lose command of good English and sight of her feet and Agatha's life thus far had very much been curious and even curiouser. It has been said that the days one has been most inquisitive are probably the best days of a life ,they certainly had been for Agatha, although they had mostly been the days when he found himself up crap creek without a boat to float.

Spurred on by Dutch courage, an inquisitive, perhaps nosey disposition and more than a degree of plain stupidity Agatha stumbled out of the car into the night and onwards to enlightenment,or perhaps oblivion. He slumped down behind a fallen tree, threw up and had second thoughts, but then saw an intriguing sight, two circles of people in loose flowing white robes danced in the candle lit grove. The inner circle were men spinning in one direction, the outer ,women going in the opposite direction and then as a group they collapsed to the ground all jabbering away in strange languages from what he could hear,but then he was tipsy. Watching intently he became increasingly drowsy and slipped into the warmth of sleep and cosy world of dream and the morphing of here and there. Perhaps he woke, maybe he didn't what ever, he was in an erotic wonderland,

145

wherever he looked naked couples were frolicking and fornicating in any and every combination and fashion. Now Agatha had been around sin a good few times as is the case in rock'n'roll, sure the name itself is an old blues men's expression for casual and wild sex, but this was way beyond anything he'd come across on the road. So many people having it away willy nilly in the darkened woods lit only by flickering candles which cast sinister shadows among the shrubbery.

Agatha woke the following morning in the woods with a powerful headache, dew soaked clothing and a brand new sense of wonder.

He was full of it, telling everybody and anybody the whys and wherefores of the phenomenon and vision, but he was obviously hung-over and T.J.s bent metal gave little validity to Agatha's wild ravings and his track record of all things incredible and unreliable were not in his favour.

Only Lucy accepted his story, but then she would, wouldn't she? But she wouldn't go down to the woods this day, or any day soon for fear of strange interferences both material and spiritual.

She whipped out her tarot cards, crystals, consulted all the astrological internet sites, double checked everything and anything with Sidarthur, who offered 'enlightenment is cosmic and has little regard how it is obtained.' and added, ' A deeper and more profound understanding, subscribe to our premium gold service on special offer for the next twelve hours at 50% discount.'

Mutton and T.J. were down that way the next day with Rory, who borrowed a tractor to tow the car out of the ditch and all three ventured down to the glade to have a poke around and see what fetched up.

'What d'ya reckon then?' Mutton had noticed a few drops of wax on the ground and the vegetation had certainly been flattened in many places.

'I'd say they were fierce heavy little people, but awful tidy after themselves.' Rory was prodding a stick under shrubs to lift them a bit for closer inspection.

'Just because the grass is flattened a bit it doesn't mean there were people here, you know what Agathas like, he's forever seeing demons and ghosts, mostly when he's blitzed.' T.J.'s mind was mainly on his car and how the damage,' could easily have been deer, or foxes.'

'With candles?' Mutton was rolling the wax between his fingers and sniffing it, akin to Sherlock Holmes on the case.

'That doesn't mean a thing,' T.J. said dismissively,' Lucy is always down here and I bet she brings candles down here and incense as well I wouldn't wonder.'

'Well I don't know, there's more than a few have seen lights and people do say there are some mighty strange things happening over this way.' Rory smiled,' you wouldn't catch me here too late into the night.' He added mysteriously,' there's been talk over the years about this place, not just since you lot moved in. You know of course what happened to the people that lived here before you.'

'No what?' Mutton was all ears, or at least he turned his hearing aid up a touch.

'Sure, do you really want to know?' Rory was enjoying the craic,' I'm not so sure I would if I didn't already know and was living here.'

'What are you saying?' T.J. was getting interested and increasingly uncertain about the glade, he shivered,' it's getting a bit cold here.'

'There was a yank looking at this place before your man came ferreting about, he was all for it until . . .'Rory was gathering pace with his tale and enjoying the telling of it. ' Then it happened and he was away like a scalded Kilkenny cat.'

'What happened?' Mutton fought feedback and intermittent volume to hear what was said.

'There's no way of knowing, he left that fast, but it must have been mighty ferocious to spook him like that, they say he wasn't the same man entirely.' Rory grinned,' If it hadn't been for your man, there's little hope this place would have sold in many a month of blue moons.' He sat on a fallen tree trunk and rolled a fag,' it's a tribute to O'Malley that he sold this place at all. But then the man is a born dealer, isn't it himself that has the place you got your vehicle?'

' . . . And a right pile of shit that is,' lamented T,J.

' My very point, the man could sell garlic to vampires in broad daylight and then off load a bag of silver crosses.' Mutton was befuddled and not thinking in tune with the times,' So hang on, do you think it's vampires?' Rory exploded into laughter and slapped his palm on his thigh,' Did you never hear tell of black pudding?' 'Betty puts that in my breakfast sometimes, she says it's good for me.' Mutton was concerned.

' Argh sure that it is.' Rory looked direct at Mutton,' During the famine they'd nick into the cows neck on a Sunday and drink the blood for nourishment. They say the Kerry cow still knows a Sunday and won't settle near a man on the Sabbath to this day.'

'Lucy's been looking a bit peaky of late, I thought it was just cos she's a vegetarian.' T.J. pitched in.

'Argh right enough again,' Rory was entertained,' she might be a vegetarian, but your vampire is all blood and guts, don't ye see?'

'Have you had vampires here for long?'

'Now a man wouldn't know that for sure, but the man Styx is doing right enough out of it all over the county.' Rory tapped the side of his nose and gave a knowing wink.

'He's always around here asking how we're feeling,' Mutton shuddered,' gives me the creeps.'

'They say he's measured half the people in the county, so he doesn't get caught short if there's a fever and keeps it all in a black book.'

'About these vampires,' Mutton continued,' does anybody know who they are?'

'There's this floozie that gets in O'Flahertys, she's a powerful set of teeth on her altogether.' Rory said straight faced.

'And?' T.J. was hooked.

'Now that I think about it, I've never seen her in daylight,' Rory fingered the crucifix necklace,' I'd say this is what's saved me so far.'

'Yea, I've come across a few chicks like that on the road myself,' T.J. cast his mind back,' there was this one in L.A. we called her the black widow sucked guys in and spat out the empty husks, no bread, no head, brain dead.'

'That crowd you were with got around a bit didn't ye?' Rory never tired of hearing their rock'n'roll stories, the furthest he'd been was on holiday to Spain twice and Dublin a dozen more times.

'That we did, but a lot of it was truck, airport, gig, hotel and white line fever,' T.J. said ruefully,

'If I got five nights sleep in a week it was luxury and the drugs were a necessity, not that I'm saying their wasn't enjoyment in them.'

'And the women?' Rory asked enthusiastically.

'Ah. . .the women.' T.J. was thoughtful, ' The women . . .best a man could have , God did I love the women. . . mind you a lot of them were old dogs, as good as harlots or jail bait, but then . . .' he trailed off.

'The others. . . what of the others?' Rory was a dog with a bone, loathe to bury it until he'd had the marrow out of it.

'Now you're talking turkey, some were like celestial virgins. . . well never virgins, but celestial none the

148

Less . . . I met a few who were so brainy and beautiful that I never could understand why they'd hang around with the likes of us. But then that sort like a bit of rough and tumble.' He scratched his head,' Nick once said he thought they felt guilty for coming from privileged backgrounds. You know private education, nannies and the pony club sort of thing, but then what do I know! Their sort of people are stuck up hooray Henries without street credibility. I suppose some of the chicks eventually got to see them for the brainless prats they really were and wanted to hang out with common people who knew where it was at.'

'Maybe they just liked a good fuck!' Mutton added wistfully, having not had so much as a feel of tit for over nine months as Betty had not just gone off the boil, but well and truly frozen over.

"That's the way off it, screw 'em while you can and run for it before they start getting broody and wanting to have your children. My grandad once told me if ye keep a jar and put a punt, sure he was an old timer, in it for every time you get your leg over with yer wife until your forty and take one out thereafter for every time you get a lay there'd always be the good few coins in the jar to fall back on.'

Rory smiled,' sure t'is an awful eejit that gets married, with so many fish in the sea. They don't mature well, get bloated and the scales fall off.'

Mutton and T.J. nodded in agreement, although there had been times in both their lives when they felt that regular sex without all the hassle of chasing tail was no bad thing. T.J.

'One time I was with a band that supported Rob Throb's Mob. . . the birds really got off on him, he was a pretty boy. . . never of the front covers of the girlie pop magazines.' T.J. reflected.' We gave their crew and the bouncers a hand. . . we lined up between the birds and the band, but they just charged straight over us pissing their knickers as they went. . . talk about golden rain, I was soaked.

Mind you a good few didn't have their knickers on in the first place, they'd already thrown them at the stage. . . glorious sight for sore eyes . . . they stung for days afterwards. . . all that salt you know.'

Rory looked up at the darkening sky and then around the woodland seeing shadows and reflections jumping from tree to shrub and then the glint of the gentle rolling water in the stream. 'I'd say it'll rain, or get dark before morning, likely enough both.'

'Is that a fact?' T.J. grinned and he then peered around and although skeptical felt menaced by a strange Atmosphere. ' Guess you're right enough, time to be getting back, don't you think?'

'Yea, Betty will have the kettle on,'

'Good enough, that'll do nicely and then I'd better get the old tractor back to Donnely before he notices it's gone.'

Rory winked.

HEARTS AND MINDS.

Dapper had been in love before, pretty much every day with any fetching face in passing, the sway of hips, glimpse of cleavage, or shapely body, in fact anything that set his heart and imagination racing. But this was strangely different, he thought about Shabin all the time, her almond eyes, her svelte body and the gentle, almost ethereal way she glided through life. Perhaps it because he hadn't bedded her, after months of courtship passionate kissing was the limit of their physical intimacy and somehow this new experience had him in its grip and moreover he had grown to enjoy it. Sex was all in the head anyway, the actual mechanics were pretty much the same, it was the imagination and emotion that charged the encounter and in most cases it was domination, submission, power and raw animal lust. Now it was still in the mind, but his vision had soared to new heights and with each passing day it reached further into some sublime ecstasy always promising more. He hoped and guessed she was a virgin and believed he was the first to romance her and it gave him deep happiness and a strange satisfaction. He couldn't for the life of him ever remember encountering a virgin, untarnished by another, completely pure and unsullied by the vulgar and wanton cravings of a predatory male. Once or twice he'd wondered if, apart from the saviors mother, any virgin had ever been born on this planet and then he remembered Miss Whitehouse, his prim and proper teacher.

Dapper was elevated from the mundane, the usual drudge of life and the living of it weren't noticed, he'd even forgotten Nuala was up the duff and hadn't been around the place for a few weeks. Her family were so shocked and embarrassed and feared further shame as her condition became more apparent, so had shipped her off to a maiden aunt in Manchester.

Betty and Molly could see that Dapper had changed considerably, his bluster and bombast diminished, his demeanor was more mature and gentle. He'd always been a dandy, labouring over sartorial elegance, dyed hair, manicured nails and near perfect teeth, but now it could be hours before he felt ready to step out from his ensuite chambers. They hadn't felt brave enough to ask Dapper if he'd lined up Shabin for marriage and the few times they'd commented on her ring, Shabin had just smiled and changed the subject. They speculated and considered what and where the domestic arrangements might be if they'd guessed right, unsure if Shabin would fit in, or be comfortable in their midst, but conceded it would be uncommonly convenient to have a resident doctor among their aging population.

However, it did rankle that amidst them Shabin was young, alluring and yet to reach her prime, while for them it was terminal decline with the aches and pains of deteriorating bodies and the inconvenience and embarrassment of gynecological problems. It was further galling that Dapper, who was around about the same age could still strut his stuff and do the business, even if he might need the aid of pharmalocigal miracles, but there was no doubting his potency.

Walking the strand at Inch had become a favourite haunt for Dapper and Shabin, here they could more or less escape the whispers and intrigue and only have eyes for each other while they courted and sparked. Dapper skimmed stones on the sea, while Shabin searched for shells and delighted in each others small success's, just to be together was enough, which for Dapper was a unique feeling.
'Mrs Hennassy told me that the first tea in this area was salvaged from a wreck out there,' She pointed out beyond the boiling surf,' apparently they stewed it for two hours and then ate the leaves.'
They both laughed and looking along the Strand watched three collies playing with the white horses barking and snapping as the waves broke, now and again checking on the solitary figure trailing behind and intent on beachcombing.

'When I was a child back home in Tibet my father told me about the sea,' They sat on a grass topped sand dune watching the water reslentlessly lap at the sand,'. . . of course I knew it was a lot of water, but I never imagined. . .'
'Do you miss Tibet?' Dapper ventured gently, slightly afraid he might upset Shabin.
'Tibet. . . yes, and no. . . I miss the people, the mountains and . . . yes the snow,' Shabin's eyes misted over and she stared hard at the sea,' . . .but not the Chinese.'
Current world affairs and past politics were not Dapper's forte, but word of the Chinese invasion of Tibet and the exile of the Dalai Lama had filtered down to him, although to date he had not formed any opinion.
Then Dapper hadn't formed much of an opinion about anything beyond music, sex and women and on these he had very strong and vociferous ideas. He also had a strong, if biased feelings about the laws relating to divorce, marriage and parental responsibility, not that he had any real animosity towards any of his ex wives or his numerous offspring. He did, however loathe and detest lawyers, considering them voracious vultures feasting on the distress and misunderstandings of the emotionaly vulnerable with cruel conceit and callous conniving.

152

Shabin a vegetarian had brought a picnic in the form of fruit, a few carrots and some sticks of celery which Dapper, a confirmed carnivore struggled to eat as a concession to his lady love.

'What's in the bag?' Dapper a born optimist hoped Shabin might have slipped something more substantial into her bag for life, a little something he could get his teeth into.

'Let me see . . .' She teased delving into the bag as if the contents were unknown,' Bananas, figs, apples,celery, carrots. . .what do you fancy?'

The old style Dapper would have had a ready, if uncouth retort to that, but he was a reformed character and trying hard to be the perfect suitor and although nothing really appealed, settled for a fresh fig.

Thus they sat a fresh wind blowing with Dapper sucking out the luscious fig while Shabin nibbled on a banana and laughed at the mess on Dappers face from his efforts to eat the moist and ripe fruit.

She reached into her handbag and took out a wet wipe and gently mopped his face like a devoted mother fussing over her messy child, normally such things would annoy him, but he was a changed man and blown away by her tender affection.

Had Shabin been a more cynical, a worldly western woman she might have noticed the demure attitude of Dapper and taken advantage and treated him like the fool in love that he was, but she had that delicate grace and modesty so common in Asian women. She did however have that inscrutable aura that kept Dapper guessing as to her true feelings, although her gentle and soft nature was in no doubt.

One of the collies came bounding up, tail wagging excitedly and snuffled around them inquisitively, before coming close to chance a lick at them.

'Hello dogdaze.' Dapper reached out to pat the dog.

'CHARITY COME HERE!' Skeeter called, but the wind whipped her voice out to the Atlantic, and her other two dogs, Hope and Faith ran up to join Charity.

'Whoa!' Dapper and Shabin were overwhelmed by damp and very friendly dogs.

Skeeter ran the 50 yards, trundling heavily up the last few feet of the sand dune,' GIRLS, GIRLS, COME HERE,

I'm sorry, they won't hurt you!' Skeeter rested her bag of seaweed which she had collected to bathe in, one of her therapeutic indulgences which toned both skin and hair. turned her bath water murky and left her with a lingering smell of the briny and the odd crab that eluded the filtering.

'I can see that,' Shabin said between being heavily licked,' don't worry their fine,' although in serious danger of being flattened, she continued,' their lovely dogs and have wonderful names.'

Skeeter reached across and pulled the dogs off one by one,' Settle girls, behave.'

'Are they sisters?' Dapper asked mildly curious.

'Yes, their usually very good, but sometimes they carried away with themselves,' She recognized both of them, but thought it might be indiscreet to mention it,' I'm Skeeter.'

'John and this is Shabin, good to meet you at last, I've seen you around town and didn't you come to our barn dance?'

'Yes, it was good fun.' Skeeter felt a little more confidant,' Your the doctor aren't you?' she said to Shabin.

'Yes, I'm sorry, your not one of my patients are you? I have to admit I don't think I've seen you at the surgery.' Shabin apologized softly.

'No you won't have, I'm not on your register.' Skeeter couldn't help but let her curiosity lead her on,

' You live at the rock house,' she nodded towards Dapper.

'The rock house, is that what they call it?' He laughed.

'Some do, there are a few names for your place.'

'and us no doubt,'

'It's their way, I suppose you've heard what they call me?' Skeeter smiled weakly and noticed the dogs had lost interest in the humans and were eager to romp away, but obedient enough to wait for the off.

Shabin noticed the kelp spilling out of the bag,' can I ask what you do with the seaweed?'

'Oh that . . . I put it in my bath. . .' Skeeter pulled a wrack of kelp and handed it to Shabin, who took it Tentatively between thumb and forefinger.

'Yea, I like a bowl of seafood chowder myself.' Dapper joked.

Skeeter smiled weakly and Shabin gently elbowed him in the ribs,' please excuse my friend, it's his age you know. . . . he's rapidly approaching his second childhood.'

'Perhaps he never left it in the first place.' Skeeter quipped. 'I don't think men ever stop playing with their toys . . . in my experience they just regard women as boy's toys anyway.'

Shabin laughed, ' Maybe you're right.'

154

Dapper was somewhat abashed and frowned.

Skeeter noticed and felt she might have spoken out of turn, 'I'd better go, the dogs want more mischief, nice to meet you.' Skeeter offered her hand,' No doubt I'll see you around town, bye.'

'What do they call her?' Shabin asked as they watched Skeeter and the girls race on towards the cafe at the main entrance to the strand'

The scarlet woman!'

'Why?'

'I've no idea, as she said that's how they are.'

A handful of courageous, if perhaps foolhardy figures rode and wrestled the surf on boards in their shiny black wetsuits, looking much like dolphins , Dapper shivered at the thought of the pounding and doubtless icy waves. 'you'd be better off in a washing machine. . . .at least the water would be warm!'

WEIRDIE BEARDIES.

'Do you know the way to the rock house?' The wreck of a first generation transit van, pulled up at the Milltown crossroads and a weirdy beardy shrouded in an aromatic mist leaned out of the drivers window. John Patrick Brandon was taken by surprise as he had been lurking behind a hedge watching the day pass through with no thought of ought in his head,' . . .what's that sir . . . rock's is it?'

'I'm looking for the place where the rock cats live,' a great puff of heavy and pungent grey smoke wafted from within the van and engulfed Patrick, he inhaled deeply, coughed a little to clear his throat,'Rock cats is it you want?' J.P surveyed the rusty van, noticing the much faded graffitti that adorned it and wondering at the message.

'Suzy loves Micky.'

'Angie adores Jake, please phone me I'll do anything you want.'

'Toby I love you.'

'Micky Epsom is fab love Joan.'

Were just a small selection that J.P. scanned and puzzled over as he considered what the rock cats were, ' and these cats. . . is it a zoo?'

'So old timer do you know them?' The weirdies head was joined by a hippy dippy of uncertain nature, so that two heads peered quizzically at him.

'Now, it's the wrong road you're on right enough and if it were me I'd start from another place,' Patrick thought deeply,' The rock cats you say?' He tipped his cap back with the long finger and scratched at his bald head, cautiously eying the strange fruit that had dropped into his day.

'Yea grandad you must know them.'

'Well now,' J.P. rubbed his stubbly and grubby chin thoughtfully,' I might and then again I might not. . .I've heard talk about a strange thing over Dunquin way. . . but then there are those that say there's often a strange thing there abouts'

'Yea man, go on, where's dunwhatsit?' A further disheveled head joined the other two,' cool a real gone dude, check out his threads.'

J.P. stared at the three monkeys, who were not at all wise and definitely saw, heard and spoke evil to some degree in his estimation,' Argh right you are, well now let me see.' He further scratched his head under his cap and cast a sly eye over his tormentors once more,' go to the left,' he indicated with his right hand,' then by the turf take the bog road to the right,' he indicated with his left hand,' its a bog road, but a good one right enough and watch for Clover She's inclined to wander and dawdle in the road, but don't mind her at all, she has a sweet nature on herself.' With that he swung his leg over his rusty bike and pedaled hard in the opposite direction, with a cheery backward wave,' grand day for the viewing, sirs.'

Many hours later after many detours, deviations and deep ditches the tired vehicle and occupants crawled up the drive in a cloud of choking black smoke from without and a aromatic grey smoke within.
'Hey man dig the pad,' a tussled head hung out of the passenger window with a far gone grin on her face,' what a cool scene.'
'Go on the lads, I knew they'd get it sorted, this'll do nicely.' Derby took his hands off the steering wheel and rubbed them together,' Agatha will be knocked out to see us, I can't wait to see his face.'
Derby had knocked about a bit, a couple of years as a free lance muso, he never got paid and was well shafted by likely lads. Before dropping out entirely to find his soul and then travelling and dealing in just about anything that fell to hand, or failing that just fell off the back of a lorry.
The van itself had been the original band wagon of a band he formed way back in the mid 60's,the 'Good Intentions' could have gone all the way, but they lacked talent, integrity and real commitment. Mostly they played free festivals, underground gigs and quasi political rallies designed to rattle the establishment and kick out the jams, their only regular income was the dole and what the individual members made from dealing dope and liberating the capitalist property for the people from shops, leaving in place a sticker which proclaimed 'PROPERTY IS THEFT MOTHERFUCKER!'
By necessity the actual line up of the band was fairly loose as individual members were either to stoned to be arsed to turn up for gigs, or doing a stretch for theft ,shoplifting, or dope.
'I think I'm gonna like it here,' Joan gave the house a once over and smiled,' Agatha you say, I don't remember you mentioning her before.'
'Me and Agatha go way back and he's a real cool cat, met him at the Roundhouse in London, some benefit gig. A real gas everybody was tripping, you should have seen it,' Derby crashed the gears of the van and pumped the brake pedal desperately hoping it might just work,' He borrowed a £5. off me and said he give it back next time I saw him.'

157

'What! . . .That was nearly forty years ago!' Joan was blown away.

'Yea, must be, I guess,' Derby shrugged,' I only just found out a few weeks ago where he was living.'

'You mean we've come all the way over from London to get your fiver back?'

'Well yea, it must be a good bit now with the interest,' Derby winked,' and anyway I reckon we could do alright here, check it out.'

'Did you see those horses in the field near the gate, I've always liked riding horses.' Joan ran a hand through her greasy dreadlocks and tied a scarf around her head.

'More than riding me?' Derby elbowed her in the ribs.

'Spider Joe gave a hollow laugh from the back where he was rolling another joint from his stash of weed,' I hope this Agatha's got some dope man, I'm into my last ounce.'

'Bound to man, that cat always had a stash on him.' Derby cut the engine and coasted the last few yards.

' Did you hang out with him for long?' Joan leaned out of the window to open her door carefully as the lock didn't work from inside the van and was only held on by one hinge.

'Only met him the once, but he was real cool . . . really laid back.'

'What the fuck is that!' Betty, like most in County Kerry had heard the van coughing and wheezing its way up the drive, backfiring every few yards with a blown exhaust adding insult to audible injury as it belched black acrid smoke into the otherwise fresh air.

'Looks like hippies, or pikies, best hide the valuables either way.' Molly joined Betty at the window and looked on in horror as the ragamuffins fell out ingloriously.

'Jesus Christ, that's all we need!' Betty darted her head back in,' MUTTON. . .MUTTON, WHERE ARE YOU.' She sprinted for the front door,' quick lock it before they have everything away.' Betty had self respect and was scornful of freeloading travellers, considering herself several classes above such idle itinerants. 'MUTTON, MUTTON WHERE THE FUCK ARE YOU?'

' WHAT DO YOU LOT WANT?' Molly boldly shouted from the safety of the open window.' WE DON'T NEED IT. . . WHATEVER IT IS!'

Derby looked around searching for the source of the voice, then saw her and grinned broadly, 'Hello Duchess, I'm looking for me dear old mucker, Agatha.'

'Don't you duchess me,you scoundrel. . . who are you anyway?' Molly yelled back belligerently, she thought quickly,' We've never heard of her, there's no Agatha here.' She waved wildly,' There's a pub about three miles further on they might know her. . . they get all sorts in there.'

She was just about to slam the window shut, when the catalyst of calamatity emerged.

'Somebody call my name?' Agatha stepped out from the shrubbery, still zipping up his flies and rubbing the damp patch on his strides.

'Hey man, hey Agatha my man, remember me?' Derby grinned broadly,' You ain't changed a bit friend.'
Agatha was bewildered as normal,' I haven't ? . . . Do I know you?'

'Aw come on Agatha you must remember, The roundhouse in 67, it's me Derby, you said to look you up sometime.' Derby grabbed Agatha with open arms and gave him a bear hug,' so how you been man?'
'Yea. . . great . . . I think.' Agatha tried hard to remember who this was,' When did you say I met you?'
'Roundhouse 67, great gig, the Floyd, Move, Mighty Baby, Soft Machine, you must remember. Jesus was there banging his tambourine and Mr Natural strutting his stuff, we got stoned and that acid was mind blowing, I didn't come down for a week.' Derby's enthusiasm was all consuming,' this is Joan, she's my old lady.'

Joan stepped forward a swathe of colour, velvet and patchouli oil and kissed him on the cheek,'Derby's always talking about you, he reckons you're like a soul brother. . . his spiritual twin.'

Agatha was speechless, which was rarer than hens teeth, he glanced at the van and then at the slowly spreading pool of oil leaking from beneath it and then back to the van, aghast as two more colourful clowns emerged blinking from it in a waft of smoke and a not unpleasant aroma, which slightly cheered Agatha up.

'So man, ain't you gonna invite us in it's been a long strange trip, there's some really weird people around here.' Derby took off for the front door,' come on cats, I need a piss.'

Agatha normally accepted the bizarre and eccentric as the order of the day and more especially the night as he and most of his associates were night owls, but even he was horrified by his visitors and their implied intentions.

Betty earth mother as she was, could be a tigress when her home and kith and kin were under potential threat from a prolonged siege of ne'er-do-wells. She was a veteran of several squats and communes and well knew what to expect. Recognising the warning signs of opportunistic infiltrators with malice aforethought she stridently challenged. 'And how can I best help you?' Standing leg sastride and arms

159

folded defiantly, with a face that would instantly curdle the milk of human kindness. She had already decided how she could best help them in a short, sharp and painful fashion.

Molly loyally at her side also with a scowl that could wither fruit on the vine and make the devil seek imminent salvation with the Lord.

Even Beaver, had turned out for the confrontation and hissed and spat, with ears pinned flat back and tail swishing from side to side like a scimitar. The cat was considered a good judge of character, never having taken to Rock and clawing his hand on the only occasion Rock had reached down to brutally shove it off his laptop case.

'Hello princess, I'm an old mate of Agatha here and thought I might look him up and bring him good cheer,' Derby liked to think he had a quicksilver tongue and a winning smile,' He never mentioned the beautiful ladies he was shacked up with, kept that one close to his chest. . . The old goat!'

Betty eyed Agatha like a panther about to pounce, he shrugged helplessly not knowing what to say, or do for the best. 'WELL?'

Half a dozen residents had turned out from late beds attracted by the rattle and hum of events in motion and looked on in wonder, although none were tempted to intervene, but stood fascinated by the fun and furore.

T.J. stepped forward and bent down to inspect the unexpected oil well developing on the graveled drive at source and was astounded as so little of the floor of the van was untarnished by rusty holes,with sheets of rotting chipboard spread over them resting on the odd solid pieces of chassis. He whistled softly and had to admit a grudging respect for somebody willing to risk life and limb and travel in this aging death trap.

'Travelled far?' T.J. asked viewing the new arrivals with a mixture of fear and loathing, he and the others had a good thing going and weren't about to share their goldmine with scruffy chancers. Nice wheels!'

'We're from over the sea and far away.' Joan answered; she liked to think of herself as a romantic poet forever lost in the mists of a muse and ever searching for a perfect poem. She was a mystic for whom the humdrum routine that passed as the practice of people was abhorrent to her spirit and a complete downer.

'Oh right.' T.J. regretted asking, he would better have asked, 'what planet.'

No matter how unorthodox, or peculiar one set of people may be, they maintain in their own heads the belief that what they are and how they appear is perfectly normal and often feel superior in someway to those that would view them askance. By the same token they view many others as socially unacceptable and are prone to criticize and distrust such with a legitimacy borne out of blind hatred and an inability to comprehend that which is different.

More pragmaticaly, once bitten twice shy and the survival of the fittest is paramount in most minds and an inherent reluctance to forget and forgive is ever present.

Once more Agatha was deep in the doo doo, blinking wildly, silent and wishing a large hole would suddenly open up beneath his feet and swallow him.

' I'm sure Agatha would love to take you into Dingle to show you the sights and socialize, I'm afraid it's inconvenient to visit here at present,' Betty thought quickly,' we've an outbreak of. . . of leprosy.'

It stretched credibility, but was the first thing she thought of,' we're all in quarantine.' She looked pointedly at the hapless Agatha,' Wouldn't you?'

He glanced at his assembled peers, who glared back unmercifully,' yea. . .yea I'm thinking that's a grand idea.'

'Slight problem.' Derby countered, himself rebuked and rejected as a matter of course for the better part of his life and having developed the speed and wit of a survivor,' old Vivian here has come a cropper, I think she's not suited to the rocky roads around here.' he indicated the rusting heap cluttering up the drive.

'Reminds me of our first bandwagon, all those lipstick names and numbers.' Mutton said affectionately, ' Do you know, now that I think of it, I'm sure I knew Bertha from Bognor.' He pointed at the faded pink inscription on the wheel arch.'I remember Paula from Petersham, great plater, got her number off the side our van.'

Betty sharply elbowed Mutton in mid reminisce,' shut up you old fool.'

Tic Tac was quick off the mark,'No problem T.J. will take you in and you can arrange a tow in from Beehive autos, how's that?'

' I need a piss.' Derby insisted and moved forward,' aw shit!' He looked down at his down at heel boots with holes in the sole which let in water and saw he was standing in fox crap.

'He's definitely taking it.' Molly mumbled to Betty, who smiled,' Too right, the fookain fox strikes again'.

161

BANDITS IN THE BOGSIDE.

Wild rumour and grim half truths filtered back to Dungiggin regarding the foraging and plundering of the unwelcome beardie weirdies around the peninsula.

' A terrible plague and invasion of outrage upon house and home.' Was one of the more charitable comments Betty was meant to overhear as she browsed the freezer cabinets in Supavalue on the Friday food forage. 'T'is an affront to all decent folk, something must be done and done quickly!'Helen who sadly wasn't blessed with a face that would launch a thousand ships, if lucky the odd patched currach might be forced out on a stormy night to salvage her, was rarely without opinion on any matter and no shrinking violet in voicing it. The witches coven centered around the medical center, had all their best misgivings and dire warnings of the end of civilization affirmed. Took this as confirmation that the heathen Visigoths amidst them now were only an advance guard for the great unwashed barbarians that would shortly sweep in from that unholy country of oppressors over the sea.

The guardai were run breathless by complaint, investigation and indignation and regarded the unwelcome intrusion into their sleepy and happy patch as nothing less than a conspiracy and a far worse threat then fully armed tinkers intent on meeting to dance upon the graves of rival tribes.

Derby and Joan had little regard for the antiquated laws of ownership, believing possession to be little more than theft of communal assets and as such anything left unattended was rightfully available for redistribution among the deserving and down trodden.

With such conflicting opinions and the belligerent attitudes of a lifetime, never the twain would meet in compatible resolution and neither sought such, this was class war, although what class of war was debatable and volatile in the extreme. Farmer owners discovered livestock and arable crops missing, landowners complained of wilful damage and trespass. The local good and worthy felt afflicted and violated by the uncompromising attentions and harassment of the unkempt and unwashed pikeys and demanded immeadiate retribution.

Although none at Dungiggin would have any truck with the travelling hooligans they were tarred with the same brush from the locals point of view, as they were not far removed from the general appearance and unorthodox attitudes. Even Agatha was aghast and vigoursly argued his innocence. Firmly insisting that he had never associated in any way with them and wasn't at all sure that he had ever met them before and even if he had, he'd definitely not invited them to blight the home.

'This can't go on, we'll be hounded out of the county, it'll be like the troubles in the twenties we'll be burnt out and turned onto the road.' Betty had called a meeting and for once everybody came, bar Cuddly Bubbly who was desperately ill and had been for a good ten days. So bad was she that Betty and Molly had taken to nursing her along with hot broth, good cheer and sympathy, but despite all ministering she showed little sign of turning the corner and was fit to fade away. She was sallow skinned, a waxy yellow like ancient parchment, struggled to maintain any interest in anything beyond her own troubles, lacking appetite, morose and deeply depressed. But life goes on in spite of those that fall by the wayside and the curse of the anarchists was a pressing threat to their future security and demanded immediate attention.

' I think it's down to Agatha to deal with them!' Molly demanded uncompromisingly,' they're his raggle taggle gypsieo's after all.'

'I keep telling you, their not. I never met the loike in me life, sure I'd remember wouldn't I?' When cornered, Agatha was prone to mumbling in a thicker accent to further add confusion.

'C'mon Molly, be sensible. Agatha would be hard put to solve the crossword in the Sunday Sport, even with Mondays edition in front of him,' Betty was strident,' no we've all got to sort this between us and before too long.'

'Oi, I am here you know and I'm not pig ignorant, sure.' Agatha protested indignantly,' wasn't my granddaddy the travelling interpreter for the courts?'

'More likely he was forever in the courts defending the indefensible!' Molly again attacked with caustic sarcasm.

Mutton sat glumly by the range warming his socked and soaking feet, as his wellies had perished where the sole joined the uppers and as ever fiddled with his hearing aid and squirmed to ease the burning itch of his farmers.

'Just how do you solve the problem of uninvited aliens polluting the environment with their toxic ways and means.' pondered T.J. aloud and to nobody in particular. He was more the creator of problems and well used to hastily moving on before the excrement hit the fan along with his companion in chaos.

'We could kill them, you know get them up the cliffs and sorta nudge them off.' Agatha enthused.

'Get real,' T.J. countered,' somebody would notice, you can't fart around here without some lurking local getting wind of it.' after a moments thought he continued,' mind you over at Brandon Point there's a place or two that might better do the trick.'

Betty and Molly exchanged knowing glances, but then neither expected anything better, or indeed realistic from the rabble and flights of fancy were normal fare.

' Hello hello earth to Agatha, earth to Agatha come in please and don't forget to bring your brain. . . Let's get back to the real world shall we. . . any ideas?'

Bemused and bewildered they exchanged silent glances, which was then broken by a wet fart from Tic Tac, ' What? . . . What?' He responded as all eyes turned accusingly on him,' haven't you ever felt that something died inside you and better an empty house than a bad lodger.' He giggled inainly and looked for approval from Agatha and T.J.

'If you've nothing more constructive to contribute then a lot of putrid hot air, butt out!' Molly told it like it was and didn't give a fig for tact and when talking to Tic Tac such finesse would be casting pearls before swine, although pigs did have certain redeeming features.

'Can't the guardai do something?' Tit Bits asked.

'Such as?' Betty felt they were getting nowhere fast.

'I don't know, evict them or something.' Feeling a bit hot in her leathers, Tit Bits shifted from her seat near the blazing log fire, feeling sweat in unforgiving places, she hated the chaffing of damp leather on her unmentionables. But liked the look and the affect it had on men, and had learnt the hard way that a girl must ouffer for her oino and indeed there wao a oertain oatiofaotion in the bump and grind of a hot man in enoited exercise.

'Don't be silly, they keep moving anyway, that's part of the problem,' Betty was exasperated,' by the time anybody discovers anything's missing they upped and shifted somewhere else.'

'Don't worry, it will all work out, the laws of universal karma are at work and it is wise to let this matter blow with the wind.' a small voice from nowhere. They'd all but forgotten Lucy Lastic was with them, which she often was in body, if not in spirit. She sat wrapped in her hand knitted psychedelic knee length cardigan, a project that had outgrown the pattern and perhaps gone on far too long and was reading from her phone,' I texted a new site, Karma unlimited. It's very good, you it's a new app I downloaded, they know all the answers and it only costs £2.32 a minute. It's magic, you should all get it.'

'Yes sweetie, I'm sure we all get it. But we haven't all got super dooper mobiles, have we luvvie?' Molly stung as waspish as ever and equally Lucy was burnt having never managed to brush aside her barbed attacks.

'C'mon everybody, giving each other a hard time isn't a great help is it?' Betty often found herself to be the only sane and balanced person among a crowd of lunatics, or so it seemed to her. At such times she ruminated once more on how it could have been, not how it should have been, if only, if only what? Then she would look at the others and oddly enough she didn't feel so bad after all.

As is often the way events overtake the general run of things and on the other side of the peninsula the yahoos had ventured beyond the pale and come upon simple country folk who wouldn't tolerate strange ways. They looked after themselves, had no truck with any authority, especially the guardai and certainly didn't need any help in dealing with gypsies,thieves and vagabonds.

Derby and Joan had been caught liberating most anything that was unguarded and not firmly attached and with five full grown strapping lads to back him up Joe Mcgee and Mary dealt rough justice without the complications of the legal weasels.

'Will I break his legs Da?' Joseph Patrick had hold of Derby by his collar and J.P. was a big boy, so Derby was on his tip toes and feeling the pinch. Brothers Brian, Aidain, Tiernan and John James also shared a no nonsense attitude and living and working with livestock weren't squeamish about blood and gore.

Joan and Spider Joe were corralled, scared and anxious to be away, but the Mcgees thought different and had never liked the English since the Black and Tans rampaged through the land and killed the grandad in an ambush that was ambushed.

Joe had his gnarled cudgel in hand twisting it menacingly within his fist and a fiery ferocious glint in his eye, he was an old fashioned culchie who enjoyed a fierce fight and wasn't fussed if it involved relatives, neighbours or strangers as long as it was good blood sport. Mary was not squeamish either, being born and bred in a farming family that had lived close to the land since before Cromwell visited murder and mayhem upon the land of saints and scholars. She routinely wrung chickens necks, delivered lambs and calves and supported her family, right or wrong, through thick and thin and appreciated a good ruck as much as her husband.

Had Derby the luxury of time and peace of mind to entertain the finer points of his predicament he might have felt empathy with a fish on a hook, as he squirmed and wriggled to release himself from the vice like grip of J.P. who held him aloft by one hand whilst teasingly prodded him with the clenched fist of the other. Between agonised gasps and snatched breaths he attempted to talk his way out of a tight squeeze as was his way, but what words were coherent fell on deaf ears and minds set on grand entertainment and an all too rare opportunity to spread a little grief and gristle.

Joan was a vegan and the prospect of an encounter red in tooth and claw was unsettling at best, she was prone to pass out on sighting a nose bleed and would panic and run rather than watch an animal in distress. At this moment in time the animals in potential distress were the travelling trio and an eye for an eye and a tooth for a tooth were two of Derby's anatomical parts that were quite likely to suffer some extreme form of punishment. ' She's pretty,' Aidain suddenly announced. He was stoutly built with a ruddy complextion and a large round face topped by a mop of wild ginger hair, which was a mystery to his dad as he had once boasted dark hair and both his wife and other sons had dark hair. Aidain was also slow on the uptake, rather lumpish in gait and stuttered when excited or nervous, unlike his siblings who were upfront, aggressive and quick witted when it suited. 'I like her hair.'

Mary sighed and gave her husband a weary look, Aidain was her special boy, but his strange ways could be tiresome and she constantly worried about him and his unpredictable nature. His brothers smirked and winking mischievously nodded, ' Oh aye, himself has a fancy again. . . better that than sheep with the nice faces though.' Joan started to worry, she seen films about rednecks, hill billies and the odd and earthy ideas and inclinations of country folk, but still clung to a vague hope that all would be well as long as they didn't pull their banjos out and start playing with them.

Spider Joe, who was routinely so laid back that it always took him a good few minutes to catch up with the present circumstance which had always moved on by the time he arrived and spoke with a slow drawl as he struggled to keep one thought in mind and find the words to communicate it. His mind and body had long been addled and compromised by copious amounts of puff, acid that had blown his box and charlie that had burned his nose. He sensed something was amiss, but then that was pretty much normal and things can always get better, he'd clung to that belief for nigh on thirty years now and knew it was only a matter of time, after all even

166

a stopped watch was right twice a day,however briefly.

The suspense was killing, Joe wasn't one to make spur of the moment decisions, quite liking to leave things dangling to enjoy the best dramatic effects, he was well aware that his captives trio quietly crapping themselves as their imaginations ran riot. His sons didn't have the subtlety and appreciation of raw emotion that Joe had garnered over the years, he enjoyed the game savouring the intricate twists and turns as his victims envisioned the noose tightening and slowly resigned themselves to their fate.

Often it is the anticipation that is worse than the actuality, the slow passage of time that seems to stretch interminably allowing the agony to increase inexorably second by second and each passing moment appears to endure for hours.

Her mind, filled with visions of rape and murder, caused Joan to sweat and her stomach to cramp with fear.Increasingly aware of the lecherous stares of the brothers, who she imagined with some justification were mentally stripping her of clothes and dignity as they conjured up depraved and lustful thoughts and deeds. She began to sob, at first softly, but as her self control evaporated, Joan started to quake and then she lost it and wet herself, much to the amusement of the sons of the sod.

'Jaysus, she's pissed herself, would you look at that!'

Aidain was stupefied and just stared at the damp patch around her feet and then at her and back to the quietly steaming pool.

Although very much a rude mechanical, Mary was moved by the degrading and embarrassing plight of another women, for her it was a step to far, although she still couldn't relate to Joans lifestyle .'Joe, enough, let the woman be.'

'Argh, I'll not let it be said that Joe Mcgee, OR ANY OF HIS SONS,' he emphasised the point,' ever took advantage of a defenceless woman.'

Any relief that Derby took from the words, believing he was off the hook, were quickly and violently dispelled as J.P. gave Derby a sharp kidney punch to show his frustration as his crude sexual fantasies were crushed. Summoning up every ounce of bravado and not a little stupidity Derby pleaded,' look nothing is missing, you got it all back before . . .ooff, aw fuck!'

J.P. landed another kidney punch,' will ye shut up, afore I give ye another good belting!'

Joe eyed the old van, wondering if it was worth the taking, but closer inspection showed it to be far worse than

167

his old Nissan and he dismissed the idea, but felt that beside his few pounds of flesh he still wanted some other compensation. 'Have ye any money?'

With some effort Derby shook his head, as did the others, although Joan had forty odd pounds tucked into her bra, as little something to fall back on in hard times. Despite their predicament Joan was loathe to even consider giving away her nest egg, which she'd managed to keep secret, even from Derby when he drunkenly fumbled her boobs before passing out on numerous occasions.

'No money is it?' Joe was flummoxed, much as he enjoyed the sport of a good beating, he liked the satisfaction of a grand profit at somebody else's expense and with a crap van and nothing of value to their name the craic was tarnished.

A cock crowed in the yard as Joe's eyes narrowed as inspiration dawned and raising his black cudgel, gently stroking his chin with the thick end as he contemplated and then a wicked grin spread across his face,' I have it. . . I have the very thing.'

All eyes turned to him some in glorious expectation, others in terror,' What Da, what?'

'Ma, d'ya have the bag of feathers?'

Mary plucked the feathers from the chickens once she had wrung their necks to stuff pillows and duvets.

'Tiernan . . .the tar.'

Joe waved his schtik menacingly at Derby,' sure I haven't had cause to do this since my youth. . . that traitor Oliver was acting the maggot with the guardai . . . we showed him right enough.'

CLUCKING AROUND.

'Good luck Mr Gorsky.' Neil Starmong called after a tourist as he left Dick Macs, not that Neil was a local man himself, as he was an occasional blow in arriving to crew a trawler when work was available. Mr Gorsky, an American with his beloved Patty was on a tour of Europe, intent on discovering her roots, as she considered a chance to connect as this could be the last time as she was in her eighties. She was desperate to make amends with Teddy having given him a rough ride through most of their marriage,refusing him a full sex life beyond the mundane and requiste monthly missionary. It had been a terrible blow to his masculine pride, which had withered his libido and all but brought their marriage to a dysfunctional head more than once. In all other ways their marriage had been successful, lasting fifty seven years thus far, with no issue inherit their goods and chattels they were indulging in a dream holiday.

Teddy had popped into Dick Macs to enquire about the Molloys, Patty's maiden name and if any of that name were still living in Dingle. It was a longshot as no one from her family had been back to the old country since her great grandfather had upped and left in the famine. Nobody in the bar could help Teddy, but he had a Guinness, a packet of pork scratchings and bought a round for the half dozen regulars hugging the counter, letting them know his big claim to fame. His neighbours son was the first man to walk on the moon and Teddy had let him clean his car on a weekly basis for $2.

With the yank away the old contemptibles, as the toxic trio had christened the regulars could get back to passing the day in the age old way, blowing the breeze, spinning mighty yarns and nursing pints. 'D'ye see this?' Sheehan nodded towards his paper and then read out the front page,' The guardai acting on information received discovered two men and two women naked in the back of an old van outside Tralee. All four were coated in tar and feathers and one was found to be heavily bruised. A spokesman for the guardai made an official statement to the effect that it was the first such case of tarring and feathering since the troubled twenties. He added that they were not pursuing further enquiries, but had arrested and charged one of the men with various motoring offences, including an untaxed vehicle, no mot and no valid driving licence. The guardai confidently predicted that the wave of petty crime that had blighted the County over the past month was now ended.

Agatha and T.J. arrived in a somewhat sombre mood to drown their sorrows and toast Cuddly Bubbly who had succumbed to liver cirrhosis passing in the night to the next great adventure.

Although not unexpected it was still a shock and a reminder of their vulnerability and the depressing fact that the birth was little more than the start of an indeterminate death sentence and that nobody, however wealthy or privileged managed to evade the reaper, or buy anonother day.

'Who do you think will get her room?' Agatha asked, as Cuddly Bubbly had lived in one of the best and three ensuite bedrooms in the house, overlooking the walled garden.

'No idea, but I don't think I want it. . . . Man, she died in it and I bet she haunts the place.' T.J. groaned, 'can you imagine, waking up at three in the morning to the sound of bottles clinking together and by the side of the bed is Cuddly wanting to share another last drink with you.'

Agatha looked horrified, ' Jaysus, I never thought of it like that. . . and she smelled like a sewer towards the end.' He shuddered,' Holy Mary it gives me the willies. . . sure, not that I'd be scared of course.'

'Like fuck you wouldn't. . . what about them lights in Lucy's glade. . .you crapped your kecks, right?' T.J. prodded Agatha in the ribs,' right hero to zero, you can get the first round in for that!'

'What !. . . aw c'mon.' Agatha floundered, once more his tarnished tongue and mercurial mind had banjaxed him yet again to his cost.

'Hey lads, it's yourselves.' Sheehan called from the bar,' did ye hear the news?'

'What news is that then?' T.J. wasn't at all sure he could take any more news, good, bad, or indifferent. Sheehan lifted the paper up and shook it, ' I'd say it's your muckers.'

'What mucker's is that then?' T.J. was curious, but cautious.

'Dem pikeys that was on the knock off here abouts.' Sheehan had caught them up to no good with a box freshly landed prawns and was relishing the newspapers report, having shown them a novel approach with crustaceans himself.

'No mates of mine. . . Hey Agatha! . . .They've been kicked out by the jams.' T.J. sneered.

Agatha was methodically counting out his change on the bar. patting his pockets in a desperation for another 75 cents,' didn't I tell you I never met them before they turned up like.'

'Yea, pull the other one,' T.J. grinned,' How would they know who you were and where to find you?'

'Sure, I was thinking about that and I'd say that Gypsy Joe put them up to it,' Agatha nodded,

'He reckoned he owed me one, there was a little misunderstanding over a thing, or two.'

Betty was collecting eggs and reflecting on Cuddly Bubbly's death which had unerved her. She sat down on stool amid the straw and talked to the chickens,' so, Memphis Minny,'. All her chickens were named after blues singers, her particular favourites being a little red rooster called WillieDixon and a gold laced Polish with an impressive crest called Sister Rosetta Tharp. ' well chicks, another girl done gone and the valley of shadows is close.

Do you know what worries me, Muddy, these things happen in threes.' The buff Plymouth briefly looked up and then returned to pecking around the yard for juicy worms and beatles.

Cuddly Bubbly was three years younger than Betty and it bothered her, almost every week she heard, or read about some icon of her generation, a film star, writer, whatever who had popped their clogs, often in desperate circumstances.

'It's o.k. for you all you do is scratch about and lay a few eggs.'

Betty picked up a stick and idly drew patterns in the dirt, a young bantham called Blind Blake on account of losing an eye in a cock fight became curious and strutted up. ' Between you and me girls I often wonder who's got the better scene.' The hen seemed mildly interested, then scratched a little before shuffling off in a full chuck.

Bettys soothing tone always drew a crowd of fowl, she couldn't be sure they understood a word, but her regular chats and a handout of grain at the end of them was too good to miss.

'Here's me hard nose to the highway just to get by and not one of you has done a days work, or had anxiety in your lives.' Betty found it quite therapeutic to voice her thoughts and concerns to a captive audience and it was less expensive than talking to a strange shrink. ' It should all have been different you know, I had a voice. . .a real talent they said and believe it or not I wasn't that bad looking . . .' One of the chickens clucked sympathetically. ' It's easy for you to say that, you've never had to deal with men and their wild and wilful whims and fancies. It's a mans world you know and a woman's gotta make sacrifices just to stay in the picture and I mean sacrifices, do you know what I'm saying?. . . The most you get to worry about is a fox on the run and you all know that Rory built you the best roost in the county. I guarantee you that the fookin fox will never get a look in and definitely not ever get his paws on you girls. Not like Rock who had his paws and worse probing every little feminine secret a women likes to pamper and protect from carnal lust. I bent over backwards

171

and then some to satisfy that ego, I should have been queen bitch in the court of the rocky horrors if there was any justice in this world. But what do I get . . . Mutton. . .he doesn't need a lover so much as a mother.' Betty laughed,' do you know what girls, I've been stuffed more times than the average hen and it wasn't with sage and onion I can tell you.'

'Ah here you are!' Molly had an edge of relief in her voice,' we missed you, nobody's seen you for hours.'

'I needed a walk to sort things out. . . you know Cuddly was younger than me. . . and you come to think of it as the Reaper's repeatedly knocking at the door with a shopping list ticking off names and one day. . . one day!'

'It's hit you hard, hasn't it?'

' It's a bit close to home, it could have been any of us.' Betty reached into her pinny pocket for a hankie and blew her nose.

"No. . .no that's not true, she was an alky. . . and didn't look after herself. you know that.' Molly said pragmatically.

'We should have helped her more,' Betty started to weep,' made her eat properly and stuff.'

'You can take a whore to culture. . .' Molly didn't do tact or diplomacy and spoke as she saw, conveniently forgetting that she was no angel and was as much a whore as any groupie could be judged by a dispassionate voyeur.

A trio of hens assembled expectantly at Betty's feet and she smiled and addressed them,' why Miss Frankie, Ida Cox and Blue Lu Barker I do believe you understand, thank you I appreciate it.' She took a handful of grain from the sack and they pecked it from her open palm.

'Betty, you make too much of those birds, get to friendly with them, give them names and personalities and you'll never be able to wring their necks and stuff them with Blind Lemon Jefferson.' Molly smiled and was quite taken with her wit and the fact she could even remember the name of a blues singer.

Betty laughed,' you're right I don't think I could take a contract out on the girls. They listen to me as much as the bees do.'

' Birds and bees hey.' Molly was getting a bit philosophical, something she was mostly a stranger to,' at least they don't go around repeating secrets, unlike some I could name.' She scanned the hens,' reckon that one would make a good roast tonight, shall I do her in?'

Betty was appalled,' You can't kill Fanny May Goosby. Honey where you been so long. Just look at her she knows what you said.' The hen in question had scooted off to the far side of the run in a flap.

'I ain't superstious, well a little bit I suppose, but these things come along in threes and I just worried about who's next.' Betty looked across at Molly,' Know what I mean.'

'Naw, it's just a stormy monday and lightening has to strike somewhere, it's tight like that, but just random.' In truth, Molly wasn't that happy with the idea, for all her words of comfort she too had noticed that things have a habit of coming in threes and also wondered who was next.

'Come into the kitchen, we'll dust the broom and rattle the pots and pans like always and everything will be fine, believe me, we're gonna make it till the end of days.' Molly smiled encouragingly.

Away in the distance but closing rapidly could be heard the blown exhaust of T.J.'s car as they returned in high spirits having consumed a skinfull of beer and whisky and therefore hazard to themselves and any foolhardy enough to share the roads with them. They'd been drinking to Cuddlies memory and intent on giving her a rousing send off, not that they ever needed an excuse for a drink.

The fact that it was drink that killed her was lost on them as was the very real possibility that it would also see them out, they weren't strictly alcoholics, or suffering any noticeable symptoms of alcohol abuse, but few days passed without copious amounts of the stuff passing their lips.

As they slewed to a halt on the drive and Betty saw them spill out of the wreck of a car singing tunelessly, she was pulled up in a sharp reality check. She suddenly realized just where she was at, but for the naming she was an aging hippie living in a lunatic asylum among raving morons that would never mature. Even Mutton was adrift and all were just kicking around in the dog days of their lives waiting to cross the river. Perhaps the worst part was that only she was aware of it, not one of the others could see further than the next meal, or drink and the most appalling thing was that they didn't seem to care. Then again as she thought on, it suddenly dawned on her that until this moment, she too had been coasting along lulled into that false sense of security when her world was the little bubble of baking, gossip and small inconsequentials of a life in terminal decline. Life was life and if considered for more than a few moments one could see it for what it was, a depressing and demeaning circle of drab and meaningless repetition and humdrum activity to deceive and disguise the ultimate truth that all desperately evaded. Little wonder so many suffered from depression and other

173

mental illnesses, perhaps they were only too aware of what others couldn't or didn't wish to recognize which was the hopeless plight that humanity really faced. She thought back to Cornish John's funeral and how things were for all of them then, isolated, enduring and existing in a limbo and how her grand dream had gathered them together, giving them the support and comfort of companionship. Maybe she had been too ambitious and filled with a false idealism which wasn't shared by the others, they didn't want a cohesive community, they just saw Dungiggin as an opportunity to further their carnival of bacchanalian cavorting.

She wasn't blind to her wild youth and hedonistic lifestyle, but felt and hoped she had matured and moved on, although she did have regrets and still enjoyed some secret pleasures which she found impossible to reject entirely. Mutton was now all but impotent and pretty much lost interest in her both as a lover and a woman, a chasm had opened up between them with neither having anything of consequence in common. The only time she ever saw him these days was when he needed feeding and he rarely shared the same bed with her as his snoring was akin to a foghorn and he needed to have a pee several times a night, which disturbed what little sleep she managed ,as she suffered from chronic insomnia herself. She felt the guilt of a pubescent teenager, but was unable to resist the urge to pleasure herself as she tossed and turned through the long dark hours.

Close as she was to Molly she couldn't even contemplate letting her best friend into her guilty little secret, although she had often wondered if Molly still felt the same drives and compulsion to comfort and satisfy herself.

Normally positive and optimistic the changes that Cuddly Bubblies death had imposed on her were dramatic and unwelcome, she suddenly felt vulnerable, mortal and depressed by the realisation.

Although convinced by reincarnation, the near presence of death was disturbing, made worse by death bed, as Betty had been comforting Cuddly when she slipped away. Betty and Molly had taken it in turns to be with her in her last days, although it wasn't a pleasant experience for either patient or carer, Cuddly was bloated, jaundiced and frequently vomited blood.

It was a serious reality check for Betty, who had perhaps been lulled into an almost soporific lifestyle, drifting through the days with little to significantly challenge the status quo. She felt she was at yet another crossroads in her life, each time the circumstance was strangely familiar and each time and more urgent.

Betty believed that this must be the major theme in her life and she had previously failed to correctly address it, so it would continue to return until she did. She had read in a book of eastern philosophy that when confronted by a problem it was human nature to take the easy option, the smooth road ahead in preference to the one seen to the rocky road. However if one conjured up the courage to take the rocky road it quickly became the mellow yellow smooth brick road that led on to enlightenment. She mused on the word enlightenment and wondered what exactly it was, she couldn't see the likes of Agatha and T.J. suddenly becoming sages and for that matter she didn't feel that she was spiritually worthy of profound wisdom. She'd heard that God loved a sinner and why wouldn't he in his line of work, after all with no sinners to repent there wouldn't be a lot of point to his own existence and the world would be surplus to requirements.

KISSING THE PINK.

'Now don't you worry yourself at all, she's in safe hands, we'll make sure she has a grand send off.' Jerimiah rubbed his hands, he'd waited a good while to impress the blowins with his unique calling.'Sure we do this sort of a thing all the time, you could say people are dying to have us take care of them.' He chuckled and rubbed his hands together once more,' now rest assured, the deceased always do, it's our specialty.'
Betty had asked for an environmentally friendly funeral with a wicker coffin and a cremation, Jerimah explained that it was still a rarity in Eire and that the only crematorium was in Dublin and the body would have to be sent there and the ashes returned later.
'There is an extra cost of course, but don't you worry yourself at all, sure it'll be very dignified and if you want to travel up to Dublin we can supply a limousine and driver for the journey. ' Jerimiah despite his brimming confidence was perplexed as he'd never been asked for an environmentally friendly funeral, let alone a wicker coffin. 'Oh and don't worry about the death notices we'll organise that and the lying in.'

Betty busied herself with all the arrangements as there were no relatives and although Jerimiah was very reassuring, she was still anxious, something told her there might be problems ahead.
T.J. and Agatha gallantly offered to sort out the wake and were full of bright ideas, but she politely declined, well aware the neither were capable of organising a pint of the black stuff on St Paddys day at St James's Gate. Memories of the chaotic farce that was the housewarming were still fresh in her memory, but a true Irish wake was always a confused carnival as indeed was life, especially Cuddly Bubblys.

Her body had been removed for preparation by Jerimiah and Betty steeled herself to sort out what little of Cuddlys personal affects remained, it was of course a sad thing to do and even with Molly's support, Betty was desperately distressed. ' Look at it!' She waved her arm at the pathetic pile of clothes and assorted items,' Fifty eight years, a battered suitcase, enough pills to start a chemist and three boxes are all she had to show for it. . . and all the pills were for pain, not pleasure.

176

'Maybe she wasn't in to possessions, after all she wasn't really short of money. . . She was definitely a minimalist as far as clothes went.' Molly was rarely emotional, always fractious and her sense of empathy was limited, but it could help in stressful times.

Betty leafed through a shoebox of papers and odds and sods,' Well I'll be !'

'What ?. . . what have you found?' Molly was intrigued,' let's have a look.' She narrowed her eyes and tried to focus, but to no avail it was still a blur.' Well what is it?'

'It's her plectrum necklace and a stack of backstage passes,' Betty smiled ruefully,

'She only ever serviced lead guitarist, never a bass player, or a rhythm guitarist and she wouldn't even look at a drummer or a keyboard player.' She laughed,' she used to say she was a specialist and always claimed a plectrum for her necklace.' Betty flicked through a few, recognizing some on her trophy choker that they shared in common.

'No head no pass.' Molly said like a mantra,' no head no pass. . . humph if you knew how many roadies dicks I sucked to get into the big boys gigs and pants.'

'Tell me about it,' Betty giggled,' do you remember that spotty Herbert that said he was with The Stones?'

'Yea. . .now you mention it, he promised to get me into the Windsor jazz and blues festival if I gave him a blow job. Wham, bam, not even a thank you mam, just did a runner, bastard. . . hope his cock caught caught in his zip!'

Betty doubled up laughing,' Did the same to me at Glastonbury and then I found out the closest he ever got to The Stones was cleaning their car in Mapesbury Road when Mick and Keith lived there.'

They both laughed until they wet themselves and then laughed more because they had.

'God I needed that.' Betty confessed.

'A little light relief hey?' Molly offered.

'Yea, you could say that. . .well a little relief anyway. . .now I'll have to change me knickers,' Betty stood up and saw the damp patch on her dress,' and my dress as well. . .thank you Molly, thank you.I feel a lot better.'

'You know cuddly wouldn't want you on the floor, apart from the last few days she was always flying. . '

'You can say that again, she was always high as a kite.' Betty smiled at the memory,' I reckon Bolly would have gone bankrupt if it wasn't for Cuddly.'

'I bet Jimi, Phil and Keith are well pleased, their little super group has got a champion attitude adjuster and

177

boozer to match their input.' Molly tried to remember if Hendrix and Cuddly had ever jumped each other, but knew she wouldn't really have got up close and personal with Lynott and Moon, but the trio would have made a cracking band and Molly wouldn't have turned down the opportunity to service any one of them in their hey days.

'Yea your right, I bet there's an incredible festival happening up there and our best musos are being plucked to form amazing super groups and they'll need crew and attitude adjusters to service them. . .'

Betty paused,' mind I ain't in a hurry to get there myself, know what I mean.'

'That I do sister, that I do.' Molly opened the suitcase and rummaging through it found a half empty bottle of Stolly.' Hey look Cuddly must've forgotten about this one.'

'Or left it for us to toast her journey . . . what'd'ya say?'

'I'm up for it, if you are.' Molly spun the cap, took a long swig and passed it over.

Betty glanced into the suitcase and gasped,' Lookie here.' She pulled out a device and sniggered,' A juice extractor, if I'm not mistaken!'

Molly snatched it from her hand and turned it on,' and it works!' She nodded her head towards Betty,' when was the last time you had a decent orgasm?'

Betty looked thoughtfull,' Molly! . . . Are you saying what I'm thinking you're saying?'

The next hour passed in a lazy haze of memories which are always better in the telling than the event, they could now laugh at embarrassing disasters, catastrophic mistakes and there but for the grace of God near misses. Their sisterly and sympathetic cuddles, reassuring hugs and girlie kisses combined with the emptying of the vodka evoked the closeness of yesteryears when their daring dash for glory and good times entertained and enthralled a good few rock gods and gave them great pleasure. Both had missed the erotic embrace, thrill and whispered encouragement of kissing the pink and the passing of Cuddly was a pressing reminder that life's pleasures were fleeting and any opportunities should be grasped and gasped.

' You two look a bit flustered,' Mutton caught up with Betty and Molly at the foot of the main staircase, 'I've been looking for you for hours, I'm hungry, where have you been?' Mutton tweaked his hearing aid to stop the whistling feedback,' have you eaten yet?'

Betty and Molly looked at each other and laughed.

'What did I say?' Mutton was perplexed.

CAMP DAVID.

'Hello sweetie I'm David, you wouldn't be a darling and pay the ferryman!'

Agatha was aghast, the biggest blackest bloke in a pink feather boa, floppy purple felt hat with a wide brim and outrageous floral shirt with puff sleeves, a snakeskin tie with an indian head for the knot and badly dyed ginger hair blocked the sun from the door.

'I'm a bit short of the necessary at present, do be a luvvie. . . Oh and while your there you wouldn't bring my impedimenta in from the boot. sweetness . . do be careful not to damage the smaller pink Calabrese, it's got my make up in,' David flounced in,' I'll make my self at home will I ? . . . oh and don't forget to tip the driver, he's such a treasure.'

Agatha looked to O'Malley who stood by his taxi with the biggest and widest grin on his face,' will it be stopping at all sir?' and then back to the retreating figure,who ran a finger across the hall furniture checking it for dust, tutted and minced into the sitting room.

Agatha had never trousered a wedge in his life and was perennially parted from the filthy lucre and the mere thought of shelling out for anything could bring on cold sweats and require therapy.

'Hey Betty. . . Betty!' He rushed to the kitchen,' somethings turned up!'

They were days away from the funeral and Betty was up to her eyes in arrangements and despite his best reassurances she wasn't entirely convinced that Jerimiah was really on the case, as he had phoned a good dozen times to either confirm or question the more unusual aspects of an environmentally friendly funeral. So when Agatha burst into the kitchen all agitated Betty knew yet another gremlin had thrown a spaniard in the works.

'Betty, Betty something's here. . .'

'What now?'

'Eh. . . you'd better take a look, c'mon quick.' Agatha was all of a dither hoping from one hot foot to the other and flapping his arms uselessly like the last desperate Dodo who'd just spied a man with a gun.

Betty was halfway up the hall when the unexpected visitor reappeared from the living room,' it really won't do Wedgewood blue is so passé ,so fifties.'

Betty did a double take, sucked in her breath and then cried out,' Well I'll be. . .I don't believe it. . . Camp David. . . I thought you were in San Francisco.'

'Betty. . . My God you're looking in the pink. . . Betty honey, so good.' David sashayed towards her kissed and hugged her,' It must be twenty years and you haven't changed . . . ' He stepped back and looked her up and down,' well perhaps you've filled out a touch here and there, but you were always so painfully thin anyway.'

Betty recovered from the surprise,' So how come. . .I mean what are you doing here?'

'Well,' he sucked in his breath,'As you know I've been in Frisco since. . . well a good long time. . .too long perhaps. ..I think I outgrew it, it can be so parochial.' David tapped his lips with his index finger as if choosing his words carefully,' you know how it is Betty, so beyond. . . such bitchy queens. . .if you're make ups not just so, or . . . oh I don't know, you've been there haven't you?'

'So how long have you been back?' Betty led the way into the kitchen,' Coffee?'

'No dear, it's the caffeine. . . green tea. . .you do have some, don't you . . . of course you do I was forgetting, aren't you the original earth mother. . . why your every thought and deed are so deeply organic and environmentally friendly. . .don't you just love that phrase?. . . organic, it's so near orgasm and who doesn't need a daily orgasm?

David turned to Agatha,' and what about you petal? . . . do you?''

Agatha wide eyed and speechless, and all but sat on Beaver who had purloined the most comfortable Windsor chair next to the range and was a tad reluctant to be shooed off and showed it by flashing his tail and arching his back.

'Green tea, white tea, chamomile tea and decaf your choice. . . you were saying .'

'Oh this is divine. . .I can really see myself in here and that range, so country set.' David swept around the kitchen delving and probing drawers and cupboards,' I was getting so bored and to tell the truth I think I was homesick. . . the States is o.k., but the yanks can be so tiresome, so gung ho. You do not what I mean, of course?. . . If only they could lighten up and cotton on now and again. . . I mean, they're so beyond, honey, beyond.' David swept his hair from his eyes with a petulant sweep of his hand. 'Then of course Scott flounced out and took the red eye to the Windy City. . . chasing some new kid in town with attitude. . . .well I said. If that's how he wants it after all those comings and goings. . . well I ask you. . . it's not as if I'm desperate!. . . is it?'

'Betty. . .Betty there's a cab outside.' Agatha glanced back to the front door where O'Malley hovered 'Argh don't ye worry about me.' O'Malley was fascinated by the house and the residents, he'd heard talk of the place, but this was his first occasion to visit, having been away in Dublin and missed the housewarming. He slowly inched his way up the hall peering into each room as he passed and anyway the waiting time was clocking away and he had all the time that the good lord had invented to satisfy his curiosity.

'But how are you here?' Betty had the big old black kettle settled on the top of the range and was setting out the cups.

'Coffee for me, five sugars Mrs.' O'Malley had caught up and was seating himself in a wheelback chair, the better to enjoy the cabaret, which was already proving to be the best entertainment he'd had for many a year.

'I caught up with Rock when he was over in June. . . took him by surprise, he was quite shocked to see me again. . . do you know I do believe, just for a moment he felt. . . well it was the look in his eye and that way he always had, just a hint of youthful vulnerability.' David laughed at the memory and helped himself to a slice of banana bread from a plate on the table and O'Malley followed suit.

'I can imagine.' Betty nodded smiling at the thought.

Agatha sat in the chair still open mouthed like a hungry goldfish, just staring at David much as he would a visiting alien fresh from Alpha Centaur, having never seen the like before, which was saying a lot.

Beaver settled in a corner on the fresh washed laundry, had a quick yawn and licked his paws between glaring at Agatha menacingly.

' I don't really think he was best pleased to be reminded of those few days we spent together, but I still had the photos and of course I mentioned the diary, I've treasured them and when I showed them to him. . . well you should have seen his face, it was a picture. . . he was so sweet then.' David smiled at the memory,' such a popit.. . Why he even offered to buy the pics off me. . . what a darling . . .Do you know,I think there was a tear in his eye. . . people just don't know how emotional he can be.' David placed a finger across his lips,' he used to let _ slip his little secrets. . . you know the gin sins and pillow talk. . .well I mean, as if. . . don't we all have indiscretions and skeletons rattling in cupboards.'

Agatha's eyes nearly popped from his head, ' Rock ?. . . you mean Rock Sturdy?'

'Oh yes, you wouldn't have known him then. . . he was so young and naive and pretty, you wouldn't believe. So innocent and trying anything to find out who and what he really was himself.' David reached for another slice of banana bread,' yours Betty? . . . of course, who else has that light touch?'

Agatha whistled softly.

O'Malley had no idea what they were talking about, but no matter the cup of coffee and bit of cake was grand all the same and the meter was still clocking up the waiting time with no expense of petrol for him and the company was fair play. He was also feeling a little light headed and in grand humour and in no hurry to leave, he reached for yet another slice of the cake.

'Well I told Rock how it was and I was jaded and homeward bound . . . I mentioned the idea of writing my memoirs once back and he was really interested.' David drank his green tea with some style, gripping the handle between thumb and forefinger, the little finger extended stiffly.

'Betty smiled,' I get the picture. . . I imagine Rock wanted to help you out.'

'Well yes, how did you know?'

'Oh just a guess!' She smiled sweetly and winked conspiratorially.

' Well that minion of his called me up the other day and said Rock had the perfect place for me, quiet, a home from home with old friends and away from the temptations and stresses of London. Well to tell you the truth I was quite beside myself with the excitement. Oh the thrill of it all, it happened so fast.

Rock was obviously very concerned to help.' David caught sight of his reflection in a mirror and checked his look, pursing his lips,' Oh look at me aren't I a sight? . . It's the long journey, my eye liner's run. . . I look like a clown.'

'I just bet he was.' Betty added.

Agatha and O'Malley were fascinated.

The kitchen door opened and Molly, just back from a long and muddy walk stepped in with encrusted wellies and stained Barber and did a double take,' GOOD GOD! . . . I thought you were dead. . . . Didn't you have A.I.D.'s or something?' Molly could always be relied on to be blunt and boldly go where wise men fear to tread and fools leap blindly.

Betty gasped and put her hand to her mouth,' MOLLY!'

'What?' Molly was blind to her faux pas.

David was stunned into silence momentarily and just stared at Molly, then recovered,' Why Mucky Molly in the flesh, you always did grub for maximum exposure!' David was no back page in the lexicon of insults and years of sneers had given him the skin of a rhino and taught him the wit of Wilde.

While Agatha and O'Mally looked on with fascination, not quite au fait with the run of things, or the implications, but never the less enthralled.

'I think you owe David an apology.' Betty almost ordered.

'For what. . .I was just saying. . .I thought it was common knowledge!' Molly snorted,' What you can't tell the truth these days, or something.'

'You're beyond the pale Molly and you know it.' Betty turned to David,' I'm sorry. . . er Molly's been under a lot of strain lately, what with Cuddly going.'

'No I'm Not and stop apologizing for me. . .I'll say what I like, when I like and to who I like. . . you're not the matron here, although you act like it.' Molly reacted angrily to being reprimanded and didn't believe in apologizing for anything, if people didn't like what she said or did that was their problem.

She turned on her heel and flounced out slamming the door behind her with such force that a pane of glass shattered.

O'Malley was warming to the place, it was a grand craic altogether and he regretted not visiting sooner,sure the entertainment was mighty and still his meter ran on.

'Any danger of another coffee?' Agatha piped up.

FERRY ACROSS THE RIVER.

It was a sad soft day in September, already a distinct hint of summers passing and the fresh approach of Autumn wafting gentle magic in the warm breeze. St Mary's was already packed and there were more outside, some spilling from Dick Mac's across Green Street where they had dropped in for a stiffener before the sombre service. The hearse was drawn up outside with Jerimiah in close attendance and Enoch swaying from an early fortifying brandy and fingering his lucky silver dollar was arranging the wreaths, with customary afore thought Jerimiah had arranged a few of his business cards within handy reach of the mourners.

A knot of people had gathered to point and stare at a swarm of bees that had settled on the church wall just below Harry Clarkes stained glass window. A wise women who kept bees herself was happy to reassure those wary of the visitation.'t'is a mark of respect, bees attending a funeral. . . rare enough all the same, but not unknown in these parts,'

Manuka was every bit an agricultural class of a women, never out of wellies, her weathered and mud stained raincoat tied with red baling twine and her scarf of many colours knotted tightly beneath her ruddy and stubbly chin. God had declined to grant her femininity and instead bestowed country wisdom and an indomitable spirit. Word had spread around town and many had turned out to satisfy curiosity or as a mark of respect and a few were there for the craic and the prospect of a grand wake, even though few of the locals had the foggiest idea who the deceased was.

Cuddly had been a good customer at Dick Mac's and a wreath from Oliver and staff was prominently displayed in the bar ready to be taken over as soon as the ad hoc pre wake was interrupted for the main event in the church.

Both Agatha and T.J. had made an effort and turned out in their best bib and tucker, although the more discerning would have been hard put to notice the difference, but as ever it's the thought that counts and to be fair they both had a limited wardrobe to choose.

Camp David whose flair for the outrageous was blatently apparent eyed the talent and asked those that took his eye ' if they were a friend of Dorothy,' which intrigued all and worried Dorothy Baum especially as she had no idea who the dark lunatic was and what interest he had in her acquaintances.

'Ah Betty, I was hoping you might tell me a bit more about Bunty,' Father Cayetano probed, never having knowingly met her,' she was a good Catholic, no doubt?. . . God rest her soul . . . I can't remember her face, was she in the congregation regularly?'

'Well lately she's hardly managed to get from her bed, but she spent a great deal of time here and at the grotto outside before that,' Betty fudged, bemused at the thought of Cuddly embracing anything other than the bottle and a good time.

'Argh good my child, the lord will welcome her to his bosom sure enough, grand so' He surveyed the assembly and nodded approvingly, ' she was popular all the same, it's a grand crowd.'

Betty glanced around, not knowing more faces than she recognized,'it looks that way.' She replied evasively and was saddened that no close relatives had come, although in truth she didn't know if any existed.

She'd contacted Bunty's solicitor to inform him and he's said he would do what was required. It was only then she found out that Elizabeth 'Bunty' Edwina Edwards was Cuddly's name and the solicitor released funds to pay for her cremation asking that Betty make the arrangements and enclosing a small payment for her trouble.

The toxic trio were early arrivals making sure they had cat bird seats with an unrivalled view of all and sundry and would be all the better informed, so, Morena had already scanned Cuddly's medical records and they had been dutifully scandalized as the outrageous strumpet that the good lord must surely turn away from eternanal salvation, less she taint the righteous minority.

'May the Holy Father in all his compassion forgive her sins and point out the error of her ways.' Nora made the sign of the cross and gave the good father an appraising eye,' he's a fine man with a gentle touch.'

Morena gave Nora a double take, noting her friends obvious and inappropriate interest in the priest,' Jesus loves a sinner. . . God knows there's enough of them. . . his work will never cease'

Those that could seated themselves in the pews and settled to watch the mourners while they waited for the service to begin, taking particular interest in the hotchpotch of Dungiggin residents.

'Isn't that your fella Morena?' Kitty pointed to the front row where Pat was consoling a very distraught Lucy, one arm dangling around her shoulder while he offered a half bottle of Powers whisky with the other hand.

Enoch swaying all the more had been guarding the coffin and arranging last minute adornments to the coffin lid passed up by close drinking chums, spotted the bottle and lurched over to offer further comfort and support.

'Sure he's a powerful man with great compassion, a strong shoulder to cry on.' Morena blustered attempting to convince herself as much as any other, barely concealing her true embarrassment and contempt for him.

The good father moved to call order and the coughing and spluttering began to decline, although the whispering continued unabated and babies and small children were heard if not seen and Lucy sobbed. The service progressed at a snail's pace and it became increasingly apparant that Father Cayetano had no idea who Cuddly was and how her life had unfolded, he talked of her great piety, strength of spirit within (which was 40% correct in a certain sense) and characteristic probity.

Tic Tac wedged in a corner happily played with his new super phone, which allowed him to surf the net for the latest horse racing results, watch unlimited porn, even out in the bog, or on a desolate clifftop and in this case in the house of the Lord.

'What did yer man say?' Agatha whispered to T.J. as he hadn't understood one word and was feeling desperate for a pee,' how long does this thing go on for?'

T.J. had nodded off and had began to snore, so Agatha gave him a good natured elbow in the ribs.'you're missing the main event.'

Tic Tac gleefully watching a spider torment a fly in a web until he grew bored and poked his chubby finger into the middle and destroyed it before switching his attentions to the oriental porn on his mobile phone and then to scrutinised the boobs of the women.

Mutton fidgeted uncomfortably in his seat as his little problem below had decided to tease and torture his ring of fire, which was hot as hell, besides which his sciatica was at him and his left leg was increasingly unbearable. Shabin had booked him an appointment in the county hospital in Tralee, meanwhile she had prescribed pain killers and a walking stick, which he tapped irritably while wishing he was elsewhere.

Betty scanned the crowd and noticed that the local congregation were more in tune with the service than those that knew and lived with Cuddly and wondered how it had got to this and began to have misgivings about their isolation from the cut and thrust of the city. Betty groaned inwardly as she recognized Mrs Harpy, the professional mourner and rapacious predator of wakes and post event refreshments. She glanced at Molly who was playing with her mobile, she'd never had much time for Cuddly and made no bones about it, having only come to the service as a favour to Betty, she didn't feel it necessary to make any further pretense beyond her presence. Betty then looked at each of the others from Dungigin and saw that not one was taking any interest, or paying any reverence to the ceremony, bar Lucy who was still weeping copiously, but then she would have been equally upset if she's happened across a roadkill rabbit. As she sat listening to the priest waffling away and going through the motions of ceremony, Betty began to drift into a muse, pondering the true meaning of friendship and just how much the years of companionship really meant.

Would she really mourn the passing of Mutton, or he her passing, whichever way around it happened? What of Molly, Lucy, or any of the others?
Then again was the ceremony of funeral, the tears shed and the beating of breast at the parting of the ways more about those still living rather than those that had slipped from the agonies of life.
What did it all mean anyway and did any of it actually mean anything to anybody, or anything?' She was dizzied with the whirlwind of anxieties, doubts and thoughts.
The priests grand and seemingly profound words seemed so empty to her, he talked of the glory of things to come, but she wondered how much he truly believed in what he pontificated and then a passing thought that he might be exploiting the devoted and indulging his pecadilos with the naieve and vulnerable.
Suddenly it dawned on Betty that she no longer believed in anything and questioned the validity of everything. Relationships were so transitory and trite, truth was relative and never absolute, she even doubted her own existence and worth, was the dream called life really worth the angst and suffering of living it? Sure enough there were high points when emotionally your soared to the stratosphere but they were all too rare and always unbelievably brief, while the times of hardship and struggle appeared endless.

Sadly Betty was no stranger to the black dogs of depression, they had stalked her on and off over the years. These days, perhaps because so many friends and acquaintances seemed to pass away almost monthly, her dark days seemed more frequent and lasted all too long. She wondered if the others felt the same, she knew Molly had other, perhaps more pressing problems and dismissed Agatha, T.J. and Tic Tac as being too limited in intellect and sensitivity. Lucy was fey to the nth degree and a swatted fly or squashed ant would plunge her into the depths of despair, but then she would rationalize it in her own way and say something like,' well I suppose it will reincarnate and return as something higher up the evolutionary tree.' And be nice and easy and bright and breezy and consult her new internet site. 'Ask Jesus' a live and interactive website where an virtual

Jesus in robe and crown of thorns would ponder the problem and offer guidance.

Lost in thought she had quite lost track of the service and although she had been constantly people watching, the text and progress of the ceremony had moved on without her active participation.

'Miss Crocker.'

Molly nudged Betty,' pstt Betty the sky pilot is calling you!' less of a whisper more of a call to arms.

'I believe Miss Crocker, a very good friend of the late Elizabeth would like to say something.' Father Cayetano smiled graciously and extended the hand of friendship and welcome.

Betty had suddenly lost the confidence and courage required to eulogize Cuddly, but knowing if she didn't then no other would she summoned up the aplomb and stepped forward. Standing next to Cuddly's coffin she silently cast her eyes over the sea of faces, wondering how many would have known Cuddly had she staggered past them in the street. Although a good few had turned out through idle curiosity, others just because there was a service in the church, she felt the vast majority were good people who had made an effort to pay their respects to the passing of another soul, no matter they didn't know her. She was moved and felt the tears welling up and saw that some had noticed and smiled warmly and reassuringly. Sniffing back the tears Betty searched her sleeve for a hankie, blew her nose and dabbed her eyes, cleared her throat and,' er. . . thank you for coming. . . .

'Cuddly, er sorry Bunty would be so touched. I don't really know how many of you actually knew her and in truth those that did would know she had many challenges, which I think she tackled with great courage and good humour. . . . . I'd like to read you something written by a Brian Chalker, it's called A Reason, Season, Lifetime and I think that it's quite appropriate in the circumstances.' She cleared her throat and took a look at the congregation, who shuffled and coughed as one expected.

'People come into your life for a reason, season, or a lifetime. When you figure out which one it is, you will know what to do for each person.' She paused, hoping they understood her message and continued,' When someone is in your life for a reason, it is usually to meet a need you have expressed. They have come to assist you through a difficulty, to provide you with guidance and support, to aid you physically, or spiritualy. They may be like a godsend, and they are! They are there for the reason you need them to be.'

Betty noticed Agatha and T.J. acting the goat and fixed them with her best withering look.

'Then, without any wrong doing on your part or at a convenient time, this person will say or do something to bring a relationship to an end. Sometimes they die, sometimes they walk away. Sometimes they act up and force you to take a stand. What we must realize is that our need has been met, our desire fulfilled, their work is done. The prayer you sent up has been answered. . . and now it is time to move on.'

Pausing briefly to gather her breath, she nervously scanned the crowd,'. . . When people come into your life for a season it is because your turn has come to share, grow, or learn. They bring you experience of peace or make you laugh. They may teach you something you have never done. They usually give you an unbelievable amount of joy. Believe it!. . . It is real. . . But only for a season.' The sound of sobbing was audible and she saw Lucy Lastic in tears and being comforted by Pat and his hip flask, with Enoch adding his shoulder to cry on whilst swigging from the flask.

'Lifetime relationships teach you lifetime lessons; things you must build upon to have a solid emotional foundation. Your job is to accept the lesson, love the person, and put what you have learned to use in all other relationships and areas of your life.' With a deep sigh of relief she finished,' Thank you very much for bearing with me, I hope Bunty's passing has taught us all something.. . . I know she would have been delighted that her years were not wasted. . . once more thank you for coming, it is appreciated.'

Away over in a far flung corner Tic Tac had obviously found something very satisfactory to drool over on his phone and Betty was in no doubt as to the nature of it.

Ten minutes later Jerimiahs lads carried the coffin to the hearse and the congregation followed, Enoch had drawn the short straw and was to drive the coffin to the crematorium in Dublin. As the door of the hearse closed and Cuddly started her last long journey the swarm of bees spun into the air and buzzed off en masse causing anxiety, astonishment and awe in equal measure.

Betty lingered long after the hearse and Cuddly Bubbly departed sitting on the bench by the Holy Mary where Cuddly had spent so much of her last few months in desperate hope of some sort of reprieve or salvation, if nothing else. Standing she studied the Virgin Mary and wondered IF? for a few moments, but then turned on her heel and crossed the road to Dick Macs and the bacchanalia which the wake would undoubtedly be. All the usual suspects and a few unsuspecting visitors blowing through, wassailed the night through in ribald, risqué and licentious bawdry. The joint was reelin'an'a rockin as Cuddly would have loved it, wine, women and song, music and laughter, she was remembered for her good times, her warmth of spirit, generosity and toasted repeatedly until Agatha pointed out that she was indeed on her way to be burnt to a crisp. This thought sobered the wake briefly and Tic Tac quipped that by choosing cremation she was cheating the devil, the burning pits of hell and the fires of damnation for all eternity this black humour broke the ice and stoked the warmth of the rave.

'Oh Tic Tac how could you? Lucy sat in as corner feeding pork scratchings to Puck who was never one to miss a celebration, especially one that included food, but even his sensibilities' were seemingly offended by the coarse comment and he upped, pissed on Tic Tacs leg and had it away down Green Street.

'Oh bravo, bravo.!' Triumphed lucy clapping like a performing seal in appreciation.

Amid the cacophony and confusion a blind couple that had somehow blundered into the chaos stood squashed among the revelers but obviously enjoying themselves, somehow it was discovered that the blind couple could sing and play the whistle. They were cajoled and coaxed and finally relented and began. A reverential silence descended and not even a cough or clink of glass broke the sublime song and shrill of pipe that touched heart and soul in a moving lament that told of life won from despair and finally lost in heroic hope and the ultimate triumph of the soul. A very familier tale of Eire through the ages and her people who seemed forever destined to strive through disaster and disappointment for freedom from the constraints and limitations often imposed for no good reason and always to rise again, when within a whisker of succes

'Yea, according to the doctor I'm no human.' Agatha passed around a letter from Shabin's surgery that clearly stated,' the test results on your specimen sent to Tralee hospital for tests indicates that you are a fox. Could you please make an appointment to further discuss this development.'Agatha chortled gleefully and glanced around his merry pranksters for approval.

'O.k., so what's the story?' T.J. asked as expected, playing the straight man in their double act.

With the mischevious glint in his eye of a joker enjoying the attention and sure of grand acclaim, Agatha took a deep breath,' I was farting like a muck spreader with a blown gasket. . . jeez, even I couldn't stand to be near myself. . . So I was away down the doctors. . . did you ever see such a creature as herself on the desk?' Agatha noticed his pint was drunk and nodded to Tic Tac,' You're round I think!'

Tic Tac glanced around in astonishment,' Not me man, I bought the last but one round.'

The wrangling continued for a few moments, until Tic Tac reluctantly conceded that perhaps he was mistaken, but delayed the assault on his wallet as best he could,' Go on man, tell us then.'

'Now so, the doc asks a few questions. . . I'm thinking she's sweet on Dapper you know?' As ever, Agatha's mind was loosly connected and sparked randomly.

'AGATHA!. . . The entire County knows that.' T.J. admonished.' You were saying'.

'She say's I need tests. . .'

Everybody nodded,' I've said that since the day I met you'. T.J. grinned.

' She gave me a little plastic tube to crap into. . . I ask you, how does a man do that?' Agatha shrugged,' anyway I couldn't get the train out of the tunnel and hadn't seen any old friends off to the coast for yonks.' Agatha meaningfully eyed his empty glass and then Tic Tac. 'I like the Doc. . . didn't want to upset her and she said the sooner I gave her some crap the quicker I get sorted. . . Well now what could I do? . . . Then as I'm walking near the barn it comes to me. . . I stepped in the fookain fox's crap didn't I?'

Even T.J. veteran of many a good craic was silently open mouthed gawping like a goldfish. When he eventually recovered the power of speech,' You didn't? . . . you mean you. . .'

'And why not?. . . crap is crap init?'

The day was old as were most of the mourners in body, but the night was young as were the mourners in mind and spirit, and a good few were far beyond the reason of sound sanity, some having spent their lifetimes on the outer rings of sobriety and society.

GOING ACROSS THE RIVER.

'Hey girls how's it going today?' A peep of chickens flocked around Betty's legs expecting grain,' argh Speckled Hen I haven't seen you around for a couple of days, I was beginning to think the Fookain Fox had gobbled you up.' Betty threw a handful of grain down,' well girls did you lay some eggs for me?'
Betty was back from the wake and more than a touch adrift of her moorings, but felt the need to spend some quiet time with the girls down at the chickin' shack.

Her peace was shattered by the insistent ring tone of he mobile which she fumbled for in her apron pocket, 'Hello. . . who?. . .Jerimiah. . .yes. . . WHAT!' She almost dropped the phone and was speechless for a good few seconds as her world spun and twisted,' what did you say?. . . No, no that can't be. . . you are sure. . . that's unreal. . . how could it happen?' She slumped down among the dirt with one hand holding the phone and the other massaging her brow,' I don't know what to say. . . I mean I just don't believe it. . . I can't take it in. . . it's so bizarre. . . you are sure? . . . no, no, yes I'm sorry I do believe you . . . and Enoch. . . how sad, I'm sorry, yes I'll be alright I'm sure, thank you. . . thank you for telling me. . . I'm so sorry, yes goodbye and thank you again.'

Betty sat among the chickens for what seemed an eternity turning things over in her mind, the whole thing was just so weird, things like that weren't meant to happen, but happen they did.
How could anyone ever understand such freaky events?
In a fraction of a second everything could change and the whole world, or at least how one saw it could be so different, it made no sense, but then did anything ever really make sense?
Everything and anything just was and that's how it happens.
Do animals try and make sense of things, or do they just take it as it comes and get on with it, live or die?
Humans, the so called pinnacle of the food chain try and rationalize things, find a pattern, a reason why and worry at a thing until they think they understand, but do they ever, or are they forever deceiving themselves?

Back in the security of her kitchen she met Molly, 'Good God woman you look like you seen a ghost!'

192

Betty just burst into tears and was all of a fluster and fumbled with inconsequential in the kitchen, trying to shake off the shock and perhaps wake from some nightmare and find that she was actually in bed sleeping off too many G & T's.

'Hey, hey what's up. . . come here, sit down,' Molly put her arm around Betty's shoulders and guided her to the chair by the range,'What is it, what's happened?'

' Betty waved halfheartedly,' no, it's o.k., I'm alright, it's just. . . it's, it's Cuddly, there's been an accident. . . '

'AN ACCIDENT, how, what. . . Betty, she's already dead!' Molly was very worried, 'c'mon it's been a long day, what with the service and the wake and everything. . . it's not good to be drinking in the day. . . you're just overtired and emotional . . . look I'll make coffee, you just sit there and warm yourself.'

'No ,no you don't understand, there's been an accident. . . the hearse crashed. . . Enochs dead. . . the hearse caught fire, it's dreadful.' Betty sobbed.

'Molly stared,' what are you saying?' She shook the kettle to check if it had water in it and then placed it carefully on the worktop to give herself a little time to think.' Where. . . how?'

Betty sighed, took a deep breath and reached into her sleeve for a hankie,' They crashed into a milk tanker on some bridge over a river and Enoch was thrown over into the water and carried away. . . the hearse burst into flames and. . . burnt out.' She blew her nose, sniffed and blew it again.

'But that's. . . how weird.' As it sunk in Molly suddenly realized what Betty was saying,' how bizarre!' She had to suppress a nervous giggle,' and Enoch's dead?. . . yes and he was still clutching his lucky silver dollar. A ferryman pulled his body out of the river . . . Don't you see?' Betty looked scared.

'See what? . . that his lucky silver dollar wasn't that lucky!' She replied cynically.

'It's the second death and it's linked to Cuddly. . . I'm worried Molly. . . who's next?'

After a few moments thought Molly smiled reassuringly,' no, it's just a strange coincidence . . . you're reading too much into it. . . it's been a long day, like I said.'

Coffee and banana cake ,Betty's magic cure all elixers calmed feelings and relaxed jangled nerves and slowly,but surely laughter the final refuge of the desperate returned, even though it had a bizarre dark side.

'Do you think we'll get the money back. . . I mean. . . we'll she won't need the crematorium in Dublin now. . . she's burnt toast already. . . know what I mean?' For once Molly meant well and was strictly business as usual.

Betty didn't hear, or pretended not to and busied herself making blueberry muffins to keep herself occupied and take her mind off the negative thoughts that threatened to engulf her. As she emptied the blueberries from the plastic packet a few took it upon themselves to roll away onto the floor,' Damn!. . . do you know Blueberries and honey fight free radicals and are a bit like that themselves. . . The berries always make a futile dash for freedom and end up squashed on the floor and honey is always trying to escape from the jar and make a sticky mess somewhere.' Chatting nervously about inconsequentials helped, but she was just a few tears and a deep breath or two from sobbing into her apron.' Do you remember when we were free radicals? . . . We thought we knew it all and our dash for freedom from the stifling grip of the old greys was sex, drugs and rock'n'roll.. . . . and now look at us. . . two old wrinklies once degenerate, now just decayed!'

'I try never to think of dried apricots and prunes, it's so depressing. . . I'm still a juicy peach in my head and you should think the same,' Molly was quick to move on,'Do you think Styx will give us a refund?' Molly persisted, hoping to evade deep reflection on advancing age and physical decline.

'MOLLY. . . you're outrageous,' then Betty laughed,' really, whatever next?'

'Betty, Betty.' Lucy burst in through the back door, which still had hardboard replacing the glass that Molly had broken in her fit of temper, ' I've had a dream.'

'That's called your life,' Molly quipped,' you're in a perpetual daydream if you ask me.'

' You're having a go at me again,' Lucy cried,' Why ? . . . What did I ever do to you?'

Molly glared at Lucy,' You really don't remember do you?'

Betty looked quizzically from one to the other, wondering what Molly meant,' Molly?'

Lucy was equally puzzled,' remember what?'

'That's for me to know and you to worry about and it suits me for you to stew until either your memory returns or I decide to enlighten you.' Molly was evidently getting a huge kick out of having something on Lucy,' they say revenge is a dish best served cold and as yet it ain't icy enough.. . . I'll wait for the hard winter of your discontent.'

'Revenge?. . . revenge for what?' Lucy was perplexed,' I've never done anything to you. . . this isn't fair!'

'Molly. . . she's right. . . if there is some issue between you then it's best out in the open.' Betty appealed.

'Never give a sucker an even break and I'll break you yet sucker..' Molly hissed.

Lucy burst into tears and ran out of the kitchen.

'Molly what's wrong with you?' Betty was seriously concerned, over the past few months she noticed that

194

Molly was increasingly cantankerous and tended to forget the simplest things, like unplugging the iron and turning off taps,' you might not have noticed but you've changed. . . you're intolerant and angry just about all the time and you keep forgetting things.'

'SO DO YOU!' Molly snapped.

'I know we all have senior moments and get to the top of the stairs and can't for the life of us remember why we went up them in the first place, but. . .' Betty felt awkward and embarrassed, but thought that her friend needed help,' I don't know how to say this, but I really think you should go and see Shabin. . . I'll go with you if you want.'

'There's nothing wrong with me,' Molly said defensively.

'Molly ?' leaning her head to one side, Betty smiled,' Be honest. . . I've been to the doctors with you and. . . well we've both got our little problems. . . it goes with the territory, age isn't on our side, is it?'

'I'm no wrinkled old prune, even if you think you are!' Molly snapped and turning sharply on her heal flounced out. Betty felt terrible, more than ever she believed her friend had a problem and she was convinced Molly also knew and was in denial. Perhaps her motives were selfish, but from what little she'd heard and read and if her worst fears proved correct then the long term care for Molly was going to be challenging and something she considered she couldn't handle.

Just after Dawn Betty took one of the bikes and cycled the couple of miles to the strand, there was promise in the morning, a warm sun rising, a fresh breeze and the sound of surging surf and screeching seagulls diving into a school of fish. She wandered aimlessly enjoying the fading waves wash over her espadrilles and let the strings of thoughts pop and drop through her mind at the same time watching the morning work the magic of just another day. An incredible miracle too often overlooked and unappreciated.

She remembered for no apparent reason that mad mother Jack the hat, he with the beak like nose and always the top hat with two playing cards tucked into the brim, the ace of hearts and the ace of spades seemingly always away on acid and constantly chattering about nothing of consequence. She smiled to herself as she recalled his winter adventure, driving 'Bobby on the Beat's' truck back from some far flung northern gig one bitter January night he had pulled into the Blue Boar service station on the M1 to fuel up. A group of greasy grunts on motorbikes, would be hell's angels, as he told it, couldn't help but notice the lipstick graffiti and love lorn messages covering the truck, obviously a group in transit. Before even he could open the door they were

battering the metal with fists and helmets, discretion being the better part of valor and pure self-preservation pervading, Jack shoved the truck into gear and put pedal to the metal and burnt 2000 miles off the tyres. Five minutes down the motorway the bikers swooped swerving in front of him, shaking fists and chains and intent on mayhem and perhaps murder. With the imminent possibility of serious inury or death weighing heavily on his mind Jack coaxed all speed from the tired transit and eventually outran them, or maybe they just gave up, anyway they faded out of the cracked rear view mirrors. Every experienced roadie knew about the 24 hour petrol station just off the motorway in the middle of nowhere and he exited stage left and got there just before the petrol gauge dropped from the bottom of the red into a long frozen walk with can in hand. Jack looked out into the cold dark night and turning to a quietly dozing Lewis,his co roadie,' I'm going outside,' he opened the door and an icy blast gripped him,' bleeding hell it's brass monkeys out here. . . I may be some time.'
As he rounded the rear of the vehicle he was confronted with a huge greaser standing on the rear step of the truck fingers in a frozen grip in the roof rim,' bugger me it's Jack Frost.' According to legend he was chipped off, shivering visibly within his black leather and was last seen dragging his sorry carcase into a bleak blizzard.

Funny thing random thought, each new and fleeting memory seemingly unconnected, without reference to time or place and the next as the previous just as arbitrary.
She was fascinated by the shifting and billowing cloud patterns and shadows projected onto the sea, which reflected distinct colour variations as if living and breathing like the rise and fall of a human body in breath. Here turquoise, then lilac,green and definitely light blue morphing into crashing white horses. Among the foam flecked waves, fronds of dark kelp rolling and tumbling, briefly revealed before being swallowed amid the turmoil and tempest.

Although seemingly wild, there is repetition to nature, which changes over time, but the variations are subtle and slow to human perception and not immediately apparent. It is raw, cruelly clawing every which way to impose, destroy, evolve, transform and create, however fleeting a reality for a few moments and is ultimately overwhelming. Alone on the beach Betty was confronted by the pain and constraint of thought which was often to much to bear, an unwelcome burden. The angst and anxiety always a self-induced punishment projected out of all proportion to the perceived misjudgment.
She guessed that for other living things it was different, with no apparent preconception of what the future might bring there could be no fear or apprehension, just the sudden trauma of the moment in which life might prevail,

or death overtake and then what. . . nothing. . . or another day in another way?

More often these days she found herself considering the vexed question of life and death, total oblivion or something more to come for better or worse, perhaps it was the stark fact that she was now nearer the end of this life than the beginning. She now knew more that had passed than remained and in an odd way was reassured by this, if the likes Cornish and Cuddly could just let go, then she would have no problem, but then it wasn't her prerogative to choose between living and dying.

Like all in youth the energy and enthusiasm to lead life with no thought of mortality entices one to reckless adventure without care and consideration, but accident, injury and lifestyle encountered return to haunt and torment in later years and demand due payment. All things change, but time is rarely on the side of the underdog, no matter how needy and no wealth is sufficient to postpone the inevitability of age, decline and the dying of the light.

Betty's gaze was drawn to a dark shape out at sea and she narrowed her eyes to better see, but then it was gone, she mused on the waves ending a journey of over 3000 miles from East Coast America and then saw the dark shape again. Shielding the glare with her hand she recognized the magic of a basking shark and was overcome with emotion and wonder, feeling that nature had granted her a rare privilege.

Betty rested against a rock to watch and then a cacophony of cawing and shrieking birds drew her attention a grassy ledge on the cliffs, it seemed like hundreds of crows or rooks had gathered and were chattering in an agitated manner. At first she thought a fox or dog was worrying them, but closer scrutiny showed that they were mobbing a single bird and almost like a criminal court they appeared to be directing their anger at this seemingly forlorn feathered creature. As she watched the level of acrimony seemed to increase and a number of the assembled birds started to jump of the ground flutter their wings and dart at the poor lonesome crow. Then suddenly there was chaos as what seemed the entire murder of crows did just that and tore the single bird to pieces with feathers and flesh floating and falling, a colony of gulls rose as one from their nesting sites on the cliffs and whirled and wheeled over head as if witnessing some mighty conflict. With the dark deed done, leaving Betty with no notion of what she had witnessed or why it happened the mob dispersed and a relative calm returned. She was stunned, horrified and fascinated seemingly unable to move a muscle as she desperately tried to make some sense from what appeared to be rough justice. Minutes passed and she increasingly felt a cold chill both in the wind and in her spirit wondering at the woeful world and the cruelty and callous nature of all that inhabited it. Then the gulls swarmed in to scavenge the fresh meat, fighting each other for the tastiest morsels; nothing was wasted in the natural world and life continued unabated.

The day was now into its stride and away over on the far side of the strand a lone figure walked dogs and a knot of surfers prepared to ride the waves, for Betty the best of the beach was gone and she made her way back still contemplating the big questions, but more content and maybe a touch optimistic.

RUNNING AND HIDING.

Rocks nights were long and sleep was short. No matter the distractions it was harder by night to evade the dark demons. Years of running free had spun enough rope and now the noose was inextricably tightening and he was choking on his own hogwash.

Dr Bobilad in Harley Street was only too happy to help, prescribing a course of hypnotic sleepers, which naturaly came at a cost. But Amitripyline plunged Rock further into a prolonged phantasmagoria that terrorised both night and day as the dead dogged his every moment.

He was hammered by retribution at every twist and turn with nowhere to run and nowhere to hide. Always an arrogant and aggressive island with an attitude of attack to defend a profound inferiority complex, Rock quickly developed a fierce anti social stance that alienated potential friends. Known to be aloof and stubborn the further distance he put between himself and his dwindling circle went unnoticed and without remark.

He stood alone and strangely vulnerable, like a hanging rock on a cliff, just a matter of time until a fierce storm blew it over the edge.

Patsy was obsessed and not easily distracted from her chase of the fox on the run. She could go for months with no hint of intrigue, or slacious scandal about Rock and then something juicy and nasty would crawl from the woodwork and inflame her passionate pursuit.

Whispers in the wind, morsals discreetly overheard, the grumblings of the many disenchanted and the malicious intent of those teased and tortured over time. The sleazy and sordid sewers that hacks trawled for stories inevitably polluted them in turn.

Having bathed far too long in such swamps, the graduate from university eager to right injustice and expose the wicked for the betterment of mankind had become soiled herself and blinded to truth. Patsy no longer saw trees, only dense woods where mischevious shadows lured the lost deeper into deceit and desperation. Where once she shrank from unreliable tittle-tattle and deliberate falsehood, now she would willingly embrace all, reasoning that the ends justify the means.

It's said that everybody has their price for betrayal and sometimes it's not just the money that whistleblowers crave. Revenge, envy and the rejection of love, are powerful inducements. Although few will turn down financial compensation to ease conscience and enhance recovery.

PASSIONATE PROGRESS.

After weeks of emotional torment and turmoil, Shabin had made up her mind to stand by her man and give herself to him. In so doing she was willfully rejecting centuries of custom and tradition. She sincerely wished she had another woman she could consult. But alone in a foreign country she had nobody she could trust and although she had toyed with the idea of calling a friend back home, she had finally rejected it as somebody over there could have no idea of life in Eire. Also her secret might leak and her reputation and the respect for her family name and social standing back home would be besmirched. It was probably the hardest decision she had ever made and Shabin had spent many very early mornings awake in turmoil, serenaded by the early birds in search of unfortunate weevils and worms.

She was unsure how to let Dapper know without sounding like a loose women; a harlot losing all self respect and dignity and was even more concerned about the actual emotional and physical mechanics of the exercise. She of course knew what went where and how it all fitted together and even the expected end result, but it was all academic and somewhat removed from the actuality and all things between were somewhat of a mystery and she had never actually handled a penis, even in the call of duty. She thought about slipping into the library and checking the sex manuals but worried that if discovered the entire peninsula would soon know and she would be an object of ridicule. It was all so difficult, she now the good catholic girls that came to her surgery in search of a little something to help them through their honeymoons. Then of course there were the added anxieties andcomplications of just what was accepted as normal and what was kinky, fellatio for instance. Did Dapper expect that and if so should she allow him to ejaculate in her mouth and if he did what would it taste like and would she instantly vomit. What should she wear and were her practical white cotton knickers just a little too sensible, maybe she should go into Tralee for something a little more erotic. Shabbin wondered if it was always so difficult for a woman or maybe it was just a conflict of moral codes and culture that complicated the issue. She was aware that Dapper was vastly experienced and very conscious that she could easily make a fool of herself as she fumbled like some naive virgin.

'Doctor I'm going now, I've to make ham sandwiches for my Pat's fishing,' Morena shouted,' You'll make sure you lock up,' Morena listened for a few moments, but got no reply and so tutting with irritation

201

climbed the stairs to Shabin's office. 'Doctor are you alright?'

Shabin sat at her desk, deep in thought and didn't hear Morena.

'Are you ill?' Morena entered the office and saw Shabin daydreaming and immediately suspected her of sampling the drugs cupboard. 'DOCTOR, I SAID ARE YOU ALRIGHT?' she bellowed,

thinking 'that's just what I need right now. A dopey doctor.'

'Sorry!. . . yes, yes. Oh it's you Morena,' Startled, Shabin replied,' Oh I'm sorry I was just thinking about something. . . did you want me?'

Morena's devious and suspicious mind crashed into gear and she considered that Shabin was pregnant,' I was just going. . . but I could stay a little longer if you want. . . is there a problem? . . . I'd be more than happy to talk it over with you, if you want.' She said perhaps a mite to eagerly.

'No, no thank you. . . I'm fine. Of course you can go home, don't worry I'll lock up,' Shabin stood up,' I'm just going myself anyway.'

Oh, well if you're sure,' Morena said with a large degree of disappointment,' your sure, I really don't mind.' Shabin made a great play of tidying her desk,' thank you, goodnight Morena. . . I'll see you tomorrow.' Morena was not one to give up easily when she scented a rich source of gossip, she had a nose for it,' I'm a good listener if you did have a problem. . . ' she probed,' they say a problem shared is a problem halved.' She smiled rather weakly,' so how can I help?'

Although Shabin was seen to be a blow in by those born and bred around the peninsula and she still felt herself to be such, but was wise enough to know that Morena wasn't to be trusted.

'I really appreciate your offer, but there really isn't any problem,' Shabin said diplomatically and then sounding much firmer than she felt,' Now I must insist that you go home to your lovely husband.' Visibly deflated Morena turned on her heal,' well don't say I didn't try to help!' she said sharply.

Shabin lived in a liitle cottage just beyond Dingle, among the Elysian fields and this was where Dapper and herself spent most of their time together. Apart from the dance and a couple of visits to treat patients too ill to come to the surgery Shabin stayed away from Dungiggin. She was well aware that her secret love was no secret anymore and the subject of much speculation and some ridicule, but love is a many splendid thing and has ever had the power to vanquish mockery. First love, for this is what it was for Shabin, is pure magic, is pain and pleasure in its seductive lure which is all embracing, nothing is quite like it and nothing is ever the same again. Lovers are united as two souls meld to stand against the world, nothing is too much to endure, as long as you are together. You all but breathe, eat and sleep as one, as you devour each other body and soul, each consumes the other in every which way and there is never enough to sate desire.

Shabin was still a ball of confusion as she closed the surgery door.

'Doctor doctor I need help!' Shabin turned and was confronted by a huge bunch of flowers,' I'm in love with my doctor, I'm desperate, tell me what can I do?'

Shabin parted the flowers to reveal Dapper,' John you fool. . .I love you.' And she kissed him.

'Here you take them they're making my arm hurt.' He trust the roses floating above a cloud of Gypsophila at her and shook some feeling back into his left arm.'

'Thank you John, they're beautiful.' She beamed and then noticing him shaking his arm, ' are you o.k.?'

'Yes my love, it's just the weight of my love. . . it's my heart that aches.' He said earnestly.

'You're heart? . . .John darling what is it?' Shabin was genuinely concerned.

'I need good lovin' quick, Doctor doctor I need your love before my heart bursts.' Dapper smiled endearingly. Shabin melted and suddenly it was all so simple,' John lets get something special for dinner, a nice bottle of wine, I'll cook us a lovely meal,' She hesitated and then said softly,' let's spend the night together.' Shabin blushed and lowered her head endearingly, hoping she hadn't sounded like a cheap slut.

Dapper looked at her, perhaps for a few moments too long and her embarrassment deepened.

'You mean? . .' His voice trailed off and he felt like a pubescent punk on a promise.

Shabing suddenly felt emboldened and looked up into his eyes,' Yes I suppose I do.'

They both smiled and then kissed.

'Would you look at that,' Nora was leaving Supavalue laden down with the weeks shop and still complaining to Kitty about the outrageous ban on carrier bags when she spotted the courting and sparking across the road,

'Trollope!'

'Flahoola,' Kitty echoed,' and she a doctor.'

'They say he has a harem up at the old bar and they get up to all sorts. . . Lord have mercy upon us.' Nora signed the holy cross.

'Would you say they do those kinky things?' Kitty ventured, feeling one of her hot flushes coming on.'and why wouldn't they? . . . I've seen the very thing in the Sunday World. . . you wouldn't think a women would do that, sure.'

'Jeez. . . Are you saying our doctor herself does that. . . disgusting,' Nora thought for a second,' Have you ever wondered what it's like?'

'NORA!. . . what ever are you thinking? Kitty admonished and then spied Pat and Willie staggering down Green Street,' Isn't that your fella Nora?'

Nora blustered with acute embarrassment,' He's, er. . . .He's not been feeling himself these days. . . he's been under the doctor. . .I think he's going down with something.'

'Oh yes, sure maybe you're right.' Kitty said in some disbelief, giving her companion a quizzical eye, friendship would be an overstatement as far as the toxic trio went. Conspirators perhaps, hyenas even ,for they would as readily prey upon each other if some tasty morsel of tittle tattle should transcend the status quo. The lovers all but floated down the road bound up in their own excitement, flowers and laughter,living for each other and the moment, the rest of the world and its woes had ceased to exist. Dapper began to sing,' Zipa de do dah, zippa de day, my oh my what a wonderful day. . . .' and bluebirds and doves circled their heads in their dreams.

A crocodile of kids in fancy dress, all giggles and mischief, with a harassed novitiate struggling to maintain order passed haphazardly on their was to a school pantomime, chanting their lines with a few impish ad libs and in fine form.

'Brian, Lindy behave. I told you two before,you can canoodle when schools out and you're off the premises', Sister Sadie admonished, she trucked no abuse lest one of her headaches plague her and then she might lose all sense of balance and tumble into freefall. 'Jimmie, you too. I saw you pinch Virginia's bottom, please don't interfere with the girls in public. . . you make such a spectacle of yourself.'

Dapper and Shabin watched, amused and entertained.

A few moments later they spied T.J. wheeling a Supavalley shopping trolly along Green Street with Agatha sprawled in it and were stopped in their tracks.

'John, do you think he's had an accident?' Shabin gripped Dappers arm,' Should we find out?. . . Maybe I can help.'

'I think it might be a bit late for that,' Dapper considered,' The only accident that moron's had is birth.'

As they watched a guardai officer approached and they moved within earshot.

'Of course you'll have an explanation for this.' Officer Boyle offered.

Always busking and ever ready T.J. countered,' It's his birthday.'

'Grand. . . and?' Boyle had heard it all before, but with a view to retirement was minded to write his autobiography and was collecting tale tales to spice it up. ' No doubt drink's taken.'

Catching sight of the guardai, Agatha mumbled and struggled to get out.

'Only a few jars, but I think it's the medicine from the doctor,' T.J. shoved Agatha back into the trolly,' he's been a bit strange the last few days'

Shabin looked at Dapper and whispered,' But I haven't seen him for a few weeks, the last time was to send a sample for analysis and I haven't prescribed anything.'

'No your alright. . . he self medicates and anything you might give him wouldn't touch the sides.' No stranger to their mania, but always fascinated Dapper placed a finger on his lips,' listen up, it'll be worth it.'

Boyle was not short of humour,' Fair enough,' He studied the trolley,' is it your coin in there?'

'Yea. . . of course,' T.J. pushed Agatha back,' I was only getting him from Dick Macs to the car park on the harbour.'

Boyle had better things to do and the thought of al that paperwork to add to his already overloaded intray appalled him,' Grand, just you make sure you take the trolley back,' he nodded and walked a few paces and turned,' He'll not be driving?'

ROCKS HARD PLACE.

Patsy Prurient had stumbled across Julian Sandie a disgruntled and much debauched thespian who was fluent in Polari and something of an sesquipedalian. His angelic and youthful face and body had aged and crumbled, as had his confidence, only his despondency and depression had increased. Julian was down on his luck in every way. His last lover, a sailor of ill repute had returned to the sea, or at least the muddy Maldon estuary, where he had a rotting hulk to live out his remaining days with the tang of salt air wafting through the haunting sea mists.

Julians country cottage on the outskirts of town had been engulfed the by creep of urbanization and the corruption of planning laws enjendered by ever increasing populations. His rural idyll was akin to a wagon train surrounded by hostiles, in the shape of three high rise sink estates that loomed over him threatening both in presence and occupants.

On a rare visit to Soho to wallow in past glories he'd popped in for a quick one in the Ku Bar and was squiffy when Patsy and her party of pissed hacks fresh from a freeform press launch rolled in for a late laugh.and a lush. A brief encounter over a spilled drink led to the sordid revelations that Patsy now gloated over.

Sandy in his heyday had mentored his beautiful toyboy David and introduced a confused and precocious new kid on the block to the promiscurity of London's burgeoning and increasingly visible gay scene.

Camp David was flattered and intrigued to receive a phone call offering him an all expenses flying visit to London and a sizeable fee for his recollections and memories and further enjoyed the cloak and dagger secrecy of Patsy's insistence on absolute confidentiality. He didn't get out and about much in 'civilized' company and a fly by night and furtive weekend in old London was most welcome and a chance to look up a few old friends.

'WHAT'S ALL THIS FUCKING OLD COBBLERS ABOUT THEN?' Rock's voice resounded around Buck's office like rolling thunder,' YOU'RE PAID A FAT WEDGE TO CRUSH THE SHIT RUMOURS AND SMEAR TACTICS.' Rock swept the contents of Buck's desk onto the floor in an angry hissy fit of fear and frustration.

Buck was emboldened by these rumours, which in truth he had long suspected and in all honesty long jaded and tired of Rock's vainglorious prima donna tantrums,deciding to retire and enjoy the good life while he still could.

'There isn't a spark of truth to this. Is there?' he emphasized the last two words,' I mean, we wouldn't be buggered if we tried to defend the accusations. Would we?' Buck had waited many a year for his moment and meant to savor it. He spoke calmly with a quiet confidence.

Rock looked agast his mouth opening and shutting soundlessly like a caught cod gasping for life.

He was completely taken off guard and quickly detected that the not so subtle nuance and choice of words betrayed a seismic shift in their volatile and symbiotic relationship which unnerved him.

'You don't think. . . do you believe all this bollocks.' Rock waved the email from Patsy's fluff and feathers seeking a response to the upcoming Sunday shocker.

'Well Rock, in truth you were a wild thing back then.' Buck glanced down at his desk contents reaching for the photo of his nearest and dearest. Fingering the smashed glass which scarred her face, Buck immeadiately regreted it as a glass splinter pierced his thumb,' shit!' The blood and pain a sharp reminder of Rock's previous visit and a spur to his brave new attitude.

'Get an injunction. . . one of those embargo things. . . get that shark Rumpsfeld on the dog, ain't that what I pay legal eagles for?' Rock was pacing the room like a caged beast, his anxiety palpable.

'I have done already. . . he's on the case, but . . .'

'BUT, BUT, but what? . . . .it's that putrid cow Patsy. She always on my case. . . Get a private dick to dish the dirt on her. . . it's common knowledge she's an old lush and I bet she screwed her way through the gutter. . . . How else would the slimy slut get the gig?. . .' Rock chuntered on like the 6.5 special from London to Brighton on the down line.

'Camp David does seem to know rather a lot of very personal. . .quite intimate details about you,' Buck gave Rock and old fashioned look,' you have to own up to that.'

Rock looked puzzled and floundered,' For fuck's sake any motherfucker could find out things like that. . . I've done enough in depth interviews and documentaries. . . you should know.' Rock's embarrassment was obvious. Buck settled back in his comfortable chair and quietly studied Rock increasing his insecurity, uncertainty and bewilderment.

'FOR FUCK'S SAKE BUCK!' Rock implored,' what's got into you?'

'Age most definitely,' Buck savoured the moment,' and perhaps wisdom.'

Rock looked puzzled,' What the blue fuck are you on about? . . . are you on something? . . . did your quack

207

change your happy pills?' His eyes narrowed darkly.

' Rock my friend, do you want to know something?' Buck shifted slightly in his seat to make himself more comfortable.

'Know something?' Rock squirmed, perplexed at the sudden change from a mouse for Rock to tease and manipulate into the cat with a rat to torment. ' What can an old fart like you tell me.' For Rock the best form of defense was always attack, although blunder and bluster was more often counter productive and very much the tactics of a bully.

Buck studied Rock for a few moments, taking the time to choose his words and calm himself,' Rock. . . you're right, I am an old fart. . . a touch older than you and full of hot fetid air. . .and,of course I acknowledge you're an expert in the latter. . . . indeed,over the years I quite possibly taught you a good deal of what you know.'

'You what?' Rock interrupted.

'I'm sorry Rock, was I talking over your head. . . I'll try to keep to language you can understand.' Buck smiled softly,'For too long you've had the arrogance and lumpish belief that you can teach your granny to suck eggs and I for my part the greed and timidity to bend with the wind and hold my tongue.'

' And, your point?' Rock floundered, not even sure what he'd heard.

'You missed the writing on the wall. . . you remember the days when the walls in Ladbroke grove were scrawled with 'Rock is God?'

'Yea, the good old days when the kids were alright and knew where it was at.' Rock smirked.

'Wrong!. . . I gave some spotty Herbert a fiver and a handful of purple hearts to daub the walls and tenement blocks, he never heard of you and wondered why I wanted to call a bit of stone God, but money and uppers talked.' Pausing to allow Rock to take his words in, buck noticed another cherished memento on the bookshelf and reached across to retrieve it.' Remember this?' He waved a brass guitar with nun- such's name on. Rock looked at the award,' yea,' he grinned,' our first real prize!'

Buck laughed,' Now what was it,'' the group of the year as voted by our readers'', or some such crap. . . that cost us £500. to the paper. . . remember the band 'Logos?'

Rock gave a moments thought,' naw. . .who they?'

' My point exactly. . . They were the other group of the year, but they could only offer £450. to be group of the

208

year, we outbid them. . . they folded six months later.' He ran a finger over it,' bit pony really, don't you think?'

Rock stopped pacing the floor as the peaks of his career were trashed before him,' So. . . all that proves is money talks. . . cash is king?'

Buck was enjoying toying with Rock like a cat teasing a mouse,' Your first single,' Ghost in the machine' made number five in three weeks right?'

Rock was getting decidedly uncomfortable,' and?'

'Two grand, a rent boy, a Spanish whore and buying a few 45s in the right shops at the right time!' Buck was emboldened and growing in confidence by the minute, a personal quality that had long eluded him in the fog of commercial intrigue.

'I don't understand. . . ' Rock began.

'You never did. . .' Buck interrupted,' how could you? . . . You've never risen above the gutter in character, intellect or social skills!' Buck delighted in his swan song as Rock's manager, having waited a lifetime to find his true voice,' and close your mouth you look like a fish out of water!'

There was a knock on the door and Sharon poked her head, 'Refreshments?'

'FUCK OFF!' Rock kicked the door shut.

With studied deliberation Buck picked up his desk intercom from the floor, checked the leads were connected and flicked the switch,' Hello Mark, actually I would quite like a milky tea. . . You'd be best to knock before you come in, it would be a shame to spill it.'

Rock glared at Buck,' Bastard, you ain't got me rattled. . . remember I've seen you at work before. . . the old crappy chair next to the full on radiator ploy and making everybody who comes to see you stew in their nervous sweat out side your door while you watch them on the old closed circuit screen.' Snarling like a cornered carnivore with full on contempt, barely concealing his clammy fear Rock jabbed his finger wildly, mentally stabbing his antagonist.

Another apprehensive knock at the door.

'Come in it's safe enough.' Buck arched an eyebrow quizzically as he looked at Rock.

Sharon walked nervously forward, the tea slopping down the mug as she gingerly steered a course to the desk,she handed Buck an email, which he studied with an increasing grin. 'I think this is for you.' He handed it to Rock.

Sharon, might only have been youthfully naieve in most things, but she knew a storm when she saw it coming and quickly ducked out.

'Would Rock care to comment on the story that will be published on Sunday. I would be happy to meet at his convenience. Anyway, anyhow, or anywhere for an in depth interview. Love Patsy xxx.'

NEWS OF THE SCREWS.

' Camp David is staying on over... He's met an old flame in Earl's Court and their doing the rounds.' Betty pointed at the monitor,' Reckons we should buy the News Of the Screws on Sunday, he say's he's in it.'

'Can't wait... what's the old bugger been up to now?... Does he say?' Molly needed glasses, but her vanity overruled her necessities and she squinted at the fuzzy words.

'No, guess we'll have to wait and see... but he does say he's had a nice touch and has got a wedge of readies and is going to blow around with a boyfriend.'

'He'd better keep a few bob for when he gets back he owes me 50 euros.'

Betty looked up,' it's not like you to lend anybody money!'

' What are you saying. I'm the queen of mean?' Molly snapped back techily.

'Don't be silly Molly I was just saying... You've always said only mugs lend dosh.' Betty had the patience of a saint, but Molly stretched her to the limits at times and taxed their friendship with her brusque attitude and short temper.

'I'm going back to bed,' Molly coughed,' I don't need this!'

'Something bad is going to happen,' Lucy was troubled, hardly sleeping a wink all night and what little she managed was plagued with awful nightmares, that left her feeling drained and depressed.

'Something bad is always happening, we live in a nasty, cruel world and nobody gives a shit about anybody else.'

Molly snapped, her mood even blacker than normal, as her occasional waterworks problem was now a daily aggravation and she had developed an uncomfortable rash, with the constant chafing.

'You don't understand, you never have and you never will.' Lucy looked to Betty for empathy,' you know what I mean don't you?'

'Well yes, I do think there's something to Astrology... there's definitely an ebb and flow to all things.' Betty poured herself a coffee,' anybody else?'

'Yes please, decaf.' Lucy replied, reassured that Betty was taking her seriously.

'The way I see it is everything has a reason and season. . . I think it's narrow minded to think otherwise,' Betty cradeled the cup in both hands.

'You're as batty as she is!' Molly chided,' you'll be telling me you believe in her alians down in the glade next.' She banged her half drunk coffee cup down on the table and stomped out.

'Oh dear, Molly's always so difficult,' Lucy was genuinely upset, her eyes glazed,' She keeps saying that I did something to her, but I didn't! . . . You know me Betty, I'm not like that.'

' Yes, I know. . .' Betty hesitated searching for the right words,' . . . I am a little worried about Molly. She gets more difficult by the day and I think she's not admitting to herself that she's got some sort of a problem.'

'What sort of a problem?' Lucy was concerned,' something serious?'

'I'm not a doctor, but yes. . . although we mustn't start jumping to conclusions, obviously.' Betty smiled reassuringly,' . . . we can only support her and suggest things, we can't live her life for her and we must be patient.'

'Oh Betty, you're so wise. . . You should set up an advice website . . . a daily blog, I know it would be a great success and help so many people.'

Although feeling calmer, Lucy decided to have a therapy bath and gathered up the bag of specially formulated herbs that Mother Shipton had sold her and headed off for one of the bathrooms. As the slightly peaty brown water alternatively spluttered and gushed into the bath, challenging the ancient and temperamental plumbing, which loudly complained in a cacophony of whistling and banging, Lucy struggled to lock the door.

Carefully placing candles in the cardinal points and lighting incense to banish the bad karma and lingering bog odours. Lucy recited her affirmative mantras, pressed play on the cd player and Tibetan chants filled the room. Already drifting into a comfortable sense of serene serendipity, she slipped off her clothes to enter the warm waters among the floating leaves of fragrant tranquility.

Agatha had a pressing need to pee, he and T.J. had stumbled onto a cache of cheap and very rough scrumpy and dedicated their afternoon to quaffing to hearts content and bladders fill.Over the years they had subjected their kidneys and liver to extreme, exacting and often excruciating abuse in their efforts to escape reality and sate their appetite for excess. Thus far they were lucky, or perhaps undiagnosed and ignored any symptoms of a deterioration in function and fluidity, not that they had ever been totally aware of normal bodily habits and performance. They had no concept of litres in and pints out, nor safe guidelines in units of alcohol, their only limitations were purchasing power and empty bottles.

'That's it man, I gotta point percy at the porcelain!' Agatha was up and trotting, clutching his fundamentals in desperation, the bloated ache and heat of a bladder overdue for evacuation relegating any other thought, or desire to the distant margins.

Like a bull crashing unceremoniously into a china shop, Agatha burst asunder the broken lock and without further ado whipped out his member, reached one hand to the wall to support his swaying and sprayed the bowl. 'Aw Jeez. . . that's great.' He hummed a happy tune, eyes closed and relief sweeping over him.

Lucy had her head under the water and her eyes closed, at the moment, luxuriating in warm sensory serendipity, her mind adrift in cosmic comfort.

Reality came to both in sudden shock.

Agatha had turned having shaken off excess droplets, his pride and joy, hanging, it had to be said, somewhat limply from his open flies and lucy had surfaced to top up with warmer water.

'FECK!' Agatha exploded, taking in Lucy in all her naked glory, with an assortment of herbal leaves clinging to her body at random,' it's a fecking mermaid in a fruit salad, with giant knockers.' He said with some delight, then aware that all was dangling before him he reached down to tuck it away, perhaps rather too hastily,' Oh Fuck, oh holy shit!' prick and zip were as one, a flesh and metal entanglement and somewhat painfully at that. Oh My God!' Wide eyed and open mouthed in embarrassment, Lucy splashed back, like a whale after breaching, with the resultant testimony to Archimedes and his grand, if damp theory, the waters parted and gushed to flood the floor in biblical proportion.

THREE WISE MEN.

'... And I say, reality is shadows in a cave with distant voices... mere glimpses of half truths... just tantalizing illusions and dellusions that the naïve and stupid seize upon to build empires in sand.'

Franklin Rumford slammed his drained pint glass down on the beer garden table triumphantly. Bald headed, but for thin grey wispy sideburns, with thick bi focal glasses and an owl like presence, he warmed his hands by the outdoor heater. 'Do you think a child has the same sense of being and perception as an adult?... or a butterfly that of a caterpillar... what can an ant know of an elephant, or indeed the reverse?'

'I think I'll have baked Alaska for pudding & a cup of black coffee... ' Mortimer Madas, was a sensualist and a bon vivant, who'd made a fortune out of sash windows,' that soup was seriously good.'

'Do you think of nothing, but your stomach? Franklin quizzed with some exasperation,' here are we debating the meaning of life and you talk of nothing but food and drink!'

'My dear Frankie,' Mort well knew that Franklin was a stickler for his full Christian name, but delighted in winding his verbal sparring partner up,' Life is of the moment... there is no tomorrow and yesterday is gone... death is nothing, a non existence,' He smiled,' life has no meaning, and were I to discover otherwise I might well find it was one I disliked, or disagreed with.' Hawk like in looks and demeanour and always keenly aware, Mort never let opportunity elude him.

Glimpsing Geal and Skeeter sitting in a corner watching and listening carefully, he ventured,' When I was 42, I thought I knew what it was all about and then I banged my head and it knocked some sense into me.' He grinned and winked at them,' I don't suppose you're in need of some good quality sash windows?'

' No, not today... but thanks for the offer , all the same.' Geal picked up his copies of 'Golem xiv' and 'Star Diaries'. And returned his attentions to Skeeter,' read these, it's food for thought.'

'Science Fiction's not really my thing... what with being only a woman... I'm more chic lit' Skeeter tilted her head to one side coquettishily. ' What would I know about strange ideas and weird notions?'

'Oh yea!' Geal raised his eyebrows, remaining unconvinced.

A third member of the old codgers, Bobby Hooker had been silently staring into space, distracted by a distant muse. The answer to all the big questions was always on the tip of his tongue, but ever elusive to the word, which continually frustrated him. He spent his nights staring into microscopes and telescopes, had a enduring fascination for Jupiter and its moons and was proud of the fact that he'd created his own watch, which he displayed at every opportunity. Although a consummate intellectual, accomplished in astronomy and horology, he was curiously adrift in the practicalities of the secular. His belt and braces had been broken some time in the distant past and his trousers hung precariously, held aloft, only by a piece of elastic around his waist tyed with an impressive reef knot.

'I believe we are children of the stars, seeded by a superior life form as an experiment and are being studied with a view to further populating the universe.' The others were astounded, in all their regular Thursday lunch meeting, Bobby had rarely said anything of consequence, mostly he just studied his watch intently every few minutes, tapped it gently and murmered about the passage of time.

Bobby himself was as surprised as any and hardly believed he'd spoken and felt compelled to apologise, ' I'm. . er. . . I'm sorry.' He scratched at his unkempt beard nervously,' I just meant. . . er,. Well it seems to be the only logical answer, given the circumstances.'

'No, no, not at all Bobby.' Franklin stared at him, entirely unsure what to think,' I'd go so far as to say we've waited a long time for your valued opinion.' He turned, with a mischevious glint in his eye' don't you agree, Mortimer?' He emphasized his protagonists name.

'Oh without doubt, definitely most interesting.' Mort said without conviction, . . . on second thought, maybe I'll just have the fruit fool.'

Franklin had an imposing air of presence and authority, seemingly a natural leader and knew when to steer a conversation onto a new topic, before apathy and boredom set in. ' I was reading that Yorkshire men lack the social aptitude demanded by polar adventure. . . They have a dour and unforgiving nature which isn't condusive to the close proximity of companionship required when snowed in for days on end in small spaces.'

'Is that a fact.' Mort replied nonchalantly, still considering what desert to have.

'I was once in the Arctic circle, it was 41 below on occasion and on average 26 below, most interesting.'

Franklin continued unabated, with the bit between his teeth he was indefatigable and little concerned with any protestation.

Bobby was back beyond the pedestrian and only dimly aware of the here and now, having found the temerity to postulate his extraordinary theory he had again retreated to intellectual contemplation..

'Could that be the reason you have no offspring?' Mort teased,' I'd be so bold as to suggest there were few brass monkeys there abouts.'

Franklin ignored the quip and continued,' the day was as night and long enough and I read the Norse sagas by a log fire whilst imbibing a rather fine Islay whisky.' Franklin glanced down at his empty glass,' I was particularly taken with the good ship 'Naglfar', built entirely from the finger and toenails of the dead. . . You're round I think Mortimer old boy!'

Geal and Skeeter were replete, but reluctant to leave the entertainment, it was much like an existential play, 'Waiting for Godot' perhaps and they briefly wondered if Dick Macs had contrived to supply cabaret. The dogs, who had lain quietly through out, anticipated the off and were up alert and eager to be gone, as if they knew of the adventure to come.

'We'd better go, Sheehan will be waiting and fretting, no doubt about a gathering storm, or some such.'

'A storm?' Skeeter suddenly doubted the wisdom of their journey, even if it was a significant milestone in their relationship.

'No, no don't worry, it was only a turn of phrase. . . I got over alright and Sheenan had no concerns about the weather then.' Geal stood up and eased Skeeter's chair back, turning he nodded to goodbye to the triumvirate of perception. Skeeter just smiled sweetly and took off after the dogs,who's patience was exhausted.

There are some people who dismiss animals in general as mere beasts, without sentient feelings, or an intelligence based solely on instinct and reaction. These are, by and large, people who have never spent any real time with animals and are thus ignorant of what the kingdom of creatures are capable of and can teach homo sapiens. One such was Mortimer, who couldn't tolerate cats, children and dogs, and for that matter most any other living creature that didn't return a healthy profit for the time and space occupied.

Both Geal and Skeeter had noticed that he glared at the dogs from time to time, but didn't pay any heed to it,

216

taking it as no more than the mark of the man.

In leaving, Charity strayed near Mortimer and sniffed at his empty plate, he took exception to the close proximity of a flea bitten bitch invading his personal space and made no bones about the thing. 'Madame, do you mind!' He called after Skeeter, who had already passed.

Skeeter turned, perplexed, as did Geal, who had moved ahead,' I'm sorry?' She asked.

'And so you should be. . . It shouldn't be allowed. . . in fact I'm sure it isn't. . . Dogs and food, my dear, dogs and food.' Mortimers tone was as annoying as it was patronizing.

Franklin rolled his eyes heaven wards and shrugged apologetically. 'Mortimer, Mortimer I'm sure there was no deliberate intention to pester you, on the dogs part.' Franklin smiled at Skeeter,' Take no notice, Mortimer here can be a little tetchy at times, he means nothing by it.'

'Frankie, old chap. . . I'm quite capable os speaking for myself and I know what I know. . . It's just not done and you have to consider the health factor.' Mortimer stated categorically. 'Animals are biological and chemical warfare at best and as such a threat to the existence of mankind!'

'Come, come, Mortimer, don't be so dogmatic. Franklin raised a reassuring hand and patted his vexated friends shoulder,' let the planet revolve in peaceful harmony once more.'

'Look, I'm very sorry. . . Charity was just being nosey. . . 'Skeeter began.

Just then another player turned the corner and sensing some fun joined the party.

Like just about everybody in town, Geal well knew the interloper and his scampish nature,' oh great, just what we need. . . you old scallywag.' Geal reached down a gently patted Puck and then looked at Skeeter and gave her a conspiratorial wink.

Skeeter initially looked puzzled, then Geal nodded down at Puck and she realized, remembering his capricious reputation and she grinned.

'What's this? . . . Another mangy old mutt. . . Madame! . . . Are you doing this deliberately?' Mortimer was in high dudgeon and kicked out at Puck.

Puck barred his teeth, snarled contemptuously, cocked a leg and pissed on his antagonists ankle, growled and leapt off with a cheeky wag of tail.

'WHAT THE DICKINS!' Mortimer was affronted and not a little embarrassed and glared at Skeeter, searching for words.

Franklin roared with laughter and smacked his knee with his open palm, in appreciation of the mighty craic'
Quid pro quo, I believe, old man.'
'Did I miss something?' Bobby, roused from his day dreams and contemplation of all things fantastic was roused by the hullabaloo.

Dapper and Shabin were stepping out in seventh heaven as they sashayed around town. Far from the guilt Shabin had expected in losing her virginity outside marriage she was elated and all her anxieties of how it would be vanished the moment they were alone in her cottage. Everything came naturaly, there was no fumbling, no ackward moments and no embarrassing interludes in which either wondered if they were forcing the pace. Dapper all but proposed, until he remembered that he was probabally still married, although he couldn't for the life of him remember who to.

'Good Afternoon Doctor, you're looking very happy, I must say.' In mid gossip, Morena had spied Shabin and hurried across, with her sisters of slander in step and all agog to garner the gossip.
'Morena, how nice to see you,' Shabin said with some surprise,' ah I see you're with your friends.'
' And I see you're with . . . ' morena stopped herself just in time, with the words 'fancy man' frozen to her lips.
'Yes John, but then you know him, of course.' Shabin was emboldened and no longer inhibited by her reptilian receptionist and actualy enjoying the encounter.'Is your day going well? . . .a little retail therapy?'
Wrong footed and a little peeved, Morena scowled, but quickly recovered,' I'd say you're having a grand time these days, you're so much happier, together.' She emphasized the last word.
Nora and Kitty exchanged knowing looks and nodded their heads stupidly like bulldogs selling insurance.
Shabin linked her arm with Dappers and smiled broadly,' Yes Morena, we are very happy, aren't we John?'
Dapper agreed and added,' . . . and your Pat, how's he doing? . . He was roaring away at Foxy Johns the other night. He's the life and soul of the party after a pint, or three, but then you'd know that wouldn't you?'
Morena grimaced,' Well I'm sure you'll have a lot to do, Doctor. . . So I'll bid you good day.' The triumvirate of tittle tattle shuffled away mithering meaningfully.
Shabin playfully elbowed Dapper,' John!. . .You really shouldn't have said that. . . You know the poor man has a big problem.'

'Yea, his wife. . . that's why he's an alcoholic. . . I'd defy any man with a witch like that to turn from the drink.'

218

'Now that's a rare sight these days, Geal pointed to a wizened old lady in a flamboyant headscarf and turn of the century taupe raincoat belted with baling twine and a fine muddy pair of black willies. She led an ancient donkey, with side paniers up the middle of main street with fierce determination despite the irritation of many motorists, apparently oblivious of the chaos she ensued. Skeeter smiled and called out,' Hello Mrs Dealney and how are you this fine day?'

Mrs Delaney continued her trek without acknowledging the greeting, the world beyond was of little concern. She had been making the same journey from five miles outside town every fortnight for as long as any living soul in Dingle could remember and always with the same degree of disregard for the disorder and confusion in her wake. She came into town for the basics, tea, sugar and that she couldn't produce and would have no bother with anybody that she wasn't required to, in order to complete her shopping. As the years passed it took longer and longer to drag her increasingly arthritic and crotchety being to town and back and in the winter months she would leave her cottage in the dark and not arrive home until the darkness returned. Despite the best offers from neighbours and the social services, she would have none of it and chased them all away with cantankerous words and her black bog oak stick.

Some said she was a hundred years old, more said older and she herself had no idea and cared not a jot, her birth certificate, if she indeed ever had one was long lost and any official record of her birth was probably destroyed when the I.R.A. burnt the offices of the recorder in the uprising. She'd been married 58 years, a widow 30, brought up six daughters and seven sons, all now either dead, or away in the States, or Australia and no longer in touch this many years; for her they were as good as dead anyway. She hadn't the reading, or the writing, so their letters home went unread and unanswered and they assumed she had followed Joseph Patrick to the graveyard. Her nearest neighbours Hogan on the one side and Riley the other, had learnt long ago that she had no need of them and expected the same. This was her fifth donkey, all living a good age and dying through overwork and the burden of the daily chore, she was one of the last to collect the seaweed to fertilize her lazy beds for a good crop of 'tatties' and 'neeps'. She once tried racing her donkey at the beach races, but the brute would have none of it, despite the attentions of Hogan and Riley and the powerful intervention of Mary Ann Macgrew and her big old schtik. Mrs Delaney was the last of her generation and her passing would close a chapter of folklore and the old ways of doing a thing that had faded into distant memory and was only to be found in the unreliable books of historical scholars of social history.

Crossing from behind the departing Delaney and donkey, Dapper and Shabin stepping lively to dodge the donkey's doings, laughing lightly as lovers do at the avoidance and the delight of their devotion.

'Hello you two.' Skeeter called and had more luck in the response this time.

'The scarlet lady no less,' Dapper quipped. 'and of course the main man.'

The dogs bounded up, tongues and tails wagging excitedly, Charity rolled over eager for a tummy rub and Hope peed with excitement over Dapper's foot, much to his consternation, although he said nothing.

'So, how's it going?' Geal reached out to shake Dapper's hand.

'Yea, great,' Dapper looked down at his wet foot,' well mostly.'

Skeeter and Shabin set to gossiping girls stuff, leaving the lads to talk.

'Rock's on the run then,' Geal tried to sound casual, but from what he'd heard the great I am was only just ahead of the hounds.

'How do you mean?' Dapper was genuinely mystified.

'The story in the Sunday sordid! . . . Didn't you know?'

'No, what story. . . there's always a Rock scandal that's his fingerprint,' Dapper rubbed his left arm,' anyway I've been staying at Shabin's. . . no time for papers and telly, know what I mean.' He smiled.

' Yea, but I think this one might be difficult to dodge,' Geal glanced at the girls,' so you two are an item now?'

'And yourselves?' He nodded towards Skeeter and burped,' apologies I have this indigestion thing for days now, must have been something I ate.'

'Could be. . . anyway you catch up with the Rock thing. It could be serious this time and might create waves for yourselves.'

BIRTHDAY.

Betty's most intense and painful moments of deep soul searching were shared with the hens, who seemed to cluck sympathetically, but carried on pecking.

'Well Etta, you fussy old hen' A clap of thunder rolled ominously across the heavens and she looked up as the dark clouds,' stormy Monday on a Thursday, it's all so sad. . . lordy, lordy, lordy have mercy.' Etta stopped in mid stride, freeze framed for a moment in an arc of lightning, slowly turned her head and seemed to shake it in bafflement, before bwaking off in search of slim pickings.

Fear and self loathing gnawed at Bettys self esteem, time had passed since the start of this great adventure. She and Mutton had escaped the desperation and descent into the darkness of isolation in Kensal Rise, but she hadn't shaken off her angst at the inevitable ending of her days. She wondered at what point suicide and the small comfort of nothing became more desirable than the slow daily dying of waiting for an end to disappointment and the suffering of consciousness and all the anxieties and fears it creates.

She dearly wished she had Lucy's faith, Molly's indifference, or even Agatha's blissful ignorance, but she didn't and suffered the brooding distress of reluctant resignation to some ominous oblivion.

'Chick, chick, chicken lay a large egg for me,' Agatha shambled passed, the worse for drink and even worse in voice,' hey look it's a bird in a cage,' he grinned gapily at Betty behind the chicken wire.

'Hey Mama Thornton, lookie hear, it's a couple of old hound dogs sniffing about. . . Well boys, did you run out of money, or did they wise up and run you out of town?' Betty picked up an egg and placed in it her basket.

'Boiled eggs and soldiers for breakfast again.' T.J. quipped,

'Breakfast is it? . . . Do you goons know what time it is?. . . in fact do you jerks even know what year it is?' Their untimely arrival was actualy the best tonic Betty could have at that moment, as having to come on strong to those more dysfunctional than herself, restored her self confidence and banished the blues.

'Girls, you know I just realized something. . . feeling blue ain't half as bad, when you see what a sad mess so many others have made of their lives.' Betty brushed some bits of straw off her apron,' You two look like you've been up all night again, had several skinfulls and couldn't find your way home.'

221

'Agatha heard talk of somebody losing fifty Euros in town. . . he spent hours searching the lanes, but the best he got was fifty cents.' T.J. ruffled Agatha's hair,' the old eegit, he's as thick and useless now as ever he was when I first met him.'

'Who are you calling a powerful old eejit, yourself?. . . Sure I've sorted you out a good few times. . .' Agatha was all but affronted, but then drink is a powerful anaesthetic and easily dulls what little sense existed in the first place.

'Now now boys, you're both a waste of time and space and have been this many years,' Betty placed her hands on her hips and stood squarely looking at them, like some old stern spinster school maam admonishing her wayward charges. ' But then I wouldn't have expected any different, you'll both go to your grave with little idea that you were ever born.'

'That's not fair. . . I could have been great. . . .I just never got the breaks.' T.J. protested.

' At what?' Betty considered, '. . . Yea, I suppose you are a reasonable drummer, but you've never had any game plan, or sense of purpose.'

'. . .and I suppose you have!' T.J. retorted angrily.

For Molly, a roll in the hay nowdays was merely a picnic in a field after harvesting, although the spirit was more than willing, but the body was weak, wrinkled and unwanted, even for the desperate like Agatha. Anger,embarrassment and bitter regret filled her mind and days, she hated the fact that she had returned to nappy days and her always vile and volatile temper were beyond her control. Molly knew that she was now her most dangerous adversery and her main failing was her bitchy and callous lack of diplomacy, or tact. She had always just blurted things out, most times they weren't even what she really thought and in retrospect she nearly always regretted her motor mouth and the bridges burnt. She was grateful that Betty stuck by her through thick and thin and although they were bosom buddies in every stretch of imagination and had shared much more than most, Molly was only too aware that she was pushing the relationship beyond breaking point.

She painfully remembered how Betty and herself had scoffed and giggled at the ads on afternoon telly for incontinence pads, antacids and stairlifts and watched the once mighty stars of chats shows reduced to flogging life insurance.

Then she sniggered as she thought how Betty and herself decided which weather girl would be next up the duff as they seemed prone to within months of their debut. What were they up to between predictions, working up some precipitation on a cloud of stratocumulus in the fog of tropical passion with some geek, mumbling about approaching orgasams of hurricane proportion?

Molly decided there was nothing worth getting up for this day and turned over for yet another duvet day of dread and dreams.

'It's my birthday today.' Mutton proudly announced to Bodger,' I'm seventy. . . I think. . . I was born in a leap year. . . so maybe I'm only seventeen and a half. . . you know about these things. . . how old am I?'

'How old do you feel?' Bodger worked on the computer,' if you had a Euro for everyday of seventy years, you'd have 25480 Euros,. . . if you had a Euro for the seventeen and a half years, you'd have 6370. Euros and fifty cents.

. . so how old do you feel now?'

Mutton searched through his pockerts and ruefully counted the contents,'   according to your theory, I'm 23 days and whatever 32 cents is worth.'

Bodger laughed,' there is a Chinese proverb, ' an inch of time cannot be bought by an inch of gold.', would you rather life, or riches?'

'Riches!' Mutton said without hesitation.

Bodger raised an eybrow,' are you sure?'

'I've spent a lifetime being broke and it ain't no fun.' Mutton's hearing aid began to feedback.

'What would you buy that you don't already have?' Bodger reached over and tapped Mutton's earpiece,' besides a hearing aid that works.'

'That's easy, wine, women and song. . . and a nice lump of rocky.'

'There's just one little thing missing,' Bodger stroked his chin.

'Yea, what?'

'No life, no riches and no way to spend it. . . unless of course you're a dead rock star with a back catalogue of unpublished material in the vaults. . . then you fake your death and live for eternity on your royalties, if only in legend and the convulted creations of conspiritory theorists.

'So there you are you old fool!' Betty marched in with Molly and a class of a birthday cake, shaped like a guitar, with an iced brown hearing aid laid across the middle and seven candles. Agatha, T.J. and Tic Tac tumbled through the barn doors in quick succession, T.J.'s handed Mutton a fat joint.

'Jeez, you old cunt. . . you're even older than my Aunt Sally.' Agatha called.

'Yea!' Mutton replied,' how old is she then?'

'Well she was fifty nine when she died a few years ago.' Agatha tripped over Beaver, who'd been ratting in the rafters before being attracted by the rumpus,' Argh shit. . . fecking cat.'

'It's the three wise men. . . and it looks like they're bearing gifts,' Bodger theatrically glanced around,' and would you believed it, we're in a stable.'

'More like the three stooges.' Molly added,' and they were all born in a barn of uncertain breeding.'

'Yet another of Dr Strangelove's failed experiments in genetics.'

'Not one a product of a virgin birth. . . I'd say the whore escaped in heat and brought disgrace on the brothel's reputation.' Molly was adept at driving the knife deeper into an open wound and much enjoyed the sport.

'I've been insulted by professionals, dearie!' Tic Tac responded,' so some hag with soggy knickers smelling of cats piss is so much golden rain in a tarts tent.' He leaned forward and thrust something into Mutton's hand,' have one on me.' and strutted out,'see ya kids.'

Opening his sweaty hand, Mutton saw two blue diamond shaped pills with the word 'Pfizer' engraved on them.

Betty also glimpsed them and said,' Oh no you don't. . . if you're thinking about swallowing them, you can join that slimy low life in the brothel.'

Mutton looked befuddled and a little disappointed.

'Here, if you don't want them,' T.J. jumped in,' don't waste them.'

'I'll have one.' Agatha offered charitably

'Would any the one of you know what to do with a stiffie these days,' Molly chided,' if indeed you ever did

CONSEQUENCES.

The CCTV viewing the wastelands of Ladbroke Grove had recorded many bizarre sights and since the rehab unit had been established the scene got weirder.

Many of the victims in the gutters of desolation row were well adrift of authority and support in any shape, or form and a vexation to community, council and police.

Nobody loves you when you're down and out and if you're so far out that any help is seen as an act of oppression and aggressively rejected out of hand, then it's hard nose to the end game.

'What's in it for me?' Bruised and battered with a face swollen and scared beyond recognition the reject on the street addressed nobody in particular and everybody in passing.

Two busybobbies in uniform looked on from the other side with disdain and quietly slipped away,' who needs it. . . think of the paperwork. . . it'll pollute the cells and we'll have to sluice it out . . today, tomorrow and every other day. Until!!'

Yummie mummies snatched up their overburdened offspring and scooted across the road in fear and loathing,' This really won't Do. . .what's happening to the neighbourhood?'

Huddled around the school gate the tittle-tattle centred on the sleazy scum, anger and angst gathered and grew, but chitter-chatter came cheap and ladies who lunch have little time to waste on waifs and strays.

Every mothers son now damaged and destroyed, bloated and bleeding, an incident of birth nearing the grave. By accident, or intent?

Named and shamed. 'A ROCK GOD CRASHES AND BURNS' as the rain sodden posters outside the hot news vendors proclaim with tantalizing bold black headlines.

Patsy finally had her glory, the battle was won, but it was a hollow victory.

'Rock Sturdy's pink Rolls Royce had been discovered abandoned at Golden cap carpark in Dorset and a figure was seen to topple from the cliff into a storm tossed sea by an intrepid dog walker. Coastguards and lifeboats were called out, but heavy weather conditions offered little hope of recovering a body.'

The report continued with an implication that Rock had been involved in several murders and sordid and perverse underage sexual crimes.

The latter was, of course, secondhand news and hardly unexpected, but a scandal none the less and grist for the mill of public outrage and Patsy declared that her detailed scoop was only the tip of the iceberg.

For Patsy it was a crusade which had it's roots in a woman spurned, although Rock had no memory of the actual rejection as he was arrogant and stoned out of his head, but for a young cub reporter on a provincial it was devastating. It was her long anticipated big break, having previously been pegged to weddings and funerals and as an ambitious young journalist she was willing to give everything to break into the big time. Her then editor, Micky Scrooby took her at her word and allowed Patsy to entertain him in return for letting her cover the new pop sensation Nun-Such's gig at the Corn Exchange. A thrill in every sense, as she would not only get the opportunity to see her heroes in the flesh, but would get her review of their performance in the post.

Patsy's heart ran away with her head when her main chance came as their lunatic Irish roadie selected her and around ten other girls to go backstage after the show to meet the lads. Although she was deep in the counties and a good distance from the swinging cities, she wasn't as green as fields and knew what the boys expected and if push came to shove was more than happy to oblige. She was after an exclusive, wanted the low down on their plans and a candid insight into just what rocked their boat, especially Rock, who fascinated her.
From a distance he was brash, bold and a beast to behold, from close up he was aggressive, assertive and an arrogant animal, who confidently strutted his stuff in a lewd and lascivious manner. He knew what he had, wanted and demanded he got his every whim satisfied.

The dressing room meat market was savage and any naive girl soon knew her expected role in the hurly burly and it was a rude awakening to the real world. Here dog ate dog & sisterly love and solidarity was for beautiful losers soon forgotten in the feeding frenzy of free love.
The great spirit must have been momentarily distracted, or had other things in mind for Patsy when he was bestowing the gifts of looks and personality for she had definitely been overlooked, but then beauty is only skin deep.

Try as she might to make friends and impress Rock with her body and mind, Patsy failed in every respect. He rebutted her every approach and openly mocked her, to the amusement of her friends. She was abused and shamed and all but socially run out of town, unable to hold her head up in public without derision.

226

With the local barn door fiercly and humiliatingly slamming shut, her grace was soon saved as the gates to the bright lights, big city blues swung wide with a neon lit welcome sign to Fleet Street. Only the good lord would know how and why and he was temporarily out of town on a pressing matter that concerned a certain Mr B. Althazar.

Then Rock had neither the intellect, or vision to appreciate just what he'd rejected and exactly what it would cost him in long term trials and tribulations.

'Hey brother what hit you?' The cardboard friend eyed another social reject with suspicion, having woken from his stupor and peered out from his deep freeze cardboard boxroom under the Westway. He was a happy man, no obligations, a past he'd long forgotten, a future he couldn't be arsed to contemplate and not burdened with a name he could remember.

The rag and bone, ripped and torn in face and clothes was unresponsive, bar a deep grunt that rippled shit hot liquid through his system and filtered it through the already threadbare and stained trousers. Indifferent to the circumstance he jently stewed in his own obnoxious juices, his mind somewhere else entirely.

'Who man, you're something else !. . . I've been around this place for,' he hesitated,.
. . yea well, I been around ok and I ain't seen nothing like you before.' He fished deep in his box and pulled out a bottle of white lightning taking the road to further oblivion.

The reject was in another dimension; a stranger in a strange place where he wasn't needed, or welcome.
' Hey man, got a fag?'

ROCK ISLAND LINE.

'Is that somebodies grave?' Skeeter pointed to a mound of earth just outside a deserted graveyard covered by a fishing net with rusting lager cans, faded plastic flowers, model trawlers and a snow dome with the Holy Virgin inside it.

' Oh yea, that's Slipper. . . well it isn't actually, he's not there.' Geal smiled and winked, enjoying the play.

'Where is he then. . . and whose there,' she stared back the 'grave',' Hey Faith stop digging!'

' Yea. . . no bones, good dog.' Geal leant on a gatepost.

'O.K. so tell me the story then Mr Mystery', Skeeter threw a stick and all three dogs chased after it, rolling and tumbling into a muddy ditch. A sudden blast of wind howled across the sparse and rocky landscape, chilling to the soul and setting fallen leaves to whirl and dance in spirals.

'Around thirty years ago about ninety people lived here on the island and Slipper was one of nine kids born to fisherfolk.' Geal warmed to the telling of the tale and searched for the words to better give a sense of the story. While skeeter felt the cold and urged him to walk and talk, following the dogs who happily gamboled, stopping to sniff and piss.

'The father went to sea one day and never came back. . . his body washed up on the mainland and was buried in the graveyard there overlooking the island.' They'd reached a highpoint and although a fine mist of rain played along the sound, the brooding coastline could be glimpsed and he pointed vaguely,' there abouts. . . Peig Sawyers is in the same cemetery.'

' Holy cow. . . you know about Peig!' Skeeter smiled,' they made us read her book in the Irish at school.' She grimaced at the memory, ' hated the mere mention of her at the time. . . It was worse than double maths and still can't make hide, nor hair of Gaelic. Spoken, or written.'

The dogs disturbed a flock of seagulls that had been picking around a stoney outcrop, with much flapping from the birds and yapping from the excited collies chasing around in the vain hope of the catch of the day.

The fine soft rain was only the herald of a gale that increased in intensity and drove all to the shelter of the lighthouse.

'The mother took to drink. . . just a nip in hot milk to help her sleep and banish the cold and lonely bed

with no man to comfort her.' With the skies dark and the force of rain beating against the windows, Geal
stooped to stoke the log and turf fire, reached into a box by the fire and threw something on the fire; immeadiately
flames flared in many colours,' Hocus Pocus!' he cried.

'GOOD GOD!' Startled, Skeeter sat back in the sofa and stared in disbelief,' How?'

'Alchemy,' He laughed,'Settle back girl, . . . just schoolboy science. . . various chlorides, potassium
and copper powder.' But effective and entertaing none the less. . . Now as I was saying,' Seating himself in the
leather swivel chair by his desk he swung to face her with the firelight throwing shadows around the room.
'The demon drink drove her to dipsomania and her children to the colonies. Scatterred to Canada, the States and
Australia. . . They say none kept in touch, but Slipper, the baby of the siblings, who stayed home to support the
poor wretch.'

Thus far the cat '9 lives' had brooded in hiding, affronted by the intrusion of the dogs to her isolated Atlantic
outpost where she was Queen, her hissy fit was all consuming and she was hungry, a lethal combination.

'Slipper stayed, aware that his mother was gone in mind and body, but she was the woman
who birthed and nurtured him and now the mantle of responsibility fell to him to feed their little needs.
. . tea, sugar, etc. The few bits beyond self help' A slight movement caught his eye and he spied 9 Lives nooked
in a discreet cranny, he winked at the cat and would have sworn the cat winked back.
'Everyman must earn his living, for some this lies uncomfortably between a rock and a hard place and this
island is both, with no work to be found on the land.'

Intrigued by the story, now more fascinated by the teller, Skeeter found her eyes studying the man and his
mannersims and found it increasingly difficult to focus on his words.
' Like every other man on the island he trawled the sea for his livelihood and made a good go of it for eighteen
months and he and his mother lived well enough with the small returns. . . they say she turned from the bottle
and was another woman.'

Skeeter wondered why a man like this was unattached. . . perhaps he was gay. . . maybe he
had a girl in every port and secretly played the field with great aplomb. . . was she a bird on a wire?' She shifted
in her seat uncomfortably and hoped she wasn't as transparent as she felt.
'One night. . . a flat calm with the Northern lights a shifting and awesome curtain of colour, but an omen for the
Vikings, who'd sailed these waters. The share fisherman on his boat chatting in the Gaelic, called to the other

boats within distance and turning to point where green shimmered red, suddenly lost sight of Slipper on the bow. . . he was there to see, then gone. No sound, no shout, nothing but the twinkling lights of the mainland away over.'

She drew breath and reached a hand down to stroke the head of Charity, almost for reassuarance, although she never knew slipper, apart from name this day.

'Of course they searched, but there was nothing to be found, he was gone and that was the way of it and no stranger disappearance than the many others that had gone the same way over the ages.'

Pacing the moment and feeling magic of a yarn unfolding on a dreich night, Geal paused to once more poke the fire for comfort, although in truth the fuel was in good order.

'As I heard it when the folk on the island gathered there was fear that herself would be destroyed by the loss of Slipper and no body returned from the sea to bury, or grave to grieve at. . . The spirits in the bottle would be uncorked to haunt her nights and the days to wander the cliffs, searching the seas for a sighting.' Geal took a bottle of Lagavulin from a side table, pouring a generous measure for both of them, 'Without doubt she was beside herself with desperation and in denial, forever in the hope that he would walk back into her life. . . some terrible mistake. Perhaps even having washed up on the mainland with amnesia and having recovered would return with an aplogy and a story to spin over a pint in the night.'

Lifting a finger, Geal jumped up,' Hang on a moment!' He fished among in a folder of papers and sketches, ' Here.' He handed Skeeter a weathered laminated A4 sheet;

SLIPPER, MY YOUNGEST SON & SACRED HEART. LOVED AND MISSED. LOST AT SEA 7.7.77. A MOTHER WEEPS.

She read the words and reread them twice more,' poor woman. . . where did you get this?' Skeeter turned in her hand.

' It was loosely stapled to that crude wooden cross. . .it took it off as it looked like it was near to blowing away,' He shrugged,' She was back with the bottle and desperate. . . Then one day a cow went over the cliff and the people turned out to winch it back. . . dead, or alive it was a precious resource and not to be abandoned to the sea.'

' And?' Skeeter clutched one of the Afgan scatter cushions to her stomach.

'A couple of the women in the crowd saw Slipper's mother away up on a cliff and curiosity got the better of them and they snuck up and saw her talking into a bottle, then she sealed it and tossed it over to the waves below. She was a changed women from there on, a devout Catholic, teatotal and a positive and cheerful part of the community.' Geal laughed,' She filled the empty bottle with her woes and worries and threw it to the water' . . . a message in a bottle.'

'What happpened to the cow.' Skeeter asked with concern.

'Dead. . . so they pulled in on a cart around the houses and each family bought a cut of it and then the owner of the unfortunate creature had enough to buy a new cow from the mainland. . . a class of an insurance policy, don't you see?'

RETURN TO GO.

'OH SHIT!' Betty stared at the screen in disbelief, rising slowly from the sofa and spilling Badger from her lap, where he had been purring contendly as she tickled his ears. He took off like a greyhound

with a red hot chilli pepper up its arse, pausing only to let out a loud squeal and take a tumble as he collided with Lucys legs.

'Betty, Betty something nasty is about to happen,' Lucy had a new IPAD in her hands and the heady smell of patchouli oil about her,' Hatma Fracs says Mars is in opposition to Venus, Mecury is in retrograde and Scorpio is rising.

'It already has,' She picked up her mobile phone and started to text Shadow and then though better of it and phoned him instead.

'The person you're calling is unable to answer your call, please leave a message. . . '

She threw the phone on to the sofa in a tizzy and looked at Lucy,' What are we going to do now?'

Lucy was perplexed,' About what?. . . What's happened. . . How can I help?' Lucy offered her IPAD,

'We could ask Hatma. . . What's the problem? . . . I'm sure he would know the answer. He's so divine.' Her soft sweet voice was positive and comforting, but useless none the less.

Betty Smiled slightly,' It must be so wonderful to be you. . . I do believe the warning that the moon was about to crash into Earth wouldn't phase you.' Then it dawned on her, that pretty much was what was about to happen to their small world.'

'The lousy bastard. . . he did it deliberately!' Never one to mince her words. Molly swigged from her can of Pussy; a high energy drink she had stumbled across in a health shop in Tralee. She raced around like a clockwork orange with a sprung spring, but it had singularly failed to spark the parts where she'd most welcome a return to mighty action and there was little prospect of the warm glow of comfort returning anytime soon.

'Buck told Shadow that Rock was about to get nicked for murder. . . something to do with a 60's band in Soho,' With time to take stock and the chance to talk to Shadow, Betty felt calmer and the initial shock had passed courtesy of Lucy and her medicine chest of Rescue remedy, St John's Wort and a nip of brandy.

It seemed that nobody actually knew what was what and rumour and speculation mill were as much in the muddle of the media as that of the inner circle. Their world was in a spin cycle and the wash had yet to be cleansed of stubborn stains and starched for a secure future.

Betty and Molly convened the kitchen cabinet around the range and thrashed out the bits and pieces. For the present they alone knew, as apart from Lucy who had floated out to consult her oracles, the bad news had yet to trouble the others.

Not even a mythical Dutchgirl could keep her finger in the dyke for long as the torrent of news became a flood of disturbing detail. What had once seemed solid and reliable became so much warm dust in the click of a mouse.

'Oh my God!' Betty reeled back,' Camp David's body was washed up on a beach in Dorset. . . the police say they're treating it as an unexplained death.'

'Shit. . . now I won't get the 50 euros he owes me!' Molly hissed venomously.

'Molly!'

'What!. . . What? . . . I was just saying,' She shrugged and rolled her eyes,' if you ask me that bitch was always playing a well dangerous game,' She kicked out at Beaver.' always gave me the creeps anyway.'

'Molly! . . . what's got into you? . . and don't take whatever it is out on the cat.' Betty was livid, more with the abuse of Beaver than anything else.

'Maybe he was up on that cliff with Rock. . . You know a last hurrah. . . knocking one out for a last time . . came over all queer.' She sniggered,' reckon the world's better off without both of them.'

There was talk in Dick Macs and as the trio of misfits entered an urgent silence and a pregnant pause, broken only when Sheehan waved his paper under T.J.'s nose, Tic Tac was a tad diminutive and Agatha a distraction.'Yer man?'

T.J. glanced at the headlines and then snatched it up to read on,' Bloody hell!' He sat on a bar stool and his restless leg all but chinned him.

'What? . . .what's happened?' Agatha and Tic Tac chorused.'

'Three pints.' Agatha took advantage of the perplexity and prioritised a little local panic.,' Rocks missing in Dorset and Camp David is toast.'

'Good Hey?' Agatha had never liked Rock, but then who did? . . . And as for Camp David, well it was above and beyond his radar.

'Do you think?' Tic Tac questioned, then on a second thought,' silly idea, when did you ever?' he reached

233

for the pint and cadged a fag from some local loser.

'Not so fast!' The barman intervened,' Who's paying?'

A collective,' urghhmm,' and shuffling of feet and shifty glances from one to the other and then dispondantly to the floor. Tic Tacs wallet was locked down, Agatha's pockets holed and empty and T.J. searching for a lost note.

Once more Sheehan was entertained, between the arrival of Geal and the motley crew up at Dungiggin his days had brightened considerably and to his mind the pace had been in the dodrums since the filming of Ryans Daughter. Although he only remembered it through a childs eyes and the legend, a good part of which was created by the duration of Robert Mitchums residence over in Milltown and doubtless much embellished in humour and pathos.

'You didn't have to be so kind,' Betty had received a phone call from Geal out on the Island, but rarely out of touch with events on the mainlands of the world. The babble and mutterings had reached him and he felt compelled to call and express sympathy for their plight.

'Who's pickin' up the pieces?' Although Geal was only too aware that the bones would be picked clean by vulturine accountants, sharp gownsmen and before them customary tax would swoop for the lions share; pre supposing there was a carcase to feast from.

SO MUCH SHIT WASHED DOWN THE DRAIN.

'Who do you think you are, Ras-clat!' The youth lashed out at the old bloke that had lurched into him down the Grove.

Busted, broke and banished the face in the gutter was without hope and status. The detritus of community ignored, or overlooked by those still in the game and intent on staying so, in the helter skelter of the daily grind. Shunned by the hopeless hoodie of gangland, with low slung Calvin's kecks and the kacky crack of his arse end, looking like he's just be gang banged in the nick. Steppin' out with attitude as he strutted his stuff and clicked his teeth, two fingers to authority and three sandwiches short of a picnic.

Slip sliding in shit, sewer bound as icy rain slashed street and polite society who raised umbrellas to shield themselves from cats and dogs and riff raff.

Far from healing, the scar faced figure was festering, deeply wounded in body and mind, tattered rags, hand rolled and robbed by every scruff and street urchin from here to eternity. Uttering and muttering incomprehensible words without meaning, or feeling. Now lamed in every sense, beyond shame and name and just staggering to everywhere and nowhere in particular.

Who gave a Donald?

It was all Mickey Mouse anyway?

Baffled and bored the fuzz always had somewhere else to be and would be, if it wasn't for the prodding of Patsy, still intent on having the last word and poking around like a pig in shit with a sniff of a trough full of swill.

P.C.s Wood and Top had the unenviable job of guarding the scene of crime, which was no ball game on a beach of pebbles in a biting wind with the night coming on and the tide rising with their backs against the muddy cliff.

''Ere Ern, I think I've found a whatsit!' Wibur handed his mucker an odd rock.

Ern studied it in the fading light,' It's an Ammonite. . . a Cephalopoda, common in the Devonian & Cretacious period. . . maybe 432 millin years old.' His dad was an amateur fossil hunter, who married late in life to an older woman and begat his only child, son and heir, one Ernest Wood; a Virgo obsessed by detail and forensics.

235

There was actually little point to the lonely vigil of Dorset's finest, as the body had been removed three tides ago, the high viz tape was blowing ribbons in the wind, now only tethered to one rod driven ever looser in the pebbles and bar the corpse there was little, or no evidence to be gathered.

But the chief Constable 'Chummy' Tarpe had form for cock ups and cover ups and was only too aware of the celebrity connection and the high profile coverage in the big city newsprint.

Therefore his explicit instructions were, much to the consteranation of the bobbies on the beach,' let no stone be unturned in this complex and demanding case and I must immediately be informed at every step of the way.'

'Ere Ern if two went over, how come we only found one?' Wilbur Topp scanned the huge expanse of beach.

Wood considered for a moment,' Did you ever read Holmes?'

' No, no Ern. . . I only read comics.'

Grinning Ern replied,' Argh good, don't worry. . . Once you've eliminated the impossible whatever remains, however improbable, must be the truth. . . . There was only one body!'

'Brilliant Ern,' Wilbur was genuinely impressed,' you'll chief Super one day.' He ideally kicked at the cobbles.'. . . 'ere hang on a sec, what's this?'

It was a lazy day down the Lane and Fergus lingered by the door of ' Gillchrists' clothes emporium shooting the breeze.

Over time he'd seen more down and outs than George Orwell, or W.H.Auden and experienced the serendipity of seeing a few go from rags to riches, returning from the dirt of the drain to buy into the dream. Fergus experienced first hand the swings and roundabouts of fashion and with a photographic memory knew the names, faces and places and caught out a good few who falsely claimed, 'I was there.'

Watching yet another dreg drag by he thought,' I know that one. . . I've just seen a face, I can't recall the time, or place. . . but it'll come to me. . . it's a shouda, couda, wouda.'

Booker M. Steiner, an authoritive antiquarian alchemist with electric axe in hand was moving purposefully to lay down a quicksilver riff at the Basing Street studio that would soon resonate and connect with many beyond the island nation.

'Hey man, do you know that cat?' The vintage proprietor called over and nodded to the ragged trespasser on the loved streets of the Royal Borough.

Elfin in feature, ever alert and always on a mission stopped to stare,' Just another of Gods forsaken creatures going through changes.' Realising the lace on his green shoes had unravelled, he stooped and a damp fiver blew against his red velvet strides. Grinning he waved it aloft, 'A gift from God, . . he moves in mysterious ways.'

HOME IS WHERE THE HEARTH IS.

They were all in the know now and none the wiser to their future circumstance as they pondered their fate by the ferocious flames of the fire. The little more that Shadow knew filtered back, but Betty was sure he only said what he thought was in his own best interest and kept much back to protect and preserve what she could only guess at. He had danced with wolves for too long to shrug of old habits and had long gone native in the badlands of cruel contempt and only preserved his own scalp by low cunning and tricking the trixsters.

A bold mouse peered out from the skirting and seeing that Beaver was otherwise engaged and nobody had noticed his presence stopped to watch the wacky and weird world of the human beings and wonder at the thoughts behind their creation. What was the quirky intent of the great spirit of the Murine in the contrivance of such creatures? Long into the nights himself and his mischief had mused over confiscated chocolate and cheese the wisdom of such an infestation and if there was any way to trap and eliminate the menance. What positive purpose had they brought to the world? The chronicles of the venerable Troden which stretched back as a shikaca of all that had been and hinted at what was to come had only recorded the death and destruction inflicted on the planet by that race. There in lay a dire prediction that within the near future they would totally destroy the earth and the greater majority of all animal, vegetable and mineral and this greatly perplexed the mice.

In the actuality Shadow was running in circles, no wiser in truth than any other, but with an inkling to the way of the hows and wherefores and the progress of things to come. Thirty two years were past and he recalled many events and the conniving conspiracies that compounded and insidiously implicated himself into an intricate quagmire of flim-flam that was quickly unravelling.

Buck was engaged in a face saving damage limitation exercise and not available for interview, or comment and was too wily to crash and burn along with a piratical and wayward Rock supernova.

How to cover his arse and come up smelling of roses?

Near impossible for Shadow with his little personal problem and the wind up in every way.

Flight or fight, no question. The first plane out of Shannon.

With the devil in the detail and complexities that would confuse Confucious the professionals rubbed hands in Glee and raised glasses of Chatteau Le Grand in The Seven Stars in Carey Street and dared a pickled egg to soak up their pleasure. In a web of deceit with a dubious beginning and no distinct denouement they were in Easy Street for the forseeable future and perhaps until retirement, or demise.

The financial institutions were not backwards in coming forwards and quickly appointed Lucre, Greenback & Simoleons as administrators to follow any paper trails and liquidate any assests.

On behalf of Her Gracious Majesty the official receiver was equally quick off the mark and stepped forward in the guise of Alan Onne. A fastidious and fierce Scot, who favoured a daily medicinal gargle of Finlaggan and once fired up was not intimidated by fear'na' favour . If ever there was a case of too many cooks spoiling the broth; but official consternation left a few cockyleeky.

' Well, what's it to be?. . . Good news, or bad news.' Shadow was hardly in the door before the horde descended, hungrily hanging on every word. He was also much relieved, here at least he was briefly off the hook, but hadn't forgotten that Patsy well knew about Dungiggin and it was only a matter of time.

'Will either make much difference?' Betty led the way to the kitchen,much like the Pied Piper leading the bewitched children of the damned.

Molly tipped Beaver off the chair by the range and royally ushered Shadow to seat himself and warm up as the first chill winds of an early winter had touched the pensinsula. Having noticed the spin in Molley's attitude Shadow was disturbed and looked to Betty for explanation and reassurance.Beaver watched and waited his main chance as he was no backnumber and well knew where to do the dirty and who to.

'Well as you well know the man done gone. . . but as to where and how,' He shifted uncomfortably in his seat, hoping his emmisions were both silent and not deadly, but a blowback gave little hope of the latter,' I only saw him briefly a couple of days before it all erupted, but he was a worried man. But I very much doubt he either had the balls to top himself, or wish to meet the man so soon.' Shadow hesitated, as he considered if he should say what he'd just remembered, but then continued,' Do you know, for all his cockiness he seriously believed that the devil would get him one day and was shit scared. . . He told me that one time when we thought a chopper was gonna crash in fog. . . boy was he crapping himself.'

' And you weren't!' Once more Molly just blurted her thoughts out.

'You can be sure that sooner or later that old cow of a reporter's gonna get here. . . she don't think that Rock killed himself and she won't give up until she sees his body.' Shadow noticed that everybody but Bodger and Dapper were jammed into the kitchen and thought wryly that this was the best crowd he pulled for a good long time.

'I can handle her no problem!' Agatha swaggered.

'Oh yea!' T.J. elbowed him,' you and who's army?'

'Children, children this is serious,' Admonished Betty like a school mam,' Sorry about that, they will toss their toys out of the pram.'

Shadow shrugged and continued,' You're better to be out when she turns up. . . I'm off to Amsterdam for a few weeks. . . I reckon this will be yesterdays news in a couple of weeks and the Express and Sun will be back to apocalyptic weather and big tits before the week is out.'

'Ducking out hey?' Again Molly jumped in where the wise hold back.

Shadow was increasingly miffed,' FUCK OFF Molly. . . I'm not the enemy. I'm trying to do you a favour.'

For once there was a chorus of union and Molly visibly shrunk back, casting poisonous glances at Shadow.

'I'm sorry Shadow, honestly we know you're on our side and trying to help. . .it's just the not knowing. . . guess it's the same for you,' Betty smiled reassuringly,' so where do we go from here? . . . what happens to this place?'

'In the short term your best to keep a low profile. . . maybe go on holiday, or something.'

'Holiday!. . . chance would be a grand thing!' Agatha spluttered.

' Tidy. . . you're permanatly on vacation. . . you know lights on, nobody home.' Tic Tac stung waspishly.

Agatha struggled from from his seat and tripped over his shoe lace, headbutting Mutton in the stomach in the fall,'I'll have you,Welsh bastard. . . I know your mother was a dragon.'

'What mother?' T.J. entered the fray enthusiasticly

Impartial at best and hostile when push came to shove, Betty was amused by the exchange as the old goats locked horns impotently. Muttons hearing aid had dropped out in the melee and he desperately searched the floor while rubbing his aching midriff and scratching his arse.

'And the long term?' Betty patience was wearing thin,' Now boys sit quietly, or you'll have to stand in the corners.'

'Well now, here's the good part, although it's early doors. There's already a small army of bureacrats squabbling for a cut and they're at each others throats. . . talk about Spaniards in the works.' Shadow stopped and grinned.

'Yea, nicely. And?' T.J. ventured, still smarting from being slapped back.

'My guess is it'll take em years to even cotton on that this place exists and even then a few more to discover which bank if any owns the place and if you're on the case. Untold to discover you're names to evict you and re possess the place. If indeed any fool wanted to buy it and then you'd probabally have squatters rights.' There was triumph in his voice,' You know what. . . I reckon you've got it made.'

AND THEY ALL LIVED HAPPILY AFTER ?

'Just once in a lifetime,' Dapper knew it to be true for he and Shabin. Maybe he known it forever and every lady before was a dress rehearsal. He was no Lord Byron, perhaps a class of a Cassanova without the cultivation, but he definitely had passion, if not the attention span required for the duration of a season, much less a lifetime.

By now virtually the entire world had heard of the 'Marie Celeste of Rock' as Patsy had waspishly dubbed him in one of her columns. Dapper shared the perplexity of the multitude, but he had a new interest and was no longer overly concerned with how it used to be and who was there and where they might now be.

Increasingly both Geal And Skeeter felt a connection to something long past, but only half remembered and always just a short step beyond the curtain of mist called memory. A tease of truth dancing on the tongue, but as yet unspoken.

They briefly talked of the great Rock fall, but Skeeter was blissfully ignorant of the beast and Geal reluctant to give the crash of a charade the oxygen of life and there were better things to occupy their time.

Once when Geal was over in Amsterdam with Nick on a P.R. exercise to promote 'Music of the Spheres' Skeeter's curiosity gnawed at her idle hours. She'd surfed the net to better know and understand the man. She was overwhelmed by the magnitude of information, trivia and utubes devoted to him.

But one thing in particular grabbed her attention and spun her around, like a fairground attraction without breaks to catch ones breath and steady the churning stomach.

Geal had played at Eel Pie island, as had Rock on the evening she'd been knocked up in the night; co incidence, syncronisity?

The lurid speculation on Rock had reached the legendary status of Lord Lucan and Big Foot and the media happily stoked the controversy. Wanted dead, or alive he remained an elusive enigma, which is exactly what about everybody wanted. Nobody needs the disappointment of a mystery solved.

Betty felt like a yoyo with the highs and lows of euphoria and depression and it fell to her to take responsibility for all their tomorrows as it was apparent that the others were still coming to terms with their yesterdays. She regreted her mother hen status and the burden of expectation, which she doubted she could deliver on.

Old habits die hard; Dapper was a late riser, while by nature Shabin woke early despite being awake most of the night. Ready to answer the call of duty, Shabin leant over to kiss her sleeping lover and was horrified to find he wasn't breathing.

'JOHN, JOHN!' She hesitated momentarily, then panicked briefly, before professional instinct took hold and she started artificial respiration, reaching for the phone to call the ambulance.

Dispirited and feeling detached, Betty dreaded emails, phone calls and the post, expecting further bad news by the hour. The roaring silence only increased her anticipation and anguish. She repeated the mantra that no news was good news for reassurance as she steeled herself to open the latest letters.

' Betty, we've gotta do. . . ' Molly was in a tempest, then saw Betty slouched and staring at the paper in her hand, ' Betty! . . . what is it?'

Molly gently teased the letter from Betty,' CRIKEY!'

'I had no idea.' Betty smiled.

'Are you gonna tell the others?'

'Of course. . . and I think I know what to do with it.' Betty put a finger to her lips,' Don't say anything will you?'

'How is he?'

' Skeeter. . . How kind of you to call. . .Yes John is here in the hospital. . . A heart attack of course. . . he's on life support.'

'Oh Shabin I'm so sorry. . . Is there anything we can do? . . . Would you like me to come over?'

' Thank you, but no. . . the next few hours are critical. . . The team here are very good.'

'If you're sure. . . I'd really like to support you though. . .You must feel terrible, so far from home and Dapper with no family in Eire.'

'No really Skeeter. . . I appreciate it, but we'll just have to see.'

For once everybody turned up for the house meeting.

'Listen up. . . We've gotta get out of this place for awhile, otherwise we've got double trouble.'

'Great, but how, where. . . we ain't got no dosh.'

'Yea Betty easy said. . . '

' O.K. . . fair enough. . . there's a way. Cuddly left us something in her will. She didn't have a family.'

'How much?' Agatha and T.J. had already spent it in their heads.

'Here's the thing. It's for all of us, but nobody gets a wedge.'

Moans and groans rippled protest.

'I've been on the internet and talked to Shadow. . . he's sorted out something in Amsterdam. . . If you're all up for it.'

'THIS IS MY STORY AND IF THERE IS A WORD OF A LIE IN IT, THEN SO BE IT!   PEIG SAYERS. 1873 – 1958 (with gratitude and respect)

© 2010.Anon E.Mouse. (A Mischevious-Mouse Fantasy)